continued . . .

"Excellent action sequences . . . excellent helicopter-borne commando raid and firefight on the Chinese air base . . . excellent carrier and air-to-air action. The book is richly populated with interesting characters. But nobody is better than Gandt at describing the ambiance and occasional loneliness of life on an aircraft carrier. . . . Bob Gandt is not only an effective action writer, but he can be a very funny man."   —*The Hook*

Acts of Vengeance

"As exciting as the first book. Readers are immediately drawn in and kept on edge. . . . This is a great story . . . another marvelous, action-packed tale . . . with its all-too-real dangers. It is sure to increase his well-deserved following."
                                      —*Flight Journal*

"Gandt, who knows his stuff, provides the reader with a plethora of whiz-bang, techno-action and old-fashioned knife and pistola duels. . . . The real excitement is in the fast-paced action. There is something for most military junkies here. . . . The climactic dogfight is authentic in action and terminology. . . . But the main enjoyment in this book is Gandt's pleasurable storytelling and authenticity."
                                      —*The Hook*

"Gandt is a rare treasure, a Navy jet jock with the rare gift of being able to tell a compelling story in a believable and exciting manner that leaves the reader exhausted at the end. If only some movie studio mogul would take this book—I guarantee you everyone would forget *Top Gun*."
                                      —*Pacific Flyer*

With Hostile Intent

"I thoroughly enjoyed [*With Hostile Intent*] . . . characters are believable . . . combat scenes are excellent. Great job!"
                                      —Dale Brown

"A red-hot aerial shoot-em-up by an aviation pro who has done his homework." —Stephen Coonts

"More thrilling than a back-to-back showing of *Top Gun* and *Iron Eagle*, this red-hot piece of military fiction is certain to keep readers riveted . . . some of the most suspenseful battle scenes in recent military fiction."
—*Publishers Weekly*

"There's no doubt that Gandt knows what it's like in the cockpit, and he takes his readers there with flair."
—*Miami Herald*

"*With Hostile Intent* is especially topical, and you do not need to be a naval aviator to enjoy the description of flight operations and life on board an aircraft carrier. Gandt is as good an author as he is a pilot, and that's high praise."
—*Aviation Week*

"Bob Gandt is known for a half-dozen nonfiction books, including the well-regarded *Bogeys and Bandits* that tracked an FRS class through Hornet training. In his first novel he builds on that knowledge to produce a solid tale about modern carrier aviation, warts and all. . . . It's a roller coaster ride." —*The Hook*

"Informative, compelling, and thought provoking, [Gandt] offers an insider's perspective on what it takes to make the grade, and a number of interesting insights on key events and trends in today's Navy." —*Sea Power*

SHADOWS OF WAR

ROBERT GANDT

A SIGNET BOOK

SIGNET
Published by New American Library, a division of
Penguin Group (USA) Inc., 375 Hudson Street,
New York, New York 10014, USA
Penguin Group (Canada), 10 Alcorn Avenue, Toronto,
Ontario M4V 3B2, Canada (a division of Pearson Penguin Canada Inc.)
Penguin Books Ltd., 80 Strand, London WC2R 0RL, England
Penguin Ireland, 25 St. Stephen's Green, Dublin 2,
Ireland (a division of Penguin Books Ltd.)
Penguin Group (Australia), 250 Camberwell Road, Camberwell, Victoria 3124,
Australia (a division of Pearson Australia Group Pty. Ltd.)
Penguin Books India Pvt. Ltd., 11 Community Centre, Panchsheel Park,
New Delhi - 110 017, India
Penguin Group (NZ), Cnr Airborne and Rosedale Roads, Albany,
Auckland 1310, New Zealand (a division of Pearson New Zealand Ltd.)
Penguin Books (South Africa) (Pty.) Ltd., 24 Sturdee Avenue,
Rosebank, Johannesburg 2196, South Africa

Penguin Books Ltd, Registered Offices:
80 Strand, London WC2R 0RL, England

First published by Signet, an imprint of New American Library,
a division of Penguin Group (USA) Inc.

First Printing, November 2004
10 9 8 7 6 5 4 3 2 1

For Phast Phil,
little brother, best buddy

ACKNOWLEDGMENTS

Life continues to imitate art. When the Brick Maxwell series was conceived, the fall of Iraq and America's pursuit of terrorists were only fictional themes. Since then, the novels have displayed an uncanny tendency to foreshadow actual events. How much this story resembles real life remains to be seen.

Another round of thanks to the Maxwell mission control crew: Lt. Cmdr. Allen "Zoomie" Baker, fighter pilot and consultant, for his counsel on matters literary and technical; Doug Grad, editor extraordinaire, for his special insight into the craft of military fiction; Alice Martell, literary agent and friend, who always goes the extra mile; Vernon Lewis, good bud, critic, and eagle-eyed proofreader.

To the Americans lost and fallen in the war against terrorism, a salute and a moment of silence. They will not be forgotten.

"The Lord your God will send the Hornet among them until those who are left, who hide themselves from you, are destroyed."
Deuteronomy 7:20

"I always knew that if I was in trouble you'd come for me."
William Tecumseh Sherman to Ulysses S. Grant

"The only chance of life lies in giving up all hope of it."
Sun Tzu, The Art of War

TURKEY

SYRIA

Caspian Sea

Tehran •

IRAN

Baghdad • Dezful air base

IRAQ

Tigris

Euphrates

• Mashmashiyeh

Shatt-al-Arab waterway

KUWAIT

USS *Ronald Reagan*,
1145, 11 March

Persian Gulf

SAUDI ARABIA

BAHRAIN

QATAR

| 0 Miles | 200 | 400 |
| 0 Kilometers | 400 | |

© 2004 Jeffrey L. Ward

THE MAN WHO
DIDN'T EXIST

I am writing this as fast as I can. In the passageway outside my cell I hear the sound of boots. They are coming to interrogate me again.

Though I officially died on 17 January, 1991, the body of the man known as Raz Rasmussen continues to breathe air and perform physical and mental functions. One of those functions is to write in this book. Keeping a journal is the only thing that distinguishes me from an insect or a rat.

It is unlikely that anyone except my captors will ever read this journal. It no longer matters to me. The only purpose of writing in the book is that it forces me to think about what I did each day.

I was interrogated yesterday. They wanted to know about the mission control computer of the F/A-18. I told them everything I knew. It is a joke, after this much time. Memory is one of the things I have lost in captivity, like teeth, hair, eyesight. Torture does not refresh memory. It kills it.

They say they are being kind by allowing me to have this journal. And in a way, they are. Of course, they take it away from me every day to see what I have written. It must amuse them to read my notes about life in prison. I learned early in my captivity to be careful what I write. My captors are paranoid. If I write something unflattering, they drag me back to the interrogation room.

If I believed in heaven or hell, I would have to assume that I have been sent to hell. If so, it's not all that terrifying. Torture is an overrated method for extracting information. The truth is, pain eventually loses its power to terrify. I have learned to detach from my physical self. Since I am already a dead man, they can't hurt me.

This knowledge gives me an immense advantage over my captors and, for that matter, over everyone else in the world. I have nothing to hope for. Nothing to lose. Nothing to fear.

I hear them coming now. They will ask the same old questions, and I will give the same old answers. They waste their time. I remember nothing of value. The only part of my life I recall with perfect clarity is the night I died.

CHAPTER 1

FOXBAT

Southern Iraq, 31,000 feet
0145, 17 January, 1991

"Contact! Zero-four-zero, thirty-five miles, angels thirty, hot."

The call cut like a scythe through the radio chatter. Raz Rasmussen's scan snapped back inside the cockpit. He squinted at the greenish radar display. *Where? Zero-four-zero from whom? Is it a MiG?*

"Foxbat!" he heard someone call. "Twelve o'clock, twenty-five miles." Someone was getting an EID—electronic identification—on the contact.

Rasmussen's heart rate accelerated another twenty beats per minute. A Foxbat was a Russian-built MiG-25. He had it tagged in his own radar now, and, yeah, damn right it was a Foxbat. Nearly level, coming at them nose on. His hands began to sweat inside the flight gloves.

"Anvil Four-one has the bogey, nose hot, twenty miles. Request clearance to fire."

Rasmussen recognized the voice of his flight leader, Lt. Cmdr. Gracie Allen, in the F/A-18 Hornet two miles to the left.

"Which Anvil?" answered the AWACS controller in the E-3 Sentry, on station over Saudi Arabia. There were a total of sixteen Hornets with the call sign "Anvil."

"Who's requesting clearance to fire? What bogey?"

"Anvil Four-one. I've got a bogey on my nose at twenty miles. I need clearance to—"

Bleep. Another radio transmission cut him off.

"Anvil, do you have positive ID? State your—"

Bleep.

Radio discipline was going to hell. No one could complete a call before somebody cut him out.

The Foxbat was in range of the strike group.

It was Night One of Operation Desert Storm, the largest American air combat operation since Vietnam. Coalition warplanes filled the night sky over Iraq. Everyone was hyped, and the adrenaline was crackling like electricity.

Lt. Cmdr. Raz Rasmussen—call sign Anvil Four-three—was the second element leader of the four-ship flight. Anvil Flight's job was to shoot HARMs—high-speed antiradiation missiles intended to kill Iraq's air defense radars. The mission was critical because the inbound strike aircraft—other F/A-18s, F-15s, F-111s, B-52s—depended on the HARM shooters to take out the barrage of radar-directed antiaircraft guns and surface-to-air missile batteries.

To Rasmussen's right was his wingman, Anvil Four-four, a cocky second-tour lieutenant named John DeLancey. To his left was the lead element—Lt. Cmdr. Gracie Allen and his wingman, Lt. Brick Maxwell.

Rasmussen could see Baghdad glimmering in the distance. Tiny flashes pulsed like heat lightning just above the horizon. Tracers were arcing into the sky over the city. Tomahawk missiles and F-117 Stinkbugs were already hitting the target area.

Then Rasmussen saw something in the radar that made his blood run cold. He waited two more sweeps to be sure. *Another bogey.*

Not one but *two* goddamn Foxbats out there. No

question about it. Two targets at twelve o'clock, fifteen miles, closing fast.

But he couldn't shoot. Not until he'd gotten clearance. He silently cursed the idiotic Rules of Engagement. An electronic ID with the Hornet's onboard radar was not considered accurate enough to tag a bogey as a hostile fighter. There were too many allied warplanes in the same tiny airspace.

The tactical frequency was clogged. The AWACS controller wasn't getting through.

Twelve miles. The Foxbats were close enough to shoot their own—

"Anvil Four-two is spiked!"

Rasmussen recognized Maxwell's voice. He was reporting that he was targeted by the MiGs' radar. In the next instant, Rasmussen saw a tiny flash of light in the dark sky in front of him.

A missile in the air.

Grunting against the seven-G break turn, Maxwell felt the perspiration pour from inside his helmet.

He knew the hard turn was taking him directly beneath the three other members of Anvil Flight. He hoped they maintained altitude so that he would pass a couple of thousand feet under them.

His RWR was warbling like a deranged parrot. *Damn!* A radar-guided missile—an AA-6 Acrid—and it had him locked. *How did we let the MiG take the first shot?*

He hit the chaff dispenser, releasing a trail of aluminum confetti to confuse the Acrid's radar guidance unit. Maxwell had a nagging doubt that the stuff really worked. Even Russian radars weren't that stupid.

Maxwell felt like a blind man. He couldn't see the Foxbat, and he couldn't see any of the Hornets in his flight. It was like knife-fighting in a blackened closet.

With zero visual reference, he was completely on instruments.

This Foxbat pilot was no amateur. He'd taken his shot at Maxwell, out at the far left of the six-mile-wide formation. Now, if he was smart, he would try to sweep around behind the rest of the formation.

Over his shoulder, Maxwell got a glimpse of the missile. A white torch, arcing toward him.

Pull! Hard right and down. Beat the missile. Put the spike at your nine o'clock.

The good news was that the AA-6 was perhaps the least maneuverable air-to-air missile the Soviets had made. The bad news was it had the largest warhead.

He rolled wings level and stabbed the chaff dispenser again.

Brick Maxwell was a nugget—a new fighter pilot on his first squadron tour. He'd been in the squadron three months when it sailed for the Persian Gulf. This was his first combat mission.

"Just stay cool, pal," his best friend in the squadron, Raz Rasmussen, had told him before the mission. They were walking across the darkened flight deck toward their jets. "Stick with ol' Raz. This is gonna be a walk in the park."

Some walk in the park. Maxwell felt like he was getting mugged. If he lived through this, he'd tell Raz he was full of shit.

The warbling in the RWR changed pitch, then ceased altogether. Over his shoulder Maxwell saw the white torch of the Acrid. It was veering to the left, behind him. Going for the chaff. Hey, the stuff worked! Thank you, God.

Where was the rest of Anvil Flight? Above him somewhere. Close.

Where?

He saw the flash of another missile launch.

*   *   *

Screw the Rules of Engagement.

The AWACS had still not identified the bogey as a bandit. By definition, a bogey was an unidentified target. A bogey didn't become a bandit until he was identified as a bona fide hostile aircraft.

Rasmussen wasn't waiting any longer. He didn't need any more identification. One of the bogeys had just taken a shot at Maxwell. That made him a bona fide no-shit bandit who needed killing

His AIM-7 Sparrow missile leaped from its rail like a runaway freight train and went scorching into the night sky.

He keyed the microphone to transmit a "Fox One" call, signaling the launch of a radar-guided missile.

Bleep. He was cut out again.

The radio chatter was overwhelming. Hornet pilots were calling bogeys, yelling for clearance to fire, blocking each other's transmissions. It sounded like feeding time in the monkey cage.

Then he caught a flash of light in his peripheral vision. Another missile launch. *Who?*

"Anvil Four-four, Fox One." He recognized the voice of DeLancey, his wingman.

Rasmussen saw DeLancey's missile arcing off into the sky, in the trail of his own Sparrow missile.

Two seconds later, Rasmussen saw an orange blob appear at his eleven o'clock position, slightly low. The blob pulsed like an amorphous creature, then turned into a trail of fire.

His Sparrow missile had killed the Foxbat.

Then another explosion. A white flash ignited briefly inside the flames of the destroyed Foxbat. DeLancey's missile had targeted the same MiG.

Before he could key his microphone, he heard De-Lancey's triumphant voice. "Anvil Four-four, Splash One!"

A flash of anger swept over Rasmussen. DeLancey

was taking credit for a MiG he didn't kill. When they got back to the ship he would—

Something else was out there. A bright blue torch where the Foxbat had been.

The second Foxbat. He was seeing the bright plumes of two Tumansky afterburners. The Foxbat had just seen his partner get hosed and he was getting out of Dodge.

Or was he?

The plumes vanished. *Where did he go?*

Rasmussen was still searching with his radar, scanning the empty sky for the missing Foxbat when he heard the sudden screaming of his own RWR. A wave of fear swept over him.

He knew where the Foxbat had gone.

Capt. Tariq Jabbar shoved the throttles of his MiG-25 up to the afterburner detent. The extra thrust of the big Tumansky engines felt like the kick of a mule.

He hated giving away his presence with the glow of the burner plumes, but he needed to close the distance between him and the oncoming Americans. Speed was his only defense. Speed was life.

The enemy fighters had just obliterated his friend and squadron commander, Lt. Col. Tawfiq Al-Rashid, with a radar-guided missile. The fireball had nearly blinded Jabbar, causing him to hunker in his seat, waiting for the next missile. The one that would kill him.

Instead, the second missile followed the first. Both had struck Al-Rashid's MiG-25.

"Make your peace with Allah," Al-Rashid had told him back at Al-Taqqadum air base before they took off. "We will be joining him tonight."

Jabbar had just nodded. He had no illusions about his longevity as a fighter pilot in the Iraqi Air Force. The war with America was about to begin, and his life expectancy could be measured in minutes.

Soon after takeoff he had been shocked to see on his

radar the armada of aircraft sweeping northward toward Baghdad. As it turned out, Al-Rashid was the first to join Allah.

As Jabbar flashed past the oncoming American fighters, he pulled the throttles out of the afterburner detent and hauled the nose of the MiG-25 up and around in a hard turn, back toward their tails.

The silence of his *Sirena* radar warning receiver told him that he was not targeted. They had lost him, at least momentarily. In their own confusion, they were not yet aware that he was behind them. Perhaps his own appointment with Allah would be postponed. The trick was to not lock any of them up until he was ready to fire his missile. Shoot quickly and run. *There.* He saw it in his radar—an enemy blip in the middle of the spread-out formation. If the geometry of his turn had been correct, it would be the same one who killed Al-Rashid.

Which was appropriate. An eye for an eye, an American for an Iraqi. Let one of them join Al-Rashid in eternity.

He commanded the radar to lock, then squeezed the trigger. The airframe of the aging Russian-built fighter rumbled as the Acrid missile roared off its rail and streaked away like a fire-tailed comet.

He waited, watching the missile vanish in the darkness. His own *Sirena* continued its silence.

They still didn't know he was there.

Maxwell saw it first. "Anvil flight, missile in the air!" he called. "Six o'clock!"

It had to be another Acrid. The flash came from beneath and behind him. The missile was targeting one of the Hornets up ahead.

It was the fighter pilot's nightmare scenario. Someone shooting at them from behind. It had to be another Foxbat. A wingman. After his leader was killed, he had merged with Anvil Flight and performed what was called a stern conversion—sweeping past the oncoming Hornets, then reversing course to put himself at their six o'clock.

Aimed at their tails.

Two thousand feet beneath the other three Hornets of Anvil flight, Maxwell scanned the black sky where he had seen the missile flash.

Nothing.

He hauled the nose of his Hornet to the left, probing with his radar. Still nothing. *Where was the Foxbat?*

Missile in the air. The most dreaded words a fighter pilot could hear.

As if triggered by his own adrenaline, Rasmussen's RWR was warbling at a high, urgent pitch.

He was targeted.

Rasmussen's years of training kicked in. He rolled the Hornet into a hard break turn, dumping the nose and hauling back on the stick. His left hand found the chaff dispenser. *Pull. Turn into the missile. Make it overshoot.*

Grunting against the Gs, trying not to gray out, he peered over his shoulder. He saw it. A flicker of light, a faint zigzag motion behind him.

With a grim certainty, he knew what would happen next. He tensed himself and waited.

As he expected, the impact came from behind. Rasmussen was dimly aware of the explosion, a blinding wave of flame that engulfed the Hornet and turned the darkness into a scarlet hell. He knew his life had ended and his remains would be scattered over the ancient dirt of Iraq.

Captain Jabbar watched the fireball of the Hornet plummet like a meteor toward the floor of the desert. Al-Rashid had been avenged.

It was enough. Jabbar knew that he could stay here and maybe kill another enemy Hornet, perhaps two. It would also mean his own certain death. At any moment now, one of them would find him on his radar. The enemy fighters would pounce like dogs on a rat.

He shoved the nose of the MiG-25 down and eased the throttles back. He would stay under the enemy formation, let them continue on their mission toward Baghdad. He would live to fight another day. Martyrdom was for fanatics.

As he descended, he glanced again at the burning hulk arcing downward in the night. He wondered about the pilot. Was he a frightened young man on his first mission? Or was he a veteran, one who had seen combat before? Jabbar guessed that he was probably a man like himself—willing to die for his country, not willing to throw his life away for nothing. He had dreams, hopes for the future, a family who would miss him.

Jabbar pushed the thought from his mind. This was war. It wasn't wise to have such thoughts about the man you had just killed.

Rasmussen's numbed brain accepted the finality of his death, but his body did not.

Following a script he had rehearsed a hundred times in training, his hands reached for the ejection lanyard between his legs. His head slammed back against the headrest. With both hands, he yanked the lanyard upward.

The ejection seat fired. Rasmussen catapulted like a cannon shell from the roiling fireball of the Hornet. A nearly supersonic wall of air slammed into his body.

Downward he tumbled through the thin air of the stratosphere, the automatic features of the SJU/5A Martin-Baker ejection seat performing as advertised. Its occupant hung slumped and unconscious in his straps.

At ten thousand feet, precisely on schedule, the main parachute canopy deployed. Borne on a twenty-five-knot wind, the inert body of Raz Rasmussen drifted toward the floor of the desert. He was not aware of the descent, nor did he feel the thunk of the landing.

Still in the parachute harness, he was dragged by the wind for another two hundred meters until the canopy wrapped itself around a pair of jagged boulders.

When he regained consciousness, Rasmussen thought he was blind. Then he realized that his eyes were swollen shut. He was lying against a rocky slope, still wrapped in the canopy and shroud lines of the parachute. When he tried to move, waves of pain shot like jolts of electricity through his limbs.

For several minutes he lay where he was, assessing the damage. Though every bone in his body ached, nothing seemed to be fractured. He wasn't blind, but he could peer only through a pair of crusty slits.

He released the Koch fasteners on his torso harness, freeing himself from the chute. He rose creakily to his feet, taking a few small steps, testing each limb. Everything still worked. It just hurt like hell.

Nothing made sense.

His brain was processing information at about one-tenth its usual rate, but that was to be expected. He was in no hurry. He was alive, and they'd come to get him. He'd get out of this place. The thought gave him comfort, and he clung to it. He'd get out.

How will they know where I am?

Simple. He'd tell them. Which was why he had the PRC-112 survival radio. It was his ticket home. He could communicate with other aircraft, give his location, call in the SAR helo. It was the new model they'd just issued, which he'd taken the trouble to put in a Ziploc bag and stuff right here in the vest pocket of his . . .

His hand felt inside the pocket. The flap was already open. The pocket was empty.

No radio. In the violence of the ejection, the damned thing must have flown out of his pocket and whirled off into space. The pocket was designed for the older

PRC-90. The PRC-112 was taller and thinner, and didn't quite fit in the standard vest pocket. The survival experts didn't think it would make any difference in an ejection.

So much for the experts.

Rasmussen fought off the sense of desolation that settled over him. *Okay, think. They know where you went down. They'll be searching for you.*

Then another thought. Wasn't there an emergency locator beacon in the seat? He tried to remember, then it came to him. Yes, an ELT was installed in the seat, but the air wing brass had ordered the things disabled on the eve of the strike. They'd gotten intelligence that the Iraqis had their own homing devices and would track the signals from a downed American jet.

Of course, he could go looking for the seat and activate the ELT. He discarded the idea. The seat separated from him in the descent at ten thousand feet. It could be anywhere in a twenty-mile radius.

The cold night was coming to an end. A pale light had begun to illuminate the bleakness of the desert. Through his slitted eyes Rasmussen could make out the irregular shapes of boulders and low ridges.

He was gathering his equipment, stuffing the chute and life raft out of sight behind an outcropping, when he sensed movement behind him.

He turned and saw them. They had approached without his hearing them. They were no more than twenty feet away, a dozen of them, and each had his rifle aimed at Rasmussen.

CHAPTER 2

DREAMS OF A DISTANT LAND

Virginia Beach, Virginia
1435, Wednesday, 10 March
The Present

She was having a nightmare.

That had to be it. One of those terrible dreams she used to have. She thought she'd finally gotten over them, but it was happening again.

Maria lowered the phone and looked around. Through the twelve-foot living room window she could see across the sloping green lawn. *Her* lawn. She saw a car drive past. Someone—her neighbor's son—was riding a bicycle on the opposite sidewalk. All very normal. Nothing at all nightmarish.

Oh, dear God, I'm not dreaming.

She spoke into the telephone again. "Who are you?"

"It's necessary that I remain anonymous," said the caller. He had some kind of accent that she couldn't place. "I'm sorry if this upsets you."

"Upsets me?" She was losing control of her voice. It sounded shrill and tinny. "A stranger who won't identify himself calls to tell me my deceased husband might still be alive. Why would a thing like that upset me?" She knew she was becoming hysterical.

A moment of silence. "I'm sorry, Mrs. Rasmussen."

"How could you possibly know such a thing about . . . my husband?"

"I have a source. It is very reliable."

"If it's true, why doesn't our government know about it?"

Several more seconds of silence. "I can't answer that."

She could feel her heart pounding in her chest. She realized she was hyperventilating. *Oh, sweet Christ, get control of yourself.* "Why are you telling me this?"

"I don't know. An act of compassion, I suppose. You are a wife, and you deserve to know the truth."

You are a wife. That much was true. Maybe twice true.

"I don't believe you," she said.

"You may believe whatever you choose. I'm just delivering—"

She slammed the phone down, then stared at it as if it were a snake. She had heard enough. It was a crank call. Had to be. There was someone out there with a sick mind. It couldn't be true.

After a minute had passed, it occurred to her to check the caller ID log. The call was tagged as UNKNOWN CALL. No surprise there. Of course, it would be unknown. Could it be traced? She didn't know.

She stood in the kitchen with her arms clasped around her. Any minute now the kids would be home. She had to think. Joey had lacrosse practice at five. Lisa would want to talk about school. Frank would roll into the driveway in another hour. He always came home before six.

Frank. She could imagine the look on his face when she told him. It wasn't fair. He was a good man, a loving husband, a surrogate father to her two children. Frank didn't deserve this. No one did.

Ten years they had been married. It was hard to believe. Frank Gallagher had come into her life at the time when she most needed him. He was a successful Virginia Beach businessman, fifteen years older than she, with grown children of his own. Frank was good-looking, intelligent, and compassionate. Best of all, he was not a fighter pilot.

Losing Raz was like losing a piece of her own life. Like most young married couples in Navy fighter squadrons, they had discussed the unthinkable. The "just in case" scenario. Neither expected anything bad to happen, but in the dangerous world of naval aviation, bad things sometimes happened. They were realists.

Two weeks after he was reported missing in action, she received a letter. "If you're reading this," Raz wrote in his barely legible left-handed scrawl, "then it means you already know that I'm not coming back. You know I love you beyond what words can express. And please remember that you must be strong and build a new life, not just for yourself but for Joey and Lisa."

It had taken nearly a year for the Navy to change "Missing in Action" to "Killed in Action." Every piece of evidence corroborated the report. Raz's Hornet was shot down by an Iraqi fighter. He did not survive the explosion.

It was official, she told herself, pacing the kitchen floor. She had the paperwork from the Navy to prove it. She was a widow, and she had already gone through the torment of hoping otherwise. Raz was dead. He'd been dead since 1991, and that was that.

Or was it? She stopped pacing the floor as another wave of anxiety swept over her. *Oh dear God, what if the caller was telling the truth? What if . . .*

She had to talk to someone. Who? Not Frank, at least not yet. She couldn't bear it. Who, then? The anxiety was pressing on her heart like a heavy weight.

She resumed pacing the kitchen, trying to think. She needed to speak with someone who could do something. Someone who knew Raz, a friend she could trust.

It came to her. Yes, if only she knew how to find him. It had been several years, but she thought he might still be in the Navy. If she could find Brick Maxwell, he would know what to do.

Mashmashiyeh, Iran

Gunfire.

Col. Jamal Al-Fasr flinched at the rattle of the automatic weapon. *What was happening?* The shots came from somewhere inside the village. He heard it just as his Land Rover crossed the bridge over the river, entering Mashmashiyeh. The village was supposed to be secure, pacified and controlled by the *Sherji*—the guerrilla troops of his Bu Hasa Brigade.

He and his driver, Shakeeb, had just returned from Tabruz, where his *Sherji* had seized two SA-2 antiaircraft sites from the inept Iranian Revolutionary Army troops who manned them.

They had been lucky. With their new equipment, they were able to target a flight of British Tornadoes patrolling the border between Iraq and Iran. He doubted that they'd done any damage, but they accomplished the desired effect.

Now a punitive mission would come, probably Americans from one of the carriers in the Gulf. They would be convinced that Iran was targeting allied jets. The Iranians would receive the wrath of the mighty United States.

Since the humiliating defeat of Saddam Hussein, the Americans and British had occupied most of Iraq. Most of the freedom fighters—*terrorists,* as the Westerners insisted on labeling them—that Saddam supported had fled eastward toward Iran.

Now there were too many for the Iranian government to control. The western third of Iran had become, for the most part, a lawless hodgepodge of private fiefdoms. While the government in Tehran still pretended to be in control, it had already ceded authority to the bands of fedayeen and mujahedeen operating along the Iraqi border.

It was a fertile place for Jamal Al-Fasr to reconstitute his Bu Hasa Brigade. He had staked a claim to the strategic village of Mashmashiyeh, along a navigable stretch of the Shatt-al-Arab waterway, yet far enough inside Iran to be out of the reach of the American occupation force in Iraq.

"Stop here," he snapped to Shakeeb. He jumped from the Land Rover and trotted to the shelter of the first stucco hut, ignoring the pain in his right leg. Shakeeb joined him, carrying an AK-74 from the Land Rover.

Another short burst. It came from the center of the village, and now Al-Fasr recognized the weapon by the distinctive crackle. Another Russian-made Kalashnikov AK-74, an advanced derivative of the classic AK-47. *Ours,* he realized. *At least, it better be.*

Then he saw the sentries; a pair at the far end of the bridge, two more watching him from a hut at the perimeter of the village. One of the sentries waved, apparently not interested in the nearby gunshots. It meant that the village wasn't under siege. It was safe to enter.

He gave Shakeeb the nod to go ahead. With his SIG Sauer semiautomatic in his right hand, he followed the sergeant along the brick-lined path to the clearing in the center of the village. They passed two more sentries— *Sherji* with their Kalashnikovs slung over their shoulders. They gave him the palm-upward *Sherji* salute, showing no sense of alarm.

The pathway led to the large open area in the village center. As Al-Fasr approached the edge of the clearing, he could see the bodies. There were half a dozen, sprawled like bundles of laundry. A dark pool of blood oozed over the worn courtyard.

Another group of a dozen or more—Al-Fasr could see by the coarse brown *gellebiahs* that they were local villagers—huddled against a far wall. Their hands were bound behind them, and they were tethered to a rusty-wheeled cart.

Al-Fasr stepped into the courtyard. Twenty meters from the tethered prisoners was a cluster of *Sherji*, at least twenty, smiling and watching him as he stormed across the courtyard. With them was his second-in-command, Abu Mahmed.

Abu saw him coming. He lowered the muzzle of his AK-74.

"What is happening here?" demanded Al-Fasr.

"It is a local matter," said Abu. He, too, was smiling.

"Why were those men killed?"

"To teach the others a lesson. They were resisting our occupation of Mashmashiyeh."

"Resisting? In what way?"

Abu pointed to one of the bodies sprawled on the cobblestones. "That one refused to turn over his boat to us for transporting supplies up from Hawr Umr Sawan. He deliberately sank it."

"So you executed him?"

"And his family. Those are his four brothers and his father lying beside him."

"The others, those tied to the cart? Do you intend to execute them also?"

"Of course. They were all supporting—"

"Enough!" Al-Fasr felt the fury boiling up in him like hot lava. He snatched the weapon from Abu's hands. In a single furious gesture, he yanked the magazine out of the automatic rifle and sent it clattering across the courtyard. "We did not come to this country to execute the population. There will be no more killing of civilians. Is that understood?" He glowered at the silent *Sherji*. None were smiling now. They stared back at him with sullen expressions.

Al-Fasr felt like using the Kalashnikov on Abu. *The arrogant, murderous imbecile!* By slaughtering the local villagers he was contaminating the very ground they needed to build a new base. A new Babylon.

He had chosen Abu Mahmed as his lieutenant because he needed the loyalty of the mujahedeen who had fought with Abu in Afghanistan. Since Al-Fasr's own defeat and rout from Yemen, his Bu Hasa Brigade had been decimated and reduced to a band of ragtag guerrillas. He needed Abu's veteran fighters, even though most were illiterate and vicious as wild dogs. They were also Islamic fanatics, which made them even more dangerous.

Abu was a fanatic, but he was not an illiterate peasant like the others. The son of a prominent Cairo physician, he had attended medical school before joining the jihad a dozen years ago. He was ambitious and just as vicious as the mujahedeen. In the name of Allah, Abu was willing to execute the population of an entire village.

It wasn't the killing that infuriated Al-Fasr. He had no sentimental scruples about executions. In his life he had slain hundreds of his enemies, some for tactical reasons and some for the pure pleasure of watching them die.

But this was different. This was Babylon. He could not afford to turn it into a killing ground.

The smile was gone from Abu's face. He was watching him with dark, accusing eyes. "Jamal, you have no right to—"

"Do not presume to give me orders." Al-Fasr threw the empty Kalashnikov on the ground at Abu's feet. "I am still in command of this Brigade." He glowered at the sullen *Sherji*, fixing his gaze for a moment on each leathered face. "Is that clear to all of you?"

None answered.

He turned to face Abu. "You," he said. "Come with me."

Kifri, Iraq

The prisoner heard the clink of the key in the cell door. He didn't look up. He continued scribbling in his notebook, ignoring the clang of the iron door as it swung against the wall.

Someone entered the room. The prisoner heard the scrape of boots on the rough concrete, coming toward the table where he sat writing in his notebook. He ignored the visitor.

"Gather your things," said a voice that sounded like gravel. "You're leaving."

The prisoner didn't respond. He took his time, finishing the passage in the notebook. He closed the notebook, then laid the ballpoint atop it.

Finally he gazed up at the visitor. The man wore the mottled green fatigues and broad leather belt of a former Iraqi army officer. A holstered semiautomatic dangled from the belt. The officer looked vaguely familiar. What was his name? The prisoner couldn't remember. Maybe he never knew. He no longer concerned himself with such things.

"Where am I going?"

"Don't ask," said the officer. "Be ready in half an hour."

The prisoner continued staring at the officer. It was coming to him now. He remembered the face, but the name still eluded him. He'd been present back in the old days, at one of the interrogations, one of the bad ones. The officer had stood there, hands clasped behind him, observing with a pitiless, blank-faced expression while the interrogators extracted the answers they wanted.

He was wearing that same expression now. For another long moment, the prisoner locked gazes with the officer. Abruptly the officer turned on his heel, making another grating noise on the concrete. He clanged the door shut behind him.

A rush of trepidation swept over the prisoner like a winter chill. *Leaving? Why?*

He remembered leaving Abu Graib prison and being taken to this place, somewhere in the northeast of Iraq. How long ago had that been? Two years? Three? Perhaps more. He had lost his ability to measure time.

All he knew was that he didn't want to leave. It wasn't a rational thought, but he'd abandoned rational thinking years ago. This cell was his only security. Not at all rational, but he didn't care. It was his reality.

For several minutes he sat there, not moving. He peered around at his surroundings—gray walls with splotched plaster, a single high, barred window, narrow cot along one wall. In a corner stood a greasy wooden table with a basin for bathing. Another table served as his writing desk.

For a quarter of his life he had lived in such a place. First Abu Graib, then Kifri. He no longer thought of it as a cell. It was a burrow, a nest, a hiding place. He was a subterranean animal, hidden like a mole from the eyes of the world.

Be ready, the officer had said. *Gather your things.* Was that a joke? Everything he owned he could carry under one arm. His possessions amounted to an extra pair of coarsely woven brown trousers, a couple of chambray shirts, a few toiletry items. And there were the ballpoint pen and the spiral notebooks.

Why am I leaving?

He could only guess. Long ago, before the government of Iraq fell to the Americans, they had moved him from Baghdad to this place. They wanted to keep his existence a secret, he presumed.

Now they were moving him again. Why?

So they can execute me.

That had to be it. It was the fate that he had expected since the first few weeks of captivity, after they'd gotten what they wanted from him. During the worst of the interrogations, he had begged them to execute him. They didn't oblige him.

Now it didn't matter. After this many years in captivity, nothing mattered.

CHAPTER 3

INCIDENT OVER IRAN

Tabruz, Iran, 31,000 feet
1145, Thursday, 11 March

What the hell are we doing here?

It was the question that always came to Brick Maxwell's mind at times like this. Five miles below lay the vast brownness of Iraq—or maybe Iran, it was hard to tell from up here—spreading beneath him like a great empty moonscape. Except that it wasn't empty. Somewhere in the mottled terrain were angry men with an abiding hatred of all things American. They were armed with exotic weaponry, some of it capable of bringing down sophisticated jet fighters.

Which was what they had attempted to do to a flight of four British Tornadoes a couple of hours earlier during a reconnaissance sweep up the Shatt-al-Arab waterway, along the border between Iraq and Iran. Someone—Iranians, ex-Iraqis, or some new team in the league—had targeted them with acquisition radar.

It lasted only a few seconds. Before the Brits could respond, the radars went dark. From the brief emission signature recorded by the Rivet Joint RC-135 controlling the fighters, the best guess was an SA-2 missile site.

Whose missiles? wondered Maxwell.

The cast of players in the region of the Tigris and Euphrates valleys had become confused. The Iraqis were no longer a threat to allied aircraft. The shaky Iranian government had so many internal problems that it paid only scant attention to the allied fighters that patrolled their border. The central government was giving way to factions, and the entire region—Iran and Iraq—was in danger of becoming Balkanized.

But somebody down there definitely had an attitude. The Russian-built SA-2 missile—NATO codename Guideline—was the same basic missile that brought down Francis Gary Powers's U-2 over Russia in 1960. Its analog signal processor was ancient technology by the standards of modern digital warfare, but the Russians had made sure it was the best analog system available. Despite its age, the continually updated SA-2 was still a lethal high-altitude killer.

"Snow King, Runner One," called Maxwell, "say the picture."

"Picture still clear, Runner." "Snow King" was the call sign for the weapons controller on the AWACS, a four-engine Boeing E-3C Sentry, on station over the Persian Gulf. He was reporting that the radar picture was showing no threats. Maxwell recognized the voice—a young Air Force first lieutenant named Surofchek.

Maxwell acknowledged. The AWACS was now their only source of data from the ground below. The Rivet Joint, whose sensors and antennae were best suited for distinguishing surface activity, had used up its loiter time and gone home. The KH-13 reconnaissance satellite that linked imaging data, via the AWACS, to patrolling fighters, was on the back side of its orbit. The next one wouldn't pass overhead for another ninety minutes.

A mile to the left, Maxwell could see his wingman,

Lt. B. J. Johnson, in a combat spread formation. Somewhere off to his right was a section of two more Super Hornets—Cdr. Bullet Alexander and his wingman, Lt. Pearly Gates.

In addition to their two external fuel tanks, Maxwell and Alexander were each carrying a Mk 83 thousand-pound laser-guided bomb and an AGM-88C HARM antiradiation missile, plus their air-to-air loads of two AIM-9 Sidewinders and two AIM-120 AMRAAM missiles. The two wingmen, Johnson and Gates, carried the same weaponry except for the HARMs. Each jet contained a full bay of twenty-millimeter cannon ammo.

On his center multifunction display Maxwell could see every member of his flight. Each jet had FFDL—fighter-to-fighter data link, or "fiddle." Even when out of visual range they could maintain awareness of each other's position. Fiddle was the modern fighter pilot's secret weapon.

They were nearly at the northern end of the sweep. Peering at the image of Alexander's Hornet in the display, Maxwell had to laugh. He knew that at this moment Alexander was praying that someone—*anyone*—down there would light up a targeting radar long enough to qualify as a bona fide hostile.

It was unusual that a squadron skipper and his XO would be on the same flight. XOs didn't fly as wingmen—at least in normal circumstances. When Alexander learned that Maxwell was taking out an armed reconnaissance flight to look for SAMs, he couldn't stay out of the action. Maxwell understood Alexander's frustration. Even though he was a commander and the executive officer of the Roadrunners, Alexander's career timing had caused him to miss every critical combat activity. He wanted to make up for lost time. Bullet wanted to—

Tweet . . . tweet . . . tweet.

Maxwell's RWR—radar warning receiver—was

chirping an intermittent signal. Not a strong, steady warning, just a low-energy alert.

"Runner One, Runner Two," called Alexander. "Are you getting hits?"

Maxwell punched up the page in his display, checking the targeting radar library. *There.* He saw it, flashing at irregular intervals.

"Affirmative. Looks like a Fan Song acquisition signal." Fan Song was the codename for the SA-2 system's acquisition and missile control radar. Once it acquired a target, it then transmitted the guidance data to the SA-2's tracking radar.

Everyone knew the Rules of Engagement. Anything short of a steady warning from an air defense site was not grounds for an attack. This was a spurious signal, as if someone at the missile site was playing with them, flipping the radar on and off.

Just to piss off Bullet Alexander.

It was working.

They're yanking my chain, Alexander fumed. *The little peckerheads are just begging to have a HARM fired into their hooch.*

He guessed that the fire control site was somewhere around Tabruz, just inside Iran. It was close—about fifty miles—to the Iranian air base at Dezful. *Careful,* he told himself. It could also be a sucker play.

There was one way to find out.

"Runner One, Runner Three," Alexander called. "How about we make a pass over Tabruz with the FLIR, just to see what they've got cooking." The FLIR—Forward-Looking Infrared—could pick up the telltale heat signs from vehicle exhausts and generator plants around a launch site.

Several seconds passed, and he knew Maxwell was studying the situation in his display. Alexander and

Gates were nearly on top of Tabruz, while Maxwell was forty miles to the west.

"Go for it, Runner Three," said Maxwell. "Hard deck is twenty thousand."

"Runner Three, roger the hard deck."

Twenty thousand feet was the minimum altitude mandated in the Rules of Engagement for overflying a potentially hostile site. It kept the jets above most of the small-caliber AA fire and high enough to counter a SAM launch.

Or so they hoped.

Actually, thought Alexander, a little hostile intent from the switch-flippers down there would make his day. They just needed to show enough bad attitude to qualify as bona fide targets.

Alexander made a quick check outside, seeing the gray silhouette of Pearly Gates's jet, still a mile off his right wing. Exactly where he was supposed to be.

He guessed that Pearly was unhappy about being bumped back to dash four in this flight. Alexander had pulled rank and inserted himself into the flight, removing the junior pilot, Hozer Miller, and bumping Pearly back to the dash-four spot. Instead of being a section leader, Pearly was now Alexander's wingman.

Tough shit, thought Alexander. *Who said life was fair for junior officers?* He'd make it up to Pearly with a few beers at the Gulf Lounge in Bahrain.

He eased the nose of the Super Hornet over, letting the airspeed build as he descended to the level-off altitude of twenty thousand. Coming up under the nose was the brown patchwork of Tabruz, an ancient village in the foothills of Iran's Zagros mountain range.

He wanted to get a look at this place, scope it with the FLIR. If his guess was correct, he'd surely pick up a—

"Check twelve o'clock, XO," called Pearly. "We'd better start jinking." "Jinking" was evasive maneuvering to throw off antiaircraft gunners.

Alexander snapped his attention out of the cockpit. *Shit.* Directly ahead of his jet—four puffs, black and roiling like ugly mushrooms. *AA fire.*

He yanked the nose up and to the left. *Get your head out of the cockpit, Alexander.* He'd been focused inside and damn near flew into a flak trap. Now he owed Pearly more than a couple of beers.

Still jinking, he hauled the nose of the Super Hornet back to the right. A quick glance to the right confirmed that Pearly was doing his own very enthusiastic jinking.

"Runner Four spiked at twelve," yelled Pearly, signaling that he had just been acquired by a hostile radar. Alexander saw Pearly's jet rolling left, slicing beneath him. A stream of chaff was spewing behind the diving Super Hornet.

Alexander followed his wingman, breaking hard to the left. With his left thumb he toggled his own chaff dump.

What the hell is it? he wondered. *A SAM? Or AAA fire control radar?*

He was checking his display again when he heard Pearly's call. "Burner Two hot! Hot on Runner Four."

Burner Two was code for an SA-2 surface-to-air missile. Hot meant it was airborne and targeting Pearly's jet.

Still rolling hard to the left, trying to keep Pearly's jet in sight, he peered toward Tabruz. Something down there caught his eye—like a Roman candle with a long orange plume.

Another missile—it had to be a second SA-2—just leaving the launcher. The first one was already out there tracking Pearly.

His own radar warning receiver was singing now. He glanced down by his right knee, to his RWR display. He saw a flashing numeral 2.

Now *he* was targeted. Two more missiles were coming from a second site.

Four goddamn SAMs in the air.

"Runners egress!" called Alexander. "It's a trap. Take heading two-zero-zero."

He had a good view of the first SAM now. It looked like a telephone pole arcing into the sky, trailing a long, thin plume of fire. It was flying a classic pursuit curve toward Pearly Gates's Super Hornet.

Alexander jammed the yellow-and-black-striped button labeled EMERGENCY JETTISON. He felt a rapid series of thumps as nine thousand pounds of fuel and weapons departed the jet, making the Super Hornet instantly lighter, more maneuverable.

He yanked the nose back to the left, following Pearly in his own missile defense. He issued instructions to himself, willing himself to stay calm. *Get to the beam. Put out chaff. Make the missile turn. Bleed its energy.*

The first missile was still on an intercept course with Pearly. Not far behind, Alexander knew, was the second pair—the ones with *his* name on them.

He could see Pearly's jet maneuvering below and to his left. Pearly still had his external stores. "Runner Four, emergency jettison," Alexander called. A second later he saw Pearly's external tanks and weapons separate and whirl away in the fighter's slipstream.

For a fleeting moment it occurred to Alexander that the jettisoned HARM might be recovered intact by the Iranians. Just as quickly, he pushed it from his mind. Let the gomers have it. It was more urgent that they get away from these SAMs flying up their butts.

"Runner Four," he called, "continue left, limiter pull, egress heading one-eight-zero." A limiter pull—cranking the Hornet into the tightest turn that the computerized flight control system would allow—was their only hope of beating the SA-2s.

Alexander rolled out above and to the right of Pearly's jet. The turn had put them tail-on to the on-coming SAMs.

Now what? Break turn into the missiles, try to outturn them? Or continue and try to outrun them. He estimated they had to be near the edge of the SA-2s' range limit.

Run. At least until the missiles got *very* damned close. Maybe the SAMs would be out of effective range before they caught up with the Hornets.

"Runners, gate," he ordered, and pushed his throttles to maximum afterburner. As he felt the thrust of the two afterburners kick in, he peered again over his shoulder.

The missiles were still there. Closing fast.

Maxwell saw them too. Near the top of his own HARM display was the big, bright 2—the symbol for an active SA-2 missile.

He did a quick assessment. By the Rules of Engagement, he required clearance to fire his HARM antiradar missile. The weapons controller on the AWACS would have to ask the ACE—Airborne Command Element—who had stand-alone authority to issue a clearance.

But he knew this ACE—an Air Force major named Hatch. Hatch was a cautious type who would get on the line to his boss, the Joint Task Force Commander, a three star based in Riyadh, and they would discuss the situation. By the time they issued clearance to fire HARMs, Bullet and Pearly would be puffs of smoke.

To hell with the clearance.

He flipped the MASTER ARM switch on. In his HARM display he assigned the seeker to the numeral 2—the SA-2 site that was tracking them. He waited two seconds until a steady box formed around it. He mashed the pickle button with his thumb.

The HARM roared off its station beneath the Hornet, trailing fire like a Roman candle.

"Magnum, magnum," he called, using the brevity code for the HARM launch. At the same time he saw the time-to-go digital countdown begin in the HUD: *Twenty-five seconds . . . twenty-four . . .*

He still couldn't see Bullet or Pearly's jets, but in the distance he could make out the ominous black smoke trails of the SA-2s. He could also see the fiery tail of his own HARM missile, just passing the apogee of its flight path, arcing downward toward Tabruz.

There was nothing more he could do. He called the AWACS controller. "Runner flight engaged by Burner Two, vicinity Tabruz. Three and Four defending, One and Two beaming south, Magnums in the air."

That'll wake them up, he thought. Somebody had just fired HARM missiles at an unidentified target in a supposedly nonhostile country. *And, oh, yeah, sorry about that. I didn't bother with a clearance.*

Several seconds passed, then he heard the controller's strained voice. "We copy that, Runner. Green south. Air picture clear."

Good, thought Maxwell. The egress to the south was clear. The discussion about the HARM shot would come later.

Bullet Alexander's voice came over the radio. "Skipper, say the HARM time to go."

Maxwell glanced at the countdown on his HUD. "Ten seconds."

"Too long," said Alexander. "The first SAM is—"

The transmission abruptly ended.

"—less than ten seconds out."

Alexander couldn't hear the last words of his own transmission. He was talking into a dead microphone.

The goddamn radio! It had just quit. So had his RWR. *What the hell is going on?* His multifunction display was flickering on and off like a cheap motel sign. His jet was turning into a bag of electronic junk.

He had seen the first missile overshoot Pearly's jet. The hard break had outturned the SAM. The second missile had gone stupid during their turn to egress, chasing the chaff cloud. Pearly was home free.

But not you, Alexander. You're in a world of shit. The second volley of missiles—the ones with *his* name on them—were coming like homing pigeons with their asses on fire.

And he couldn't communicate.

One thing was certain. The SAMs would kill him in less than ten seconds. That was how much time Maxwell said was remaining on the HARM countdown.

He keyed the mike again to call Pearly for another break turn. Nothing. The radio was dead as a dog turd.

No time left. He racked the Hornet into another max-G break turn to the left. Grunting against the G forces, Alexander peered over his shoulder, looking for the killer SAM. The turn would take maybe five seconds. He was buying time. *Keep turning, make the SAM turn with you, throw it off. Run out the clock . . .*

Kabloom! He felt the concussion through the airframe of the jet.

Alexander tensed himself, ready to eject. *How bad am I hit?*

He waited, counting the seconds. Nothing happened. No warning lights, no fire, no failures—except the goddamn radio that had already gone tits-up.

Gradually he let himself realize that he had escaped. The SAM had come close enough to detonate its proximity fuze, but the whirling, gnashing cookie-cutter teeth of the warhead had not sliced through his Hornet.

He was okay. He realized he was holding his breath, still grunting against the force of the max-G turn.

In the next instant his RWR came back on. After the momentary BIT check, the display was clean. No more targeting. Maxwell's HARM must have landed. Somewhere in Tabruz, what used to be a SAM-2 launching unit was now a bonfire, and the gomers who tried to kill him were crispy critters. Alexander felt like whooping and rejoicing—and then he caught himself.

Shit. Something else was going on. His radios were

still dead, and the displays were flickering like a video game. But that wasn't all.

Smoke. A dark, acrid cloud was seeping up from the consoles.

Time to get out of Dodge, Maxwell decided. They were still a hundred fifty miles inside Indian country. "Runners egress south," he ordered on the radio. "Heading one-nine-five."

As he started his turn, he saw B. J. turning her jet to the south, staying with him. By the indications on his own display, the missile battery was no longer emitting. "Anyone still spiked?" he called.

"Runner Two naked."

"Runner Four naked."

The HARM had done its job. Neither B. J. nor Pearly was getting hits from the missile battery radar.

Bullet hadn't replied.

"Runner Three, say your status."

No reply.

"Looks like Runner Three has a problem," called Pearly. "He's NORDO." NORDO was the brevity code for "no radio."

In his display Maxwell could see the datalinked symbols of Alexander and Gates's jets. They were only twelve miles away, closing. "Pearly, you take the lead, and we'll join on you. Maintain angels thirty on a one-nine-five heading."

He called the AWACS. "Snow King, are you copying all this?"

"Snow King copies," answered the controller. "Do you require assistance?"

Maxwell considered for a moment. They might need the SAR—Search and Rescue—helo if Alexander had to get out and walk.

"Stand by. I'll let you know."

Keeping a constant bearing on the two symbols in the

display, Maxwell set up an intercept. The link with Alexander's jet was intermittent. At a range of six miles, he picked up the two specks of the Hornets, slightly low, at his ten o'clock.

What the hell is going on with Bullet's jet? The F/A-18E had not one but two UHF radios. He'd never heard of a dual failure in the Super Hornet before, but—

"Runner One from Four. Three just blew his canopy. I think he's going to eject."

Uh, oh. "Snow King, Runner One. Tell Sandy to scramble. Launch the SAR helo. And with it, the A-10 armed escorts."

He could see the other two Super Hornets clearly now, Bullet in the lead, Pearly flying a loose wing position on his left side. Alexander's jet looked like a cabriolet, the big Plexiglas canopy gone. He could see Bullet hunched down in the cockpit, trying to keep his bulky shape out of the violent wind blast.

Why did he blow the canopy? Maxwell wondered.

"Runner Four, start a descent now," he called. They were still at twenty-eight thousand feet. Alexander's cockpit was unpressurized. He needed to get down into thicker air.

As the flight of jets slanted downward, Maxwell came close alongside. He ordered Pearly and B. J. to move out to a loose tactical formation.

Maxwell could see Alexander peering at him through his black helmet visor. As Maxwell slid in close, Alexander pointed to his oxygen mask with his left hand, tapped the side of his helmet, then he gave a thumbs-down.

No transmit, no receive. Alexander's radios were shot. They had to communicate by hand signal.

Maxwell signaled that he was taking the lead, and Alexander dropped back to a loose position on Maxwell's right wing.

As they exchanged more air-to-air hand signals,

Maxwell began to get the picture. Alexander had some kind of electrical problem. Smoke had filled his cockpit, which forced him to blow the canopy for ventilation.

Alexander was signaling again, this one nonstandard. He was holding up a middle finger, waving it around the cockpit.

It took Maxwell a second to get it, then he had to laugh. *This jet is all fucked up.*

He nodded back to Alexander. *Roger that.*

At ten thousand feet, he leveled off. Only seventy more miles to feet wet—the safety of the open sea. All they had to do was get back to the *Reagan*, then make a two-ship approach with Alexander flying his wing. At a quarter mile out, Alexander would detach and fly his own pass to the deck. Routine.

But first, they had to get out of Iran.

"Runner One," called the ACE. "For your info, Sandy is airborne. They'll hold at the border until cleared in. What's your status now?"

Maxwell glanced at Alexander's topless jet. *Status? Royally fucked up, thank you.* "Looks like we'll make it feet wet."

"Copy that. Suggest you change heading twenty degrees right. Your present course will take you over a possible triple-A threat."

"Runner copies, coming right twenty." A good call. At ten thousand feet, they were sitting ducks for large-caliber antiaircraft guns.

He eased the throttles forward, nudging their airspeed up to 450 knots. It was a hell of a ride for Bullet in his topless cockpit, but the sooner they got out of hostile territory and to the ship, the better.

He saw movement off his right wing. Alexander was coming alongside again.

As he came close, Maxwell saw him giving another hand signal. Electrical failure. Same problem, thought Maxwell. So why was he—

Bullet held up a blank briefing card. Maxwell could see the grease-penciled letters: FIRE.

Mashmashiyeh, Iran

By the time Al-Fasr reached his command building—a stucco hut festooned with antennae for Sat-Comm and the data link to the missile batteries—the pain in his right leg had worsened. It was throbbing as if his thigh were on fire, forcing him to walk with a limp that he could not conceal.

The damaged leg was the price he paid for escaping from a shattered MiG-29 at zero altitude. A half swing in the parachute, then he had slammed into the hard dry earth of Yemen. But the worst damage had occurred during the day and a half he spent in a horse-drawn wagon before his fractured femur could be attended by a clumsy village doctor.

It was a miracle that he had survived. It was an even greater miracle that he and half his *Sherji* managed to escape Yemen before the Americans could hunt them down like wild animals.

Jamal Al-Fasr sometimes wished he could attribute such miracles to Allah. It would be a blessing to possess the blind faith of zealots like Abu and his men. Whatever happened, regardless of their mistakes, it was the will of Allah.

One of their cherished beliefs was that death in battle entitled them to a reward in heaven that included seventy virgins. The image always forced Al-Fasr to suppress a laugh. Seventy virgins. It was a cruel myth, but it had enticed thousands of Arab men to become martyrs.

He could not let the Brigade sense his true feelings. They had to believe that they were engaged in a holy war. They mustn't suspect that Al-Fasr's mission was something else, and that it had nothing to do with virgins or the fear of Allah.

He entered the command building and flopped into the padded chair at his desk, extending his aching right leg straight out. Abu followed him inside while Shakeeb took up his station at the doorway, watching both men from beneath his dark, hooded eyebrows.

Abu stood in front of Al-Fasr, his shoulders hunched forward in a combative posture. "Jamal, you have gone too far. You have humiliated me in front of—"

"You are impertinent. A subordinate may not address his senior by his given name. In public, you will address me as 'Colonel.'"

"This is the Bu Hasa Brigade, not your emirate air force. We have no rank here."

"We have discipline here!" Al-Fasr slammed his fist on the desk. "We are soldiers, and we will conduct ourselves like soldiers. That means you will not carry out the execution of civilians without direct orders from me."

"You were not here. As second-in-command, I made the decision."

"You made a mistake, Abu. Let us hope it was not an irreparable mistake."

Despite his anger, he forced himself to soften his tone. Abu was a prideful, swaggering figure who coveted authority. This was not the time to turn him into an enemy.

"You are a good soldier," said Al-Fasr. "I want you to stay focused on our mission. We wish to establish a permanent base in this country, and it does not serve our purpose to alienate the people who live here."

Abu nodded, apparently placated by Al-Fasr's change in tone. "How would you have me deal with those who resist our occupation?"

"Regard them as stubborn children. The day will come when they will thank us for restoring their land."

"What about those we have rounded up to witness the executions?"

"Release them. They may hate us, but they will be thankful to be alive."

Abu nodded again. His expression showed that he did not agree. "And the attack on the Americans? When will you give the order to proceed?"

"Soon. The timing is critical. The nature of the attack must leave no doubt about where it comes from."

"What if the enemy is not deceived?"

"They will be. The Americans are very predictable. They are obsessed with retaliation."

"Al ain bel ain sen bel sen." The words seemed to amuse Abu. "An eye for an eye, a tooth for a tooth."

"Ironic, isn't it?" said Al-Fasr. "We will cause them to behave like Arabs."

At this, Abu laughed and relaxed his hunched posture. *"Inshallah,"* he said. "If God wills it."

Al-Fasr laughed with him. The crisis had passed— for now. Al-Fasr dismissed him with a wave, and Abu left the command building, still laughing to himself.

From the doorway, Shakeeb watched with narrowed eyes. When Abu was gone, he turned to Al-Fasr, who was massaging his leg. "He is not a loyal comrade, Colonel."

"It doesn't matter. He is a good soldier."

"I am not so sure. I hear things from the *Sherji*."

Shakeeb had been at Al-Fasr's side since their years together in the emirate air force. Al-Fasr trusted Shakeeb more than anyone in the Bu Hasa Brigade.

"What things do you hear?" asked Al-Fasr.

"Tiny things. Insignificant perhaps, but they cause me concern. Abu is ambitious. He is a dangerous man."

"We are at war. I need dangerous men."

"Do not trust this one, Colonel. He is a smiling snake."

Southwest Iran, 10,000 feet

Bullet Alexander was pointing to his watch, making a landing gesture with his left hand. *I need to land.*

Maxwell nodded his understanding. Bullet had a fire, and they were running out of options. He would have to eject if the fire worsened or if he lost electronic commands to the Hornet's fly-by-wire flight control system.

They were almost feet wet—out of Iran and over the water. Ahead he could see the slate gray void of the Persian Gulf looming like a colorless blanket. Returning to the *Reagan* was becoming a bad idea. The ship was a hundred and fifty miles down the Gulf. Setting up the two-ship approach to the ship would take too long, and Alexander had too many problems to add the demanding task of a carrier landing.

"Snow King, Runner One," he radioed. "A change in the game plan. Runner Three has an electrical fire, and we're diverting to Kuwait City." Kuwait was less than a hundred miles away, almost in view.

No immediate reply from the AWACS.

Maxwell scrawled a big black note on his own briefing card and held it up for Alexander to see: KUWAIT. Alexander flashed him a toothy grin and a thumbs-up.

"Runner One, this is Hammer." Maxwell recognized the voice of Hatch, the ACE. "Be advised that diversion to Kuwait City is not approved. The general says he doesn't want any military aircraft at the international airport."

Maxwell felt a flash of anger, but he kept his voice calm. By now the general was probably monitoring the channel. And Hatch knew it, too, which was why he was being an asshole.

"Roger that. We'll use Al Jaber then. It's almost as close." Al Jaber Air Base was a Royal Kuwaiti Air Force installation just outside Kuwait City.

"Ah, Runner One, that's not approved either. The general wants you to divert to Dhahran."

Maxwell did a quick calculation. Dhahran was in Saudi Arabia, across from Bahrain, another two hundred miles south. The general was concerned about politics. Kuwait was going through a fresh wave of anti-American demonstrations. Armed U.S. warplanes dropping in for a visit would stir up more trouble.

"Hammer, Runner One. Does the general understand that my wingman is on fire?"

"He's aware of your problem, Runner."

"Please advise the general that I know he's the boss. But with all due respect, Runner Three will not—repeat, will not—make it to Dhahran. Advise Kuwait control we will land at Al Jaber in one-zero minutes."

An ominous silence came over the radio. He knew Hatch was having a one-sided conversation with the general. *Kiss your job good-bye, Maxwell.*

He took advantage of the break and detached his second element—B. J. and Pearly—to return to the *Reagan*. He saw the two Hornets pull up and start a turn to the left, back toward the southern Persian Gulf.

Hatch was still keeping his silence. Listening to the general have a tantrum, Maxwell guessed. Air Force generals didn't take it well when their orders were flouted by Navy pilots.

Finally the ACE's voice came back on the tactical frequency. "Runner One, Al Jaber has been notified you're inbound." Hatch sounded subdued now. "Your IFF mode four is confirmed and the MEZ is cold."

Maxwell acknowledged. Mode four was the discrete radar code that identified them as friendlies. The MEZ—Missile Engagement Zone—was the field of fire for the Patriot missile batteries. Also good news.

"Runner One, contact Kuwait Approach Control on two-five-eight point three."

"Runner One switching. Thanks for the help." *And give my regards to the general.*

Thirty miles from Al Jaber, the approach controller switched him to the Al Jaber tower frequency.

"Lucky for you that you're coming to Al Jaber," said an American voice. "You've got U.S. Air Force controllers here in the tower, and the Louisiana Air National Guard waiting for you on the ground."

"We're going to close your runway for a little while," said Maxwell. "My wingman will take the approach end cable. How about keeping the parallel taxiway clear in case I need to land there?"

"You've got it, Runner One. Emergency crews and equipment are standing by."

Because of his mechanical problems, Alexander would be landing without flaps, adding extra knots to his approach speed. Stopping the troubled jet would be a problem. He'd have to use the Hornet's tailhook to engage Al Jaber's approach end arresting cable.

The airspeed was rolling back through three hundred knots, two-fifty, back to the maximum alternate landing gear extension speed.

At fifteen miles, Maxwell gave Alexander the hand-crank signal—the cue to lower the landing gear. Alexander would have to use the alternate gear extension because of the electrical failure.

A few seconds later, Maxwell saw the wheels extend from Alexander's jet and lock into place. Then the tailhook came down.

So far, so good.

On short final he passed the lead to Alexander, then stayed on his wing as Alexander aligned his jet with the centerline of the runway. They were descending through three hundred feet.

Twenty seconds to touchdown.

Something wasn't right. As they swept low over the sand-covered terrain, Alexander's jet was making erratic pitch changes, descending rapidly, then over-correcting and pitching up too high.

Fifty feet off the desert, still descending.

"No lower," Maxwell yelled into his mask, forgetting that Alexander couldn't hear him. "You're too damned low."

The jet descended nearly to ground level, then lurched back into the air, climbing a hundred feet. The Hornet was wallowing like a torpid fish, nose oscillating up and down, wings rocking.

Two hundred yards to the runway.

Descending again. The main wheels bit into the earth, sending up two geysers of sand behind the Hornet. The jet pitched upward again.

Maxwell watched helplessly from his own cockpit. *You're losing it.* He saw the jet's nose pitch down again. *Punch out, Bullet. Eject.*

Alexander was still in the cockpit. Maxwell was flying ahead of the stricken Hornet now, watching over his shoulder.

The Hornet caromed once again off the ground, kicking up a cloud of brown dirt, then it pitched upward in a sickening, nose-high roll to the left.

Maxwell tensed himself, knowing with absolute certainty what would happen next.

A mushroom of flame and dirt and metallic debris erupted from the threshold of the Al Jaber runway. Even through the insulated capsule of his own cockpit, Maxwell could feel the impact of the twenty-ton fighter hitting the floor of the desert.

He pulled up in a tight climbing turn, circling back to the runway. He forced himself not to look at the billowing black mushroom cloud as he swept back over the end of the runway and landed on the long concrete strip.

Damn you, Bullet. Why didn't you eject?

CHAPTER 4

A PLACE CALLED BABYLON

Kifri, Iraq
1305, Thursday, 11 March

Maybe they weren't going to execute him.

The thought passed through his mind as they led him into the open yard behind the prison. Rasmussen peered around. No firing squad, no troops with ready weapons, no grim-faced executioner. Just the Iraqi officer and a pair of bored guards who didn't bother to unshoulder their carbines.

They were taking him somewhere. At the far end of the courtyard, near the gated entrance, he saw a tarpaulin-covered truck. The back flap was open, and several rag-tag troops stood around the truck watching him. Three battered Land Rovers were parked in random order around the enclosure.

On all four sides he could see the cell blocks with their rows of barred windows. He hadn't had such a view of the compound since the day they brought him here.

He had had the distinction of being the first combat loss POW, shot down the opening night of Desert Storm and captured the following morning. During the next few weeks, as the war sped to its inevitable conclusion, he became aware of other prisoners in the Abu Graib prison where he was being held. Sometimes he could hear their voices across the courtyard—Americans, Brits, even voices speaking French.

One day he heard a newly captured pilot arguing in the courtyard as they hauled him in, telling a Republican Guardsman to go fuck himself, getting a rifle butt in the head for his trouble. The other prisoners cheered and whistled, giving the newcomer a round of applause.

For reasons never explained to him, he wasn't allowed to mix with the other POWs, not even to exchange snippets of information about who was there, why they were shot down, how the war was going. All the while he could hear the sirens outside, the boom of the antiaircraft guns, the exhilarating *whump* of incoming bombs and Tomahawk missiles. Baghdad was taking a pounding.

It would be a short war. They were going home soon.

One day the sirens were quiet. The *whump* of the bombs stopped. A silence like the inside of a tomb settled over the prison compound. It took him a while to realize that he was no longer hearing the voices of other prisoners.

Because they weren't there.

Why? What happened? His interrogators wouldn't tell him. He ordered himself to stay calm. If the war was over and prisoners were being exchanged, his turn would come. It had to come. He would go home.

Weeks passed. His turn didn't come. With a growing sense of dread, he sensed the truth. He wasn't going home. He had been left behind.

Months passed, then years. He lost track of how many, but somehow he held on to his sanity. He was moved to another prison outside Baghdad, and then he was moved again, the last time to this godforsaken place called Kifri, in the east of Iraq.

One day, about five years into his captivity, his handler, an Iraqi officer named Hakim, brought him an English-language newspaper. It was the *Norfolk Courier*, a month old, and in the social section was a photograph that leaped off the page and pierced his heart like a dagger.

A pretty, black-haired woman, wearing a long white gown, was on the arm of a man he didn't recognize. He was tall, with wavy gray hair, handsome in a dark cutaway and vest. The happy couple was exiting a chapel while smiling friends showered them with rice. According to the caption, the newly married Mr. and Mrs. Frank Gallagher had just exchanged vows in the Virginia Beach Episcopal Church.

For the rest of the day he sat in his cell, holding the photograph, staring at the chipped plaster wall, unable to focus his thoughts. He felt as if he were peering through a veil into another world. The world of the living.

Widowhood hadn't suited Maria. She needed a man in her life. The anchor of a good husband. Their children—a daughter and a son—were rushing into adolescence and they needed a father.

It made sense, he thought with a numb acceptance. They were alive. He was dead.

Sometime after his last move, another war had come. He heard the distant thud of bombs, the high dull rumble of jets. With his gradually increasing knowledge of Arabic, he overheard from his guards' conversation that the Americans had invaded Iraq. Saddam was gone. The Iraqi army had been defeated.

For a brief while he allowed himself to hope. *The Americans were coming.* He would be free.

But they didn't come. No one came to this abysmal hole on the frontier. He was still a prisoner.

His new captors were former Republican Guard officers and Baath Party members—old Saddam loyalists—who, he gathered, were waiting for an opportunity to seize power again in Iraq.

Why were they still holding him captive?

After a few months, he stopped speculating about such things. It was too painful. Better for him to remain dead.

The man who didn't exist.

Now he was leaving. He stopped in the middle of the courtyard and tilted his head back. He peered straight up. Darkness had descended on eastern Iraq, and stars were twinkling in the hazy night sky. When was the last time he had seen stars? He couldn't remember.

"What are you waiting for?" said the Iraqi in the officer's uniform. He nudged the prisoner. "Keep moving."

As they approached the truck, a man stepped out of the darkness. He wore a dark, shirtlike *gellebiah* over camouflage trousers and army boots. A blackened semi-automatic pistol hung from his hip. He didn't look like an Iraqi.

"My name is Abu," said the stranger. "I am taking you away from here."

The prisoner didn't reply. He had expected a firing squad. Instead, they were taking him somewhere. They had done this once before, moving him from Baghdad to this remote place in the northeast of Iraq. It was more than he could comprehend.

"Where are we going?"

"To a new place. You will be treated well."

He felt another wave of gloom sweep over him. *A new place.* He was right. They were taking him into the desert to kill him.

No, it didn't make sense. Not the Iraqis. They were too lazy. They'd just shoot him here on the spot and be done with it.

"What new place?"

"It's better if you don't know."

He didn't ask any more questions. He climbed into the back of the truck, where he was joined by half a dozen unsmiling men in *gellebiahs*. They didn't look like soldiers. Each wore a beard and a kaffiyeh, the ubiquitous Arab headdress. Each lugged a Kalashnikov assault rifle over his shoulder.

Abu got in front with the driver. The truck chugged off into the night, followed by a pair of Land Rovers filled with more armed, bearded men.

The procession wound through the darkened streets of Kifri, an impoverished village near the Iranian border, then departed the village southward, into the desert night. The prisoner didn't care where they were going. It didn't matter. He leaned against the back of the bench seat and fell asleep.

While the truck lurched through the night, he dreamed that he was in a distant green country with no guards, no prison cells, no brown-hued desert around him. He dreamed that he was with a raven-haired woman named Maria and their two freckled children.

Al Jaber Air Base, Kuwait

"We have to keep this stuff hidden because it's not allowed in Kuwait," said the tech sergeant. "Not the real stuff, anyway."

They were inside one of the tents the U.S. Air Force contingent at Al Jaber called their "hoochs." The front flap was closed, and the portable air conditioner at the far end was straining to keep the inside temperature under eighty Fahrenheit.

The sergeant wore desert fatigues, and his blue name tag identified him as CHALMERS. He reached outside the rear tent flap and pulled back a tarpaulin on the ground, exposing the top of a buried garbage can. He stuffed his arm inside the can, through a layer of floating ice and

Cokes and 7-Ups, and fished around the bottom until he came up with a glistening green can.

"Real Heineken," he said. "Not that near beer crap they sell in town. Got this from the loadmaster on the C-17 out of Ramstein yesterday."

Bullet Alexander popped the tab on the can and slurped down half the beer in one long swallow.

Chalmers and his tent mate, another tech sergeant named Soileau, watched appreciatively. "Yeah, we figured you could use a cold beer," said Chalmers. "Considering how you got out of that jet."

Alexander nodded as he drained the can. He handed the empty to Chalmers, who promptly resupplied him.

Chalmers and Soileau had been in the armada of crash trucks that came rumbling across the sand toward the burning jet. One of the trucks had nearly run over Alexander while he was lying in his parachute, still too stunned to move.

He tried to recall the sequence of events. The final minute of the flight was like one of those nightmares every fighter pilot had. He was trying to control a jet that was overresponding to his inputs. Everything he did produced an exaggerated effect. And then he had no option except to leave.

The Super Hornet's flight control system had degraded when he began having electrical problems. From normal computerized control, the system reverted to DEL—direct electrical link—where every stick movement was an input to a control surface, without computer refinement. Sometime during the final approach, it degraded further to MECH—mechanical operation. It meant that he could only move the two angled stabilators on the tail. There was a fair amount of lag in the flight control response, and when the response did come, it was a big one. Too big.

It was a precarious way to control the jet. To the best of his knowledge no one had ever actually landed a

Super Hornet using MECH. Alexander had just proved that it was a lousy way to fly.

The truth was, he reflected, he'd stayed with the jet too damned long. But the runway was right there, so close he could almost feel the concrete under him. Another ten seconds and he would have made it. The Super Hornet would be parked here on the ramp, still worth most of the sixty million bucks the taxpayers paid for it.

He had never ejected before. He knew that in an airborne emergency the pilot went through a critical phase of denial, then analysis, then decision. He had denied too long, decided too late. It had almost cost him his life.

Thank you, God, he thought to himself. Then another thought. *Thank you, Martin-Baker, wherever you are.* Martin-Baker ejection seats had been saving U.S. Navy fighter pilots' lives for half a century.

"I don't suppose you have any more of these?" he asked, holding up another empty can.

"As many as you want, Commander," said Sergeant Chalmers. He was fetching another beer when the front tent flap burst open.

A man in a sweat-stained, desert-colored flight suit appeared in the open entrance. A leather-holstered Colt .45 hung around his shoulder, and the lines of an oxygen mask were still imprinted on his face.

He stared wide-eyed at Alexander as if he were seeing a ghost.

Alexander gave him a broad grin. "Hey, Skipper, welcome to Kuwait. How about a beer?"

USS Ronald Reagan

The Air Wing Commander was waiting in the passageway when Maxwell came down from the flight deck. Capt. Red Boyce was wearing his battered leather flight jacket. A much-gnawed cigar, unlit, protruded from the corner of his mouth.

Though Boyce's official title was Air Wing Commander, he went by the traditional but extinct label of "CAG"—Commander, Air Group.

"I've got good news and bad news," said Boyce.

Maxwell pulled off his helmet and shook hands with his boss. "I already know the bad news. The general is going to court-martial me."

"Of course," said Boyce. "What do you expect when a Navy jock tells a three-star blue-suiter to go get stuffed?"

"What's the good news?"

"Admiral Dinelli, who also has three stars and runs the Fifth Fleet, sends a well done. He says you did the right thing going to Al Jaber."

"So? Do I get court-martialed or not?"

"You know how the game's played. One attaboy cancels one oh-shit. It's a wash."

They descended the ladder to the O-3 level where the Roadrunner ready room was located. Boyce stopped outside. "How's Bullet?"

"A little beat-up, but okay. He's coming back on the COD on the next recovery."

"Does he know what happened to his jet?"

"Only that the electrical system started unraveling about the time he engaged the SA-2s."

Boyce gnawed thoughtfully for a moment on his cigar. "It makes a big difference to your squadron whether it gets written off as combat damage or an aircraft mishap. I don't have to remind you that you guys are having enough trouble keeping jets in the air without one of them self-destructing from an internal problem."

Maxwell knew where Boyce was going with this. His squadron, the VFA-36 Roadrunners, had won the Battle "E" last year as the most combat-ready Super Hornet

squadron in the fleet. But this year the Roadrunners'
record was dismal. They were having trouble keeping
the jets in the squadron airworthy and ready to fly.

"We'll know something soon," said Boyce. "I'm con-
vening a mishap board right away, and a team will go to
Al Jaber to examine the wreckage. In the meantime,
you're wanted in the flag conference room. Someone
named Maria wants to talk to you."

CHAPTER 5

RUMORS

USS Ronald Reagan
Northern Persian Gulf
1915, Thursday, 11 March

She hadn't changed. Same raven-black hair, same large brown eyes with the oversized lashes that she knew how to use with devastating effect. She still had the high cheekbones and fine, chiseled nose of her French-Canadian ancestors.

"How have you been, Brick?"

"Fine. I'm doing just fine, Maria."

Maxwell hadn't seen Maria Rasmussen's face for— how long? Something over seven years. It was at a re-union back at Oceana when they laid a wreath in Raz's memory. Raz had been the only casualty the squadron suffered in the first Gulf War, and now a plaque with his name on it hung in the Strike Fighter Wing head-quarters.

"You look wonderful," she said. "Congratulations on getting command of your own squadron."

Your own squadron. They both knew that was some-thing Raz always talked about. It was the only thing he said he wanted out of the Navy. Command of his own squadron. If circumstances had been different, Maxwell thought, he would have already gotten it. By now he might be an air wing commander like Boyce.

He was alone in the *Reagan*'s flag conference room. The live video conference had been set up by Capt. Gracie Allen, who had been Raz's flight lead the night he was shot down, and who now commanded the Atlantic Strike Fighter Wing back in Oceana. Chief Lester, the flag staff yeoman, had showed Maxwell how to run the console and how to position himself for the video monitor. Then he exited the compartment and closed the door behind him.

Video conferencing was spooky, he thought. It was almost—but not quite—like being face to face with the other person, except there was this half-second delay in response. The image on the screen moved with a jerkiness like an old silent movie.

Maxwell could see only her face and slender neck in the video screen, but he was sure that she still had the slim-waisted, willowy shape that made all the heads turn at the officers' club swimming pool. Maria had a knockout figure. Raz loved going to parties with her, strutting in with her on his arm, making the single guys eat their hearts out.

She told him about the anonymous phone call. She was almost through before she broke down. Her voice caught, and she dabbed at her tear-filled eyes.

Maxwell nodded, trying not to show his own tangled feelings. He remembered the day back in 1991 when Iraq released the prisoners they had captured during the Gulf War. At Maria's request, he had gone to Kuwait City to see the POWs deplane from the C-130. They were the last, according to the Iraqis. Six Americans had been released the day before, fifteen more on this flight. Twenty-one captured, twenty-one released.

Maxwell recognized some of them. Three guys were from the *Saratoga*. They looked pale and undernourished. Some had noticeable bruises, or arms in slings.

One walked with a limp. All wore huge grins, happy to be alive and free.

He waited until the last had exchanged salutes with the senior officers and then boarded the bus to the hospital ship *Mercy*, where they would be examined and treated.

Raz Rasmussen was not among them.

Maxwell was not surprised. Raz's name had not appeared on the Red Cross list of prisoners. The Iraqis declared they had never heard of him. No body had been found, and no evidence turned up to change the KIA— killed in action—to MIA—missing in action.

That night Maxwell called Maria and told her that Raz wasn't on the airplane. Her husband wasn't coming home. Every bit of evidence indicated that he had died in the cockpit of his Hornet in the predawn hours of 17 January. Maria should get on with her life.

For years after Desert Storm there were rumors. There were always rumors after POWs were repatriated. Many Vietnam veterans clung to the belief that POWs were still being held in Hanoi thirty years after the war ended.

Maxwell didn't believe the rumors. They had to be a cruel hoax. *But what if they weren't?*

"Who was it that called?" he asked.

"Nobody that I know. At least, I didn't recognize his voice."

"Did he say why he was telling you this?"

"He thought I deserved to know."

"What does your husband think about it?"

"Nothing. I haven't told him." At this, she began to cry softly.

Maxwell waited for her to compose herself. *No way,* he told himself. *It has to be bogus. No way could Raz have survived the fireball.*

"Is it possible?" asked Maria. "Could he be alive?"

Maxwell thought for a second, then told her the truth. "I don't know."

"What should I do? What do I tell the children?"

Maxwell could hear the pain in her voice. She was young when Raz was shot down, still in her twenties. Too young to be a widow. She had needed help raising her children. Maria was a woman who needed a man in her life.

"You don't have to tell them anything, Maria. These things happen. Some crank wants to harass you. Unlist your number and get caller ID."

"What about Frank?"

Maxwell had met her new husband only once, several years ago. According to Gracie Allen, Frank Gallagher was a decent guy with a solid reputation and a thriving business in Virginia Beach. He was good to Maria and the kids. They seemed to be a happy family.

"Tell him the truth. That the CIA did a year-long investigation into Raz's case and determined that he was killed in action."

"Would the CIA lie to us about Raz?"

He didn't answer for a moment. The same thought had occurred to him. *Not unless they had a good reason.* He couldn't think of a good reason, so he said, "I don't think so."

He could see Maria chewing on her thumbnail, still uncertain. "You were his best friend in the squadron, Brick. Would you . . . please look into it? For my sake?"

This was the part of video conferencing that was most unsatisfactory. He wanted to squeeze Maria's hand, give her reassurance. He couldn't because she was six thousand miles away. "I'll do everything I can, Maria."

"Promise?"

"I promise."

The screen went blank.

For several minutes Maxwell sat there alone, staring at

the empty monitor. It still glowed with a gray background, but the camera on the other end had been turned off.

He thought about Maria's husband. Frank Gallagher had fallen in love with a woman who thought she was a widow. Now someone was telling her otherwise. And if it turned out that she really *wasn't* a widow, that the ghost of her husband came back in the flesh, then how was he supposed to handle it?

That was Gallagher's problem, but it was one that Maxwell understood perfectly. It was a problem that they had in common. They both loved women whose husbands had vanished somewhere in the barren maw of Iraq. Gallagher loved Maria Rasmussen, who was married to a ghost named Raz. And Maxwell loved Claire Phillips, who was married to someone named Chris Tyrwhitt, who had also gone to Iraq and become a ghost.

Maxwell rose from the video console, turned off the master switch like Chief Lester had showed him, and left the conference room. Walking through the hangar deck, he could see through the open elevator bay. He stopped to watch the brown shoreline of Bahrain glide past, framed like a picture in the great steel frame of the elevator bay.

The *Reagan* was making a port call. When the anchor was dropped and the watch list and admin business were sorted out, Maxwell would turn the squadron over to his XO, Bullet Alexander, and go ashore.

Claire Phillips was waiting for him in Bahrain—or so he hoped. She was supposed to be on assignment from her network, covering the escalating tension in the Persian Gulf. That was the good news.

The bad news was that she was no longer a widow. Her husband was no longer a dead man in Iraq. He was back, very much alive, and Maxwell couldn't stop wishing that he was still dead.

* * *

Bullet Alexander took a seat facing the board members.

The day before, the team from the *Reagan*'s air wing had arrived at Al Jaber air base to sift through the remains of Bullet's Super Hornet. To no one's surprise, they found no telltale clues—no obvious combat damage or evidence of a mechanical failure—in the twisted and incinerated wreckage.

The AMB—Aircraft Mishap Board—convened in the air wing conference room. Maxwell appointed Cmdr. Gordo Gray, skipper of the *Reagan*'s F-14 squadron, senior member of the board. He also named Cmdr. Craze Manson, squadron maintenance officer, Lt. Cmdr. Hairball Shepard, the safety officer, and the air wing flight surgeon, Lt. Cmdr. Knuckles Ball.

The first witness the board called was the pilot of the crashed jet.

"Step us through the mission, Bullet," said Gordo Gray. "From briefing until they picked you up off the sand."

Alexander took a moment, reflecting back on the events of the previous day. So much had happened that it seemed like a week. He started with their briefing back in the ready room on the *Reagan*, the launch, the rendezvous with a KC-10 tanker, the ingress to the threat zone.

He was describing the first RWR hits from the SAM site when Craze Manson interrupted.

"I'm missing something here," said Manson. "How did it happen that the squadron CO and the XO were scheduled on the same sortie? Especially a combat sortie? Isn't that against air wing doctrine?"

Alexander shrugged. "I saw that the squadron was tasked to fly an armed reconnaissance, so I put myself on the schedule."

"Doesn't it seem like your place would have been back here running the squadron in his absence?"

"That's between me and the skipper. Why don't you stick to the mishap?"

"Nothing's off limits in a mishap investigation. I'll ask any question I think is pertinent."

Alexander took a deep breath and held back his anger. Manson knew perfectly well why Alexander had flown the mission. Craze was grandstanding for the other board members. He never passed up a chance for an easy shot at Alexander.

"The skipper ran it by CAG, and he said go for it. You got a problem with that, Craze, take it up with CAG."

"We don't need any more of that," said Gray, giving Manson a warning look. "We're here to determine what happened to Bullet's jet, not why he was flying it. Bullet, get to the SAM engagement. Describe how you started losing systems."

"Well, that's the odd part," said Alexander. "While we were defending against the SAMs, I tried to transmit—and couldn't. Both radios had gone tits-up."

"Are you saying the radios went out *before* the SAM exploded?"

"Yes, sir, at least that's the way I recall it."

Gray shuffled through a stack of papers. "Here's a record of the transmissions from you and your flight recorded by the AWACS," he said. "According to the tape, you asked your flight lead for the time to go before the HARM he had just fired reached the target. He reported 'ten seconds.' You replied, 'Too long. The first SAM is—' And then your transmission ended."

Gray looked up from the report. "Isn't that when the missile exploded behind your jet?"

Bullet tilted back, scratching his memory. He felt the gazes of the men across the table on him. "I know what you're suggesting, Gordo. Sure, it's possible, but that's not the way I remember it. The radios went sour while I was still turning with the SAM."

"So when did the rest of the failures occur?" asked Hairball Shepard. "The electrical smoke and the fire?"

"After the warhead went off behind me."

"Did you feel an impact when the missile exploded?"

"No. I felt and saw the explosion, but I didn't feel anything hit the jet."

Craze Manson was leaning forward on his elbows, a knowing smile on his face. "But the shrapnel *could* have struck something without your feeling it."

"Are you asking me or telling me?"

"Just getting the facts. This was your first time in actual combat, was it not?"

"You know the answer." *Asshole.*

"In the excitement of coming under fire for the first time, it's not unusual that you might be confused about the sequence of events."

Alexander took another deep breath and fought back the urge to choke the living shit out of Craze Manson. "I'll say it again. I didn't feel or see any direct result of the missile exploding."

"That's not unusual either. Happens to everyone the first time they're shot at. They don't know they're hit until they see a red light telling them they're on fire."

Alexander could see where this was going. Craze was leading him. Whatever went wrong with his jet was going to be attributed to the SAM. *And for all you know, maybe that's the way it happened.*

The board asked more questions about the Hornet's electrical problems. They wanted to know why he blew the canopy, why he had control problems, why he ejected when he did.

Alexander answered their questions.

"Thanks, Bullet," said Gordo Gray when they were finished. "This is one of those mishap investigations where most of the evidence comes from the testimony of the people involved and the records of the aircraft. The fact that it happened in combat conditions makes it even cloudier. Sorry if we seemed a little abrasive with you." He glanced at Manson, then back to Alexander. "Hope you weren't offended."

Alexander rose from the table, keeping his gaze on Craze Manson. "Not at all," he said. "In fact, I expected it."

Lagash, Southern Iraq

The prisoner awoke. He sat upright, rubbing the grimy film from his eyes.

The truck had stopped.

A coarse layer of dust covered everything—the truck, the bench seats, the occupants in the back. There was no breeze. He could taste the dirt in his throat, feel it settling on his skin in a fine sediment. Ancient dirt.

For two days and nights they had driven. The landscape changed from brown terrain marked by undulating wadis and mounds of sand to a jagged, boulder-strewn moonscape. Twice the procession had stopped at villages that looked like Stone Age dwellings. They refueled the vehicles, filled the water containers, then headed on into the desert.

Darkness had fallen again. The prisoner guessed by the flatness of the terrain that they had traveled southward. North would have been into high country, the rugged massif that joined Iraq to Turkey and Syria and Iran. This had to be the great desert that extended southward through Kuwait, all the way down the Arabian peninsula.

The man who called himself Abu came around to the back of the truck. "You may dismount. We have traveled as far as we will go in the truck."

The prisoner climbed stiffly down to the ground and gazed around. Once again he had the thought that they were about to execute him. He shook his head. *Foolish thought. You're delusional.* Why would they travel a thousand miles just to shoot him?

The two Land Rovers were stopped behind them. The guerrillas were unloading the vehicles, gathering their equipment into piles. In the darkness the prisoner could see only the silhouettes of low hills, a few ancient huts. Somewhere a dog barked.

"Where are we?" the prisoner asked.

Abu didn't answer. He had his head cocked, listening to something.

Then the prisoner heard it. Something mechanical in the distance, growing in volume. It sounded vaguely familiar. As he listened, the noise swelled, coming toward them. A beating, whopping sound.

In the next instant he knew. The helicopter burst over the darkened hillside, rotor blades thumping the air like drumbeats. A powerful white searchlight swept the area beneath, then fastened on the men standing beside the truck.

The prisoner froze, certain that a hail of bullets was about to find them. He looked at Abu, who was smiling. "Right on schedule," Abu said. "Now we take the last leg of our journey."

CHAPTER 6

WORKING SMARTER

USS Ronald Reagan
Persian Gulf
1050, Monday, 15 March

"Another goddamn clinker," said Boyce, peering down at the flight deck. "One of yours again."

Maxwell nodded, not bothering to answer. They stood in Pri-Fly—Primary Flight Control—watching the launch of the CAP fighters. On the flight deck down below, a tug was towing a Super Hornet off the number two catapult.

"Haul the broken Hornet to the hangar deck," bellowed the mini-boss—the assistant Air Boss—over the flight deck loudspeaker. "Move the ready spare to Cat Two."

They could see the tug hauling the backup bird from the sister squadron, VFA-34, on its way to the catapult. The other three fighters in the CAP were already airborne, heading for the tanker.

It was the second time in three days that a VFA-36 jet had missed a launch because of a maintenance discrepancy. The pilot, Lt. Cmdr. Flash Gordon, called in after engine start with an electronic glitch—an intermittent flight control system warning.

"The same thing that happened last time," said Maxwell. "The avionics crew worked all night on it. Another A799. They couldn't get the system to fail again."

An A799 maintenance code was exasperating. It meant a system failed in the air, but worked okay when it was checked on the ground.

"Well, it just did," grumbled Boyce. "What the hell's going on with you guys? Your squadron won the Battle 'E' last year, best strike fighter outfit in the fleet. You're still in the running for it this year—except for one big problem. Your jets are breaking down. The other squadrons are kicking your butt in the operational readiness department."

"We had some bad breaks, CAG."

"You had some lucky ones, too. Bullet's mishap being one of them. No identifiable evidence, so the board wrote it off as a combat loss, which doesn't count against your operational readiness score."

Maxwell nodded. He knew what Boyce was saying. The mishap might have been a combat loss. And it might have been something else. The truth disappeared in the smoking hole Bullet's jet made in the desert at Al Jaber.

Boyce jammed his cigar back into his mouth. "You're the skipper, Brick. Your squadron's got a problem. Straighten it out."

Maxwell knew the protocol. To such an order there was only one response. "Aye, aye, sir."

"What's this?" said Craze Manson when he appeared in the doorway. "A lynching party?"

"Just a meeting," said Maxwell. He and Bullet Alexander were already seated at the small conference table in Maxwell's stateroom. "Come in and take a seat."

Manson came in, glancing at his watch as he took the

remaining empty seat. "Let's make it quick, if you don't mind. I've got an appointment in a few minutes."

"It can wait," said Alexander. "This is squadron business."

"Shouldn't all the squadron department heads be present?" said Manson. "So you two can't gang up on me?"

Maxwell thought again how he wished Manson would get orders to a squadron in another part of the world. Another ship, even. Anywhere except the USS *Reagan*. There seemed to be a rule that every military unit had to have one bona fide, card-carrying asshole. His squadron had Craze Manson.

It was no secret that Manson had a deep-seated contempt for both Maxwell and Alexander. When Maxwell moved up from executive officer to commanding officer of the Roadrunners, Manson had expected that he would be named as the new executive officer, which would put him in line to succeed Maxwell as skipper.

It didn't happen. Instead, Maxwell chose a new executive officer from outside the squadron. Cdr. Bullet Alexander, who was just completing his tour with the Blue Angels demonstration team, was drafted to be the Roadrunners' new XO—and prospective CO.

Manson hadn't gotten over it. He carried a massive chip on his shoulder, and he could barely bring himself to be civil to either Maxwell or Alexander.

Maxwell slid a printed handout across the table. "This is the reason for the meeting. That's the squadron's readiness status, measured in hours flown versus training events accomplished and maintenance discrepancies carried forward. Notice the bottom line. As you can see, the other two Hornet squadrons on the *Reagan* are kicking our ass."

He gave Manson a minute to peruse the report. "You're the maintenance officer, Craze. Tell me, why aren't we flying the same number of hours as they are?"

Manson sighed. "Very simple," he said. "If we had more flyable jets, we'd fly them. We have a tech order to upgrade all the APG-73 radars, one at a time, and that's got the avionics shop tied up. Plus we've got the periodic corrosion inspections to perform. That takes each jet out of service for ten to fourteen days, and that's if we don't find anything wrong. On top of that we've got the day-to-day maintenance, just fixing the birds that our guys break." He gave Maxwell and Alexander each an indulgent smile. "That's why we're not flying the same hours. Any other questions?" He glanced again at his watch.

"Maybe you're not getting enough out of your maintenance guys," said Alexander.

"I've already switched the department from three eight-hour shifts to two twelve-hour shifts. They're working round the clock. Maybe you'd like to tell me what else we could do?"

"The other squadrons have the same problems, and somehow they're getting more service out of their jets."

"We're not getting the same parts support they are," said Manson. "We're forced to cannibalize our jets, removing parts from one to put on another. That triples the maintenance time required. Instead of just removing one part and replacing it with one from the supply chain, we have to pull the part off a good jet. The whole process just feeds on itself."

"Something's wrong here," Maxwell said. "We should never have to cannibalize our own jets. Why isn't the supply chain working for us?"

Manson looked at him and shrugged. "It's a system problem. You were never a maintenance officer, so I wouldn't expect you to understand."

They both knew it was a calculated insult. Manson still openly referred to Maxwell as a carpetbagger. Instead of working his way up through a sequence of squadron jobs, Maxwell had gone off to test pilot school

and then to NASA as an astronaut. He returned to the
fleet already wearing the rank of commander, bypassing
the lower-ranking assignments.

Alexander's eyes flashed and he slammed his hand
down on the table. "Listen, Mister, you don't talk to the
skipper like—"

"It's okay," said Maxwell. "Craze is right, neither of
us has ever been a maintenance officer. But we've been
around the air and space business nearly twenty years,
and we both know enough to depend on a good maintenance officer. I have to trust you to run the department
as efficiently as possible, Craze. That's why I have you
in the job."

For the moment, Manson was disarmed by the flat-
tery.

Alexander was still glowering at him. "What I'm
hearing is a lot of butt-covering about why our numbers
are bad. The bottom line is we've got more birds down
for maintenance than any other outfit."

"We've also had more combat losses than anyone
else," said Manson, looking at Alexander. "Yours in
Kuwait, plus four we lost in Iraq and Yemen. The replacement birds for those lost jets all came from the
same place. They're all maintenance nightmares."

Maxwell nodded. He had to admit Manson was right.
The replacement jets came from a squadron returning
from an extended deployment. The squadron's aircraft
had all flunked a post-cruise corrosion inspection.
Worse, the inspectors found evidence of bogus inspections while the squadron was deployed in the Middle
East. The inquest resulted in the XO being dismissed
and the maintenance officer being discharged from the
Navy. A taint of scandal still wafted over the strike
fighter wing's maintenance structure.

"Okay, gentlemen," said Maxwell. "Here's the bottom line. We want to win the Battle 'E' again, but it's
more important that we do our real job. We're a strike

fighter squadron, and we're going to be combat ready. Ready to fight anytime, anywhere." He turned to Craze. "That means no more cannibalizing our jets. If the supply system isn't working for you, we'll fix it, but don't rob parts off our own airplanes."

Manson bristled. "Listen, sometimes that's the only way to—"

"You just received an order, Commander."

Manson's face reddened. He nodded acknowledgment.

"I expect you to schedule your people better," Maxwell went on. "We've got to get more airplanes flyable."

"You're saying you want me to work them harder than they're already working?"

"Not harder. Smarter."

Manson showed by his tight expression that he didn't agree. He shoved himself back from the table and rose to leave. "I have the message. Will that be all?"

"I certainly hope so."

He gave both officers one last glowering look, then turned on his heel and left.

Alexander waited until he was gone. "Whaddya think, Skipper?"

"About what?"

"Craze. Would it change his attitude if I punched his lights out?"

"That's not the textbook method for dealing with a subordinate officer."

"I seem to remember your telling me that you did it once."

Maxwell smiled. It was true. Back when he was the new squadron XO, Manson walked out of a department head meeting, deliberately flouting Maxwell's authority. Maxwell followed him into a deserted passageway where he rapped Manson's head against a steel bulkhead hard enough to make his eyes glaze over. Before

Manson could protest, he banged his head again, then once more for effect.

"It didn't work," said Maxwell. "Trust me, Craze will never change."

Carpetbaggers, thought Craze Manson as he descended the ladder to the second deck, where the VFA-36 maintenance spaces were located.

Manson's stomach was still churning. *Alexander and Maxwell.* Carpetbagging, showboating, political suck ups. Their combined fleet experience didn't add up to as much time as Manson alone had in the fleet. In the *real* Navy, not the celebrity service.

It started when Maxwell, hotshot test pilot and astronaut reject, checked in to the squadron with zero qualification and in less than a year moved from ops officer to XO to CO. He made it for no reason except that his old man was an admiral and—something that Manson never understood—the Air Wing Commander thought he shit gold bricks.

Even worse was Alexander, who knew how to play the minority card and was where he was for no reason except that he was one of the few senior black officers in the air wing. Instead of working his way up the hierarchy as a squadron officer and then a department head, he lived a pampered life in grad school and then a tour on the Blue Angel showboat circuit.

It wasn't goddamn fair. By all rights, Manson thought, *he* should have been the one assigned as executive officer of the Roadrunners, not a poster boy for the NAACP like Alexander.

It was insulting enough that as a newly promoted commander he still had the job of maintenance officer. Bat Masters, who was junior in rank to Manson, had been assigned as operations officer, the number three slot in the squadron. Maxwell's reasoning was that Craze had the most experience in maintenance and he didn't want to change things in the middle of a deployment.

Which was bullshit, of course. Manson knew the real story. Maxwell hated his guts and wanted to sabotage his career. Keeping him out of the most senior department head job would make him look bad when the command screening board met next month. Unless the board included Manson in their list for upcoming squadron command, he could kiss his career good-bye. He would retire in some obscure staff job at some suckhole air station in the lower Midwest.

Fuck that.

One of the truisms about Navy politics was that your career could get trashed by a commanding officer who didn't like you, but such an action could be negated if it turned out that the skipper was an incompetent who was out to get you. Well, Maxwell was definitely incompetent, and he was being propped up by an even more incompetent executive officer. It was just a matter of time before both Maxwell and Alexander showed their true colors and got their butts shipped out. Manson would be vindicated and receive his own command.

He reached the second deck, beneath the sprawling hangar bay, where most of the squadron shop spaces were cloistered. Manson's office was a tiny adjunct of the avionics shop.

As he entered the compartment, he saw the Maintenance Master Chief Petty Officer, Master Chief Piltz, in a huddled conversation with Lt. Splat DiLorenzo, the Maintenance Material Control Officer. On a stand in the corner stood the ubiquitous coffeepot, half-filled with thick Navy brew.

"How'd it go, Boss?" said DiLorenzo. "They try to give you a ration of shit?"

DiLorenzo was older than Manson by a couple of years. He was a "mustang," meaning he had risen through the enlisted ranks before being commissioned

as an officer. His duty specialty was aircraft maintenance.

"Just like we thought," said Manson. "They want
more airplanes available so they can fly them more so
they can make themselves look better."

"Did you tell 'em where to stuff it?" DiLorenzo liked
to disparage senior officers in Manson's presence to im-
press Master Chief Piltz. Manson found his manner ir-
ritating, but he let it go. DiLorenzo was one of his few
allies in the squadron.

"I told them we'd tighten up the work shifts in order
to get the corrosion inspections done and still have
enough ready aircraft."

"No way, Boss," said DiLorenzo. "Not if we do those
inspections according to the tech order. Each single jet
stays grounded for at least a week. We're out of manpower."

"They want us to work the crews smarter, not
harder." He said it with enough sarcasm that the two
men understood his disdain for the order.

"Yeah, right." DiLorenzo looked at Master Chief
Piltz. "Who gets to tell the troops they gotta work
smarter?"

"Not me," said Piltz. Piltz had been in the Navy
longer than either Manson or DiLorenzo. One of his
sons, a second-class petty officer based in San Diego,
was as old as some of the squadron pilots.

"Listen, you two," said Manson, putting an edge to
his voice. "It doesn't matter how you or I or the troops
feel about it. Somehow this department is going to produce better results, or all our careers go down the crap-
per. I don't care how you do it, but you're going to put
more airplanes on the schedule."

Piltz nodded sullenly. DiLorenzo went to the coffeepot and refilled his mug.

A silence fell over the space. Manson took a seat at
the desk he shared with DiLorenzo.

"I gotta get the second shift organized," said Piltz, grabbing his hat from the hook on the bulkhead. On his way out he added, almost under his breath, "I'll be sure to tell 'em the part about working smarter."

DiLorenzo waited until the master chief was gone. "You know, there's more than one way to skin a cat, Boss."

"Yeah? What are you suggesting?"

He peered into his coffee mug, deliberately avoiding Manson's eyes. "I know a way to get those inspections done faster."

Mashmashiyeh, Iran

Rasmussen blinked his eyes, surfacing from a fitful sleep. He sat up and gazed around the room.

Nothing was familiar. For a moment, he felt a sense of panic. *Where am I? Why am I here?* His comfortable reality had been destroyed like a bulldozed anthill.

The room contained the cot on which he sat and an ancient wooden table with two chairs. In the corner was a primitive latrine and a tall bucket filled with water.

It didn't look like a prison cell. At least it didn't look like the kind where he'd lived for most of a decade.

Shafts of pale sunlight streamed through the high, barred window. Through the top of the window he could see the tiled roofs of adjacent buildings. From somewhere nearby came the wheezing sound of an underpowered vehicle—a motorbike or ancient automobile.

In a corner of the room were his possessions—a change of clothes, eating utensils, a packet of writing materials.

And his notebook.

He felt the anxiety subside. He was in no immediate danger. Since they'd removed him from the cell in Kifri, nothing bad had happened. No beatings, no maltreatment, no interrogation. They had even fed him. It was some kind of unidentifiable porridge, but it was the same that Abu and his guerrillas—they called themselves *Sherji*—had eaten. He had been treated humanely.

He walked across the hard-packed floor and tried the door. It was locked, which was no surprise, but it didn't look all that substantial. He guessed that a hard kick would probably break the hinges.

He looked up at the window. The crisscrossed bars were wooden. They didn't look substantial either.

He retrieved his notebook and opened it. The last entry was two days ago, while he was still in the Kifri prison. How far had they traveled? In the darkness he hadn't gotten a good look at the terrain, but he knew it was flat and covered with vegetation, not the parched desertscape of northern Iraq. They were in the south somewhere, probably the Tigris-Euphrates delta.

Near the Persian Gulf.

Rasmussen was wide awake now, his mind whirring with new energy. Thoughts were inserting themselves in his mind without his bidding.

He was not in a prison. That was obvious. No maximum security complex with iron doors and guards watching his every move. Nor was he in the interior of Iraq with a thousand miles of desert separating him from the outside world.

Somewhere out there, not too many miles distant, were people like him. Westerners.

Americans.

He looked again at the wooden bars over the window. An idea was germinating in his mind. He had not had such a thought since the first weeks of his captivity. Not since he'd accepted the fact that he was a dead man.

He could escape.

The idea terrified him. And exhilarated him also. It was so alien to his usual thinking that he tried to push it away, but it kept returning to his consciousness.

Freedom.

If I see an opportunity, he told himself, *I will seize it.*
The thought made him almost sick with fear, but he reminded himself of another truth. *Why not? You're already a dead man. What have you got to lose?*

Nothing, of course. All he had to fear was—

The door opened behind him.

He whirled, his heart pounding, terrified that he had
been caught in the act of thinking forbidden thoughts.

One of the guerrillas, a dark-skinned Bedouin whom
he hadn't seen before, came through the door. He was
followed by a man in creased fatigues, a leather-holstered
semiautomatic pistol at his hip. He had lean, handsome
features, his slicked-back hair and mustache revealing
traces of gray. Rasmussen noticed that he walked with a
slight limp.

For a long moment, the man regarded Rasmussen
with an intent, curious gaze. Finally he said, in English,
"You are a military officer?"

"I was."

"A U.S. Navy commander?"

"Lieutenant commander."

"A fighter pilot, correct?"

Rasmussen nodded. He should have expected it. The
interrogations were beginning again.

"Very good," said the man. He smiled, displaying a
row of perfect white teeth. "We have something in
common. My name is Al-Fasr. Col. Jamal Al-Fasr."

CHAPTER 7

BAHRAIN

Northern Persian Gulf
1935, Tuesday, 16 March

Abu Mahmed watched in silence as the boat sliced through the black water. The thirty-knot wind over the streamlined bow snatched at his hair, whipping the sleeves of his padded jacket. The deep-throated rumble of the two diesel engines reverberated off the water like the growl of an angry beast.

The hull of the boat was slapping the crests of the three-foot swells, making Abu's stomach churn and his knees weaken from the repetitive bumps. He wished now that he had refused Al-Fasr's order that he command this operation. He was a land warrior, not a seaman. In daylight the sea made him uneasy. At night it terrified him. He wasn't a good swimmer, and he had been told that there were venomous sea snakes in this part of the Gulf.

In the darkness he could barely make out the silhouette of the second boat, running on a parallel course with them thirty meters away. They were now nearly twenty kilometers into the Gulf, keeping radio silence.

Akhmed Fayez, the lead boat's captain, was peering into the green-lighted radarscope, nodding his head in

satisfaction. "Another ten degrees to starboard," he
barked at the helmsman. He looked across the cockpit at
Abu and pointed to the scope. "There it is, eight kilometers away, just as we expected."

Hanging onto the brass rail on the bulkhead, Abu
wobbled over to the cockpit and peered into the scope.
Akhmed was right. The single large, yellowish blip on
the screen was unmistakable.

Akhmed flicked the radar off again. "No more radar.
We'll have visual contact in a couple of minutes. No
need to alert him that he's being targeted."

Both craft, old Teryer naval speedboats built by the
Zelenodolsk Bureau in Russia, had been seized in a
commando raid from the Iranian navy's river base at
Abadan. Even though the two boats were constructed of
fiberglass, Abu had no doubt that they were already visible on radar.

He still marveled that a giant vessel like the *Bayou
Queen* would be unprotected. Could it be possible that
such a ship would have no escort, no antiship weapons?
The idiot leaders of the Western countries never learned.
Not since the Iraqi-Iranian war had oil tankers in the
Persian Gulf been escorted by naval warships. Not until
one of their precious assets—an airliner or an energy
plant or one of their monolithic high-rise buildings—
was actually destroyed in a surprise attack did they
bother to take defensive action. Then they would leave
something else exposed.

Like an oil tanker.

"I see it, dead ahead," called the sentry in the bow
station.

Abu peered into the darkness, squinting against the
wind. Yes, there it was, the hulking shape of the *Bayou
Queen*. She was a modern 200,000-ton, double-hulled
supertanker, built three years ago in New Orleans. Like
many such tankers, she operated under a Marshall Is-
lands flag, but she was owned by the Sanders Oil Com-

pany of Houston, Texas. Her captain and most of the crew were American.

He could see the white-lighted superstructure and red running lights on the port side. The giant ship was steaming southward from Kuwait, toward the strait of Hormuz, delivering oil to the corrupt infidels of America.

As he watched the big tanker swell in the night, Abu saw a white beam of light flash down from the bridge of the big vessel. They had picked up the incoming boats with their own radar and were probing with a searchlight.

"Left ninety degrees," Akhmed ordered. "We parallel their course for half a kilometer. Let them think we are staying clear."

Akhmed waited until the shape of the tanker began to drop behind their starboard beam, then barked another order. "Right ninety degrees. Signal the attack boat."

The crewman on the port deck sent a series of quick flashes with his signaling lamp. From the second speedboat came an answering pattern of flashes.

The second speedboat—the attack boat—surged ahead. Abu could hear the big diesels bellowing at full throttle. Akhmed let his own boat drop behind while the first boat bored through the night on a direct course for the *Bayou Queen.*

This was the critical moment. The two men in the attack boat—the only crewmembers aboard—must be certain their boat was locked onto an intercept course with the tanker. Then they would set the autopilot to hold a steady heading. When everything was precisely correct, they would abandon ship.

A quick series of flashes from the attack boat.

"They're in the water," said Abu. Akhmed was already throttling back, letting the boat decelerate in the choppy sea. "Find them quickly. They're out there somewhere, close to us."

It took less than a minute. The two crewmen from the attack boat were no further than a hundred meters ahead, bobbing on the black water in their inflated vests, flashing the dim yellow beams of their survival lights. Akhmed idled the speedboat toward them, swinging the starboard bow around so that the pair could grab the rope ladder.

Abu was glad they didn't have to search for long. He had no scruples about leaving the two in the sea. Their usefulness was over, but it would be very bad if they were picked up by the Americans, who would soon be swarming over this piece of sea like birds of prey. The true identity of the attackers must remain a secret.

While the two sailors were clambering up the rope ladder, Abu peered into the darkness after the attack boat. He could still hear the high-pitched growl of the diesel. Without the wind in his eyes, it was easier to keep the faint silhouette of the *Bayou Queen* in his vision.

The crew of the tanker knew something was happening. Searchlights were sweeping the sea, looking for the target that had been detected on their radar. One of the lights found the fast-moving speedboat, holding it fixed in its beam. In the distance a voice boomed over a megaphone, demanding that the intruding boat turn about and keep its distance.

While the two dripping-wet sailors flopped onto the forward deck, Akhmed shoved the throttles forward and swung the bow back toward the east. Abu looked back over the stern, through the spray of the boat's wake. He saw all the searchlights on the tanker fixed now on the incoming boat. Sporadic orange flashes were twinkling from the deck of the tanker.

Gunfire, Abu realized. Small arms, probably .30 caliber at the most. Too little and too late. It would take an armor-piercing round to penetrate the fortified hull of the speedboat where the two hundred kilos of high explosives were loaded.

He wished he could hear the dialogue on the tanker's bridge at this moment. The captain would be demanding to know what the hell was going on, receiving no clear answer. By now his gaze would be riveted on the specter of the boat that was bearing down on him like an avenging angel.

Abu waited, counting the seconds. *What happened to the boat?* It should have impacted the tanker by now. In the inky blackness he could see only the vague shape of the *Bayou Queen*. Searchlights were still sweeping the surface. From the port deck came the continuous little orange blinks of gunfire.

A pall of gloom fell over Abu. They had failed. Either the guns stopped the boat, or it missed its target altogether. After all the planning and risk, they had failed to—

"Look!" cried Akhmed. "Allah has answered us."

So he had. An orange sphere of flame appeared on the waterline at the tanker's bow. As the men on the speedboat stared in awe, the ball of fire swelled like an amorphous creature, engulfing the entire forward half of the tanker. The fireball mushroomed high into the night sky, bathing the sea in a shimmering orange light.

Flaming debris spewed like Roman candles from the burning ship. The tower of flame gushing from the tanker's hull lit the horizon as brightly as a new dawn. The stark silhouette of the stricken tanker was etched against the rim of the sea.

It took nearly twenty seconds for the loud *whump* of the explosion to reach them. A primal cheer erupted from the *Sherji* on the speedboat. Even Abu screamed in triumph. With the orange glow of the burning *Bayou Queen* shining in their faces, the men of his little unit had reason to cheer. After all the humiliation—the routs from Yemen and Afghanistan—they had managed to inflict real pain on the enemy.

"Aircraft!" The hoarse sound of Akhmed's voice cut through the cheering. He was hunched over his radar display. "They know where we are. Aircraft are coming after us."

The cheering abruptly stopped. Abu scrambled across the cockpit to peer into the radar scope. A little yellow blip winked back at him, moving on a steady track toward the escaping speedboat. Where was it coming from? A shore base or from a U.S. warship? A patrol plane or an attack jet?

It didn't matter. He would deal with them.

He swung to Omar, stationed on the upper front deck. "Ready the Igla battery," he ordered.

U.S. Navy fleet landing, Manama, Bahrain

Some things never change.

To Maxwell, the fleet landing in Bahrain looked like every other dock in every other port in the Middle East. Same row of sputtering taxis waiting to haul sailors to the city. Same gaggle of hawkers pushing carts filled with scarves and brassware and cheap jewelry. Same smell of oil and seaweed, the distant whiff of sewage.

It was late afternoon and a cool breeze swept in off the Gulf. The *Reagan* lay at anchor a mile out in the harbor. Like all hundred-thousand-ton U.S. Navy ships, the big carrier never tied up to a dock in the Middle East, not just because of its immense size but for other reasons.

American warships had become the most coveted targets of terrorist organizations.

As the senior officer on the boat, Maxwell was the first to step ashore. He was wearing his standard in-port liberty garb—khakis, blue knit shirt, deck shoes. In the bag were the blazer and cotton shirt he'd wear tonight. He set his faded canvas weekend duffel bag down and gazed around.

She didn't come. Oh, well, she was busy with network stuff, probably setting up a shoot.

Not until he'd walked out to the street, about to hail a taxi, did he spot her. She was standing in the shade of the same towering palm where they'd met during his first cruise aboard the *Reagan*. Around her neck was the silk scarf he had bought for her in Dubai. She wore it like a talisman whenever she came to meet him after a long separation.

She waved, and he picked up the bag and trotted across the street, dodging a honking taxi and a motorbike. He set the bag down and took her in his arms. He kissed her for what seemed like minutes but was, in fact, only thirty seconds. She held him tightly, her hands entwined behind his neck.

When she came up for air, she looked at him. "Wow."

"Is that all you have to say?"

"I had a cute little speech prepared. I forgot it."

He saved her the trouble of remembering by kissing her again. For the next minute Maxwell forgot about the war on terrorism and the USS *Reagan* and the thirteen Super Hornets of his squadron that were now lashed down on the hangar deck. None of it mattered. Not for three glorious days would any of it matter.

He tried to remember how long it had been. Three months, a couple of weeks, and some days. They had last been together at Oceana Naval Air Station in Virginia, standing in a cold rain, wives and kids snuffling and waving little American flags, the pilots of his squadron looking grim before flying out to the *Reagan*, which was already at sea, bound for Gibraltar and the Middle East and another confrontation with America's enemies. Another farewell in what seemed like an endless litany of farewells.

"Come back to me in one piece, Sam Maxwell,"
Claire had said.

And so he had, at least as far as Bahrain, where the
Reagan was taking a week off from war. Claire had e-
mailed him about her assignment to the Gulf. And yes,
she would most definitely be in Bahrain when the *Reagan* came to town.

"Where are we staying, Sam?"

"The Al Hazra, a little hotel in Sitra. Off the beaten
path."

"Will I have you all to myself?"

"For three days."

"Three whole days," she said, shaking her head. "We
have to hurry. Life is short."

Northern Persian Gulf

Skimming the sea at only a hundred feet, Lieutenant
Jay Pfeiffer could see the choppy water through his
night vision goggles as clearly as if it were daytime. The
spectral glow of the blazing tanker was lighting up the
Persian Gulf for a radius of at least fifty miles.

Pfeiffer and his two crewmen were manning the alert
helo when the call came. The big Sikorsky SH-60R helicopter had been launched from its pad on the Aegis
cruiser USS *Richmond*, less than two minutes after the
Bayou Queen reported being attacked.

Attacked by what? Pfeiffer was still wondering. One
of the several varieties of nutcase terrorists in the Middle East, he guessed. There were no reports that the
Iranian navy had gunships in the area. But it had to be
some kind of small boat. Whose?

This appeared to be the same stunt Al Qaeda had pulled
in Yemen against the French oil tanker *Limburger*. Somehow they were able to get in close enough with a boat full
of explosives to light off a tanker full of crude oil.

According to the surface watch aboard *Richmond*, two boats had been spotted. One was the bomber, and the other was now hauling ass back toward Iran. It was Pfeiffer's job to catch him.

"Wizard One-one, the target is confirmed hostile. You are weapons free, acknowledge."

"Wizard One-one copies weapons free." He couldn't keep the tension out of his voice. He had rehearsed this dialogue a dozen times in fleet exercises, but never had he received a no-shit clearance to fire on an enemy.

"Target bears zero-seven-zero, fourteen miles," reported Lt. junior grade Jazz Mulligan, the ATO—Airborne Tactical Officer—from his station in the aft cabin. Mulligan was busy correlating the information that was being datalinked from the Surface Warfare Commander aboard *Richmond*. "What are we gonna whack him with?"

"We'll shoot the 2.75 rockets to stop him in the water, then move in close with the M60 gun. We're just supposed to cover him until a boarding party gets here from the Saipan. They want these guys alive, whoever they are."

Though the Seahawk was armed with the new AGM-119 Penguin ship killer missile, such a weapon was gross overkill against a small target like this one, which was probably some kind of fiberglass- or wood-hulled speedboat. There'd be nothing left but an oil slick.

The prospect of using the M60 machine gun caused Pfeiffer's pulse rate to kick up even higher. Damn, this was cool! There was nothing like the hard, visceral feeling you got from hosing a surface target with a machine gun.

He had often regretted his decision back in flight training. He'd opted for helicopters instead of flying pointy-nosed jets off carriers. Then he learned the dismal truth: Fighter jocks were the only ones who ever saw real combat.

Until now.

"Ten miles, twelve o'clock," reported the ATO.

"I'm looking," said Pfeiffer, peering through the NVG. "No visual ID yet."

Over his shoulder he glimpsed Buddy Jenkins, a second class petty officer and third member of the Seahawk crew, positioning himself in the door with the M60. Jenkins's normal assignment was "Senso"— sensor operator—in charge of the helo's submarine detection equipment. Pfeiffer felt a twinge of envy. Firing the gun was going to be the best part of the mission.

Still, he was the guy who would shoot the 2.75s. The trouble with them was that they were folding-fin rockets. After they left the launching tube, the little fins were supposed to extend and guide the rocket to where you aimed it. In Pfeiffer's experience, they came out like a covey of quail, and accuracy was a matter of luck.

There. Straight ahead, something on the surface, trailing a white ribbon of wake. The burning tanker was over twenty miles behind them, but the orange glow was reflecting off the fast-moving object. Pfeiffer could make out the shape of a boat. It was heading due east at something over thirty knots.

Pfeiffer toggled his weapons display, selecting the 2.75 pod on the starboard pylon. He flipped the master armament switch on, then adjusted the reticules in the HUD gun sight. It wouldn't take much to stop the boat. After one or two of the 2.75s ripped into them, the Iranian crew would go over the side. The trick was to not kill all of them.

He could see the boat clearly now. It was about thirty feet in length, wide in the beam with a slick, tapered prow. Pfeiffer nudged the nose of the Seahawk off the inbound bearing a few degrees. He would make his attack from an oblique angle, rolling hard into the target, firing a couple of the rockets for effect, then let Jenkins pacify them with the M60.

The fight would be over. All they would have to do then was—

Something flashed from the deck of the boat. *What the hell? Are the bastards shooting?* If they were that crazy, he was going to give them a dose of—

Armstrong's voice crackled on the intercom. "Flares! They've got a missile in the air."

A wave of fear surged through Pfeiffer like an electric shock. *Shit!* He could see it—a reddish pinpoint of light, zigzagging like a goddamn bat. Coming at them. *Why didn't I use the Penguin missile?*

He stabbed the button for the flare dispenser. At the same time he threw the Seahawk into an evasive turn. In his peripheral vision he saw the luminous glow of the flares igniting behind the helicopter. Helicopters were easy targets for surface-to-air missiles.

Dear God, make it go for the flares. That's what flares are for, fooling heat-seeker missiles into . . .

The missile wasn't fooled. The reddish point of light was swelling in intensity, pulling lead to intercept, zigzagging ever closer to a collision course with the Seahawk. Pfeiffer dumped the nose of the helicopter and reversed the turn. *Make the missile overshoot.*

It wasn't working. Pfeiffer watched the oncoming missile make its correction, then home in on the heat signature of the Seahawk's port engine.

For a long instant he had a view of the Igla through the windscreen, as if it were suspended in time. He glimpsed the control vanes that made the missile flit through the sky like a bat. He could even see the IR seeker head that guided it precisely to the heat-emitting turbine engine.

Strange, he thought. He felt as if he were a detached witness to a calamity. The destruction of the Sikorsky helicopter seemed to be happening on a stage separate from him, playing in slow motion.

It took, in fact, four seconds. The Igla missile detonated inside the compressor section of the port turbine engine, taking out the gear assembly and severing the rotor components. The front section of the Seahawk separated from the main fuselage. Alone in the cockpit, Pfeiffer watched the dark surface of the Persian Gulf whirl toward him.

CHAPTER 8

RECALL

Manama, Bahrain
1945, Tuesday, 16 March

A red-and-white checkered cloth covered their table. The flame of the yellow candle flickered on the table between them, casting dancing shadows on Claire's face. From speakers hidden behind the curtains, Placido Domingo was hitting the high notes of the "Nessen Durma," from *Turandot*. A half-empty '96 Gevrey-Chambertin rested in its cradle.

Coming to Cico's had been her idea. If they were going to spend three whole days together, they would begin with a romantic dinner, which, in Bahrain, meant Cico's. It was the undisputed best Italian cuisine in the Middle East.

Darkness had descended over Manama, but it was still early evening. Only half the tables were filled. Officers from the *Reagan* wouldn't start trickling in until later, after they'd made a sweep of the Hilton garden bar and the Gulf Hotel lounge and the downtown clubs.

Maxwell didn't want to see anyone from the air wing tonight. Or for the next three days. *Life is short.* Claire had said it herself.

She touched her glass to his. "To us, Sam."

"Just us? No one else?"

He saw a cloud pass over her face, and wished he could take it back. It was the subject most on his mind—and the one that he promised himself he wouldn't bring up. Her husband.

He and Claire had fallen in love years ago when he was a lieutenant in test pilot school at Patuxent River, Maryland, and she was a fledgling reporter in Washington. For reasons neither of them understood—youth, ambition, geography—they separated. Each married someone else.

Maxwell's wife, an astronaut and cardiologist named Debbie Sutter, perished in a training accident one blazing afternoon at Cape Canaveral. Claire's journalist husband, Chris Tyrwhitt, was a charming and dissolute character who covered Iraq for an Australian news syndicate. He earned for himself the label "Baghdad Ben" for his pro-Saddam reporting.

By the time Brick and Claire found each other again, she had already initiated divorce proceedings. Before the marriage was officially ended, though, she was informed that her husband had been killed in Iraq by army guards while he was trespassing in a forbidden area. Claire was a widow—and a free woman.

She and Maxwell resumed their old romance. They spent all their free time together, and when the *Reagan* returned to the U.S., she transferred back to the Washington bureau so she could be close to him. They talked about getting married.

And then their world was turned upside down. Chris Tyrwhitt returned from the dead, rolling like a flash flood back into their lives. He hadn't died, and he wasn't the dissolute journalist Claire thought him to be. He wasn't really a pro-Saddam toady. It was possible that he might even be something of a hero.

"I'm still married, if that's what you mean."

He nodded. That was what he meant, but he knew

better than to push it. "Sorry. I promise not to bring it up again."

She reached across the table and took his hand. "I don't blame you for being impatient, Sam, but you can't rush me. I need time to work it out."

He wrestled with his feelings, forcing himself to keep his mouth shut. Time? Was she divorcing Tyrwhitt or not? Or was she stringing them both along, not sure whom she preferred? The military officer in Maxwell resisted stalemates like this. Every conflict was supposed to have a resolution. Why wasn't this one resolved? It was like the Korean War. These were questions he needed to ask.

But not now. Tonight was their first together, and he didn't intend to spoil it. He wanted to preserve in his memory the yellow candle flame playing on her face, showing off her freckles, making her eyes sparkle.

Relax, Maxwell. He was a lucky man, he told himself. Sitting across from him was the woman he loved. If she needed time to sort out her life, then so be it. He would wait as long as it took.

The waiter arrived with the antipasti. In the background, Domingo had segued into an aria from *La Boheme.* Claire was watching him from across the table, smiling a knowing half-smile.

Life is short, he reminded himself. Tonight was special. In another hour they'd be on their way to the Al Hazra, where they'd be together for the next three days.

The wine was relaxing him. He felt a warm glow of contentment settle over him. Tonight he and Claire would—

The thought froze unfinished in his mind. He saw a change in Claire. Her eyes were no longer gazing at him but staring at something across the room.

Someone coming toward them.

Maxwell felt the contentment dry up inside him. He knew by the look in Claire's eyes who it had to be.

Northern Persian Gulf

From the stern of the Teryer speedboat, Abu watched the burning helicopter plunge into the sea. A small sheet of flame blazed on the surface for half a minute, then extinguished. The blackened carcass of the Sikorsky slipped beneath the waves, leaving nothing but an oily splotch.

For a while no one in the boat spoke. Akhmed kept the throttles pushed all the way forward. He kept peering into the radar, then back over his shoulder where the helicopter had vanished.

Finally he said, "Killing the helicopter was bad. It means the Americans will not just retaliate. They will seek revenge."

"So much the better," said Abu. "Let them take their revenge on Iran."

"They are not stupid. They will come after us."

"Shut up," snapped Abu. "Your task is to get this boat back into Iranian waters. Do not concern yourself with matters that are beyond your knowledge."

Akhmed locked eyes with him for a long moment, then returned to his radar. From time to time he looked up and shot a baleful scowl at Abu.

Abu took a seat in the aft cockpit, keeping his eye on Akhmed and the others in the front. His right hand remained close to the trigger guard of his H&K MP-5 submachine gun—another item of hardware liberated from the Iranian base at Abadan.

Akhmed had become a problem. He was a Red Sea fisherman whom Al-Fasr had recruited in Yemen because of his skill with small boats. Since joining the Bu Hasa Brigade, he had stayed with the *Sherji* from the Yemen campaign, most of whom remained loyal to Al-Fasr. When he was around Abu, Akhmed was surly and argumentative.

He had had enough of Akhmed. His usefulness was

nearly over. After tonight's mission, Abu would find a way to dispose of him.

In the distance he could see lights twinkling on the Iranian shore. Another ten or so kilometers and they would be inside Iran's territorial waters. The demoralized Iranian navy seldom bothered to patrol their coast anymore. If they came out to intercept them with one of their decrepit patrol boats, Abu would blow them to hell with another missile.

He wondered how Omar Al-Iryani's mission in Kuwait had gone. If Omar failed and he and his *Sherji* were killed or captured, the whole reckless scheme tonight would have been for nothing. It was a clumsy operation at best, leaving a trail of death that was supposed to point to Iran.

Much as he hated to admit it, Akhmed was right. The Americans weren't stupid. Arrogant, satanic in every respect, but not stupid.

In the final analysis, he reminded himself, it didn't matter. Whether the Americans linked the attacks to Iran was not important. They only had to be informed of the identity of their real adversary. They would know where to find him.

Manama, Bahrain

Maxwell had never seen her flustered before. As a broadcast journalist Claire Phillips was trained to stay cool. Now her training left her.

"Chris? What are you . . . how did you—" she stammered, then ran out of words.

"You mean, of all the gin joints in all the world, why did I have to pick this one?" Christopher Tyrwhitt flashed a toothy grin. "One of Bogie's greatest lines. This could be a scene right out of *Casablanca*, don't you think?"

Maxwell had never met Tyrwhitt, but he recognized him from photographs. Ruddy complexion, fading reddish beard and hair. About Maxwell's height with a solid build, a few pounds overweight but not enough to be a pushover. He wore a lopsided, roguish grin that Maxwell guessed women found charming.

Standing at Tyrwhitt's side was a burly, square-jawed man with a short haircut. He kept his eyes on Maxwell, giving him a critical stare.

Maxwell felt his earlier contentment sink like a raft in a storm. Claire still wore a wide-eyed expression, her face frozen, as Tyrwhitt gave her a noisy kiss on the cheek.

Then his mood hit bottom. He heard Claire say, "Would you gentlemen please join us?"

No! he wanted to say. *To hell with these—*

Too late. Tyrwhitt was pulling two chairs over from the adjoining table. "Let me introduce my colleague, Ted Bronson. This is my wife, Claire Phillips. And this chap, I believe, is a Yank from one of those ships in the harbor."

Maxwell and Bronson exchanged perfunctory handshakes. Tyrwhitt didn't bother proffering his hand.

Claire had recovered some of her composure. "Bronson?" She shook his hand and said, "Haven't we met somewhere? At the embassy maybe? One of the press briefings?"

He didn't blink. "Perhaps."

She turned to Tyrwhitt. "Okay, never mind *Casablanca*. What are you doing here in Bahrain?"

"Just a little freelancing."

Her eyes narrowed and she thought for a moment. She turned back to his colleague. "Bronson? Now it's coming to me. The CIA station chief in Bahrain, right?"

"It's possible." Bronson's expression didn't change.

She looked at Tyrwhitt. "And what's this about freelancing? Let me guess who you might be freelancing for."

Tyrwhitt shrugged. "Everybody needs a job."

"Sounds like the same job you had before. Are you still pretending to be a journalist?"

"Why not?" Tyrwhitt's eyes shifted from Claire to Maxwell. "Basically, we're all whores, right?"

A heavy silence fell over the table. Maxwell saw Claire's face redden, and he felt a rush of anger. It occurred to him that this would be an excellent time for Tyrwhitt to get his balls kicked into the next country.

He was pushing his chair away from the table when he felt Claire's foot rap his ankle.

"Good old Chris hasn't changed a bit," she said, her voice mellow again. "Sensitive as ever."

Tyrwhitt grinned back at her. "That's me. A candidate for sainthood."

After that, she tried to keep the conversation light while she and Maxwell pecked at their dinner and Tyrwhitt ordered more drinks. He rambled on about current events in the Middle East, how Islamic fundamentalists were threatening the stability of some of the old monarchies, including Saudi Arabia and even Bahrain. From time to time Bronson would break his own silence to correct him on a fine point.

Claire seemed to have gotten over the shock of seeing her estranged husband. She was laughing at his jokes, adding her opinions. She seemed to be enjoying herself.

Maxwell's mood darkened. He knew little about Claire's husband, only that he was an Australian and that his cover had been as a journalist who was sympathetic to Saddam Hussein. Not until he was shot and imprisoned by the Iraqis for spying did Claire learn that Tyrwhitt had been working for the CIA.

And, apparently, still was.

There was a lull in the conversation. Bronson looked

at him and said, "And what are you doing in Bahrain, Maxwell? You're off one of the Navy ships?"

Maxwell didn't like the patronizing tone. He was about to tell him his job was cleaning up messes made by assholes like him and Tyrwhitt, but he saw Claire giving him a warning look.

She said, "Sam is the commanding officer of a fighter squadron on the USS *Reagan*."

Bronson nodded, showing by his expression that he wasn't impressed. He didn't ask any more questions, which was okay with Maxwell. Bronson was like many professional intelligence officers he had encountered. Condescending, pushy, filled with little secrets that they would never share.

And then Maxwell had another thought—the video conference with Maria Rasmussen. *Would the CIA lie to us?* she had asked. Good question.

"Have you been stationed in the Middle East for long?" Maxwell asked.

Bronson gave him a wary glance. "A number of years."

"Since before Desert Storm in '91?"

He nodded.

"Do you know anything about what happened to the Americans taken prisoner in Desert Storm?"

Bronson's eyes narrowed. "Why do you want to know?"

Tyrwhitt and Claire were both watching him now. Tyrwhitt was leaning forward, chin on his fist, a curious expression on his face.

"Just wondering," said Maxwell, "whether you'd heard rumors about a prisoner who might still be there."

Bronson's face remained frozen. "As a military officer, you should know better than to discuss such things in a place like this."

"Why? Is it classified?"

"It's nothing I've ever heard of."

"There's a story that Saddam kept one of our pilots from the first Gulf War. Someone listed as killed in action, but in fact he was alive and left behind. His name was Rasmussen."

"Rasmussen?" Bronson scratched his chin. "No, there was never anyone like that—"

"That reminds me of someone," interjected Tyrwhitt. "Back when I was a guest of Saddam, after the buggers shot me and patched up the holes and chucked me into Abu Graib prison. While I was there, I had a brief conversation with a chap in the cell next to mine. I'm sure he was a Yank because he—"

"Not a chance," said Bronson sharply. Gone for an instant was the frozen expression. His eyebrows lowered over his eyes as he glowered at Tyrwhitt. "There were no American prisoners left in Iraq." He cleared his throat, then went on in a lighter voice. "That's an old myth that keeps popping up like those Hollywood CIA conspiracy movies. It happens after every war. We did an exhaustive search of the country after Operation Iraqi Freedom, and I can assure you there were no living American prisoners in Iraq."

Tyrwhitt just nodded, giving Bronson a curious look.

Maxwell watched the two men. There was a peculiar chemistry between them. Tyrwhitt was definitely not a CIA company man like Bronson. He had a big mouth, and his boss had just shut him up.

Tyrwhitt was sitting back in his seat, nodding his head, pretending to be chastised. A sly grin had crept over his face.

"Stories like that do everyone a disservice," continued Bronson, "because they undermine the credibility of the intelligence services. And they cause unnecessary pain for relatives."

That much was true, Maxwell thought. Maria Rasmussen and her kids didn't need any more pain. But he didn't mind prodding Bronson, maybe cause *him* a little pain. If nothing else, it might prompt him to check into the matter further. Maybe—

He became aware of another presence at the table. Someone standing behind him, and it wasn't the waiter. He turned to see a barrel-chested man in khakis and an ugly, flowered sport shirt. He had wispy red hair, and he held an unlit cigar in his hand.

"Please forgive the intrusion," said Red Boyce. He gazed around the table. "Evening, Claire. It's good to see you again." His eyes rested on Tyrwhitt for a moment. "Well, if it isn't Baghdad Ben. What are you doing now that your pal Saddam is out of work?"

"Oh, I do odd jobs." Tyrwhitt winked at Claire.

Maxwell sighed and said, "Care to join us, CAG?" *Why not? Everyone else in Bahrain is.*

"No, thanks. You and I are leaving."

Maxwell felt his world getting darker. "Ah, Claire and I are planning to—"

"The helo is waiting at the fleet landing pad. We've got orders Baksheep." "Baksheep" was an old Navy term. It meant "back to the ship," and Maxwell used to think it was funny. Now it infuriated him.

He'd been in the Navy too long to say what he really thought, at least in front of civilians. *The hell I'm leaving! What could possibly be so goddamn urgent that I have to leave now?*

Lots of things, actually. This was the Middle East. Boyce was giving him that look.

"How much time do we have?"

"Five minutes. My driver's outside."

Claire was looking at him with large, stricken eyes. It wasn't fair, he thought. It wasn't fair to either of them. War sucked. The Navy sucked. The whole frigging Middle East sucked.

He took a deep breath and rose from the table. He

didn't bother saying good-bye to Tyrwhitt or Bronson. Claire rose and followed him outside.

Boyce's car, a black, unmarked Ford Crown Victoria from the fleet motor pool, waited across the street. They stood on the sidewalk and she took his hand in hers.

"Have you ever considered another line of work, Sam?"

"I'm open to suggestions."

"You'd be a good dentist. Or an accountant. You could work regular hours and be home every evening. You wouldn't have to fly off in the night like this."

"Good idea. I'll tell Boyce I quit."

The restaurant door flew open again, and Boyce appeared on the sidewalk. "Took me a minute to figure out who the other guy at the table is. That's Bronson, the head spook in the region. What the hell's he doing here?"

"He came in with my husband. His boss, I presume."

Maxwell noted the "my husband." Not ex, or former, or about-to-be split. She didn't sound like a woman in the process of divorce.

"They probably know more about what's going on than I do," said Boyce.

"What *is* going on?" Maxwell asked.

"This is the Gulf. You can figure it out. Something's up, and the *Reagan*'s hoisting anchor."

Maxwell nodded. It had something to do with jihad. Or Al Qaeda. Or the villain du jour. The Axis of Evil never slept.

Boyce crossed the street and climbed into the car, giving them a moment alone.

"Promise me you'll be careful," Claire said.

"I'm always careful." He knew it sounded brusque, but he couldn't get over his annoyance at being plucked out of the restaurant by Boyce. But it wasn't just leaving Claire that bothered him.

He was leaving her with Tyrwhitt.

He kissed her, then he held her for several seconds, trying to find the words to tell her what was troubling him.

They wouldn't come. He turned and crossed the street to the waiting car. He saw her watching from the sidewalk as the Ford pulled away.

CHAPTER 9

PROVOCATION

Kuwait, northern frontier
2145, Tuesday, 16 March

The night sky lay like a canopy over the desert. On the southern horizon, Omar Al-Iryani could see the glow of the lights from Kuwait City.

Omar's patience was dwindling. He settled himself into the depression beside the road and looked again at his watch. In the darkness across the road, concealed in a narrow wadi, were the other *Sherji*—Ali and his two Omanis, and their prisoner.

The vehicle with the relief border guards was late. He had been assured that the Kuwaitis rotated detachments at the border outpost every night shortly after midnight. This was the only access road to the post on the border between Kuwait and Iraq.

While he waited, Omar wondered how Abu's mission had gone. On the scale of danger, it was even more hazardous than his own assignment. Out there on the open Gulf, Abu and his party were easy prey for enemy naval craft and airplanes. Why were they doing this? All to satisfy the fantasies of their commander, who was becoming a toothless tiger.

Omar didn't know what the outcome of tonight's action would be. He only knew that Abu, who was a holy warrior and his true leader, had ordered him to execute this mission. If death was to be the outcome, then it would be the will of Allah. He was prepared to join the martyrs in heaven. He heard the low grumble of an engine.

Omar hunched down again in the depression. The dim yellow glow of headlights appeared on the road. As it approached, he could make out the low profile and wide body—an American-made HMMWV, the thing they called a Hummer. Another bauble bestowed on the fawning Kuwaitis by their American patrons.

Omar waited until the Hummer was only fifty meters away, coming toward him. In the dim light he could see four occupants in the open-topped vehicle.

Omar opened fire. He aimed a short burst into the forward quarter of the vehicle, pinging rounds off the thick steel body.

The driver slammed on the brakes and the Hummer skidded off the road, onto the soft shoulder. The front wheels buried themselves in the deep sand, and the vehicle ground to a stop.

Perfect, thought Omar. He fired another burst, again hammering the hard metal side of the stalled vehicle.

It produced the desired effect. All four battle-dressed soldiers scuttled out and hunched down behind the Hummer. Each was fumbling with his weapon, trying to get a line of fire on his attacker.

Omar almost laughed out loud. The three guards were Kuwaiti soldiers, relief troops for one of the outposts on the border. The enlisted troops of the Kuwaiti army came from the least privileged stratum of the oil-rich country. They were mostly young Bedouins with little education and no real skills.

The other, the one who was *not* fumbling with his weapon, was probably one of the American soldiers seconded to the inept Kuwaiti defense force.

From behind the Hummer came the familiar dull crackle of an automatic weapon. One of the soldiers— was it the American?— was firing at Omar's position.

Excellent, thought Omar. An H&K MP-5 submachine gun. Just like the one he held in his hands, courtesy of the Iranian navy. The scenario was playing out just as he hoped.

Bullets were kicking up the sand around his sheltered ledge. Time to end this charade. The Hummer was equipped with a radio, and the American would be summoning help.

It was time for Ali Massouf to emerge from concealment. He was supposed to move up with the RPG-7 grenade launcher. With the bullets pinging around him, Omar's impatience swelled. *Why isn't Ali*—

The exploding round from the Russian-made weapon made a metallic sound, like a collision of freight trains. Omar saw something, perhaps a door from the Hummer, careen through the air. Someone screamed in agony. A cloud of greasy smoke billowed into the air.

He rose from the depression to check the results. Ali and his squad were emerging from the wadi, approaching the destroyed Hummer.

The enemy soldiers were a mess. Two were dead, badly mutilated. The American was writhing on the ground, his right leg nearly severed at the knee. One of the Kuwaitis was on all fours, dazed and wounded, trying to crawl away.

Ali watched them without pity. He cradled his submachine gun in his arms and looked across the smoking Hummer at Omar.

Omar nodded. Ali turned to the crawling man and fired a burst into him. He moved over to the American with the damaged leg. The wounded man—a sergeant, Omar judged by the black insignia—glowered up at him. Omar finished him with a burst to the forehead.

"Where is the Iranian?" said Omar. "Bring him

quickly." One of the *Sherji* trotted back to the wadi where they'd concealed themselves. Seconds later he returned, pulling a stubble-bearded man by the elbow. The man's wrists were bound in front, and he wore the shabby blue uniform of the Iranian navy.

Omar picked up the MP-5 that lay next to the dead American. He checked it, then walked over to the Iranian prisoner.

The Iranian sensed what was coming. His eyes filled with terror. "Please," he said in Farsi. "In the name of Allah—"

The dull crackle of the MP-5 drowned out his words. The Iranian toppled backward, his chest stitched with the burst of nine-millimeter bullets. He lay spread-eagled on the desert floor, his eyes staring straight into the sky.

"Untie his wrists," ordered Omar. "Position him with a weapon over there, across the road." He threw the MP-5 back on the ground next to the body of the dead Kuwaiti soldier.

At that moment he heard it. The first faint whopping noise.

Rotor blades.

He cocked his head, listening. The other *Sherji* watched him anxiously.

"Ours or theirs?" inquired Ali.

He listened for another several seconds to be sure. Yes, he was certain. It was the distinctive thrum of a French-built helicopter's blades.

"Ours. The Dauphin, coming back for us."

The Dauphin was an armed utility helicopter. It was the sole remaining war bird in the inventory of the Bu Hasa Brigade.

While he waited for the helicopter to arrive, Omar surveyed the carnage around him. One dead American and three Kuwaitis. A good count, he reflected. Too bad they weren't all Americans.

Manama, Bahrain

"Welcome back, old girl." Tyrwhitt raised his glass. "Now that they're gone, let the party begin."

She saw that he had ordered another bottle of wine. Bronson's own glass was still half full. He looked bored.

"Something must have happened," said Claire. "Why would the *Reagan* be going back to sea so quickly?"

"Ask him," Tyrwhitt said, nodding to Bronson. "I'm not supposed to know such things, at least in public."

Bronson gave her his dead-eyed gaze. "Your news bureau has the story by now," he said. "A terrorist action. A nasty one against an oil tanker."

"What will the *Reagan* battle group do? Retaliate?"

Bronson gave her a humorless chuckle. "Even if I knew, do you really think I'd divulge it to a reporter in a restaurant? Get serious, lady."

"You could tell me off the record. Chris can tell you that I respect confidentiality."

"Your husband isn't qualified to decide such things."

Whatever that meant, she guessed it was an insult. Tyrwhitt didn't seem to mind. He tossed down half his wine and said, "Your boyfriend seems rather antisocial. Don't you find him boring?"

"Not at all. Sam was annoyed that we weren't alone this evening."

"Pity. Were you going to spend the night together?"

She bristled, but she kept her voice level. "I know it's difficult, Chris, but try not to be obnoxious."

"Well, since the poor chap's been called away, I'll step forward and do the right thing. I'll take his place."

"Chris, you're unbelievable."

"Does that mean yes?"

"It means you're a presumptuous ass." She said it too loudly. The group at the next table was staring. A waiter carrying a tray of dinners stopped and gave her a wary look.

Tyrwhitt was pleased with himself. He set his glass on the table and gave her a round of applause. "That's my girl. Another classic performance."

He'd done it again, she realized. It was an old trick of his—getting her riled up with some outrageous insinuation, pushing her crazy button and watching her go ballistic.

She'd obliged him as usual, and with that thought she laughed, too. For all his faults, Chris Tyrwhitt was one of the funniest men she'd ever known. That was one of the reasons she fell for him back in Washington several years ago.

It was after she'd broken up with Sam Maxwell, and he'd gone off to NASA. She'd only known Tyrwhitt for a couple of months before they were married. He was good-looking, witty, and, when he felt like working at it, could be a competent journalist. What she learned later was that Chris Tyrwhitt seldom worked at anything except drinking and philandering.

Some of that, she realized now, was a front. The philandering and drinking part was all true, but there was a side to him that he hadn't revealed. The side that caused him to disappear inside Iraq and be shot as a spy. Tyrwhitt was a better man than she had believed.

Careful, girl. She had fallen once before for that disarming, Down Under humor of his; the way he turned everything around and made you laugh with him. Chris Tyrwhitt could charm a girl out of her knickers.

Be careful, she warned herself again. *You learned your lesson.*

Or did you?

Persian Gulf

"Where are the others?" asked Akhmed, sticking his head up from the aft hatch. "Muhammad and Yusef and the other *Sherji*? Where have they gone?"

"I sent them to the rendezvous point," answered Abu. "We're late. If the helicopter crew doesn't see us, they won't wait."

They had made it to the ancient port of Bandar-e Basht just before dawn. As Abu expected, no one occupied the drab dwellings of what was once a fishing village on the extreme northern coast of Iran. The village had been deserted since 18 March, 1981. That was the day an officer of Saddam Hussein's army fired a canister of sarin gas into the Iranian garrison bivouacked in the village.

Since then Bandar-e Basht had been considered uninhabitable. In the view of the few surviving villagers, the village would be forever unfit to live in.

Which was why Abu Mahmed had chosen this place to dock the boat. The village was close—less than an hour's helicopter time—to Mashmashiyeh and the safety of the low marsh country. At exactly sunrise, the Dauphin was supposed to retrieve them from the old road intersection on a plateau above the village.

But time was running short. Already the eastern sky was pink with the first glow of dawn. Abu still had business to conclude.

He regretted giving up the boat. It was too risky to take it all the way upriver to Mashmashiyeh. There was no way to conceal it from the airplanes and satellites and unmanned spy craft of the Americans. By daylight, they would be scouring the Gulf for the speedboat that attacked the *Bayou Queen* and killed one of their helos.

The boat would have to be sacrificed. But Akhmed

didn't know that. Not yet. Like all peasant fishermen, he had a sentimentality for boats, even ones that he had stolen.

"Secure the boat," Abu ordered. "You and I will sweep the cabin for traces of evidence that could identify who used the boat."

"I have done that already."

"Do it again. We can't be too careful."

Akhmed glowered at him from the hatch, giving him another of those insolent looks, then turned and went back inside. Abu suppressed a smile. He wanted to freeze that insolent expression in his memory. It would be the last recollection he would have of Akhmed Fayez.

Carrying his canvas satchel over one shoulder, he followed Akhmed down the hatch and into the main salon. "Check the forward cabin," he called. "I will look in the aft."

He waited until Akhmed disappeared inside the forward cabin, then he entered the aft cabin and lifted up the hatch that exposed the engine compartment and the fuel tank. The reek of oil and diesel fuel and stagnant water struck his nostrils like a wave of polluted seawater.

He could hear Akhmed rummaging in the forward cabin, opening lockers, slamming the doors of compartments.

Now.

He reached inside the satchel and felt the hard oval shape of an RGO-78 fragmentation grenade. It was the same old Warsaw Pact weapon procured by every guerrilla organization since the 1980s—the mujahedeen, Al-Qaeda, Hamas, Shining Path. And the Bu Hasa Brigade.

Wrapping one hand around the grenade, Abu squeezed the spring-loaded grip. He reached inside with his other hand and pulled the safety pin free. Glancing up, making sure Akhmed was still in the forward cabin, he released the grip and lowered the satchel onto the greasy shelf between one of the engines and the main fuel tank.

The grenade was armed and counting down.

Forcing himself to be quick but deliberate, Abu exited the aft cabin and ascended the short ladder to the boat's cockpit.

As he stepped onto the old stone ledge that served as a dock, he heard Akhmed's voice behind him. "Did you forget something?"

Abu continued walking. "No."

"Your satchel. Where is it?"

Abu didn't stop walking. Over his shoulder he said, "In the main cabin. Get it for me."

Akhmed was replying with something unintelligible—a Yemeni insult—when the muffled *whump* of the grenade obliterated his words.

Then came the secondary explosion. The fuel tank.

Abu whirled in time to see the deck of the speedboat levitate from the hull. From the bowels of the boat erupted a pulse of flame, spilling across the gray surface of the harbor and lighting the dawn sky. Inside the blaze Abu glimpsed the dark shape of something human—Akhmed Fayez—arms outstretched, his scream lost in the roar of the inferno.

For several minutes Abu watched the boat burn. Soon nothing was left except a charred shell, which finally yielded to the weight of the two diesel engines, tilted, and slipped beneath the surface. A smoking oil slick spread over the harbor where the speedboat had been.

Abu turned his back on the empty mooring. The sun was just breaking the horizon above the village. In the distance, up on the plateau, he heard the first faint beat of helicopter blades.

Manama, Bahrain

"Share a cab?" said Bronson.

"No, thanks." Tyrwhitt set off down the street, leaving Bronson standing in the street in front of Cico's.

To hell with Bronson, he thought. He felt like walking anyway. After you'd been in a prison like Abu Graib, the act of walking alone—no guards, no leg chains, no escorts, in any damned direction you pleased—became one of life's sweetest pleasures.

An even sweeter pleasure, of course, would be having Claire with him. That wasn't an option tonight, but he had the impression that she was coming to her senses. She was getting over the infatuation with the fighter jock. One of the unexpected results of his being shot and imprisoned by the Iraqis was that Claire seemed to have a new appreciation of him and their marriage.

Not that he hadn't given her cause to judge him harshly. He hadn't exactly been a model spouse. But she knew that his dalliances were always brief and never serious—the occasional consul's wife, a flirtatious stewardess, a nightclub singer. Nothing of consequence.

In any case, that was behind him. Since his wounding and capture, he had been forced to look at his own mortality, and he had decided to change his ways. Living a more or less chaste life with Claire made a lot more sense than the old days of wretched excess. For Claire he would mend his lifestyle. She was worth the sacrifice.

He walked at a brisk pace, following Salmaniya Avenue through the center of Manama, past the rows of closed merchant shops and into the yellow-lighted section of the old city. The evening was warm, a fresh wind rolling across the narrow expanse of water that separated the island of Bahrain from the Saudi mainland. As he walked, his leather soles made a crunching sound on the graveled roadside.

His thoughts returned to the conversation at the table in Cico's.

The prisoner. Where had Maxwell gotten the idea that there might be such a prisoner? It had to be more than a coincidence.

Was it the wife?

He wondered again what possessed him to place the call to the woman in Virginia. Gallagher was her name. Formerly Rasmussen.

The idea had been germinating like a seed in his brain for weeks. He was unable to erase from his memory the recollection of a prisoner—it had to be the American pilot—with whom he'd had a brief dialogue that night in Abu Graib. The Iraqi guard had overheard them and given them each a beating. But the American's voice had remained with him, still clear in his memory.

Why should I care?

That was the strange part. He *shouldn't* care. Prisons in the Middle East were filled with lost souls who had vanished into the maw of Arab politics. One more made no difference.

But something had compelled him to make the call. He wanted to tell the woman that her lost husband might still be breathing the air of this world. It was a way of expunging from his memory the guilt of knowing a prisoner was there—and left behind. He fantasized that the call might trigger a succession of events, leading like a string of dominoes all the way to Bahrain.

The thought made him smile. If Bronson knew that the true source of the rumor about an American prisoner came from inside the CIA, he would be apoplectic.

Tyrwhitt walked the outer circumference of the roundabout at the King Faisal Highway, then headed westward again toward the center of Manama. He doubted that anyone was tailing him, but if they were they'd be in for a tiresome hike.

He glanced at his watch. Almost ten o'clock. Technically, he was in violation of Bronson's standing order that all meetings with outside agents be cleared by him. But Bronson would have nixed this meeting, citing his distrust of freelancers like Mustafa.

Mustafa Ashbar was an Iraqi whose services Tyrwhitt had used off and on since his early days in Baghdad. He trusted Mustafa for personal reasons. The Iraqi had saved his life on two occasions.

Tyrwhitt made one pass by the Sabah bar on Zubara Avenue, then doubled back and went inside. He found Mustafa at his usual table in the back corner, hunched over an Arabic newspaper, sipping at a tall drink. Tyrwhitt snorted. Mustafa had been corrupted by his years of exposure to western culture. Now he had an abiding fondness for Jack Daniel's whiskey.

Mustafa looked up. "Were you followed?"

Tyrwhitt shrugged. "Does it matter?"

Mustafa smiled, showing an uneven row of yellow teeth. "You're the one who should worry, not me."

Tyrwhitt ordered a beer and pulled up a chair. In many ways, he thought, he and Mustafa were alike. Mustafa worked both sides of the street. While he accepted payments from the CIA, he was probably in the pocket of the Iranian secret police. Maybe the Kurds. Maybe even the Israeli Mossad. Mustafa was a pragmatist, not a patriot.

Tyrwhitt guessed Mustafa's age at somewhere around forty, maybe older. He came from the primitive marsh country of lower Iraq. His face had the leathered, gaunt look of a Bedouin, but his hair and mustache were jet black, and he moved with a young man's easy agility. Tyrwhitt knew for a fact that Mustafa could kill with the speed of a cobra.

Mustafa produced a pack of Marlboros. Another Western corruption. He lit one and exhaled a stream of smoke from the corner of his mouth, a mannerism lifted from old American gangster movies.

"So?" said Mustafa. "The American aircraft carrier has just arrived in Bahrain. Now it is leaving already. A very short visit. Something bad must have happened."

Tyrwhitt nodded. "It will be in the newspapers and television in the morning. A rocket attack on a tanker, and a killing of some border guards in Kuwait."

"Who was it this time? Not the Iraqis. They've lost their taste for terrorism. Iran, perhaps? Or one of the jihad groups? The game never ends, does it?"

"Do you still have contacts in Iran? In the Bu Hasa Brigade?"

Mustafa swirled the last drops of whiskey in his glass. "Perhaps."

"Someone willing to talk to me?"

"It depends on what you wish to talk about."

"The usual things. Weather, politics, football."

Mustafa smiled. "It will require many thousand dinars. Such people take football very seriously."

"Can you arrange it?"

"Of course." He tossed down the remainder of the Jack Daniel's. "Enough business. Let's have another drink."

Masmashiyeh, Iran

Al-Fasr's anger had reached the flash point.

"You made a grave mistake," he said, glowering at Abu Mahmed. "Why did you destroy the American helicopter?"

"There was no choice. He would have attacked us. He would have stopped us in the Gulf, and we would have been taken prisoner."

Al-Fasr didn't reply. He turned from Abu and glared out the window, trying to control his anger. In his heart he knew Abu was correct. The helicopter *would* have opened fire on the boat, stopping it so it could be boarded. That would have been unfortunate.

It was bad luck, the helicopter arriving when it did. He had expected that the boat would make it to Iranian waters before the Americans reacted.

Setting the *Bayou Queen* afire was one thing. It amounted to a small loss of life, a few hundred thousand liters of expendable oil, a replaceable tanker. Nothing more. Same thing with the Kuwaiti border patrol. A pin prick.

When you killed American military personnel, it became something else. That was the lesson he learned from the Yemen campaign. After he downed three U.S. Navy aircraft, trapped a contingent of Marines inside Yemen, then nearly sank their precious aircraft carrier, the *Reagan*, the Americans came after him like banshees from hell. His plan to seize Yemen and its wealth of oil went up in smoke.

He barely escaped with his life. He would always have the pain in his shattered right leg to remind him of the disaster in Yemen.

But the helicopter was not the true source of his anger. Something else was happening. He could sense it, feel it in his bones. Something troublesome.

He looked at Abu. "What happened to Akhmed Fayez?"

Abu did not avert his eyes as the other *Sherji* did when Al-Fasr turned his gaze on them. He held eye contact with Al-Fasr and said, "He was disloyal. Akhmed defied my authority, and he put the unit in danger. As commander of the mission, I made the decision to eliminate him."

For a long moment the two men regarded each other, both knowing that Akhmed Fayez's loyalty, at least to Al-Fasr and the Bu Hasa Brigade, was never in question. He had fought bravely at Al-Fasr's side throughout the Yemen campaign, then remained with him during the escape across the Saudi peninsula.

No, thought Al-Fasr, it wasn't loyalty. It was something else. "Akhmed was a brave soldier."

"He would have betrayed us."

"When I assign one of my best soldiers to serve under you, I don't expect you to execute him."

"If I am to be your second-in-command, I must exercise my own authority in such matters."

Al-Fasr nodded, not wishing to pursue this argument. Later, he told himself. Whether or not Akhmed Fayez had to be killed was something he would not debate.

The truth was, he could not afford an open clash with Abu Mahmed, who held the loyalty of at least half the new Bu Hasa Brigade. He would save the clash until after they had secured control of Babylon. For the moment he needed Abu's support. Despite his fanatical religious fervor, Abu Mahmed was a competent soldier.

Al-Fasr tried to make his voice conciliatory. "You should get some rest. We will know soon whether the provocation has succeeded. The Americans will either attack Iran, or they will come looking for us."

"If they do, we will deal with them."

Al-Fasr nodded, wondering where the younger man's overweening confidence came from. His Islamic faith? Did he really believe that Allah would protect him from the full might of the American military?

Or did he envision some other scenario?

He turned back to his desk. The pain shot through his right leg like a hot spike. He longed for the day when he would no longer be in the business of war. Instead of destroying, he wanted to build. He wanted to construct a bright new world.

Babylon. It existed only in his dreams, but he could see it as clearly as a fresh new dawn. The image of a magnificent domain built on these historic ruins was what kept him alive, gave him the strength to fight his enemies.

He had to win the next battle. Just one more. Perhaps it would be his last.

*   *   *

Abu drove the Land Rover out of Mashmashiyeh, over the ancient bridge and down the narrow road to the *Sherji*'s eastern defense perimeter. He made a show of checking the positions, the disposition of the forward fire teams, then he returned to the Land Rover and sat alone.

He pulled out the Cyfonika satellite phone, punched in the twelve-digit code, then waited.

It took five minutes. After the standard exchange of authentication, a man's voice came on the line. "You weren't supposed to kill Americans."

The voice sounded tinny, the result of being scrambled, relayed 150 miles into space, then bounced back to Abu's receiver in western Iran. Still, Abu recognized the voice.

"The helicopter should not have pursued us. They would have attacked us."

"There will be repercussions. The reprisal operation is larger than we expected. An entire battle group will be assigned, including a Marine expeditionary unit."

Abu considered for a moment. The stakes were going up. It meant that he would have to be extremely careful.

"When?"

"Soon. Probably the morning after next."

"Do they believe that Iran was behind the attacks?"

"No."

Abu shook his head. Just as he predicted. "Why is that?" he asked, knowing the answer.

"Because the U.S. military intelligence community has a very reliable source of human intelligence in the area."

"And that is . . . ?"

"You're talking to him."

Abu nodded to himself. "And where will the Marine unit land?"

A pause. "Wherever they can best engage Al-Fasr."

"I understand. You will receive that information to-morrow."

"I'll be waiting."

Abu punched the yellow CANCEL button. The Cyfonika went dead.

CHAPTER 10

TERRIBLE SWIFT SWORD

USS Ronald Reagan
Quebec Station, Persian Gulf
0925, Wednesday, 17 March

Lt. B. J. Johnson knew she shouldn't be having these thoughts. She couldn't help it. Walking up behind Maxwell, watching him fire his ancient Colt .45 at the paper target suspended on a boom behind the *Reagan's* fantail, she felt the familiar old stirrings inside her.

Get over it, she commanded herself. *He's taken.*

Actually, she *had* gotten over it, at least the silly schoolgirl crush she once had on him. It was not only unprofessional, it was a guaranteed career-trasher to get emotionally involved with a senior officer in your squadron. Especially if the senior officer was your skipper.

Anyway, it was common knowledge that Maxwell had a romance going with a high-profile broadcast journalist named Claire Phillips. She was a beauty with a long-legged, willowy figure, chestnut hair, and the kind of face men would die for.

Everything, thought B. J. Johnson, that she wasn't. Men like Maxwell didn't fall for girls in baggy flight suits and klunky boots and with oxygen mask outlines on their faces. But she was okay with that now. She was over it.

Right. So why did her heart still skip a little beat like this when she was around Maxwell?

Well, maybe she wasn't *completely* over it. It didn't hurt to fantasize that maybe, just maybe, Maxwell might someday be free and available. In the meantime she wasn't going to get all google-eyed and fluttery like she used to when he gazed at her with those icy blue eyes.

He was holding the Colt in both hands, taking his time, popping away at the silhouette on the target. B. J. had to suppress a laugh. He was a klutz with the pistol. Maxwell's ineptitude with the old Colt .45 had become a squadron legend.

He fired the last round, and the slide remained open. The seven-round clip was empty. As he laid the pistol down and removed the ear protectors, he saw B. J. standing behind him.

"Good thing you fly better than you shoot, Skipper."

"What do you mean?" said Maxwell. He reeled in the target from the boom. "Hell, I'm a marksman with this thing."

"Yes, sir. But you'd do better if you'd trade that antique in for one of these." She pulled out her Beretta. The Beretta nine millimeter had long ago replaced the oversized Colt automatic as the Navy's service pistol.

"Old dogs like old toys," he said. "It's a family thing. My dad hauled it around for two tours in Vietnam, then gave it to me. It's kept me out of trouble."

"More or less."

"You don't believe me? Look at this." He held up the target. Daylight was showing through several holes in the black silhouette.

She nodded in appreciation. "That's good, Skipper, because you may get a chance to shoot it again."

"How's that?"

"CAG sent me to find you. He wants all commanding officers and strike leaders in the flag briefing space. He said to tell you it was showtime."

"So?" said Craze Manson on the phone. "Why not get a replacement radio from the parts pool?"

"That's the problem," said Splat DiLorenzo. "They say they don't have one, at least one they can get their hands on in time."

Shit, thought Manson. He was due to brief in ten minutes for an air intercept training sortie. He and Jasper Johns, a nugget lieutenant, were going against a pair of F-14s on a radar exercise.

Leroi Jones had just landed with his number-one radio inoperative. He'd used his "back" radio, the number-two radio, which worked okay. But the aircraft was scheduled for an immediate turnaround. And no replacement radio was available.

"Do something," said Manson. "Whatever it takes."

They both knew what that meant. The replacement radio would come from one of the "rob" birds—airplanes that were already grounded and were being cannibalized for parts. Parts like radios.

The problem was, Maxwell had given the order to stop cannibalizing the squadron's jets. There weren't supposed to be any rob birds. But what the hell did Maxwell know about being a maintenance officer? He didn't have a clue what it took to keep airplanes flying.

Well, damn it, this was the real world, not Rocket City. If the supply and logistics system didn't work for you, you had to get creative. You took parts where you found them.

DiLorenzo knew what he meant. "Consider it done," he said, and hung up.

Manson put the matter out of his mind and headed for the ready room to brief his flight. Jasper was waiting for him in the briefing cubicle at the back of the ready room. The two Tomcat crews were there too, eager as usual to prove that their aging fighters could still kick some serious Super Hornet butt.

Ten minutes into the briefing, the duty officer summoned Manson to the phone again.

"Ops just threw us a curve," said DiLorenzo. "You know the rob bird we took the radio out of? They just made it a go bird for the next sortie—the one you guys are flying."

Manson moved away from the duty desk, over to a corner where he couldn't be overheard. "No big deal," he said. "Someone will have to fly it with one radio, that's all." Technically, the Hornet required *two* functioning radios to be cleared to fly, but Manson didn't mind pushing the rules. One radio was all you really needed to fly the mission. "Just make the paperwork look right, that's all."

"That's the problem," said DiLorenzo. "Someone already cannibalized the front radio. It's not in the maintenance record, of course, but now the sonofabitch doesn't have *any* goddamn radios. And it's already on the elevator headed for the flight deck. Our asses are in a sling, Boss."

Manson noted the *our*. Falsification of maintenance records was a career-threatening offense, and DiLorenzo was not about to be a martyr. "Okay, I'll handle it. The jet will launch, and nothing goes on the squawk sheet until it comes back with a multiple failure. Got it?"

"If you say so."

Manson returned to the briefing. When they were finished, he followed Jasper Johns into the flight gear room. He made sure they were alone, then said, "Listen, Jasper, you're new to this game, but I can tell you're a team player. This squadron is trying its damnedest to win the Battle 'E,' and we do what we have to do, understand?"

"Ah, understand what, sir?"

"That your jet may have a radio problem. If it does, I want you to discover the fact after you're airborne. All you have to do is stay welded to my wing until the fight starts, then blow straight through the merge. I'll join you on the opposing station, and we come back to the ship together. I'll do the talking for both of us."

Johns looked dubious. "Ah, I don't know, Craze. That doesn't sound like a good—"

"Look, Lieutenant, this isn't a discussion, it's a briefing. Just fucking do it, understand?" With nuggets like Johns, sometimes you had to use a little intimidation to make them get it.

Johns got it. "Yes, sir." After a moment, he said, "But how am I supposed to fill out the training matrix? Since I won't be actually doing anything . . ."

"Put down exactly what I put down."

"But what about my training?"

Manson was already headed for the door. "What about it?"

As usual, Boyce was pacing the flag briefing space like a caged bear. His gnawed cigar jutted at a rakish angle from his teeth. He looked up and saw Maxwell come into the room. "I hear you were out on the fantail punching holes in the air with that blunderbuss of yours."

Maxwell held up the target. "Six out of seven in the black."

Another voice boomed from across the room. "Pretty good for a squid. Of course, any self-respecting marine would put all seven in the bull's-eye."

Maxwell turned to see a man in sharply creased BDUs with a graying buzz haircut, wire-framed spectacles, and colonel's eagles on his collar. "Colonel Gritti. We heard you were going back to the Pentagon to put on a star."

"The Pentagon can wait. So can the star. If you guys

get your asses in a wringer again, I'll have to bail you out like I always do."

Col. Gus Gritti, CO of the 43rd Marine Expeditionary Unit, was a legend not just in the Marine Corps but throughout the military. He was a mud-crawling infantry commander who held a masters in humanities from Stanford, spoke four languages, and, without prompting, was prone to vocalizing snippets from Puccini arias.

Maxwell shook Gritti's hand, then endured a rib-bending bear hug from the burly marine.

The room was filling with flight-suited strike leaders and the squadron skippers from the *Reagan*'s air wing. In one corner a cluster of intelligence specialists, military and civilian, was huddled over a stack of briefing material.

Maxwell was about to take a seat in the second row when he recognized one of the civilians. He wore a short-sleeved, button-down shirt and tie, and he had an unmistakable look about him. Spook.

Ted Bronson. He was deep in conversation with a man with shaggy red hair and a wrinkled bush jacket.

Bronson caught Maxwell staring at him. He turned and mumbled something to the man in the bush jacket, who peered across the room at Maxwell.

"Look who's here," said Chris Tyrwhitt. "Small world, isn't it?"

Too damned small, thought Maxwell.

He took a seat with the other skippers in the second row, a jumble of unwanted thoughts flowing across his mind. Tyrwhitt had a knack for showing up at the worst possible times, like a pimple on prom night. First he wouldn't stay dead, then he wouldn't stay away from Claire. Now he wouldn't stay away period.

Maxwell couldn't see Tyrwhitt's face without thinking of Claire. Tyrwhitt having breakfast with Claire. Tyrwhitt married to Claire. Tyrwhitt in bed with Claire.

For an instant Maxwell imagined throwing Tyrwhitt off the fantail of the *Reagan*. Using *him* for target practice.

Knock it off, he told himself. Jealousy wasn't one of his usual weaknesses. He forced the image from his mind as Boyce strode to the podium to begin the strike briefing.

In the front row sat Adm. Jack Hightree, the *Reagan* Battle Group Commander, flanked by Capt. Sticks Stickney, the *Reagan*'s captain, and Capt. Guido Vitale, the Battle Group Operations Officer. Col. Gus Gritti sat with another marine, a lieutenant colonel, at the end of the row.

Most strike briefings were conducted by intel specialists or operations officers, but Hightree usually yielded the stage to Boyce, who liked to keep the focus on tactics. Neither he nor Hightree had any use for long-winded intel officers.

Standing at the side of the compartment were the two civilians, Bronson and Tyrwhitt. Tyrwhitt kept glancing in Maxwell's direction, giving him that annoying grin.

"Good afternoon, gentlemen," said Boyce. "This briefing is classified top secret. Neither the subject matter nor the contents disclosed herein may be repeated or revealed to anyone outside this room without specific written clearance." The standard classification and disclosure spiel.

On the screen behind Boyce appeared a backlighted map of the Persian Gulf. Boyce whapped the map with his pointer and said, "Last night, in this vicinity"—he pointed to a spot off the coast of Kuwait—"a pair of gunboats approached the tanker *Bayou Queen*. One of them, filled with explosives, rammed it and lit off three hundred thousand gallons of crude oil, killing thirteen sailors. When a Seahawk from the *Richmond* went chasing after the second boat, the bastards shot down the helo with some kind of SAM, probably an SA-16. Three Navy crewmen lost.

"At almost the same time, another bunch came across the border in Kuwait and took out a Hummer with three border guards and an American special ops advisor in it.

"Both attacks came from the east, in the direction of Iran, with whom, as you know, we've been having some serious disagreements. The gunboat escaped back to the coast of Iran. The shooters in Kuwait got away in some kind of helo, back across the Iraqi border, then the Shatt-al-Arab waterway, also into Iran."

Boyce paused and examined his cigar while the pilots stared at him.

"So what's it mean, CAG?" said Rico Flores, the VFA-34 skipper. "Iran is begging us to hammer them like we did Saddam?"

"Looks like it, doesn't it?"

"So we're gonna turn Tehran into a gravel pit?"

"We're not gonna turn Tehran into anything. Much as the Iranians might hate us and cheer the ragheads who are shooting at us, they didn't pull this one off, despite the way someone wants it to look." He paused for a moment and looked over at Bronson.

The CIA officer gave him a tacit nod.

Boyce went on. "Courtesy of the CIA, we have solid intelligence on who really did it and why."

The map of the Gulf on the screen vanished. In its place appeared the smiling face of a handsome Arab man with black hair and mustache, wearing a military uniform with wings on the breast.

"Anyone recognize this guy?" Boyce said.

A murmur went through the assembled officers. "That sonofabitch," said Gus Gritti in a low growl.

"For those of you who weren't with us in Yemen," said Boyce, "may I present Col. Jamal Al-Fasr, commander of the Bu Hasa Brigade and terrorist extraordinaire."

Seeing the face on the screen, Maxwell felt a chill run through him. *Al-Fasr.* Another ghost.

"Since getting kicked out of Yemen," Boyce continued, "Al-Fasr has set up camp somewhere in Iraq or Iran, in the marsh country. He wants to suck us into a shooting war with Iran so he can take control of a piece of the country."

"Just like he sucked us into Yemen," said Gritti.

"Yeah," said Boyce. "Except this time we're going to hit this guy with maximum force. That means a Marine Expeditionary Unit, plus every asset of the battle group."

"What about Iran?" asked Cmdr. Butch Kissick from VF-31, the Tomcat squadron. "How are they gonna feel about being invaded by the U.S.?"

Boyce glanced at Admiral Hightree, who just nodded. "Tehran is already denying that they had anything to do with the attacks on the tanker and in Kuwait. At the same time they're beating their chests and saying they will repel any invasion by foreign forces. That's more bravado than fact. The truth is, Iran couldn't repel the Salvation Army.

"The bottom line is this. Iran is hosting a terrorist group that has attacked Americans, and according to our Commander-in-Chief, that makes them fair game. The Rules of Engagement will specify that Iranian military assets will not be attacked—unless they show hostile intent. If they do they're dead meat."

Boyce switched the image on the screen back to a map of Iran. "Until the MEU is on the ground and has a command post secured, the airborne strike leader will be Commander Maxwell of VFA-36."

Maxwell felt all the eyes in the room on him. *Here we go again*, he thought. That was Boyce. He never bothered giving a warning before assigning you the mission from hell.

"When Colonel Gritti has his LZ and perimeter secured, he becomes the on-site commander. The MEU will be tasked with securing the area, destroying all Bu Hasa equipment, seizing any and all intelligence material, and delivering prisoners to the *Saipan* for interrogation and processing. We intend to be in and out of country in the same day. No assets, no personnel left behind."

Boyce flicked off the screen and looked at his watch. "That's it, gentlemen. There'll be a detailed strike briefing three hours before T-time. Commander Maxwell's strike planning team should muster in CVIC ASAP. I want all COs to provide my ops officer with the lineups."

Maxwell was on his way out the door when he saw Bronson coming toward him. "Wait a minute," said Bronson. "I want to talk to you."

Maxwell continued toward the door. He wasn't a stickler for military etiquette—except when it was flouted by a jerk like Bronson.

Bronson caught up with him. "Hang on a second, Maxwell."

"This is a U.S. Navy warship, Mr. Bronson. It's 'Commander Maxwell' to you."

"Okay, Commander. Weren't you asking me back in Bahrain whether I knew anything about an American POW who might still be in Iraq?"

Maxwell stopped. "Do you?"

"I did some checking. Called in some markers in Baghdad—human intel sources from Saddam's old prison system—and had them check the story out."

Maxwell waited for the rest. He knew that spooks loved to tantalize by withholding information. It made them feel needed, he supposed. "Okay. What did they find out?"

"Exactly what I told you in Bahrain. It's a myth. They just confirmed it. There is no such prisoner in Iraq."

"If he's not in Iraq, where is he then? Iran, or Syria?"

"He's not anywhere. He doesn't exist."

"You mean he was never a prisoner? Or he was, but now he isn't?"

"Don't read anything into this, Maxwell. I'm passing along a simple fact. No American prisoner. None. Now that I've done you a favor, leave it alone."

Maxwell wasn't satisfied, but he could tell by Bronson's dead-eyed expression that he wasn't getting anything more.

He turned again for the door. "Thanks for the information."

CHAPTER 11

STRIKE

Mashmashiyeh, Iran
1310, Wednesday, 17 March

"Game of chess, Navy?"

Rasmussen looked up from his notebook as the visitor walked into the room. He saw that the limp was more pronounced today. The leg must be acting up again.

That was one of the things they had in common—an ejection from a destroyed jet fighter. He had been luckier than Al-Fasr. His ejection seat worked perfectly. He hadn't broken anything.

As it turned out, of course, it hadn't been good luck at all. Better for him if the seat hadn't worked.

"Sure, Colonel. If you feel like being trounced again." That was the protocol they observed. He addressed his captor as "Colonel," and he in turn was called "Navy." His own rank no longer mattered. Deceased officers didn't have rank.

Al-Fasr lowered himself into the empty chair, keeping his right leg outstretched. He began arranging the chess pieces. "I trust that room service was satisfactory today?"

"Not bad. The champagne was a bit off, rather thin in body, but the caviar was superb."

This produced the usual subdued smile from Al-Fasr. It was a little game they played, pretending that Rasmussen was not a prisoner but a guest in the colonel's sumptuous hotel. The fact was, he ate the same fare as the *Sherji*—rice, fruit, sometimes fresh fish from the river. Compared to the gruel back in Abu Graib prison, it was haute cuisine.

"Whose turn to open?" asked Al-Fasr.

"Yours. I won the last game."

"A fluke. I was distracted or I would have beaten you easily."

They played in silence for a while, each giving up a pair of pawns, neither gaining an advantage. They were closely matched, Al-Fasr being the more aggressive player, but sometimes reckless. Rasmussen preferred long, slow battles of attrition. He had learned that if Al-Fasr became impatient, which he often did, he would make a mistake.

He wondered why Al-Fasr spent his time this way. He hadn't revealed much about himself, only that he had attended university in the United States and had taken advanced flight training from the U.S. Air Force. He had been an F-16 pilot in one of the emirate air forces. So how did a man like that become an international fugitive? Why was he living like a goat herder in this mud-caked village?

Rasmussen knew better than to ask these questions. That was part of the protocol. Al-Fasr controlled the conversation. If he felt like talking about military matters, or aeronautical subjects, or some abstract philosophical idea, he would ask the questions.

Which suited Rasmussen. At least he wasn't being interrogated. He'd been through all that during the early days in Baghdad and paid the price of trying to uphold the POW code of conduct. Give them nothing of value. Make them break you.

In the end he had broken, just as they knew he would.

It no longer troubled him as it had in the early days. He had given them no information of military value. Now, even if he could remember classified data, which he couldn't, it would be useless history. Expired and defunct, like himself.

Al-Fasr seemed distracted. He attacked with his bishop, failing to anticipate the threat from Rasmussen's knight. Two moves later, his bishop was gone and so was another pawn.

"You set me up for that."

"You did it yourself." Rasmussen removed the pawn.

Al-Fasr shook his head and looked away from the chessboard, losing interest in the game. He stared for a moment out the dirt-streaked window of the hut, in the direction of the reed-covered riverbank. "Do you have any idea where you are?"

"Not exactly. In the south of Iraq, or maybe it's Iran."

"Iraq is an artificial place, constructed by the British and French after World War I. So is Iran, at least down here in the delta. This country is only a quiltwork made from an ancient land that belongs to neither of them."

"What land is that?" Rasmussen tried to conceal his growing curiosity. He kept his eyes on the chessboard.

"Do you know about Babylonia? It was here, the land surrounding the rivers Euphrates and Tigris. They called it the cradle of civilization." At this he let out a dry snicker. He pointed out the window, at the chipped stucco hut next door. "Hard to believe, no?"

Rasmussen nodded in agreement. He was an engineer, not a scholar of history. Babylonia? He had only a vague idea of what Al-Fasr was talking about.

Al-Fasr went on. "In the second millennium B.C., Babylonia was ruled by Hammurabi. He was an enlightened despot who, among other things, gave his people a code—a legal system that is still reflected in the laws of most advanced countries. But the region fell into chaos, besieged and sacked by other empires. Then came Nebuchadnezzar II, who was not only a military genius but also a great builder and restorer. He rebuilt the capital city of Babylon and restored all the temples and monuments of the land. He ruled for forty-three years, and during that time Babylonia was the flower of the civilized world. But after Nebuchadnezzar's passing, it happened again. Babylonia was conquered by the Persians. It never regained its independence or its prosperity."

Rasmussen knew that Al-Fasr was using him as a sounding board. He had been through this more than once. It was Al-Fasr's way of thinking out loud. "You've studied the history of this place."

Al-Fasr nodded. "In another time, another life, I might have come here as an archaeologist and not as a warrior. It would have been a suitable calling for me. Sifting through the detritus of a lost civilization, piecing together what went wrong. Learning how the world's most advanced culture became one of the most regressive."

For a while Al-Fasr seemed lost in thought, gazing out the window at the gathering darkness. The shabby huts of Mashmashiyeh looked like gravestones in the twilight. The village was quiet except for the squawking of the night birds down by the river.

He turned to Rasmussen. "So tell me, Navy. What do you think? Why did the Babylonian empire fail?"

Rasmussen didn't know, but he had learned that such a question required an answer. "Sounds like a leadership problem," he said. "This guy Nebuchadnezzar, he was a take-charge type of leader, but no one came along after him to carry on. Babylonia became a country without a leader."

It was the right answer. Al-Fasr was nodding his head. "For twenty-five hundred years this land was divided, ignored, used by different factions as a hiding place during their stupid religious wars. Then the idiots in Baghdad and Tehran fought over the border for no reason except their own glorious egos."

A spark was glowing now in Al-Fasr's eyes. "But I tell you this. No matter what they call it, this will always be Babylon. This is a land of destiny. You can feel it in the ground. Babylon can rise again from this festering swamp into a land of greatness." As he spoke, Al-Fasr's voice rose to a feverish pitch. Abruptly he rose to his feet and went to the window. He stood there, gazing into the darkness.

"And how will that happen, Colonel? How will it rise to greatness?"

Al-Fasr continued looking outside. "As you said. It is a matter of leadership."

"Another Nebuchadnezzar?"

He saw Al-Fasr's head nod. "Perhaps."

Rasmussen looked at the chessboard again. They would not finish the game, but he didn't care. He had just gleaned two useful items of information. He knew where they were, give or take a hundred miles. And now he knew why Al-Fasr was here.

One important piece of the puzzle was still missing. Why was *he* here?

Quebec Station, Persian Gulf

She had been through this—how many times? At least a dozen, but it never got any better. There was something undignified about arriving aboard a ship this way, seated backward, strapped into a nearly window-less compartment like a crate of produce, dropping out of the sky onto the hard steel flight deck.

The others in the crew—Tony, the lead cameraman, and Jeb and Carl, the audio/visual guys—hated it even more than she did. Tony was hunched forward in a Zen-

like trance, muttering some kind of mantra, trying for an
out-of-body experience.

She felt the wings of the C-2A Greyhound COD—
Carrier Onboard Delivery—rocking in a series of quick
corrections. Then the drone of the two turbine engines
tapered back to a dull whine. The bottom fell from beneath the COD and—*thunk!*—the wheels slammed
down on the steel deck. She felt the hook snag a wire
and in the next second and a half the big cargo plane
lurched to a stop. Tony's head snapped back with the de-
celeration, ponytail flailing beneath his baseball cap.

The rest was easy. As the COD taxied to a stop beside
the carrier's island structure, the clamshell doors in the
aft fuselage swung open. The cabin filled with the din of
turbine noise, the reek of jet fumes.

A man wearing a Mickey Mouse cranial protector
and a survival vest stuck his head through the open
door. He peered around the cabin. "Miss Phillips? I'm
Captain Walsh, the ship's executive officer. Welcome
aboard USS *Reagan*."

After unloading and stashing the camera gear, she
and her crew found their staterooms. The three guys
bunked in a junior officer's stateroom, while she had her
own space in the female officers' section. Then she
found her way to the Public Affairs Office for the com-
pulsory security brief with Lt. Cmdr. Butch Fleur, the
ship's PAO.

She knew the drill. No sightseeing in restricted
spaces. No filming of anything unless it was specifically
approved. No interviews without a PAO staffer present.
No transmission of anything until it had been screened
by the PAO.

Orwellian censorship for sure, but she knew better
than to bitch about it. This was the Navy and it was their
ship. She considered herself lucky. The only other reporters on board the *Reagan* were a crew from CNN and
a couple of syndicated print journalists. Their little

clique would have an exclusive on America's police action in Iran.

Next stop, the officers' wardroom on the O-3 level. By now she knew her way around the *Reagan* pretty well. This was her third assignment during a military operation, plus she'd been aboard the carrier on several occasions as Sam Maxwell's guest. She even managed to avoid bashing her shins on the knee knockers—the hard steel enclosures positioned at every bulkhead along the passageways.

She looked around the wardroom, didn't see anyone she recognized, then helped herself to a coffee. At a corner table was a telephone. She took a seat and dialed a number she still remembered.

He answered on the second ring. "I'll be damned," said Sam Maxwell. "Claire? Is it really you? How did you . . ."

She laughed. He was always shocked when she showed up like this, without warning, while his ship was at sea. Women weren't supposed to be that clever.

"Remember our old meeting place?" she said.

"The viewing deck behind the island?

"Vulture's Row, they call it? Meet me in fifteen minutes?"

"Make it ten."

It took him five.

The *Reagan* was plowing into a northerly breeze, leaving in its wake a mile-long ribbon of foam. On either flank cruised the ships of the battle group—the Aegis cruiser *Arkansas* to the port side, led by a pair of destroyers. To the starboard, two more destroyers preceded the amphibious helicopter carrier *Saipan*. Behind the *Reagan* sailed a tanker and a resupply ship. Somewhere ahead, beneath the surface, prowled the attack submarine *Santa Monica*.

"Hello, Sam."

A smile spread over his face.

She was wearing a soft blue jumpsuit that almost but not quite concealed the curves of her slender shape. Around her throat was the beige silk scarf. Her chestnut hair ruffled in the breeze that billowed around the island superstructure.

He knew crew members were probably watching from the windowed air ops spaces above them. Let them, he decided. Later he'd remind himself that this was a ship of the line and he was a senior officer and a squadron skipper. Had to set examples and all that.

To hell with examples. He opened his arms and she came to him, pressing herself against him. He kissed her, sensing again the lack of privacy on a carrier at sea. Even though they were shielded from most prying eyes out here on the aft viewing deck, he felt as if they were on display. He still hadn't gotten used to the idea of seeing the girl he loved on board while he sailed off to war.

"You're amazing," he said. "How did you pull this off?"

"I'm a broadcast journalist. This is my job."

"You fluttered your eyelashes at some Fifth Fleet staff weenie and he gave you the clearance."

"Not a staff weenie. The Admiral."

"I rest my case."

"Aren't you glad I'm here?"

"Yes, ma'am, I'm very glad you're here."

Which was true. He was glad she was there despite the openness of the windy viewing deck and the sailors peering down at them from the glassed compartments in the aft island. The azure Persian Gulf sky seemed to cast a spell over them. ·

She put her arms around him and pressed her head to his chest. "I felt awful when you left me back in Bahrain, Sam. What kind of life is this? Is this the way it's always going to be?"

"No. Someday I'll be too old for this job. They'll give

me a desk job on the beach and I won't be getting yanked out of restaurants to sail off on a carrier."

"You'll hate it."

"Maybe." And maybe not, he thought. There were times, like back in Bahrain, when he wanted out of the Navy. The separations and hardship and loneliness were cumulative. You could take only so much of it, and then you'd had enough. Sooner or later it would be time to pack it in and stay ashore.

But not yet. This was still his life. His only life.

He was about to tell her this when he noticed the C-2A COD on the flight deck. The aft doors were open, and two men were walking from the island to the waiting aircraft.

"Look who's leaving," Maxwell said. "You just missed him."

"Who?"

He nodded toward the gray C-2A parked below them. "Your husband."

"Chris?" She peered over the rail. "What's he doing here?"

"He's with Bronson, the CIA chief. Not much doubt about who he works for now."

"Why are they out here?"

"Are you asking as a reporter or a wife?"

She glowered at him. "Don't start, Sam. I have to deal with this the best way I can."

He wanted to ask what way that was, but he didn't. He just nodded, aware of the old burning in his gut. Tyrwhitt. All it took was the mention of him and it was back.

"Sorry," he said, but it was too late. The spell was broken.

Bronson took the only free window seat on the starboard side of the C-2A. He finished strapping himself in, then looked over at Tyrwhitt, who looked like an alien in the cranial protector and float coat. He was fumbling with the harness fasteners, wearing the expression of a man going to his execution.

The sight gave Bronson a secret pleasure. He rarely saw the supercilious Australian so unsure of himself. Tyrwhitt had no experience with military airplanes, particularly those in which you sat backward and were catapulted like a cannon shell from a carrier deck.

The crew was in the cockpit, getting the Greyhound ready to launch. Bronson could hear whirring noises—inverters, hydraulic actuators, gyros coming to life.

The trip to the *Reagan* had been a colossal waste of time. Bronson's only role was to hand over the intel data, then stand there like a stuffed dummy while that windbag navy captain with the cigar took over the strike briefing. He could just as well have sent the data over the encrypted message net and stayed in Bahrain. But then he wouldn't have gotten to watch Tyrwhitt sit through a catapult launch.

"First time on a carrier, huh?"

"And the last, I hope." Tyrwhitt looked nervous.

Bronson waited a moment, savoring the next item. "Your wife is aboard the *Reagan*."

Tyrwhitt's face froze and he stared at Bronson. "Claire? How do you know that?"

"I saw her in the wardroom about half an hour ago. She arrived on this same COD that we're taking back to Bahrain."

"Why didn't you tell me?"

Bronson shrugged. "What for?"

Tyrwhitt peered through the window at the gray mass of the *Reagan*. "What's she doing here? How did she get clearance to come aboard?"

"How do you think? Connections."

"Her pilot boyfriend? He's only a commander. He doesn't have that kind of pull."

"She's got a great ass. Women like that know how to get what they want."

"What are you suggesting?" Tyrwhitt's voice was strained. "That Claire used—"

"You said it yourself, the other night in Bahrain. We're all whores. She's just more traditional about it."

For a long moment Tyrwhitt stared at Bronson. "You know something? It's a good thing for you that you're my boss."

"Why is that?"

"Because if you weren't, I'd smash your fucking face."

Bronson flashed a humorless smile, pleased that he had found Tyrwhitt's weak spot. As he suspected, Tyrwhitt's wife, or soon-to-be ex-wife, was still an issue in his life. It was useful information.

He turned his attention back to the activity outside the cabin window. Yellow shirts were scurrying around the aircraft, releasing tie-down chains, removing equipment.

Tyrwhitt was a liability, he reflected. The man didn't belong in an elite organization like the Central Intelligence Agency. He had no special education, no qualifications for being an agency operative except that he knew his way around the whorehouses and cesspools of the Middle East. It was a sign of the times that the agency had to recruit people like him.

Back in the seventies and eighties the CIA had rid itself of the rogues and thugs and sleazy criminals it used to infiltrate enemy networks. The new generation of leaders favored "surgical" military operations and spy satellites that could read license plates from low earth orbit, 250 miles up.

But then came the attacks on America and the embarrassing revelations about America's intelligence failures. Until a new cadre of professional spies could be recruited, trained, and deployed, the agency was forced to hire a corps of undisciplined amateurs.

Amateurs like Christopher Tyrwhitt.

Much as Bronson hated to admit it, Tyrwhitt *was* able to come up with useful information. He had already been shot and incarcerated by the Iraqis, and then released through a secret negotiation. He had connections throughout the Middle East—in the souks and the black markets and inside the training camps. He spoke Arabic, and he managed to get people to pass information to him.

Someday, if Bronson had his way, the CIA would return to its purest form—an elite corps of dedicated professionals like himself. They would not be answerable to know-nothing busybodies in the White House or Congress. They would not be forced to associate with loudmouthed bar flies and foreign nationals like Tyrwhitt.

Both turbine engines were rumbling at idle RPM now. The C-2A was taxiing toward the catapult. Through the cabin window Bronson could see the deck moving beneath them. The gray mass of the ship's island came into view. Bronson looked up. On the aft viewing deck, he saw two people watching the COD trundle across the flight deck. He recognized them. The woman was Tyrwhitt's wife, the reporter. The other was Maxwell.

Another useful tidbit.

Bronson felt the C-2A's nose wheel bump over the catapult shuttle. The engine noise swelled to a crescendo and, seconds later, the COD hurtled off the bow of the *Reagan*.

CHAPTER 12

TOMCATS

USS Ronald Reagan
Quebec Station, Persian Gulf
2145, Wednesday, 17 March

"Lock the door behind you," said Boyce.

Maxwell secured the door of CAG's stateroom. He blinked his eyes in the gray cloud of smoke that filled the room. "How do you breathe in here, CAG?"

"This is the only place on the ship where I can light a cigar. Goddamn clean air freaks have ruined the Navy."

Everyone knew that Boyce didn't mind breaking certain rules. The smoking prohibition was one of them.

"Want a drink?" said Boyce. That was another one— the ban on drinking. He opened the safe on his desk and slid out a tray of bottles. Boyce believed in the value of a late-night libation in his stateroom.

"No, thanks."

Boyce shrugged. "It's bad luck not to have a medicinal drink the night before a combat mission." He shoved the tray back into the safe. "You got any problems with the strike package the way we set it up?"

"Deep strikes never work out exactly the way we plan them. I keep wondering what's going to bite us in the butt this time."

"That's why you're leading the strike and I'm staying in CIC to run the show."

Maxwell nodded. He'd been through these night-before sessions with Boyce before. Boyce had something on his mind, and this was his way of getting it out.

Boyce's cigar was dead, and he paused to reignite it. He wreathed himself in another bank of gray smoke and said, "I could have picked one of the other squadron skippers, Rico Flores or Gordo Gray, to lead the deep strike. They're senior, and they've both got solid experience."

"So why didn't you?"

"There's something about this operation that's bugging me."

"You think Al-Fasr will try to suck us into another trap?"

"Not this time. We're gonna smoke his ass once and for all. It's the bigger picture I'm worried about. The environment we're in."

"You mean Iran?"

Boyce nodded. "They may be a raggedy-ass country without indoor plumbing, but they've got an air defense system and an air force with real fighters. It's not like Iraq, when they parked all their jets and turned over the sky to us. If the Iranians decide to get involved, it will turn into a cluster fuck."

"Why would they want to get involved?"

"They don't want Al-Fasr on their property any more than we do, but they most definitely don't want us Yankee imperialists doing their job for them. They got a good look at how that works when we invaded Iraq. They'll go through the motions of fighting, even if it means getting their ass kicked."

"If they come out and fight, what am I supposed to do?"

"You know the Rules of Engagement. We're not supposed to shoot unless we see hostile intent."

"Does that mean we give them the first shot?"

"Officially, it means you comply with the Rules of Engagement."

"Unofficially?"

Boyce clamped the cigar between his teeth. Squinting through the smoke, he gave Maxwell a look that he had come to recognize. "I tagged you as the flight leader because you're a guy who can think outside the box. In Iraq you passed up a shot at a MiG because it wasn't necessary to kill him. When a so-called friendly fired a missile at you, you killed him because the sonofabitch needed killing."

Boyce paused to waft a cloud of smoke into the air. "When you're out there tomorrow, I want you to do whatever has to be done."

Maxwell nodded his understanding. Some things never changed.

0730, Thursday, 18 March

The catapult officer watched Maxwell with his sad brown eyes. He was wearing the standard shooter's flight deck outfit—cranial protector, radio headset, and survival float coat.

Sitting in his cockpit, Maxwell had to laugh. Through the Plexiglas canopy, he could see the shooter's name plainly stenciled on the front of his float coat: DOG BALLS.

Dog Balls Harvey, who came to the *Reagan* from the patrol plane community, had made the mistake one day of letting the Roadrunners give him a call sign. Then he learned one of the essential truths about Navy call signs. They were like Super Glue. The more you resisted, the more they stuck.

Poor Dog Balls, thought Maxwell. The Roadrunners had raised their tormenting of him to a new level by howling like depraved hounds whenever he made an appearance in the officers' wardroom.

Nobody said life on a carrier was easy.

The pale morning light reflected off the surface of the Persian Gulf. Beyond the bow of the ship waited empty space. On the deck beneath Maxwell's cockpit, Dog Balls was giving the power up signal.

Maxwell shoved the two throttles up to the detents.

One last glance at the displays—no warning lights, no faults. The Hornet's airframe was rumbling like a freight train under the full thrust of the two GE engines. Ahead lay the three hundred feet of the number one catapult track.

In the center of the deck, between the two bow catapults, he could see the shooter waiting for his ready signal. Maxwell gave him a smart salute, then waited.

His left hand gripped the throttles, holding them at full power. His right hand was on the "towel rack"—the grip on the canopy rail that kept his hand from instinctively grabbing the stick and interfering with the computer-controlled inputs to the flight control system.

Two seconds elapsed. The ritual never failed to stir his blood.

He felt himself rammed into the back of his seat. The force of the acceleration caused his eyeballs to flatten, warping his vision. The deck of the carrier swept past him in a gray blur, vanishing behind the canopy as the Super Hornet hurtled off the bow.

Abruptly, the stroke of the catapult ended. He was flying. Sixty feet below lay the slick water of the Gulf.

The rest was standard. Right hand on the stick, nudge the nose up to a climb attitude, left hand on the gear handle, then the flaps. Even with its load of ordnance, the F/A-18E was accelerating like a runaway horse.

The strike package from the *Reagan* was launching at fifteen-second intervals from the *Reagan*'s four steam catapults. A mix of twelve Hornets and six F-14 Tomcats formed the package. Maxwell would lead the fighter sweep, a pair of Super Hornets teamed with two Tomcats from VF-31. Their task was to clear the area of all intruders, then maintain air supremacy.

Gus Gritti's 43rd MEU was lifting from the *Saipan* in an armada of helicopters—CH-53s and CH-46s—preceded by a wave of AH-1W Super Cobra gunships and half a dozen AV-8B Harrier jets. That was something the veteran Gritti had been emphatic about. Never again would his marines go into Indian country without their own air cover.

Already on station was a pair of EA-6B Prowlers, whose mission was to jam Iranian air defense radars and command centers. Also in an orbit over the Gulf was the E-2C Hawkeye command and control aircraft, with its rotating radome mounted atop the fuselage. The Hawkeye was datalinked with the *Reagan* and the jets of the strike package, and was also linked to the Purple Net, a real-time feed from Navy EP-3s, Air Force Rivet Joint intelligence-gathering aircraft, and current national asset data.

Today the Hawkeye had an extra mission. One of the three controllers was broadcasting on all the common civilian and military frequencies.

Attention, all ships and aircraft. A U.S. military operation is underway in the northern Persian Gulf area. Any aircraft that enters this airspace without clearance may be intercepted and fired upon.

Every five minutes the controller in the Hawkeye repeated the warning, in both English and Farsi, on the VHF and UHF guard frequencies and on every published air traffic control frequency in the northern Persian Gulf.

Maxwell was still joined with the KC-10 refueling

ship when he heard a voice in his earphones. "Gipper One-one, this is Battle Axe." "Battle Axe" was Boyce's call sign as the Air Wing Commander.

"Gipper One-one, go ahead Battle Axe."

"Your signal is Slamdunk, Gipper. Repeat Slamdunk. Acknowledge."

"Gipper One-one copies Slamdunk. Here we go."

Slamdunk was the go-ahead signal. The strike was on.

Maxwell knew that Boyce was hunched over his tactical display in the *Reagan*'s CIC—Combat Information tion Center—with a chewed-up cigar clenched in his teeth. Somewhere close by, peering around like a mother hen, was Rear Adm. Jack Hightree, the Battle Group Commander, who had overall command of the operation.

The Hornets of the strike package finished topping off from the orbiting KC-10 tanker, then regrouped in their assigned formations. In addition to being the overall strike leader, Maxwell was leading the BARCAP— barrier air combat patrol. His mixed flight of two F/A-18Es and two F-14D Tomcats would sweep the area a hundred miles inland from the target area, establish air supremacy, then wait for any intruders.

Maxwell called the Hawkeye. "Sea Lord, Gipper One-one checking in as fragged. Say the picture."

"Gipper One-one, picture is clear."

The controller in the Hawkeye—call sign Sea Lord—was Lt. Cmdr. Ralph Bunn, a naval flight officer and operations officer of the E-2C squadron aboard the *Reagan*. He was confirming that the radar picture was clear—no bogeys in the area.

Maxwell swung the nose of his Hornet toward the north. Ahead he could see the dark, irregular coastline of Iraq and Iran, the fan-shaped delta of the Tigris and Euphrates rivers. To the east, the high range of Iran's Zagros mountains jutted up like the spine of a serpent.

He inhaled deeply in his oxygen mask and forced himself to relax. The picture was clear, the controller had said. For how long? Where were the Iranians? Maybe the warnings were working. Maybe they were smart enough to stay home.

Shatt-al-Arab Waterway, Southern Iraq

You didn't have to sign up for this one, Gritti.

Memories of other amphibious raids raced through Gus Gritti's mind as he stared at the approaching land-mass. Through the open hatch he could feel the dank air from the marshes ahead. The rumble of the CH-53E's turbine engines swelled up from the cabin deck, through his boots, giving him that old familiar tingling sensation.

Another goddamn assault. Another shot at a posthumous medal.

He should be in Washington by now, sipping martinis at the club, letting all the other O-6s suck up to him because they knew he was going to pin on a star. His relief as CO of the 43rd MEU, Col. Chris Parente, was already on the *Saipan*, perched now at a console in the Landing Force Operations Center on the O-2 level. He would direct the battle with the cyber tools of the twenty-first century while Gritti went to war the old-fashioned way. On the ground, with guns and grunts.

Parente's voice crackled over Gritti's radio headphone. "Grits, Battle Axe confirms that our signal is Slamdunk. Acknowledge."

"Grits copies. We have Slamdunk." "Grits" was the call sign he had selected as commander of the assault force. Parente had just passed the go signal to him.

He knew the drill. Go find the gomers, kick in the door, ruin their day. Then get your people out of there alive. Simple. He'd done it a dozen times.

And it never came off exactly as he planned it.

He gazed around the cabin of the assault helo. Thirty grease-painted faces peered back at him. Before they launched from the *Saipan*, his marines had been full of themselves, grinning and shouting "Ooh-rah!" and "Semper Fi!," slapping war paint on their faces, checking their equipment, exuberant at the prospect of action.

Now they looked tense and sober. It was the look of men about to enter combat. Many of them had fought in Operation Iraqi Freedom. Some had been with him during the Yemen operation. They had lost buddies there in the hills of Yemen because some misguided official in a high place had restricted the use of all their firepower. Some dumb shit who thought he could do business with terrorists.

Well, thought Gritti, that was a mistake they weren't going to repeat. Gazing through the hatch, he could see the procession of CH-53Es that stretched for a mile behind him. Ahead of the column flew a swarm of gunships—AH-1W Whiskey Cobras—armed with Gatling guns, 2.75 rockets, and Hellfire missiles. Their escorting AV-8B Harriers had already swept past them, low and fast on the deck, loaded with "shake and bake"—Mark 20 Rockeye cluster bombs and napalm—to take out any threats to the helicopters.

Gross overkill, reflected Gritti. And that suited him just fine. It was another lesson from Yemen. Overkill was good.

Dezful Air Base, Iran

"Where are the others, Colonel?" asked Captain Zahdeh from the backseat of the F-14.

"Coming," said Colonel Shirazi, trying not to show his anger. "They will join us in a minute."

Col. Hassan Shirazi fumed in his cockpit while he

waited for the members of his flight to taxi out. The slow-moving laggards! For the first time in their careers, the young fighter pilots of his squadron had been summoned to engage a real enemy. And they were late, damn them.

Two were still starting their engines. The third, Lieutenant Bassiri, had just taxied out to the end of the runway at the Dezful air base. Shirazi could see the faces of Bassiri and Lieutenant Mahmood, his RIO—radar intercept officer—in their cockpit. Both wore the expressions of men on their way to their executions.

Which, reflected Shirazi, they probably were.

Colonel Shirazi had always known that this day would come. As a squadron commander and the senior fighter pilot in the Iranian Islamic Revolutionary Air Force, it was his duty to defend Iran against an invading enemy.

This particular enemy—Americans, undoubtedly—had even been brazen enough to transmit a warning. They were conducting an operation in the northwest sector of Iran. Shirazi guessed that it was against one of the lunatic groups that had taken root in the low country. Instead of throwing them out as they should have, the timid Tehran government had bowed to the mullahs and clerics and given the terrorists sanctuary.

Now they would pay the price.

A voice crackled in his earphones. "Jaguar leader, your number three and four pilots report that their aircraft are out of service. Your orders are to conduct the mission with your two remaining fighters."

Shirazi felt a wave of despair sweep over him. *Two fighters.* Two decrepit F-14A Tomcats to repulse a dozen or more top-of-the-line American fighters.

Shirazi loved the Tomcat. Or at least he had loved the Tomcat when both he and the fighter were in their prime. Iran had been the only country other than the United States to be equipped with the Grumman F-14

Tomcat. Seventy-nine of the swing-wing fighters, armed with Phoenix air-to-air missiles, were delivered to the Shah in the 1970s, giving Iran the most potent air force in the Middle East.

And then came the Islamic revolution. The Shah was gone, and with him half the pilots and skilled technicians of the air force. With no support or spare parts to maintain the F-14s, the air force was forced to cannibalize most of the fighters to keep a few flying.

In the war against Iraq during the 1980s, Shirazi had earned legendary status for himself by shooting down four Russian-built MiG-25s and one MiG-21—a feat that made him the only living ace in the Iranian Islamic Revolutionary Air Force. His photograph adorned the walls of every Iranian air base.

The name of Shirazi struck fear in the hearts of Iraqi fighter pilots. Saddam Hussein had gone so far as to offer a reward of a million dinars to any pilot who downed Shirazi. No one collected.

That was nearly twenty years ago. Both Shirazi and the Tomcat had become relics of Iranian history.

"What will we do, Colonel?" asked Captain Zahdeh from the backseat. "With only two aircraft . . ."

"We will do what warriors have always done," said Shirazi. The canopy of the F-14 closed with a clunk. He released the brakes and steered the Tomcat toward the runway. "We will engage the enemy and destroy him."

CHAPTER 13

ACE

Mashmashiyeh, Iran
0816, Thursday, 18 March

"We have a warning, Colonel." The technician swung away from his console. His voice was strained. "The southern sector. The battery commander reports incoming aircraft."

Al-Fasr was instantly alert. "What kind of aircraft? How many?"

The technician listened for several more seconds, then said, "Many aircraft. Different kinds. Jets, big helicopters, smaller ones, probably gunships. Coming up the Shatt-al-Arab waterway."

Americans, thought Al-Fasr. *They didn't take the bait. They're not attacking Iran. They're coming for us.* The Shatt-al-Arab waterway flowed along the Iraqi and Iranian border, which meant it was an assault force coming from ships in the Gulf. Marines, probably, preceded by a wave of strike fighter aircraft.

"Sound the alert," Al-Fasr said to Shakeeb, seated at a desk by the door. He turned back to the technician. "What's the range? Has the southern SA-2 battery engaged them?"

"He has secured the acquisition radar, the battery

commander says. He's worried that—" A frown came over the technician's face.

"He's worried about what?"

The technician shook his head. "I don't know. His transmitter has gone silent."

Al-Fasr nodded. The Americans would be armed with antiradiation missiles, HARMs probably. It was always the first target, the air defense radars. The southern sector air defense commander foolishly emitted enough radar energy to give them a target. Now his installation was a smoking hole in the earth.

"Order all battalion commanders to deploy their units," said Al-Fasr. "And summon Abu Mahmed. I need him here with me."

"Yes, Colonel."

Al-Fasr had often hoped for an assault by the Iranians. The Iranian army was demoralized and inept. The Bu Hasa Brigade would have scattered them like chickens. A victory over Iran would have cemented Al-Fasr's claim to Babylon.

But the Americans . . . The Bu Hasa Brigade had no chance of repulsing an assault by the Americans, who would be armed with laser and GPS and IR-guided weapons, flying strike fighters and helicopter gunships and assault helicopters filled with marines. Their ground assault force would try to capture as many *Sherji* as they could, eradicate the rest, then scorch the ground where Bu Hasa lived.

It was the worst-case scenario, but Al-Fasr had prepared for this eventuality. His *Sherji* would put up a fight, kill a few Americans, maybe even down some airplanes. In the end, they would yield the ground and vanish into the marshes. They would blend into the ancient countryside.

Eventually the United States would lose interest. America was losing its stomach for guerrilla warfare in places like Afghanistan and Iraq and now Iran. The wars on terrorism—one after the other—had exhausted their spirit.

When the raids were finished and the Americans were gone, Al-Fasr would still be there. Babylon would be his.

But first he had to survive the coming battle. *Where was Abu?*

"Shakeeb," he snapped to the sergeant. "It is imperative that I speak with Abu. Go find him now."

"Yes, Colonel."

While he waited, Al-Fasr went to the comm technicians' consoles. They were receiving steady reports now from the defense positions. Low-flying jets had taken out two of the SA-2 batteries. Helicopter gunships were firing on the southernmost positions.

That was to be expected, thought Al-Fasr. The Americans were dangerous but predictable. They would suppress threats to their helicopters first. Then the main assault force would land and establish a perimeter. Not until then would they engage the Bu Hasa Brigade on the ground.

By then the *Sherji* would have vanished like the ghosts of Babylon.

The sound of an explosion rattled the fixtures in the room. A five-hundred-pound bomb, Al-Fasr guessed. Then something else—the staccato belching of antiaircraft guns. It was one of the 37 mm, mixed with the rapid-fire bark of the mobile 23 mm.

More explosions, nearer this time.

They don't know where the headquarters is. They'll have to find it.

Or will they? Perhaps they know. But how?

The sounds of battle were drawing nearer. *Where is Abu?*

The plan for extricating the Brigade from the jaws of the enemy depended on Abu Mahmed. He was supposed to mount a decoy attack on the eastern flank, drawing the attention of the advancing ground forces. Al-Fasr and the rest of the *Sherji* would retreat along the bank of the Karkeh River, northward to Lake Hawr Umr Sawan. Under cover of darkness, they would disperse in airboats throughout the low, impenetrable marsh country.

At least that was the plan. It all depended on Abu Mahmed.

Listening to the whump of explosions to the south, Al-Fasr had a gnawing sensation in his gut. Something wasn't right. *Where is Abu?*

Gritti hit the ground in a dead run. Directly in front of him was Sergeant Major Plunkett, moving at a surprising rate for a man weighing nearly 250 pounds. Both men sprinted for cover, coughing on the fine dust kicked up by the whirling blades of the CH-53E.

Marines were spilling out of the helos, fanning out, setting up the perimeter defense for the landing zone. As more assault helicopters swept into the LZ, the pall of dust swelled like a storm cloud. The zone looked like it had been savaged by a tornado. A wave of AV-8B Harriers had dispensed cluster bombs, then the Whiskey Cobra gunships gave it a sweep with Gatling guns.

Gritti followed Plunkett to a sheltered outcropping of rock, then waved for the corporal hauling the PRC-119 ManPack UHF TACSAT radio. He could hear the distinctive three-round bursts from the M16A2 combat rifles, interspersed with the angry *brrrrp* of an H&K MP-5N nine-millimeter submachine gun.

No answering Kalashnikov fire that he could pick out. A good sign.

"What are they shooting at?" he asked Plunkett.

"Stragglers. The few who survived the air attack."

It took less than five minutes. Gritti saw one of the fire teams coming back into the perimeter prodding half a dozen prisoners in front of them. The prisoners wore dark *gellebiahs*—the long, shirtlike garb favored by the Bu Hasa *Sherji*. They walked with their hands on their heads, staring at the tableau around them with wide-eyed, stunned expressions.

"That's it," said Plunkett. "Colonel Hewlitt reports very light resistance at LZ One. He thinks the gomers have pulled up stakes and are already heading north."

Gritti stood up and wiped the dust from his mouth. "Time to move out. Let's set up the welcome wagon." LZ One was four miles south. The idea was for Hewlitt's force to sweep northward, driving the terrorists out of their positions around the village of Mashmashiyeh. According to the intel brief, the Bu Hasa terrorists would flee northward, up the Karkeh River, where Gritti and his three rifle companies would cut them off.

The terrorists—Gritti refused to dignify them by using their own label, *Sherji*—could join the legion of jihad martyrs, or they could throw down their weapons and come out with their hands on their heads. Either way was fine with Gus Gritti.

Western Iran, 25,000 feet

"Gipper One-one, your weapons status is yellow and tight. Acknowledge."

Maxwell acknowledged the call from Sea Lord. "Gipper One-one, yellow and tight."

"Yellow and tight" meant there was a possibility of a threat, but none was yet identified. His Master Armament switch was supposed to remain safe.

Beneath him, he could see the smoke and flame of the exploding bombs. The strike was going well, without serious opposition. The strike fighters were obliterating Bu Hasa targets like boots stomping an anthill.

Maxwell felt a twinge of envy. He was up here, removed from the action by twenty-five thousand feet. Off his left wing, in a combat spread, was his wingman, Lieutenant B. J. Johnson. To his right were the long delta shapes of the two F-14Ds from VF-31.

Maxwell's four-ship BARCAP had just finished the northwestward leg of the fighter sweep, paralleling the Iraq-Iran border. The picture was still clear, according to the controller in the Hawkeye. No Iranian fighters had come up to challenge them. So far.

"Gipper One-three, take spacing," Maxwell called.

"Gipper One-three, roger," answered the RIO of the lead Tomcat, Cmdr. Butch Kissick. Kissick had just joined VF-31, the *Reagan*'s F-14 squadron, as the new XO. His pilot was Lt. Rusty Schroeder. The second F-14 was flown by Lt. Cmdr. Big Mac MacFarquhar and his RIO, Lt. Jeff-Ro Bush. Mixing the aircraft types— Hornets and Tomcats—in the fighter sweep was Boyce's idea. They worked well together.

Maxwell watched the pair of Tomcats take their spacing, setting up the two-by-two BARCAP formation. They would begin their racetrack orbit, oriented toward the Iranian fighter bases that housed the only threat aircraft in the area.

The F-14D was still the fastest and most brutish of carrier-based warplanes, but it was in the twilight of its career. The Tomcats were being replaced, a squadron at a time, with F/A-18 Super Hornets.

The happy-hour arguments about which jet—Hornet or Tomcat—could kick the other's butt would rage on for years. The big Tomcat, with its sleek wings-retracted delta shape, could charge into battle at over twice the speed of sound. It had the fuel capacity to fly long sorties without refueling, and in its later years had been retrofitted, to the disgust of fighter purists, as a capable bomber. But the complicated airplane had become a maintenance nightmare, sucking up precious assets that the Navy needed for new aircraft.

The new Super Hornet possessed a state-of-the-art weapons package and a modular-replacement maintenance system. After a heated debate in the bureaus of the Pentagon, the Super Hornet was anointed as the Navy's all-mission fighter for the next generation.

Watching the eruptions of smoke from his perch on the BARCAP, Maxwell wondered again if the Iranians would join the battle. The threat axis for Operation Slamdunk was not well defined. If they did put up a fight, it would come from one of their bases near the western border—Isfahan, Shiraz, or Dezful.

Maxwell wished again that he had assigned himself a ground attack role. Flying BARCAP for a mission where all the action was—

"Gipper One-one, Sea Lord." The Hawkeye controller's voice broke through his thoughts. "Purple Net info reports four bandits moving at Dezful. Two on the runway now."

Maxwell was instantly alert. Purple Net was the Hawkeye's link to all the intelligence-gathering sources. "Gipper, roger. Do we have an ID?"

"Not yet. Fulcrums or Tomcats. We'll call it when we see them airborne."

Maxwell acknowledged. Forget the clear picture. If the Iranians were coming out to play, it meant his BARCAP was the only barrier between them and the assault force.

What kind of bandits? Iran's Fulcrums—twin-engine, Russian-built MiG-29s—were mostly decrepit ex-Iraqi jets flown to Iran to escape destruction in the first Gulf War. Though they had a few modernized Fulcrums imported from Russia, they weren't based at Dezful.

He turned to gaze for a moment at the two silhouettes off his right wing. What if the bogeys were Tomcats? He shook his head at the irony. Who would have dreamed back in the seventies, when the U.S. outfitted Iran with the F-14, that this day would come?

"Gipper One-one, pop-up contact over Delta, in the weeds, climbing and accelerating. Multiple contacts. Probable flight of two."

Here they come. The bogeys were airborne, low and climbing. Delta was the code for the Iranian fighter base at Dezful.

"Gipper One-one, roger."

A pause. "Sea Lord shows the bogeys as Tomcats, Gipper. Flight of two. Two more on the ground not yet moving."

Maxwell acknowledged. His own radar was picking up the contact. He was also at the end of his leg of the racetrack. "Gipper One-one, turning cold."

From the lead BARCAP Tomcat, Butch Kissick replied, "Gipper One-three turning hot." As Maxwell's nose turned away from the incoming bogeys, Kissick was turning his fighters toward them.

"Sea Lord shows the bogeys twenty south of Delta, low and fast, hot." The Iranian fighters were headed toward the ground assault operation.

"Gipper One-one."

"Gipper One-three, clean high, looking low." Kissick was reporting that the airspace above them was clear, and now his radar was scanning below them.

Maxwell stayed riveted to his own radar display. He saw the two datalink symbols representing the targets, still coming his way.

"Gipper One-three, contact twenty-five south Delta, angels ten, climbing, fast, hot."

"Those are your bogeys," answered Sea Lord. "Signal India."

India was the code for "intercept and identify."

Maxwell considered for a moment. From this angle, his number three and four wingmen, the Tomcats, were in better position to lead the intercept. He could pass the tactical lead to Kissick, and support him from the rear. That would be the safest way to run the intercept.

To hell with that. He was the flight leader. He'd run the intercept.

"Gipper One-one turning hot," he called. "One-three, turn cold and join on me."

"Three," acknowledged Kissick, sounding skeptical.

Radio chatter from now on would be minimal. Each of Maxwell's fighters had radar-datalinked information in his display. Each pilot could see the others' speed, altitude, and heading.

Maxwell's radar was showing the two contacts about thirty miles south of Dezful air base, climbing through fifteen thousand at a speed of six hundred knots. His situational display held the datalink tracks of the bogeys.

In the same display he could see the symbols of the other members of his flight. His wingman was paralleling him, maintaining a combat spread. Kissick's Tomcats were already in their rendezvous turn. He glanced outside to his left, and there they were—the delta-shaped silhouettes of the F-14s, sliding into position.

"Gippers, take wall," Maxwell called. A wall formation—all four fighters in line abreast—would maximize their firepower.

"Gipper One-one has contact thirty-four south Delta," he called. "Angels eighteen climbing, Mach one, hot. Confirm?"

"That's your bogey, Gipper," Sea Lord replied.

Maxwell was getting an uneasy feeling. The Iranian fighters were still inbound. They were too damned close to be playing identification games. In less than two minutes it would be a kill-or-be-killed scenario. He couldn't allow the Iranians the first shot.

"Gipper One-one flight committing," he called. "Off-set heading zero-eight-zero." The new heading would place him between the Iranian fighters and the target area. Flanking the Iranians would shrink their weapons envelope.

Or so he hoped.

His RWR chirped to life. "Gipper One-one spiked at ten o'clock," he called. One of the oncoming fighters was targeting him with its radar. The RWR screen was showing the distinctive electronic signature of the enemy radar—an American-built AWG-9. Twenty-some years old and still working.

"They're Tomcats," Maxwell called. "What's my weapons status?"

Several seconds passed. Maxwell knew the controller was on a direct hookup to the Battle Group Commander.

"Bravo Golf declares your weapons status red and tight."

Maxwell cursed to himself. *Red and tight.* Intercept and identify, but don't shoot.

They were three minutes from the merge. What the hell was going on?

Mashmashiyeh, Iran

Shakeeb entered Abu Mahmed's office without knocking. "You are to report to the colonel immediately," he said.

Abu lifted his eyes from the notebook computer on his desk. Shakeeb was one of Al-Fasr's desert rats, a Bedouin who had served under him in the emirate air force, then escaped with Al-Fasr when their attempted overthrow of the emir failed. Shakeeb followed his colonel around like a trained baboon, fetching tea and relaying orders in that imperious military tone as if he himself possessed some kind of authority.

"I do not take orders from sergeants," said Abu.

"The order comes from Colonel Al-Fasr. He demands

your presence in the command headquarters without delay. It is urgent."

Yes, thought Abu, it probably *was* urgent. Any idiot could hear the explosions working their way toward the headquarters. Al-Fasr's world was about to blow up in his face, and he expected Abu to save him.

"Tell the colonel I will be there when I am ready." Abu went back to the computer.

Shakeeb didn't move. "He made it very clear. You are to come with me now."

The two men locked gazes. Abu saw the cold, Bedouin eyes boring into him. The sergeant was like a trained watchdog. He wouldn't leave.

Abu sighed and closed the lid on the computer. "Very well. Take me to the colonel."

He rose and followed Shakeeb to the door.

As Shakeeb reached the open doorway, he stopped, sensing Abu's movement behind him. He turned and saw the Makarov automatic pistol. Reaching for his own weapon, Shakeeb whirled, trying to escape.

His hand was on his holster when Abu's bullet caught him in the chest. As he sagged to the floor, Abu bent over him and fired another round into his head.

Abu stopped for a moment to consider the dead sergeant. It had worked out even better than he expected. Shakeeb, the lackey sergeant, had shown no respect for the true warriors of the jihad. He deserved to be killed, and Allah had provided the occasion.

He dragged Shakeeb's body into the office and stuffed him behind a row of cabinets. Al-Fasr would soon be wondering what became of his pet sergeant.

Let him, thought Abu. By the time he knew, it would all be over.

CHAPTER 14

THE PRIZE

USS Ronald Reagan
Quebec Station, Persian Gulf
0850, Thursday, 18 March

"Goddamn it, Jack," said Boyce, "you don't have any choice. You can't send fighters into a merge with their weapons status tight."

Boyce had known Rear Admiral Jack Hightree for nearly twenty years. In the tense atmosphere of the red-lighted CIC, he could dispense with formality.

Hightree was shaking his head. "I don't like the looks of it. If your guy Maxwell gets trigger-happy, this is going to turn into a shooting war with Iran."

"We can't risk letting one of those raghead Tomcats take out our strike package. That's why we put the BARCAP up there."

Boyce knew he was pushing the limit. Hightree was a cautious battle group commander who had acquired two stars by following a nonconfrontational career path. He wanted to add a third star the same way.

Still, Boyce liked Hightree. Despite his inherent stodginess, he was an honest, no-bullshit leader who stood up for his people. He just needed a little pushing.

Hightree was frowning at the merging blips on the

tactical display. "If Maxwell blows this, somebody's going to be explaining what happened on CNN tonight."

Boyce shrugged. "What's to explain? If the gomers show hostile intent, Maxwell whacks them. Very simple."

"Not simple at all. This is supposed to be a limited police action against a terrorist group, not a military engagement with a sovereign country like Iran. If all the other Islamic countries believe that we're beating up on one of their brothers, we're up to our necks in trouble."

Boyce stuffed his cigar back in his mouth and shut up. He was glad he didn't have to concern himself with the politics of war. He could think like a fighter pilot, and right now he was thinking that someone better be taking out those Iranian Tomcats.

A yeoman came to Hightree and handed him a headset with a boom mike. Boyce watched Hightree's eyebrows raise as he listened to the voice on the headset. Hightree continued listening for half a minute. He nodded his head and interjected several "Yes, sirs."

The admiral removed the headset and stared at it. "I'll be damned," he said.

"Who was that, Admiral?"

"The boss."

"Fifth Fleet?" asked Boyce. The commander of the Fifth Fleet was a three-star headquartered in Bahrain.

"The big boss. The President."

Boyce removed his cigar. Never before had he heard of the Commander-in-Chief making a direct call to a battle group commander during a strike operation.

"No shit? What did he want?"

"He wanted to know if we were getting into a war with Iran." Hightree gave Boyce a hard look. "Well, Red? Are we?"

Western Iran, 25,000 feet

   Red and tight.
   Maxwell saw where this was going. Don't shoot. At
least, not yet. Admiral Hightree—Bravo Golf—wanted
to play it down to the wire. He was still hoping he could
bluff the Iranians into bugging out and going home.
   But these guys weren't bugging out. The two blips on
Maxwell's radar were boring straight toward him like
torpedoes on a terminal run. They were in a close two-
ship fighting wing formation—the classic old East Bloc
tactical formation—instead of the American-style combat spread. It signaled they were heavily dependent on
their GCI—ground-controlled intercept radar—instead
of using mutual support between the fighters.
   Obsolete tactics in obsolete airplanes.
   He could feel the old familiar surge of adrenaline as
he drew nearer to the merge. For an instant he thought
about the three kill symbols painted beneath his name
on the fuselage. Three MiG-29 Fulcrums—one in Iraq,
two more in Yemen. A fourth symbol was missing, that
of a Chinese Black Star stealth jet, gunned down on a
secret mission over the Taiwan Strait. Not until the operation was declassified would he get credit for that kill.
   One more kill would make him an ace, off the record.
Eventually his name would be added to the elite list of
fighter pilots with five kills.
   He tried to erase the thought from his mind. Maxwell
had no remorse about killing an adversary in combat,
but the death of an anonymous enemy gave him no pleasure. The objective of battle was victory, not extermina-
tion.
   The Iranian Tomcats were closing fast.
   He was running out of options. His first priority was
to protect the strike package. But Bravo Golf wanted to
avoid a shoot-out with the Iranians, if possible. That's
why his weapons status was still—

"Gipper One-one, Sea Lord. Bravo Golf has changed your weapons status. You're red and free. Cleared to engage, cleared to fire."

"Attention, all ships and aircraft. A U.S. military operation is underway in the northern Persian Gulf area. Any aircraft that enters this airspace without clearance may be intercepted and fired upon."

In the cockpit of his F-14A, Colonel Shirazi heard the warning again on the guard frequency. He was tired of hearing it, but it was coming over every channel he selected.

He ignored it and continued on a southwesterly heading, toward the northern Gulf.

"Jaguar Lead," said the GCI controller, "you have multiple targets, low, two hundred kilometers, bearing 230 degrees."

"Roger the low targets," said Shirazi. He knew those were the strike aircraft. They were of secondary concern for the moment. They wouldn't be out here without a fighter escort, and he had to deal with them first. He radioed his controller. "Where are the fighters high?"

He already knew the answer. His RIO, Captain Zahdeh, had a radar lock. The trouble was, he didn't trust the Tomcat's quirky AWG-9 radar. The American-made radar was two decades old and subject to a host of anomalies.

Same with the AIM-54A Phoenix missiles. The big Hughes-produced long-range air-to-air missile had been designed specifically for the Tomcat to use against incoming aircraft. During the war with Iraq, the Phoenix had accounted for twenty-five enemy MiGs. In the years since, the complicated missile became too difficult to maintain without technical assistance. Shirazi had ordered the Phoenix removed from all the fighters in his squadron.

His Tomcat still carried a load of elderly AIM-9

Sidewinders and AIM-7 Sparrows, though the radar-guided Sparrows were only as reliable as the Tomcat's own AWG-9 fire control radar.

"Jaguar lead, you have four hostile targets, bearing 220, range eighty kilometers."

"Jaguar lead concurs." Zahdeh was picking up the same targets. What were they? If they came from the American carrier in the Gulf, they were probably Hornets.

Or F-14s.

It was bizarre, thought Shirazi. He had fought other Tomcats in hundreds of mock dogfights over Iran. He knew what the fighter could do in the hands of a capable crew. He had never expected to fight another Tomcat in real combat. The American Tomcats would have newer, more powerful engines, more effective radars.

"What are the targets?" he asked Zahdeh. "What type fighter?"

"Unknown, Colonel," said Zahdeh.

Shirazi pondered this for a moment. There was another possibility. The Americans might be flying their new Super Hornet fighters. That was even worse.

Forty miles to the merge.

Maxwell knew that if he stayed with the pre-briefed intercept plan, they'd be in a furball with the Iranian Toms in a little over two minutes.

He keyed his mike. "A new game plan, Gippers. Three and Four, on my command, dump chaff and drag west. Gippers One and Two will post-hole away for the bracket. Stay radar passive to escort."

He knew Boyce and the Battle Group Commander were listening back in CIC, watching the link display, wondering what the hell he was doing.

He still had the spike from the Iranian Tomcat's AWG-9 radar. The idea was to break the Iranian radar's lock by using chaff—confettilike foil that presented a brilliant, but bogus, radar target. At the same time he'd make an aggressive vertical maneuver, diving in a tight spiral—a post-hole—beneath the Iranians' radar coverage.

Meanwhile Kissick's Tomcats would present a fat target for the Iranian Toms, dragging them northwest away from Zulu—the target area where Gritti's Marines were landing. Maxwell's flight would convert the Iranians— swing into a firing position behind them.

He waited, watching the distance close. "Range thirty, Gippers. Action . . . *now!*"

He rolled to the right and hauled the nose down, dispensing chaff as he aimed the jet toward the earth. He slid the throttles into afterburner, pointing the nose straight down. The mottled brown landscape of Iran filled his windscreen. A mile to his right, he caught the silhouette of B. J. Johnson's Hornet in a parallel dive, twin afterburners blazing like torches.

Maxwell was counting on the Iranian pilots as well as the GCI controller being confused. He was also counting on the AWG-9 radar's notorious habit of locking onto chaff instead of the real target.

The Hornets punched through Mach one, aiming toward the earth like descending comets.

It was an old tactic. Going perpendicular to the threat radars—beaming, it was called—minimized the amount of Doppler shift a radar could see, denying it a lock. Sometimes it worked, sometimes it didn't.

Maxwell glanced inside the cockpit at his RWR. It worked. No spike. The Iranian radars had lost them.

The pocked earth of Iran was filling Maxwell's windshield. He was hurtling toward the ground faster than a rifle bullet.

Twelve thousand feet.

Ten thousand.

Eight thousand. *Pull.*

He nudged the stick back and brought the throttles

out of the afterburner detent. He felt the G-suit tighten around his legs and abdomen, squeezing him like a hydraulic vise. Grunting against the force of seven Gs, he pulled the Hornet's nose toward the horizon.

He leveled at five hundred feet above the surface, still supersonic. The landscape of Iran was skimming beneath him in a brownish blur. A half mile to the right, B. J. Johnson's Hornet was leveling a few hundred feet above him.

"Gipper One's naked."

"Two's naked."

No radar spikes. The Iranian fighters had lost them, at least for the moment.

But Maxwell had *them*. Two red V-shaped chevrons were moving like glowworms across his display, datalinked from the E-2C Hawkeye. *Thank you, Dolly.*

His display also showed the symbols for each friendly fighter in the engagement. Kissick's F-14s— the bait—were fifteen miles ahead of the two Iranian Tomcats, heading two-seven-zero.

He watched the geometry developing in his display. *Go for it guys. Take the bait.*

Seconds passed. Then Kissick called, "Gipper Three, spiked at six—an AWG-9."

Maxwell studied his display for another moment. He could see the Iranians in hot pursuit now, committed to engaging Kissick's F-14s. Closing at a rate of over two thousand miles per hour.

They were going for it. Taking the bait.

The Iranian controller's voice was high-pitched and panicky.

"Jaguar Lead, you have four—no, six targets—one o'clock, ten o'clock. No, no, two targets now at three o'clock! Another at two . . ."

Colonel Shirazi wanted to strangle the hysterical controller. The idiot on the ground was screaming out targets everywhere. What was he seeing? Were the four American fighters he had called initially now only two? If so, two had vanished. Or they were multiplying like rabbits.

It had to be chaff. The screaming GCI controller was too stupid to distinguish chaff from buzzard shit. His own onboard AWG-9 radar was nearly as worthless. It hadn't been upgraded since the air force's last skilled technician fled Iran twenty years ago. The radar had great difficulty with chaff even when it was working well.

Shirazi slammed his fist against the canopy rail. "Zahdeh," he yelled at his RIO. "Where are the two lead contacts? Where did they go?"

Zahdeh didn't know.

"Jaguar Two," Shirazi called to his wingman, Lieutenant Bassiri. "How many targets do you have locked?"

"None," said Bassiri. "Our radar, it is . . . malfunctioning. No lock, Colonel."

Shirazi had to shake his head. He should have followed the Shah's example and left Iran to the Ayatollah and the crazy mullahs. He could be playing golf in Palm Springs instead of offering himself as a blind target for American fighter pilots.

"Zahdeh, do you have the lead contacts?"

"I think so. Or maybe chaff. It is difficult to tell."

Of course it was, thought Shirazi. The trouble with the ancient AWG-9 was that it loved chaff. Loved it more than a real target, which, in a way, made it predictable.

"Colonel, I have them! Two contacts, fleeing west."

"Sort them out," said Shirazi as he shoved the throttles forward. With his left thumb he chose AIM-7 SPARROW on his weapons selector. "We're going to kill them."

USS Ronald Reagan

"What's Maxwell doing?" asked Hightree. "Is he playing games with them?"

"Looks like he's bracketing to the south," said Boyce, watching the carrier's master datalink tactical display. "His two Hornets are going for an unobserved intercept from below. He's broken their radar lock, and they're blind on him."

Hightree frowned at the screen. "That's no good. The Iranians are too close to our F-14s. Tell Maxwell to stop screwing around and take them out."

Boyce looked at Hightree in surprise. This was a switch. A few minutes ago the cautious admiral was worried about starting a war with Iran. Now he was worried about losing his own fighters.

Boyce said in a low voice, "Give it a second, Jack." He had to be careful not to tread on Hightree's authority. "Let's see if Brick can pull this off."

"I don't intend to lose our F-14s because we waited too long to splash a couple of Iranians," said Hightree. "Tell him to shoot."

Boyce nodded. He knew Hightree. He was out on a limb, and he wasn't interested in going any further. "Yes, sir. It's your call."

Boyce keyed his boom mike. "Sea Lord, Battleaxe on purple."

"Go Battleaxe."

"Bravo Golf clears Gipper to kill the bandits. Repeat, cleared to kill the bandits."

While he waited for acknowledgement, a thought came to Boyce's mind.

Maxwell was going to be an ace. If he followed orders.

CHAPTER 15

THE SWEETNESS
OF LIFE

Mashmashiyeh, Iran
0855, Thursday, 18 March

Something was happening.

In the distance, he could hear the sound of bombs, cannon fire, the whoosh of jets. The two *Sherji* in Rasmussen's hut, Ali and Karim, were agitated, chattering between themselves.

Rasmussen sat at his wooden table, scribbling in his notebook. He feigned indifference. These two were still unaware that he could follow their conversations in Arabic.

"The Americans are coming," said Ali. "They are bombing the perimeter with their jets, clearing the path for the helicopters."

Rasmussen didn't look up. *The Americans are coming.* An electric jolt ran through him. He felt as if he were dreaming. His heart was pounding like a jackhammer.

"*Eeeee!*" said Karim. "We have to abandon this place. It is time to go up the river, to escape with the colonel."

Ali glanced at Rasmussen. "What about him? Do we kill him or take him with us?"

"Shoot him. It is much simpler."

Ali looked uncertain. "I will ask. You wait here."

A string of bombs detonated a mile away, followed by the screech of a low-flying jet. "Hurry," said Karim. "If you don't return in five minutes, I will put a bullet in him and leave this building."

They glanced again at Rasmussen, who continued scribbling. Ali tapped a finger to his head. "His brain is like cow dung. He doesn't understand anything."

Ali slung his AK-74 over his shoulder and left the hut, closing the heavy door behind him.

Rasmussen listened to the sounds of battle in the distance. Not since he ejected from his Hornet over Iraq had he been this close to anything that represented the United States. Even when the Americans invaded Iraq in 2003, he was far away, already moved to the squalid cell on the Iranian border.

Now they were here, so close he could hear them. Americans like him.

An unfamiliar feeling was stirring in Rasmussen's gut. A feeling from a long ago past, so remote he'd nearly forgotten the sensation.

Hope.

It was growing inside him like a living thing. He knew it was irrational, delusional probably, but he clung to it, not wanting the feeling to fade away. The mere presence of such an impossible thought was like a narcotic. It was making him giddy.

Freedom was a mile away. He could hear it in the whoosh of the jets, the thud of the bombs.

Karim was listening too. He stood behind Rasmussen, trying to peer through the slit of the boarded window. He was nervous, shifting the AK-74 from hand to hand, muttering in a low voice to himself.

Rasmussen summoned up all his resolve. He turned in the chair, gathering his legs beneath him. He felt like a disembodied person, watching his own actions from a remote viewing place.

He launched himself from the chair, driving his shoulder into the small of Karim's back. He felt himself energized with a strength he had not possessed in years. As Karim bounced off the boarded window, Rasmussen seized a handful of long hair. He rammed Karim's head against the hard stucco wall.

Like most of the *Sherji*, Karim was wiry and tough. Enraged, he wrenched himself around and lunged at his attacker. Rasmussen stepped into him, driving his fist into his face. Karim lurched backward, stunned.

Rasmussen seized his hair, yanking his head toward him, throwing an arm around him, wrenching the Arab's neck with all his newfound strength. He heard an audible crack.

Karim's body went limp beneath him. The AK-74 fell from his hands. He slumped to the floor, his legs still twitching.

For a moment Rasmussen stood over the body of the *Sherji*, his breath coming in hard rasps. He'd never killed anyone before. He thought he should be feeling remorse, or sorrow, or disgust. He felt nothing like that. Nothing but a need to be free.

There's no turning back now. Escape or die. You won't be a prisoner again.

He snatched the kaffiyeh off the dead *Sherji*'s head, then picked up the AK-74. Outside the door, he heard the sounds of running feet, hysterical chatter, orders shouted from down the street.

He pulled the kaffiyeh down low over his forehead. He cracked the door open. No sign of Ali. Holding the AK-74 in front of him, he stepped into the shaded pathway. At the end of the narrow street was the low building where Al-Fasr made his headquarters. He turned and walked briskly away, in the opposite direction, toward the sound of the bombs.

Western Iran, 25,000 feet.

Colonel Shirazi tried to control his frustration.

The idiot GCI controller kept screaming about radar contacts to their left and low. Zahdeh had obediently broken his radar lock on the fleeing American fighters and gone back to search mode, looking for the low-altitude contacts.

"Do you see any such contacts?" Shirazi demanded.

"No, Colonel," said Zahdeh. "The targets are not there. Just chaff."

Shirazi was still boring straight ahead to where the fleeing American fighters should be. With his previous closure rate, he estimated he was nearly in range for an AIM-7 Sparrow shot.

He scanned the horizon in front of him. At any moment he should be getting a visual contact.

"We will attack the first group then. Lock them up again!"

"Yes, Colonel."

Shirazi called the GCI controller. "Never mind the low-altitude contacts. Say the position of the previous enemy fighters. Give me real targets, damn it, not the decoys."

The GCI controller's voice was high and strained. "Jaguar Lead, you have targets . . . to the north of you. Eight kilometers. They have reversed."

Again Shirazi cursed the moronic controller. *Damn!* He'd had a radar lock on the two fleeing Americans. He could have destroyed them within minutes if this moron controller hadn't started reporting chaff. Now Zahdeh, his RIO, couldn't find them on his own radar.

Of course. The Americans' Radar Warning Receivers would have told them when he broke lock. They were probably cranking around, trying to neutralize him. Very clever, but it wasn't too late. He could still acquire them visually and kill them with a—

The controller's shrill call cut through his thoughts

like a dagger. "Targets, Jaguar One! Two more targets behind you. Range five kilometers, closing. They are all behind you now."

Shirazi's senses went numb. What was the idiot talking about? Targets? *He* was the target. How did they get behind him?

"Jaguar One, this is Jaguar Two, behind you! Break right!"

As he rolled into the right turn to counter the new threat, Shirazi looked over his shoulder. What he saw made his blood run cold.

A sleek, gray shape, canted twin stabilizers. It was behind Bassiri's jet, a hundred meters.

"Jaguar One," said Bassiri in a hoarse voice, "Enemy fighters. You have one at your eight o'clock, very close."

Colonel Shirazi peered over his shoulder. Yes, Bassiri was right. Another one, very close.

He drew a deep breath through his oxygen mask and waited to die.

Maxwell's finger curled around the trigger on the stick. He watched the desert camouflage–painted Tomcats swell in his HUD. In his headphones he could hear the insistent *screeeee* acquisition tone of the Sidewinder seeker head.

He took a quick glance to the right. B. J. Johnson was sliding into firing position on the second Iranian F-14.

"Gipper One-two has the trailer," she called.

"Roger, stay locked and wait for my call."

The Iranians knew they were there. The lead Tomcat was in a right turn, too late and too ineffective to defeat the Hornets on his tail.

Maxwell already had his signal. *Cleared to kill the bandits.* Down in CIC Hightree and Boyce were waiting to hear that the Iranian F-14s were splashed. He and B. J. were seconds away from killing both bandits.

He slid his Super Hornet to the outside of the lead

Tomcat, his finger poised to launch the Sidewinder. He was close now, almost too close. Any closer and he would have to switch to a guns kill.

Where are Kissick's F-14s?

He took a hurried glance at his tac display. There they were, across the Iranians' turn, out of the Iranians' kill envelope. Gipper Three and Four were one vertical move away from their own kill shots.

The Iranians were dead meat.

Sliding up from the outside of the turn, Maxwell had a good view of the lead fighter. The old Tomcat was a mess. It had a faded paint scheme with numerous dark streaks—hydraulic or oil leaks—running back along the fuselage. The two engines were spewing trails of dark smoke, making it an easy target to follow. American engine makers had long ago cleaned up the exhausts of tactical fighter jet engines.

There was something else. As Maxwell closed on the lead Tomcat, he saw markings on the fuselage, beneath the canopy. Symbols, arranged in a row.

Kill symbols.

Maxwell slid in tighter. His finger was still on the trigger, but his curiosity had taken charge. He was too close for even a guns shot now, but he knew he could put the Tomcat away in a matter of seconds if the Iranian pilot made a sudden maneuver.

He was flying formation on the Iranian Tomcat, escorting it. The pilot and the RIO in the Tomcat cockpit were staring at him.

Maxwell had a good view of the kill symbols on the fuselage. They were Iraqi flags. Five of them.

Mashmashiyeh, Iran

Sherji were running in all directions, shouting at each other, pointing to the east where a steady din of explosions rolled across the hazy marshes. No one seemed to notice the tall man in the dark *gellebiah* and the kaffiyeh, carrying the AK-74.

Rasmussen came to the edge of the village, then stopped in the shadow of a crumbling stucco building. At the east end of the village was the river and the flimsy concrete bridge. It was guarded at each end by a pair of *Sherji*.

Shit. He had to get out of the village. Had to cross the river, had to reach the Americans' positions. If he waited any longer—

Footsteps. Running, coming from behind him.

He whirled and saw them. Ali was charging down the pathway, holding his assault rifle across his chest at the ready. With him was another *Sherji*, one of the sergeants from Al-Fasr's headquarters.

They hadn't recognized him yet. The borrowed kaffiyeh was working, at least for another few seconds. It concealed his telltale shock of white hair.

He turned from them, not too abruptly, and stepped around the corner of the building. Then he ran, sprinting for the cover of the far pathway that paralleled the row of buildings. He reached the corner. As he turned to run back up the next pathway, he stopped.

A Land Rover blocked the narrow passage. It was lurching over the rough stones, coming toward him. Atop the vehicle was a machine gun mount and a *Sherji* behind it swinging the barrel as if he were searching for a target. He fixed his dark, Arab eyes on the man in the kaffiyeh.

Rasmussen saw the other man in the vehicle, sitting next to the driver. They made eye contact.

Rasmussen recognized him. Abu Mahmed.

Abu kept his eyes on him as he barked a command at the driver. The driver nodded, and the Land Rover accelerated down the street.

Rasmussen fought against the panic that welled up in him. He whirled and reversed course, running back to the end of the street, around the corner. He braced himself for the hail of machine gun bullets.

They didn't come. He heard only the Land Rover tires crunching on the rocky street behind him.

Still running, he darted around the next corner, back into the street where he'd seen Ali and the sergeant.

They were still there. Side by side, trotting toward him, looking for the American. Ali looked perplexed. He stared at the figure in the kaffiyeh coming toward him, not sure what he was seeing.

Rasmussen leveled the AK-74 and shot him in the chest with a quick three-round burst. The sergeant yelped and did a sideways dance, swinging his own assault rifle to a firing position. Rasmussen fired three rounds into him.

Behind him he heard the chuff of an engine, the crunch of tires on the crumbling path.

"Stop," said a familiar voice. "Put down the weapon and raise your hands, or I'll kill you where you stand."

He stood there holding the AK-74. The bodies of Ali and the sergeant lay spread-eagled on the gravel in front of him. His freedom had lasted, he figured, four minutes. Four minutes out of a dozen years.

A low-flying jet screeched overhead. The staccato pop of an antiaircraft gun followed it, then stopped. The Americans were coming, thought Rasmussen, but he wouldn't be here. He didn't exist.

He couldn't go back. Not after being free, even for four minutes. He would make them kill him.

He whirled to fire the assault rifle. *Take as many with you as you can.*

It was his last conscious thought before something struck from behind and blackness enveloped him.

Western Iran, 25,000 feet

"We're dead," said Zahdeh, from the backseat. His voice was flat, without emotion.

Colonel Shirazi didn't answer. He was beyond thinking about life and death. Nearly thirty years of military flying were about to end in a fireball over western Iran.

It was ironic. They were flying almost exactly over the place where he'd killed his first MiG twenty years ago. The Iraqi pilot had been an amateur, an easy kill.

This one on his left wing was no amateur.

Shirazi saw the American pilot staring at him. It was the look, he thought, that a lion gives a wildebeest. He wanted to look his victim in the eye before killing him.

Shirazi considered his options. He could make a hard break into the Hornet, maybe surprise him enough that he could get inside his turn. Or he could try to ram him.

Neither option was feasible.

Then he saw something else. On the side of the Hornet—*kill symbols.* Shirazi recognized the symbols. Silhouettes of MiG-29 Fulcrums.

The law of the jungle, he thought. Col. Hassan Shirazi, Iran's celebrated killer of MiGs, was about to be killed by a stronger opponent. It was inevitable. Maybe even appropriate. He felt a moment of regret that Captain Zahdeh, his RIO, and Bassiri and Mahmood in the second Tomcat, had to die with him.

As Shirazi waited for the cannon shells to shred his jet, he saw another specter slide into view. Below and outside the Hornet appeared another jet—an F-14. But not an F-14 like his own. This one was gray and sleek, bristling with an arsenal of missiles—AIM-9s, AIM-7s, the deadly AIM-120 AMRAAM.

Even before he glanced to his right he knew what he'd see. The second American Tomcat was sliding into firing position off Bassiri's rear quarter. The two F-14s they'd lost on their radars had somehow executed a reversal and intercepted them.

A voice in English crackled over his earphones. "Iranian F-14s entering the U.S. exclusion zone, this is Gipper One-one on guard frequency. You are being escorted by four American fighters. If you understand this transmission, waggle your wings."

For a moment Shirazi was too stunned to react. Then he gave the stick a quick left-right movement, rocking the Tomcat's wings. To his right, he saw Bassiri giving his own jet an enthusiastic wing waggle.

"You are standing into danger, Tomcat. Turn your aircraft to a heading of zero-four-zero and exit the area. Return to your base and land."

Exit the area? Return and land. It was too difficult to believe. Why would someone with three kill symbols on his jet not add two more easy victories?

He switched his UHF transmitter to guard frequency. "American Hornet, this is Jaguar One, the lead F-14 you are escorting. We understand your instructions. We are exiting the area."

The Hornet pilot gave him an affirmative nod.

Shirazi began a gentle turn to the left, and he saw the Hornet slide back. Maybe it was a trap, thought Shirazi. The Hornet could kill him anytime he chose. But if he wanted to do that, why hadn't he done it already?

"Good job, Jaguar One," said the voice in English. "Have a nice day."

Shirazi rolled out on the assigned heading. *Have a nice day?* He shook his head in amazement.

He saw Bassiri in position off his right wing. The enemy fighters were not in sight, but Shirazi knew they were back there, watching him depart.

As he descended toward his base at Dezful, Colonel Shirazi felt a sense of peace come over him. He had seen enough war. He had seen enough of Iran and its craziness. Somehow he would find a way to leave.

Ahead he could see the sprawling base of Dezful at the edge of a barren mountain range. Yes, thought Shirazi, he would leave this miserable place. He might even go to the United States. He would move to Palm Springs and play golf. Why not? Life was sweet.

CHAPTER 16

PAYBACK TIME

Mashmashiyeh, Iran
0905, Thursday, 18 March

Where is Abu?

Nearly ten minutes had elapsed since Al-Fasr sent Shakeeb to find Abu. Neither had come back. Now reports were coming in that helicopters were disgorging troops across the river, less than ten kilometers away. Abu wasn't answering his satellite phone or field radio.

Al-Fasr couldn't wait any longer. He shoved an extra magazine of nine-millimeter rounds for the SIG Sauer into a jacket pocket, then he slung an AK-74 over his shoulder.

"Shut down the equipment and set the explosives," he ordered Ali, the senior technician in the command center. The Americans would still be able to glean data from the wreckage of the computers, but that couldn't be helped.

He could hear the thunder of low-flying jets. The sound of the antiaircraft guns was a steady rumble, punctuated with the *whump* of an exploding bomb.

Time to exit.

He assembled the headquarters staff—half a dozen technicians, two cryptologists, and a sergeant. Outside the stucco building waited his command battalion, a hundred *Sherji* who were all hardened veterans of his Yemen campaign. Within the Bu Hasa Brigade he had kept these troops under his direct command. Just in case.

The *Sherji* were huddled in the cobbled pathway between rows of brown plastered buildings. They had one serviceable APC, three rusting trucks, and Al-Fasr's personal Land Rover. The bulk of the Brigade force, nearly a thousand more *Sherji*, was deployed along the southern perimeter with orders to execute a leapfrog withdrawal back to the lakes in the north.

"Has anyone seen Abu Mahmed?" Al-Fasr asked one of the *Sherji*, a captain named Akhbar.

"He's not in Mashmashiyeh, Colonel," said Akhbar. "I saw him leave in one of the fighting vehicles."

"Leave? To where? In what direction?"

Akhbar pointed westward, away from the river.

Al-Fasr kept his face expressionless while he considered this information. Abu was supposed to be commanding the eastern flank, drawing the enemy away from Mashmashiyeh and Al-Fasr's own retreat. Did Abu withdraw without waiting for orders?

He put the matter out of his mind. He was running out of time. He would deal with Abu later. It was critical that he get the Brigade out of Mashmashiyeh and make sure nothing of value was left behind to the enemy.

With that thought, he remembered an item of great value. His insurance policy.

He turned to Akhbar. "Go get the prisoner. He will come with us."

Akhbar nodded and ran fifty meters down the pathway to the hut where the prisoner was confined.

In less than a minute he was back. "We are too late, Colonel."

"What do you mean? What's happened to the prisoner?"

"The prisoner is gone. One of his guards, Karim Kouri, is dead."

Al-Fasr stared at Akhbar, still pondering this latest news, when he heard something. It was only a whisper, a fragment of sound within the din of explosions outside the village. In a millisecond of comprehension he knew where the sound came from.

"Get down!" he yelled. He was diving beneath the Land Rover when the bomb detonated.

USS Ronald Reagan

"Would someone explain to me what the hell just happened out there?" said Admiral Hightree.

Boyce shifted the cigar to the other side of his mouth and deliberately avoided looking at the admiral. Hightree wasn't a fighter pilot. He had an air-to-mud background, coming up through A-6 Intruders. Some of the finer nuances of the air-to-air business had to be explained to him.

"Looks like Brick let the Iranians off the hook," said Boyce.

"I thought I gave him the order to splash the Iranians."

Boyce kept his eyes on a spot somewhere in space. "Well, you did, but you sort of cut him some slack. I believe you said 'cleared' to kill."

Hightree's right eyebrow lifted into a question mark. " 'Cleared'? You said that, not me."

"Did I? Well, hell, Jack, it worked out the way you wanted, didn't it? We didn't lose any fighters, and we didn't get into a pissing contest with Iran. Not yet, anyway."

"Goddamn it, Captain Boyce, when I give an order, I don't expect you and everyone else in the chain of command to interpret it your own way."

"Yes, sir." Boyce knew that Hightree had to blow off some steam now. Admirals liked to be treated as admirals. After he'd huffed and puffed, Hightree would cool down and be secretly very damned glad that Maxwell had pulled it off.

Boyce settled back in his padded chair and watched the blips separate on the tactical display. The Iranians were landing at Dezful. Maxwell and his fighters were returning to their station on the BARCAP. Gritti's Marines were landing.

In the red-lighted darkness of the CIC, he allowed himself a secret smile. Hightree was right, of course. A direct order was supposed to be obeyed. He would have to chew Maxwell's ass out when he returned to the ship. But, hell, that was part of the job.

Karkeh Valley, Iran

He wasn't dead.

Rasmussen was sure of this because his head hurt like hell. And he was thirsty. Dust clogged his nostrils, and his chin bobbed on his chest, bouncing with the motion of the vehicle. He noticed with disgust that he'd vomited on his shirtfront.

Slowly, like a peephole opening in his consciousness, it came to him. He hadn't gotten off a shot with the Kalashnikov. He hadn't forced them to kill him. Someone had clubbed him from behind.

He was a prisoner again.

He gazed around him. He was in the back of a Land Rover, tethered by a nylon line to the seat frame. His wrists were bound with a plastic tie-wrap. A stream of blood from the gash on the back of his head was still wet and sticky.

In the distance he heard the deep *whump* of an explosion. He turned to look back at the village, a half mile away. A hundred-meter-wide cloud of black smoke was boiling upward from where the brown stucco buildings had been. Pieces of plaster wall and tile and rubble were flung into space like foam from a waterfall.

Holy shit. He knew what it had to be, even though he'd never seen such a weapon actually employed. An FAE—Fuel-Air Explosive. They were going to use the things in Desert Storm, he remembered. Maybe they did. They were vapor cloud bombs, a concussion weapon to pulverize the Iraqis hunkered down in the underground bunkers along the Kuwait border.

Mashmashiyeh had just been pulverized.

Abu was watching also. He wore an interested expression, like that of a man observing a firepower demonstration. "It is finished," he said. "Jamal Al-Fasr has kept his appointment with Allah. Now he is a martyr whose death we will have to avenge."

Rasmussen noticed the way Abu said it. He didn't seem especially saddened by the death of his leader.

They were bumping along in the open Land Rover, driving through a patchwork of low-hanging brush and high reeds. Abu and Rasmussen sat in the back. The driver and a machine gunner occupied the open front.

Rasmussen took his eyes off the billowing black cloud over Mashmashiyeh. "Where are we going?"

"Shut up. You have no need to know." To emphasize the point, Abu reached over and clubbed Rasmussen's cheek with the butt of his pistol.

Rasmussen shut up. Abu was right. He didn't need to know anything. He had resigned himself to the living death of captivity. It would be better if he'd been in Mashmashiyeh when the bomb flattened the village. He would be as dead as Al-Fasr.

It was odd. He could almost feel a twinge of sadness that the colonel was gone. The man was a terrorist and a murderer, but in all the years of Rasmussen's confinement, Al-Fasr was the only one who had treated him with dignity. They were fellow professionals.

Abu was something else. He was not a military professional. He had a different agenda, one that Rasmussen had not figured out. It had nothing to do with Babylon or the dream of a new country. For reasons that Rasmussen could not fathom, Abu seemed pleased that Mashmashiyeh was under siege.

More bombs were exploding to the east. Rasmussen could see the dark shapes of fighters. He recognized the distinctive twin-tailed silhouettes of the Hornets, and beneath them, working the targets like low-flying hawks, the Harriers. In the distance a pulsing sound reverberated through the steady whump of the explosions.

Helicopters. The thumping of their blades rolled over the marshes like a drumbeat. They carried troops, marines, probably. It occurred to Rasmussen that many were still in grade school when he was shot down in Iraq.

He felt a fresh wave of despair settle over him. They were so close, only a few miles. He could almost see them. They were Americans, and they didn't know he was here.

Mashmashiyeh, Iran

Al-Fasr dragged himself from beneath his Land Rover. A noise like a tornado roared inside his ears. He coughed, choking on the dust that lined his throat and clogged his nostrils. He felt a trickle of blood dripping from his nose.

He wobbled to his feet and gazed around at the tableau of devastation. His driver lay slumped over the steering wheel. The roofs were gone from the buildings on either side of the road. Bodies were tossed like bundles of laundry against the sides of buildings, into the drainage trench beside the road. A dying donkey lay on its side, thrashing its legs.

The mass of the Land Rover had saved him. By diving under the vehicle, he had shielded himself from the direct concussion of the bomb. It had to be a Fuel-Air Explosive, he thought, detonated from overhead. The bomb had smashed the village like a sledgehammer.

He felt dizzy, all his organs walloped by the impact of the explosion. His ears were still filled with the roaring noise. He tried to focus, make himself think. *Take command. Get your troops together. Execute the withdrawal plan.*

There was no one to command. Everyone he could see in the village was dead. He braced himself against the vehicle, trying to gather his thoughts, when another explosion split the air, this one a kilometer away. Across the river he could see the eruption of billowing flame and smoke.

The AAA radar command site. It had just been obliterated.

Seconds later, another explosion. And another, in a chain along the defense perimeter. They were using Fuel-Air Explosives to neutralize the defense perimeter. It was working.

Through the roiling clouds of black smoke and billowing dust, he saw something else. Dark, pulsing blobs, flying in column. *Helicopters.* His hearing was too impaired to hear the beating of the blades, but he knew what was happening.

They're coming. I've got to get out of here. Head north, up the river to the lake.

He dragged the dead driver out of the seat. The Land Rover was covered with plaster and dirt. He tried the ignition and, to his astonishment, the motor started. For another long moment he sat there, pondering what to do. His brain was still numb.

You have a way out. Follow your plan.

He put the Land Rover in gear and started down the littered path. He drove over piles of debris and shattered machinery and bodies of dead *Sherji* until he reached the edge of the village. Across the clearing he could see the old bridge over the river Karkeh. Coming from the bridge were two *Sherji*, carrying automatic weapons. Al-Fasr recognized them. They had been guards at the bridge.

"Where are you going?" Al-Fasr demanded.

They stared, not recognizing him at first. Then one said, "Is it you, Colonel?"

Al-Fasr nodded, barely hearing them. He knew he was probably unrecognizable, his face blackened from the explosion. "Get in the vehicle," he ordered. His own voice sounded distant and tinny.

"The Americans are coming, Colonel," said one of the guards. He pointed to the east. "Helicopters and gunships."

"I know. We will head north, to the lake country. Come with me."

He could see the dark blobs of the helicopters swelling in the distance. Yes, he thought, the Americans were coming. The assault force was aimed at Mashmashiyeh. It meant that their intelligence sources were better than he had given them credit for. They had not only declined to take retaliatory action against Iran, they had located the headquarters of the Bu Hasa Brigade with unerring accuracy.

How? Where had they obtained their information?

A germ of suspicion was growing in his brain, but he was still unwilling to give it a name. Not yet. He would think about it after he'd extricated himself from this snare.

The two *Sherji* climbed into the Land Rover. He shoved it into gear and lurched down the litter-strewn street to the concrete bridge. He stopped, making sure the bridge wasn't being targeted by another jet.

Nothing in immediate view. He charged ahead, speeding across the bridge, his nerves twanging in expectation of another bomb. Another earth-shuddering explosion that would rip at his guts and sear his lungs.

He reached the eastern end of the bridge.

Veering hard to the left, he drove over the embankment and down the cleft in the terrain where the river flowed. He shoved the Land Rover's front through the thick wall of reeds and swamp grass and found it—the path along the riverbank, sheltered by an overhang of scraggly trees.

The ancient path had been used for centuries by the river people and their livestock. It was barely wide enough to accommodate the Land Rover. He drove as fast as he dared without accidentally sliding into the muddy river. Perched in the back, his two *Sherji* maintained a nervous lookout for the marauding helicopters.

Five kilometers upstream was another village, smaller than Mashmashiyeh and populated by nomadic tribespeople who fished the river and raised grain in the marsh country. It would be a suitable place to stop. Perhaps he could acquire a boat and—

One of the *Sherji* was tapping his shoulder. "Colonel, ahead of us. Something coming."

Al-Fasr tried to peer through the canopy of foliage. He didn't see anything. Nor could he hear anything approaching. His ears still rang from the blast of the bomb.

Then he saw it. Through the boughs of the overhanging trees, the dark shape of a helicopter.

"Attention all Gippers, this is Grits," Gritti barked into the PRC-119. "Signal Corkstop. Repeat, Corkstop. Sea Lord, confirm that all Gipper leads acknowledge Corkstop."

"Sea Lord, roger," answered the Hawkeye controller. Gritti put down the mike and waited for Sea Lord to hear from the flight leaders. Corkstop was the signal to cease firing.

The airdales would be pissed, Gritti knew. Most of them still had unexpended ordnance on board. Back on the *Reagan* and the *Saipan*, another wave of strike jets was waiting to join the fray. They wouldn't be needed.

The air assault had gone well. Almost too well, because the *Sherji* were being exterminated faster than Gritti's marines could capture them. The marines were already inside the Bu Hasa positions, and he couldn't risk any more close air strikes.

First had come the Hornets launching HARMs against the air defense radars. Then the Harriers from the *Saipan*, which laid waste to the *Sherji* forward defense positions with their anti-personnel cluster bombs and napalm. More Hornets and Tomcats arrived with laser-guided bombs.

Then the pièce de résistance—the 550-pound CBU-72 FAE bombs.

Even Gritti, who had no sympathy for any specimen of America-hating raghead terrorist, shuddered when he saw the roiling orange-and-black clouds rising from the *Sherji* positions. It was the next best thing to a tactical nuclear weapon. The poor bastards under the vapor clouds were being transformed to Jell-O.

"What's our casualty count now, Sergeant Major?"

"Four wounded," said Plunkett. "One serious in Bravo Company. A 7.62 in the lower back. None killed. They're all on their way back to the *Saipan*."

Gritti nodded. It was better than he dared hope for in the initial assault. No matter how good your intelligence, how well you covered the contingencies, you never knew for sure what you were up against until you had your boots on the ground.

"Grits, this is Bird Dog," came another voice on the PRC-119. Bird Dog was the call sign for Lt. Col.

Aubrey Hewlitt, commanding the southern half of the pincers. "Chicago is secure," he said.

Chicago was the place name for the village of Mashmashiyeh—home base of the Bu Hasa gang. "We're still rounding up gomers, but they're mostly in bad shape. The FAE did a number on this place."

"What's the status of Capone?" Gritti asked. "Capone" was the code name he had picked for Col. Jamal Al-Fasr, his number one enemy.

"No sign of Capone yet. There's a large number of dead *Sherji* from the air strike, and we're checking bodies. He's either one of the dead, or he beat it out of town before we showed up."

"Where are you now?"

"I'm in what we think is Capone's main hooch. Hard to tell because the roof is gone and the place is blown all to hell. We're gathering intel material and interrogating prisoners. I've found something that I think may be of interest to your friend, Brick Maxwell."

"Bring it along. I'll see him in debrief."

"Roger that. Bird Dog out."

Gritti replaced the mike on the ManPack unit and gazed off to the south. From his viewpoint at the edge of the river, he could only see the flat expanse of marsh and reed-covered banks. Further away, in the direction of Mashmashiyeh, a pall of smoke was forming an overcast.

Al-Fasr was close. Gritti could sense it in the air. *You're out there, you sonofabitch. Still on the run.*

But not much longer.

Whenever he wanted, Gritti could close his eyes and see with perfect clarity the smiling, mustached face of the Bu Hasa terrorist commander. Terrorists were the rats of the world, in Gritti's opinion, and Jamal Al-Fasr was the king of the rats.

This, he would admit only to himself, was the *real* reason he had not yet turned over his command to

Colonel Parente and returned to the Pentagon to pick up his general's star.

He wanted Al-Fasr.

Revenge was sweet, but Gritti knew it was bad motivation for a military commander. It clouded your judgment, took away your objectivity. Acts of vengeance seldom worked out the way you wanted. Gritti knew all that because he had learned it the hard way.

In the case of Jamal Al-Fasr he would make an exception.

Sea Lord, the controller in the E-2C Hawkeye, reported that all the air strike flight leads had the cease-fire order. No more bombing. And the pilots weren't happy about it, just as Gritti expected.

Tough shit. He would use the Marine AH-1Ws for the finishing work, chasing down elements of the *Sherji*, hosing any remaining armored vehicles with TOW missiles and Gatling guns. The rest of the job was grunt work.

"How many prisoners?" he asked Plunkett.

"A little over a hundred. Bird Dog says he only has about fifty in Chicago."

Gritti frowned. It wasn't enough. It meant they'd killed nearly a thousand *Sherji*. Or else several hundred were still on the loose, running somewhere.

Where?

Gritti was getting a bad feeling. The assault had gone *too* well. There had been too little resistance. The exodus of *Sherji* from their positions around Mashmashiyeh was supposed to come up the river, into the—

"Grits, this is Foxhound Twenty-one." Foxhound was the call sign of one of the Whisky Cobras sweeping the river between Gritti and Mashmashiyeh. "I've got some kind of small vehicle with a gunner coming up the river road, headed your way. Am I cleared to interdict him?"

Gritti thought for a second. Something in his gut was

sending him a message. "Negative, Foxhound. Keep him tagged. I'm on my way."

Al-Fasr jammed down hard on the accelerator, no longer concerned about sliding off the road. He had a good look at the helicopter through a break in the tree line. It had the slim, menacing profile of a gunship. A Cobra, which meant it was equipped with a rotary cannon and Hellfire missiles.

The Land Rover burst into an open space, a gap of several vehicle lengths between sheltering trees. Al-Fasr saw the helicopter swivel and point its nose toward them. It had a clear shot at them.

It didn't fire.

He could see the two crewmen—the pilot in the elevated back cockpit, the gunner in front. They were watching him.

The *Sherji* atop the Land Rover was swinging the machine gun toward the helicopter. The other was setting up an RPG—rocket-propelled grenade launcher.

"Don't fire," said Al-Fasr. "Not yet."

The helicopter wasn't shooting, just keeping them in their sights. If the *Sherji* tried to fire an RPG or used the puny little 7.62 machine gun on the Land Rover, the Cobra would turn them into shredded meat.

They were toying with them. Playing some kind of cat and mouse game, not shooting, not letting him go.

If he could reach the village ahead, he would find cover. It was no more than a kilometer or two. He could meld into the warren of huts and ancient houses, find a path through the reeds, disappear in the trackless marshes.

The river made a bend to the right. For several hundred yards the Land Rover crashed through the canopy of low trees. Al-Fasr got only glimpses of the helicopter as it trailed them.

His internal alert system was shouting a steady warning. The danger level was swelling like a gathering storm. Why was the helicopter shadowing them? It was as if they were herding them, like a dog driving cattle.

To where?

Then he saw it.

Another helicopter. Al-Fasr recognized it—a UH-1W, the modernized Huey flown by the U.S. Marines. It sat in a clearing, its blades still turning. Deployed in a semicircle in front of it were a dozen troops.

Waiting for him.

Al-Fasr wrenched the Land Rover to the right, up the bank of the river. The front wheels dug into the soft earth, stalled with the wheels churning mud. Abruptly the four-wheel drive found traction and they motored up and over the embankment. They crashed through a thicket of reeds and vines, into a shallow ditch and up the opposite side.

The Land Rover burst into the clear. Ahead lay a brush-covered expanse of a hundred meters, then another stand of trees, more reeds and brush. Beyond the trees Al-Fasr could see the brown stucco of huts and scruffy buildings.

The village. Safety. All he had to do was—

Brrrrraaaaap! The earth erupted in a geyser of dirt twenty meters ahead of the Land Rover. Even with his impaired hearing, Al-Fasr recognized the unmistakable deep-throated burp of the Gatling gun.

The Cobra again. It could have killed them with a single burst, he realized. It was a warning shot. They wanted him to surrender.

They wanted him alive.

Al-Fasr yanked the steering wheel hard over, throwing the Land Rover into a skid. A shower of dirt and rocks flew up from the wheels.

"Shoot!" he yelled at the *Sherji*. "Shoot the helicopter."

He launched himself from the vehicle, hitting the

ground on his shoulder and hip, rolling over and jump-
ing to his feet. As he ran for the thicket, he heard the
chatter of the 7.62 machine gun on the Land Rover. The
Sherji were firing on the helicopter.

The burst lasted less than three seconds before it was
drowned out by the hellish din of the Cobra's rotary
cannon.

Al-Fasr didn't look back. The sound of cannon fire
abruptly stopped, and he knew how the one-sided exchange had gone. His *Sherji* had been chopped to pieces
by the Cobra's gun, but it bought him time. Maybe in
the debris and chaos of the battle, the helo crew hadn't
seen him.

He kept running. Twenty meters away lay the edge of
the thicket. He would find cover, hide, make his way to
the village. Escape to the marshes.

He was almost to the edge of the thicket when a blast
of downward air kicked up the dirt and rocks around
him, almost blowing him over. He heard the beat of helicopter blades directly over him.

He was still running when something heavy—he
thought it was the helicopter—hit him from above,
driving him headfirst into the dirt.

Al-Fasr lay facedown, stunned, the breath driven
from his lungs. He wheezed, gasped for breath. Something—whatever had fallen on him—was still on him.

He felt the weight lift from him. He was aware of
boots crunching the dirt next to his face.

He rolled to his side and gazed up at a soldier in camouflage battle dress—the one who had dropped from
the helicopter. A few meters away, the helicopter was
touching down, kicking up more eddies of dirt and dry
brush. More soldiers were scrambling out.

The soldier knelt and removed Al-Fasr's SIG Sauer
pistol. He gave him a quick pat down, taking the double-
edged Denckler fighting knife from its scabbard.

The soldiers from the helicopter walked up to them.

A man with wire-rimmed glasses said, "Hell of a jump, Sergeant. That gomer thought he was home free until you fell on him like a ton of cowshit."

Al-Fasr wheezed and sat up. Thirty meters away, wisps of smoke wafted up from the shattered Land Rover. He could see the shredded bodies of the two *Sherji* sprawled over the top. Steam was wafting from their riddled corpses.

The man in the wire-rimmed glasses wore small black eagles on his collar. A colonel, probably the commanding officer of the assault unit. He had the lined face of a man who had spent much of his career in the field. Standing next to him was the sergeant who had jumped from the helicopter. He was a heavy-set young man with a soft, angelic face.

The colonel seized Al-Fasr's collar in both hands and yanked him to his feet. For a long moment he fixed him with his penetrating brown eyes. "You look just like your picture, except for the dirty face."

"Who are you?" said Al-Fasr.

"The name is Gritti. Colonel Gus Gritti. I've been waiting a long time to meet you."

"Why is that?"

"I'm the guy you surrounded for three days in Yemen. You killed a dozen of my marines."

Al-Fasr nodded. "It was your fault. You should have surrendered."

"I'm a marine. Surrendering isn't one of the things we're good at."

"You should thank me for not killing you when I had the chance."

Gritti's face remained frozen. Al-Fasr sensed what was coming, but he was too late.

"Here's your thanks, asshole."

The blow came from behind Gritti's shoulder, gathering energy as he unleashed all the fury inside him.

Gritti's fist caught him on the cheekbone, snapping his head back like a pendulum.

Al-Fasr toppled backwards, landing spread-eagled at the feet of the sergeant who had captured him.

Gritti was standing over him, massaging his right fist, his chest heaving as if he'd just run a hundred yards.

"Are you okay, Colonel?" said the sergeant.

"Me? Never felt better in my life, son."

CHAPTER 17

THE PRIZE

Western Iran, 31,000 feet
0920, Thursday, 18 March

Right on time.

Maxwell saw the relief CAP sliding toward him from the southwest. In the distance they looked like ephemeral objects, the two Hornets slim and short-winged, gnats against the hazy Middle Eastern sky. The Tomcats stood out in contrast, massive and formidable, their folded-back delta shapes making them look like objects from space.

"Gipper One-one, Gipper Two-one and company are on station. You're off duty, Skipper."

Maxwell recognized the voice of Bullet Alexander, his XO. "Gipper One-one has you in sight. It's your show now."

The ground battle was almost over. Alexander's CAP fighters were there to discourage any more Iranian attempts to intercept the strike package as it mopped up the targets on the ground. A remote possibility, thought Maxwell. Even if the Iranians could get any more of their decrepit Tomcats airborne, they probably weren't dumb enough to challenge the American fighters.

Thirty-one thousand feet below, Maxwell could see

the veil of smoke drifting over the marshes and villages. Silhouetted against the smoke were the dark shadows of the CH-53Es lifting Gritti's marines out of Iran.

He wondered how the assault had gone. Did they really wipe out the Bu Hasa Brigade? Did they get the key leadership?

Did they get Al-Fasr?

It was too much to hope for. In the war on terrorism, the U.S. military had been efficient in destroying the enemy's bases and training camps, but the most wanted enemies—Osama bin Laden, Jamal Al-Fasr—managed to slip through their fingers. They were hard to catch, harder to kill.

Before returning to the *Reagan*, Maxwell led his flight to the tanker, a KC-10 on station over the northern edge of the Persian Gulf. After taking on two thousand pounds of fuel each, they made a long descent to the marshal point—the holding station at twenty thousand feet, fifty miles from the *Reagan*.

They spent less than ten minutes at marshal before CATCC—Carrier Air Traffic Control—called. "Your signal Charlie, Gipper One-one."

A classic clear-weather recovery. Maxwell led his flight of four around the back side of the left-hand holding pattern and started his descent. He leveled off at eight hundred feet and continued his left turn behind the ship. His flight of four Roadrunners sizzled past the starboard side of the USS *Reagan* in a smart right echelon.

Passing the bow, Maxwell broke hard to the left, grunting against the four-G pull, slowing the Hornet to pattern speed. Abeam the LSO platform he turned, extending the gear and flaps. Descending, turning across the white wake of the USS *Reagan* as he rolled onto final, he picked up the shimmering yellow "ball," the yellow optical glide slope indicator mounted on a lens at the left edge of the landing deck.

"Three-oh-one, Rhino ball, four-point-four," he
called, telling the LSO—Landing Signal Officer—that
he had the ball in sight and that his fuel remaining to-
taled 4400 pounds. "Rhino" was the call to distinguish
the Super Hornet from its smaller Hornet ancestor.

"Roger, ball," came the voice of Pearly Gates, the
VFA-36 squadron LSO.

Landing a jet fighter aboard an aircraft carrier—an
act Maxwell had performed over five hundred times—
was never routine. It was a delicately balanced maneuver requiring minute applications of stick and throttle,
backed up by the watchful eye of the LSO.

"A lii—iitle pow-werrr," called Pearly in his most
soothing LSO's sugar talk.

Maxwell squeaked on a tiny increment of throttle,
steadying the Hornet's descent toward the deck. The
yellow ball stayed fixed between the two rows of green
datum lights—precisely on glide path. The gray mass
of the USS *Reagan* swelled in his windscreen.

While he kept his eyes fixed on the lens at the left
edge of the deck, he saw in his peripheral vision the
landing deck center line, the jutting island structure to
the right, the tiny stick figures of the LSOs on the port
deck watching him. The blunt, unforgiving ramp—the
aft end of the flight deck—skimmed fourteen feet beneath his wheels.

The deck swelled to meet him.

Whump. He shoved the throttles up, just in case the
hook missed a wire. Then he felt the familiar lurch into
the straps. A number three wire, he knew. The target.

As the Hornet lurched to a stop on the deck, he pulled
the throttles back. Following the yellowshirt's signals,
he raised the tailhook, then powered forward out of the
wires and clear of the landing deck. Another Hornet—
his wingman, B. J. Johnson—was in the groove right
behind him. He taxied to his parking spot forward of the
island, then shut down the engines on signal from Mar-

tinez, the nineteen-year-old enlisted plane captain. Martinez climbed up the boarding ladder to help Maxwell unstrap.

"Message from CAG, Skipper," said Martinez over the whine of jet noise from the flight deck.

He handed Martinez his helmet and canvas navigation bag. "What message?"

"He wants you in the air wing office ASAP, sir. He says don't stop to drink, talk, or pee."

Maxwell nodded. No surprise. Boyce had been on the hot seat while Maxwell was leading the strike. He wanted to get even.

"Why didn't you shoot the sonofabitch?"

Boyce had a cigar clenched in his teeth. They were alone in the air wing office.

"There was no need to," said Maxwell. "We had the Iranian Tomcats neutralized. The trick was to make sure they understood it."

Boyce gave him that squint-eyed look Maxwell had learned to recognize. "Even though the admiral gave you a direct order to splash him?"

Maxwell felt a flash of irritation. He was still wearing his torso harness, sweat-stained from the four-hour mission. He was tired, thirsty, and in no mood for this. "You said you assigned me to the strike lead job because you trusted me to make judgment calls. Well, damn it, CAG, I made one. In my judgment, the mission was better served by not killing the Iranians. If you think I was wrong, then you can fire me."

A grin spread over Boyce's face. "Hey, that's good. That's exactly what I want you to say when the admiral gets around to reaming your ass out." He removed the cigar and studied it for a second. "For the record, you handled the intercept exactly the way I expected you to. You may consider yourself summarily disciplined for disobeying orders, and commended for doing a shit hot job. Go get a coffee and talk to the intel debriefers. Then you and I are going for a ride."

Boyce never stopped surprising him. "I just had a ride."

"A helicopter ride. You can sit back and enjoy the view. We're going to the *Saipan*."

USS Saipan

From a cabin window in the HH-60, Maxwell watched the helicopter make its approach to the *Saipan*'s deck. Like all fighter pilots, Maxwell distrusted the conglomeration of components that kept a helicopter aloft. There was something unnatural about the whirling, thumping dynamics of rotary-wing aircraft.

USS *Saipan* looked like a classic straight-deck WWII carrier. The Tarawa-class LHA assault ship had an 820-foot flight deck with nine helicopter landing spots and two aircraft elevators to the hangar deck. *Saipan* could haul an entire MEU—over 1500 marines—plus nearly a thousand crew. Its air group included twenty-four assault helicopters, half a dozen Cobra gunships, four Iroquois "Super Hueys," and a detachment of six AV-8B Harrier jets.

The Seahawk thumped down on the *Saipan*'s deck. Boyce and Maxwell clambered out and were greeted by a young marine in flight deck gear who led them to an open door in the island. Maxwell instinctively ducked under the still-rotating blades of the helo even though they were a good ten feet above his head.

Inside the passageway, they stopped and removed their cranial protectors and float coats. Maxwell was still in his sweaty flight suit, while Boyce wore his usual attire of service khakis and beat-up leather flight jacket.

"Colonel Gritti is waiting for you in the SCIF, sir,"

said the marine, a first lieutenant. SCIF was the acronym for Special Compartmentalized Information Facility—a tightly guarded compartment on the warship where the most classified business was conducted.

They wound through a series of passageways and ladders, into the bowels of the ship, to the end of a passageway. They came to a door with two sentries posted outside.

A voice from an invisible speaker said, "Put your ID cards in the tray."

They did. Half a minute passed while a video camera observed them. Boyce shuffled his feet and glowered at the unblinking eye of the camera.

Finally a buzzer sounded and they heard the sound of electronic latches releasing. The door swung open.

Gus Gritti stood in the open doorway. "Welcome to the *Saipan*, gentlemen. You should feel honored. Not many squids get invited out here to Marine Corps country."

Boyce was gazing around at the array of consoles and monitors. "What do you guys do down here? Some kind of secret Marine rituals? Orgies, human sacrifices, stuff like that?"

"You'll see. Follow me."

He led them through another door, to a smaller space guarded by two more marines armed with M16A2 combat rifles.

One of the guards opened the door. Maxwell stepped into the room, blinking in the glare of the overhead fluorescent lights.

Then he saw the man seated in the steel chair. Maxwell felt a current run through him. In a hundred bad dreams he had seen that face.

"Gentlemen," said Gritti, "allow me to introduce our guest, Col. Jamal Al-Fasr."

Boyce removed the cigar from his mouth. "Well, I'll be damned. You got the sonofabitch."

Al-Fasr gazed back at them with a sober, defiant expression.

He hadn't changed much, thought Maxwell. His hair was streaked gray, and his face had a more gaunt appearance. But the bearing was the same—the look of the supremely confident fighter pilot.

One wrist was cuffed to the steel chair. His face had a dark-colored abrasion on one cheek. He wore tailored battle dress utilities with a patch of dried blood on one sleeve.

"We've already met," said Maxwell.

"Have we?" said Al-Fasr. "Where?"

"The Red Flag competition, 1994. I was with the Navy detachment from Oceana. You were leading the United Arab Emirate fighter weapons team."

Al-Fasr nodded. "I remember."

"You scraped an Air Force F-16 pilot off on a ridge when you broke the hard deck."

"He was incompetent. He shouldn't have tried to fight me down there."

Maxwell felt the old anger coming back as he remembered the incident. Al-Fasr had been thrown out of the competition and sent back to the emirates with instructions never to return.

"We met one other time," said Maxwell.

Al-Fasr's eyes narrowed. "In the air?"

"You were in a MiG-29."

He studied Maxwell for a moment, then said, "You were flying the F/A-18?"

Maxwell nodded.

"In the canyon?" said Al-Fasr.

"I'm the guy."

"I should congratulate you. No one was ever able to beat me in a one-versus-one engagement. You were lucky. If my aircraft had not struck the ground, you would not be here."

"If your aircraft had not struck the ground, my next Sidewinder would have blown you to hell."

Al-Fasr gave him a hint of a smile. "Perhaps. Perhaps not."

The dogfight with Al-Fasr was still vivid in Maxwell's memory. He had pursued Al-Fasr's MiG through a twisting canyon in the highlands of Yemen. Al-Fasr led him into a trap—a narrow canyon bridge that looked like the eye of a needle. In an instinctive maneuver, he rolled the Hornet into a knife-edge bank and slipped through the narrow passage.

Al-Fasr had been waiting. He pounced from above, and Maxwell countered with a rolling scissors maneuver. The two jets were locked in a fight to the death, turning, depleting energy, until they were only a few hundred feet above the moonlike terrain.

And then Al-Fasr made a mistake. Dodging a Sidewinder missile from Maxwell's fighter, he scraped a wing along the crest of a ridge. In a geyser of fire and debris, the MiG-29 exploded.

Al-Fasr was dead—or so everyone thought. But at the last instant before the MiG disintegrated, Al-Fasr had ejected from the dying jet. Though badly injured, he survived and managed to escape Yemen.

"How'd you catch him?" asked Boyce.

"He got separated from his main force," said Gritti. "He was boogying for cover in the marshland. One of my marines dropped out of a helo on him like he was Hulk Hogan."

"You caught him by surprise. That's a switch. Maybe we're finally getting the drop on these assholes."

Al-Fasr seemed oblivious to the discussion. He sat with his arms crossed, examining his fingernails.

Boyce reinserted his cigar in his jaw and stood gazing down at the prisoner. "What were you doing in Iran?" he said to Al-Fasr. "Is Iran supporting the Bu Hasa Brigade?"

"Is this a discussion or an interrogation?"

"Neither. It's a question."

"Iran means nothing. It is an artificial country with no right to exist."

"So you moved in and carved out a piece for yourself?"

Al-Fasr shrugged. "I don't require the consent of an irrelevant government."

"Now that you're retired from the terrorist business," said Boyce, "who's going to run the brigade?"

"An effective military unit doesn't depend on a single leader."

"Military unit?" snorted Boyce. "Since when does a bunch of thugs who murder innocent people qualify as a military unit?"

At this Al-Fasr looked up, meeting Boyce's gaze. Before he could answer, the steel door of the compartment flew open, banging against the stop.

Ted Bronson stormed into the room, accompanied by one of the marine sentries. He was wearing khakis and desert boots, and he still had the float coat from his helicopter trip to the *Saipan*.

"What the hell's going on here?" Bronson demanded.

No one answered. Everyone in the room stared at Bronson as if he'd just landed from Uranus.

A look of cold fury covered his face. He turned on Gritti. "Who gave you the clearance to let unauthorized personnel have contact with a prisoner?"

Gritti's face darkened. "Clearance? Excuse me, but I'll remind you who captured this guy. And in case the CIA is too fucking stupid to know who this ship belongs to, let me also remind you that you're a civilian who is assisting a naval operation."

Bronson said, "This happens to be a national security operation, Colonel, and your role in it ended the moment you returned to the *Saipan*. Your orders were that any prisoners or material recovered from the raid were supposed to be handed over to the senior CIA officer in the theater. That happens to be me."

For a long moment the two men glowered at each other. Finally Boyce cleared his throat and said, "As a matter of military protocol, Colonel Gritti called his fellow strike commanders—that's Commander Maxwell and me—to a post-strike debriefing. He was kind enough to let us meet the enemy we've been trading shots with for two years. You got a problem with that, Mr. Bronson?"

Bronson swung his gaze to Boyce and Maxwell. "I want both of you out of here now. Everything you've heard or observed in this space is considered classified."

"Now wait a damned minute," said Gritti. "I'm still in command of this unit. When and how these officers leave is my call, not yours."

"Unless you want to be relieved of your command," said Bronson, "you'll butt out and leave this matter to the CIA."

It was a standoff. Gritti's eyebrows descended over his eyes. Bronson's neck turned a shade of crimson.

Al-Fasr was watching the exchange with rapt attention. His eyes flicked from Bronson to Gritti and back again. "Excuse me," he said. "I have a proposition that may interest you."

CHAPTER 18

THE GIFT

USS Saipan
1540, Thursday, 18 March

A silence fell over the room as they stared at him. Al-Fasr almost laughed at the look of surprise on their faces.

Finally Gritti, the one who took him prisoner, said, "What kind of proposition?"

"An exchange of prisoners."

"What prisoners are you talking about?" said Boyce.

"Me. For one of your people."

Another silence, more looks of surprise.

You've got them, Al-Fasr thought to himself. *You are in control.*

"One of our people?" said Boyce, exchanging glances with Maxwell. "Would you mind being more specific?"

The CIA officer, Bronson, inserted himself between them. "That's enough. Any discussions with this man will be conducted by the CIA. I want all of you out of here now."

"Wait a minute," said Maxwell. "What does he mean, one of *our* people? Did they capture any of our guys during the raid?"

"None that have been reported to me," said Gritti.

Maxwell shoved his way past Bronson. He looked down at Al-Fasr. "Okay, who are you talking about? Are you saying the Bu Hasa Brigade has an American prisoner?"

For a moment Al-Fasr held Maxwell's gaze. There was something in the American's eyes. *He knows who I mean.*

"That's correct," said Al-Fasr, still looking at Maxwell. "One whom they will release in exchange for my freedom."

"Who the hell is he talking about?" said Gritti.

"It can only be one person," said Maxwell.

Gritti and Boyce were both looking at him. "Would someone tell me what the hell's going on?" said Boyce.

"Get out of this compartment," said Bronson, his voice turning shrill. "I'm bringing charges against all of you for breach of national security."

He waved to the marine sentry at the door. "Escort these officers out of the SCIF now. They have no further access to this compartment."

Boyce said to Gritti, "Can he do that?"

"Yeah, if he wants to be an asshole about it, which he obviously does."

Boyce and Gritti turned to leave the compartment. Maxwell hesitated, still peering at Al-Fasr as if looking for confirmation.

Al-Fasr gave him a barely perceptible nod.

"Out!" yelled Bronson, giving Maxwell a shove toward the door.

USS Ronald Reagan

Petty Officer First Class Donald Carson was getting a bad feeling.

Standing behind Lieutenant DiLorenzo, watching the

officer's fingers fly over the keyboard of the maintenance computer, Carson had the feeling that he was standing in quicksand.

"See how easy it is," said DiLorenzo.

It *was* easy, observed Carson. Easier than he had ever imagined. DiLorenzo had managed to open up the LAN—Local Area Network—of the air wing maintenance department. Displayed on the monitor was the page listing the periodic inspection dates of each aircraft in the wing.

It was nearly midnight. Carson and DiLorenzo were alone in the Quality Assurance compartment on the second deck. DiLorenzo had locked the door. Though most of the ship was quiet, the night maintenance shift was at work in the shop spaces and on the hangar deck.

Carson was an AM1— Aviation Structural Mechanic First Class. He had been in the Navy eighteen years, which wasn't long enough to retire, but too long to still be only a first class petty officer. As the quality assurance petty officer in the squadron maintenance department, Carson was responsible for verifying each procedure of the aircraft corrosion inspections.

"There are the dates for the last corrosion inspections on aircraft 306, 307, and 309," said DiLorenzo. As Carson watched, DiLorenzo erased the dates from nearly a year ago and inserted new dates. Exactly seven days ago. Each of the inspection items was checked off and had the name of the quality assurance rep from each work center.

Carson's bad feeling was getting worse.

"Is it really necessary to hack into the LAN like this?" said Carson. "Couldn't we just do it the normal way and actually run the inspections?"

"This is all a paper game," said DiLorenzo. "It's about numbers. We're in competition with all the other Hornet squadrons, and we won't make the necessary numbers unless we do it this way."

"But what if there really is some corrosion in those jets?" said Carson. "What if something is wrong with them? Our pilots have to fly those things, and they trust us to do it by the book."

DiLorenzo turned from the computer and looked at Carson. "You know I would never compromise safety. That's not the issue. These jets were inspected a little over a year ago and they were clean as a whistle. This is a three-year cycle, and there isn't any way we should have to be taking them apart this soon. This stuff is all bullshit—just a game the bean counters make us play. How could these jets have corrosion? They're damned near brand-new."

Carson wasn't so sure. He wished he hadn't been dragged into this, but he didn't know how to avoid it. He was afraid of DiLorenzo. DiLorenzo had been a chief petty officer himself, and he knew ways to make life a living hell for any poor bastard who didn't do things his way.

"How many do we have to do like this?" asked Carson.

"Just these two. Getting past these two inspections will put us ahead of the other two Hornet squadrons in the maintenance production numbers. It will decrease our short-term workload by half."

DiLorenzo grinned and turned back to the computer. "Think of it like it's a pit stop at the Daytona 500. Something Jeff Gordon would understand."

Carson nodded. DiLorenzo had found his soft spot. Carson was a native of north Florida, and NASCAR was practically a religion to him.

"Okay, but what if someone hears about what we did?"

DiLorenzo's hands froze over the keyboard. He turned back to Carson and his voice hardened. "No way is that going to happen. No way. You got it? If anyone should ask about this, you deny everything. This comes directly from Commander Manson, and he's our boss."

Then DiLorenzo softened his voice and flashed another grin. "And besides, everyone on the corrosion inspection team is going to get a Navy Achievement Medal. Plus, you and I, Carson, are going to get Navy Commendation Medals. I don't need to tell you how that will look on your upcoming promotion board. So will the Battle 'E' that the squadron is going to win because of us. Medals mean promotion points, which means you beat out the competition. You're gonna have a whole new row of ribbons on your rack. You'll finally get that chief petty officer's hat you've been wanting all these years."

DiLorenzo's voice had the warm charm of a natural salesman. Carson felt himself being swept up in the officer's spell. He had never received any decoration higher than the Navy Achievement Medal, which these days was almost a rubber stamp award. But a Navy Commendation Medal! And the Battle "E." He could see the look on his wife's face at the award ceremony back in Oceana.

DiLorenzo returned to the keyboard and continued talking as he typed. "Commander Manson takes care of his people. He's about to screen for his own squadron command, you know. He'll be looking for loyal troops like us for his maintenance department. If that happens, you're not only looking at promotion to chief petty officer, but maybe even Senior Chief. How would you like that?"

He'd like it a lot, Carson had to admit. More than anything else, he wanted to put on a chief's hat. His last three evaluations by division officers had been lousy. So lousy that he had missed promotion to chief petty officer.

Now he was in a bad spot. If the Navy separated him before he got his twenty in, he would have problems getting a decent job on the outside. He might be a good aviation mechanic, but he wasn't good enough to make chief petty officer, a dismal fact that his record would reflect.

He had a teenage son still at home, and a plump and disgruntled wife who wanted nothing less than a nice new home that was far away from military housing.

Yes, damn it, more than anything he wanted to exchange his sailor's dungarees for the khaki uniform of a chief petty officer. It would be the culmination of his Navy career.

And why not? It was a fair reward for bending the rules a little. A win-win, good for him, good for the squadron.

So why do you still have this bad feeling in your gut?

He tried to ignore the feeling. "Uh, how did you manage to get into the master computer?" he asked. "I thought that was hack proof."

"Simple. I used the air wing maintenance officer's password."

"So it looks like he made the entries?"

"Sure."

"How do you know his password?"

"Guesswork. I figured that he used the same thing almost everyone else does—a family member's name. In this case, his wife. Same as you."

Carson's bad feeling was getting worse. He felt himself sinking deeper into the quicksand.

USS Saipan

"It's Rasmussen, isn't it?" said Maxwell. He glowered at Bronson. "That's who Al-Fasr is talking about, isn't it?"

Bronson ignored him and slammed the door of the compartment where Al-Fasr was confined.

"I told you to get out of here," said Bronson. He shoved Maxwell toward the main door of the SCIF. "That's an order."

"Screw your order. They've got Rasmussen, don't they? And Al-Fasr wants to be exchanged for him."

Instead of answering, Bronson seized his arm and aimed him toward the door. Maxwell yanked his hand off his arm. "Answer my question, goddamn it!"

"If you don't leave this space immediately, I'll have you confined to the brig."

"You lied when I asked you before about Rasmussen." The anger was boiling up in Maxwell. "You knew Rasmussen was alive, and you knew where he was. You're stonewalling it."

Boyce and Gritti were watching the scene with rapt attention. The marine sentry had a worried look on his face, glancing from Gritti to Bronson.

Bronson said, "You are now several fathoms out of your depth, Maxwell. Before you completely trash your petty little career, I advise you to return to your ship and keep your nose out of national security matters."

"He's right, Brick," said Boyce. "Let's go."

Maxwell wasn't finished. "Wait a minute here. A friend of mine has been left behind in Iraq for over a dozen years. And this so-called intelligence professional knew it all along. Didn't you, Bronson?"

Bronson gave him another shove. Maxwell shoved him back. "Do that one more time and I'll break your fucking nose."

"Corporal, arrest this man," Bronson said to the sentry.

Gritti stepped in before the young marine could respond. "Belay that, Corporal. I'm in charge here. Brick, we're leaving. Now."

Maxwell hesitated, still thinking about smashing Bronson's face. It would be worth it. Almost.

"We're outta here, Brick," said Boyce. "Let's go cool off and talk."

For another moment Maxwell glowered at Bronson, then he turned and followed Boyce and Gritti out of the SCIF compartment. They stood in the passageway while Maxwell tried to control the anger that still seethed in him.

The two sentries at the compartment door watched with curious expressions.

"Rasmussen is alive," said Maxwell. "Bronson has known it all along."

"Like he said, it's an intelligence matter," said Boyce. "Not our business."

"Raz is *my* business. He's *my* friend, CAG. He's one of *us*. The CIA wants to leave him behind for some reason that Bronson won't tell us."

"We don't know that it's Rasmussen. We don't even know that Al-Fasr isn't yanking our chain. The sonofabitch is a terrorist and a murderer. It's probably all bullshit."

"It's not bullshit," said Gritti.

Boyce and Maxwell stared at him.

"Excuse me?" said Maxwell.

Gritti glanced once at the curious sentries, then gave Boyce and Maxwell a nod. "Follow me."

They walked in silence to Gritti's stateroom.

Gritti closed the door, removed his cap, then took a seat at his desk. He twirled the combination to his safe and extracted a plastic-wrapped object. "This was recovered from a half-destroyed building in Mashmashiyeh this morning by one of my company commanders. The room where it was found appeared to have been used to confine a prisoner."

He handed the object to Maxwell. It was a notebook, the kind used by school children, with ruled pages and a hard cardboard cover. The notebook showed the signs of heavy use, and was warped and frayed around the edges.

Maxwell opened it to the first page. At the top of the page was a handwritten entry:

> *Volume III: The daybook of*
> *Lt. Cmdr. Allen S. Rasmussen, USN.*

The breath nearly went out of him as he read the page.

> *When I left Abu Graib this morning, the Iraqis kept the two volumes of my daybook. They obviously don't want any written record of my captivity here to leave Baghdad.*
> *My new captors—they call themselves* Sherji— *have provided me with this new notebook. I have no idea why they have taken custody of me, nor what they intend to do with me. If they try to extract information from me by torture, they will become as frustrated as the Iraqis . . .*

Maxwell had to sit down. His eyes blurred with tears. A jumble of thoughts flooded his mind as he leafed through the pages of the worn notebook. He could see ink smudges, fingerprints, tangible traces of the man he once knew as Raz Rasmussen. The entries had gaps of several days, sometimes weeks. The writer kept records of his diet, the weather, his dreams, thoughts about death and captivity. Thoughts about his wife and children.

The last entry was dated 18 March.

Today.

A chill came over Maxwell. Only a few hours ago, Rasmussen had been writing in this book. They had been so close. He could almost feel Raz's presence in the pages of the book.

Gritti said, "I was supposed to turn it over to Bronson along with all the other documents we found."

"Why didn't you?"

"I don't know. Something about Bronson bothers me. I wanted you to see it first."

Maxwell nodded. He held the notebook up. "Can I take this?"

"Sorry. Everything we recovered in Iran goes to the CIA."

"What if it disappears after you hand it over to them?"

"That possibility crossed my mind." Gritti reached in the safe again and extracted a file folder and handed it to Maxwell. "That's why I made this."

Maxwell skimmed through the folder. It contained a sheaf of pages—copies from the pages of Rasmussen's notebook.

"You don't know where it came from," said Gritti. "I'm trusting you to use it with discretion."

Maxwell held the folder as if it were a holy object. The full gravity of what Gritti was doing struck him. He was risking his career and his general's star.

"Why are you sticking your neck out like this, Gus?"

"Remember when I was caught on the ground with my team in Yemen?"

Maxwell nodded. "Al-Fasr suckered us in."

"You stuck your neck out for me. You violated the Rules of Engagement by coming down to bomb the *Sherji*, and you saved our butts. Consider this a payback."

It occurred to Maxwell that perhaps he had underestimated the marine. Gus Gritti was more than just a superb infantry commander. He was a righteous warrior and a priceless friend.

"Yes, sir. I'll use it with discretion. You have my word on it."

*   *   *

The Seahawk helicopter lifted from the deck of the *Saipan*, then lowered its nose and accelerated toward the distant silhouette of the USS *Reagan*, four miles across the Gulf.

Boyce took his eyes from the cabin window. He said to Maxwell, "Whatever you're about to do, don't. That's an order, by the way."

"What makes you think I'm about to do anything?"

"I've seen you in this mode before. You're like a goddamn terrier with a rat. Leave it alone, Brick. Let the professionals handle it."

"Meaning Bronson and his fellow professionals?"

"Meaning the CIA and the intelligence community. It's their show, not yours."

"Do you think they will exchange Al-Fasr for Raz?"

"I don't know. They don't tell me how to run an air wing, I don't tell them how to run an intelligence operation."

For a while Maxwell kept his silence, watching the deep blue water slip beneath the helicopter. In his satchel was the folder with the copied pages from the notebook. Bronson was right about one thing: He *was* several fathoms out of his depth. He should shut up and let the professionals handle it.

To hell with that.

"CAG, suppose we run this by the admiral."

Boyce rolled his eyeballs. "Hightree already wants to court-martial you for not splashing the Iranian Tomcats. I advise you to stay the hell out of his sight for the rest of the cruise."

"He'll get over that. The possibility of a missing POW is something he should know about. He can run it up the chain of command."

Boyce didn't answer. He took his time unwrapping a cigar, snipping off the end, wetting it, inserting it in a corner of his mouth.

"Hightree undoubtedly has been briefed about the

capture of Al-Fasr. Being an admiral and a political animal, he will be glad to take the credit for grabbing one of the most wanted terrorists on the planet. I'm willing to bet that he has zero interest in giving his prize back in exchange for a prisoner no one knows exists."

"*We* know he exists. Are we going to leave him behind again?"

Boyce clamped down on the cigar and shot Maxwell a look of pure exasperation. "You know, Maxwell, sometimes you are a huge pain in the ass."

"Yes, sir. So I've been told."

CHAPTER 19

INFORMER

USS Ronald Reagan
1815, Thursday, 18 March

Boyce was right. The admiral hadn't forgotten about the Iranian fighters.

"Commander Maxwell, do you have the slightest notion what a direct order means?"

"Yes, sir. I take full responsibility for my decision about the Iranian fighters. But that's not what I'm here to talk to you about."

Hightree stopped pacing the deck of the flag bridge and glanced at his watch. "I'm waiting for a call from Fifth Fleet. What's on your mind?"

"Al-Fasr, the terrorist leader we captured. In my opinion, sir, we should exchange him for an American POW the Bu Hasa Brigade is holding."

Hightree stopped in mid-stride and peered at Maxwell. "Excuse me? Am I missing something here? What's this about an American POW?"

Maxwell told him about Al-Fasr's proposition. Then he told him about Raz Rasmussen, omitting any mention of the notebook that Gritti had captured.

Hightree was speechless for a while. He took several minutes to ponder the information.

"Who else knows about this besides you?"

"Captain Boyce and Colonel Gritti. And Bronson, the CIA officer."

"Sounds to me like you've blundered into an area that's off limits, Commander Maxwell."

"Yes, sir, I may have. But Raz Rasmussen was our fellow naval aviator. If there's any possibility that he's alive and out there, we should do whatever has to be done."

"Including get into a pissing contest with the CIA?"

"If that's what it takes."

"What do you expect me to do about it?"

"Intercede. Run it up the chain of command, see if they'll approve the exchange."

Maxwell caught the look of distress that flashed over Hightree's face. The admiral turned away for a minute, seeming to search for an answer somewhere in the haze over the Persian Gulf.

Boyce was right about Hightree, Maxwell decided. He was too cautious, too sensitive to the currents of politics. He wouldn't swim against the stream.

And then Hightree surprised him.

"I'll bring it to Fifth Fleet," he said. Hightree's immediate boss, a vice admiral based in Bahrain, commanded both the U.S. Fifth Fleet and the U.S. Naval Forces Central Command. "If he's convinced that we have a POW left behind, then I assure you he'll take it all the way up the chain. All the way to the President, if necessary."

Maxwell was stunned. "Thank you, Admiral Hightree."

"Until you hear otherwise from me personally, this matter is classified Special Category Top Secret, compartmentalized. No one else is to know about it. Got that?"

"Yes, sir."

"Now get out of here before I change my mind and court-martial you for violating orders today."

"Yes, sir." Maxwell turned to leave.

"Oh, Skipper . . ." Hightree was using the familiar title for a unit commander.

"Sir?"

"I want to thank you for exercising good judgment with the Iranians today."

"Yes, sir."

"Dismissed."

"Aye, aye, sir." Maxwell left the flag bridge smiling, and closed the steel door behind him.

Manama, Bahrain

Meeting an informer, reflected Tyrwhitt, was always a crapshoot. You never knew what would happen. Even in Bahrain, which was a shrine of peace compared to Baghdad or Damascus, you could get your throat sliced.

"Keep walking," said the informer. "Follow this street through the souk."

Because of its multitude of immigrant workers, Bahrain was an amalgam of cultures—Persian, Indian, Filipino, Indonesian, and a melting pot of Arab factions, most of them in conflict with each other. Like Al-Qaeda and Hamas, the Bu Hasa Brigade had placed agents in Bahrain to glean tidbits of information from informers inside the American compounds. And just as in every intelligence-gathering group, some of the informers were double agents who worked both sides of the street.

Darkness had fallen over the souk, and in the yellowish glow from the lighted market stalls, it was difficult to see faces. With his dark suntan and scruffy beard, wearing a checkered kaffiyeh and the ubiquitous *gellebiah*, Tyrwhitt could pass for an Arab. The informer, who was a head shorter than Tyrwhitt, also wore a kaffiyeh and a filthy chambray shirt over khaki trousers.

Tyrwhitt kept walking. Mustafa Ashbar had tapped his most closely held sources to put Tyrwhitt in contact with the informer. The man was nervous, his eyes darting in each direction. He took furtive, birdlike steps as he spoke. "Here, at this corner, we turn and follow the back street."

The street was nearly deserted, all the stalls closed and their proprietors gone to the coffee house. Tyrwhitt was having a hard time getting the informer to talk.

"Okay, I'll ask again," said Tyrwhitt. "Why did the Bu Hasa attack the oil tanker and the Kuwaiti outpost?"

The informer made a sucking sound through his teeth. "Why do you think it was the Bu Hasa?"

"Bodies. Iranian bodies. Even the Iranians are not that stupid."

"Then you already know the answer. Someone wished to provoke an attack from the Americans."

"What someone? Al-Fasr?"

Another sucking sound. "Who else? Isn't that why you attacked the Bu Hasa base?"

"Sure," said Tyrwhitt. They both knew these questions were just warm-ups. Part of the game to start a dialogue. "But why did Al-Fasr want that to happen?"

"He didn't. He wanted the Americans to destabilize Iran. Perhaps topple the government in Tehran. With Iran and Iraq broken into pieces, he could establish his own state in the low country. The place he called Babylonia."

Tyrwhitt noticed the informer's use of the past tense. Al-Fasr *wanted* the Americans to destabilize Iran. Now they were getting down to the real purpose of the meeting. Did the Bu Hasa Brigade—what was left of it—know that their leader was alive and captured?

"Now that Al-Fasr's base at Mashmashiyeh has been destroyed, where is he now?"

The informer shot him a wary look. "You know."

"Perhaps, perhaps not. Tell me."

"He is nowhere. Dead, killed by your bombs."

Tyrwhitt nodded, not sure who was duping whom. Either the informer was passing disinformation, or he was unaware that Al-Fasr had been captured.

"Then who is commanding the Bu Hasa Brigade?" asked Tyrwhitt.

"It has broken down into small units since the attack," said the informer. "No new leader has come forward yet to reassemble them."

Bullshit, thought Tyrwhitt. He knew enough about terrorist organizations to know that even when you cut off the head of the snake, another head always emerged.

As they walked, Tyrwhitt kept scanning the darkened buildings. It occurred to him that the informer might be leading him into a trap. It seemed unlikely. If anything, the little Arab was more worried for his own safety. He was nervous as a bird, his eyes darting left and right.

"Tell me about the Bu Hasa Brigade," said Tyrwhitt. "What assets do they have left? Guns, missiles, how many, where they're deployed."

This was more to the informer's liking. He spoke haltingly at first, then warmed to his subject, spouting information in bursts of Arabic. Though Tyrwhitt had a basic command of the language, he was having trouble following the slurred, consonant-rolling dialect. He tried to place the accent. North Africa, maybe. Libya or Morocco.

As the man spoke, they continued along the darkened back street, turning into a narrow lane that doubled back to the main souk. At the end of the lane Tyrwhitt could see the yellow lights of the stalls in the central marketplace.

He waited while the man finished talking about Bu

Hasa's defenses—a few ZSU 23- and 57-millimeter antiaircraft guns, and some SA-7 man-portable missiles. As far as he knew, all the SA-2 batteries had been obliterated in the strike.

Tyrwhitt listened in silence. None of this was new— they already had good satellite and unmanned air recon photos of the installations—but it gave him a chance to gauge the informer's veracity.

Who was he? Tyrwhitt wondered. Why was he willing to inform? Money was always an enticement, but the ancient rite of bribery hadn't been effective with the Islamic extremist groups. They were motivated more by hate than by earthly comfort.

Maybe this one wasn't a true believer. Or maybe he was disenchanted with the crazies in the Bu Hasa camps.

Or maybe he's setting me up.

It was time to go fishing.

"Tell me about the prisoner you're holding," said Tyrwhitt.

The informer looked at him in surprise. "Prisoner?"

"You know the one I mean. The American pilot. Where did he come from? Iraq?"

The informer looked away, shielding his eyes. "I don't know about a prisoner."

Tyrwhitt could tell by the changed attitude that they'd gotten into new territory. The informer no longer had a script to follow.

"Sure you do," said Tyrwhitt. "Everybody knows about him. He was captured during the first Gulf War, then Saddam Hussein turned him over to the Bu Hasa Brigade before the second war."

He was shooting in the dark, but he could tell by the informer's reaction that he'd struck something.

"You said you wished to talk about the Bu Hasa organization," said the informer. "I have told you what I know."

"That was just for starters," said Tyrwhitt. He pulled an envelope from the inner pocket of his *gellebiah*. "This is half the amount we agreed on. Tell me about the prisoner and you will receive the rest."

The informer looked at the envelope with renewed interest. Tyrwhitt decided that he had judged him correctly. The little bugger wasn't a dedicated terrorist. Running through his veins was the blood of a capitalist.

The informer reached for the envelope, but Tyrwhitt held it just out of his grasp. "I believe you were about to mention a prisoner . . ."

The informer looked around again, then fixed his eyes on the envelope. "I may have seen such a person. In the compound at Mashmashiyeh."

"An American?"

"It is possible."

"What was his name?"

"I don't know. Al-Fasr called him 'Navy.' "

Tyrwhitt nodded, showing no expression. *Navy*. It had to be him. The missing pilot. "Why would Al-Fasr keep such a prisoner?"

The informer shrugged. "We have asked the same question. It seemed to amuse him. Perhaps he thought the prisoner would be useful if—"

He froze. Tyrwhitt hadn't been watching the narrow passageway ahead of them. He was absorbed in the tale of the prisoner. They had nearly passed the darkened entrance when he realized what was happening.

There were two of them, wearing black, one on either side, almost invisible in the inky darkness.

The informer saw them and let out a yelp. He whirled to run, but he was too late. The man in the nearest doorway intercepted him. He grabbed the informer's arm, yanking him nearly off his feet, slamming him face-first into the wall of the ancient building.

Tyrwhitt stepped backward as the second man in black bolted from the doorway toward him. He saw something glint in the darkness. *Amateurs*, he thought. They were using knives for this job. They thought they would be quiet and quick.

He watched the assassin lunge toward him, driving the knife blade from waist level at Tyrwhitt's midsection. Tyrwhitt balanced himself, waiting for the right moment. Timing was everything.

As the assassin committed his weight and energy, Tyrwhitt sidestepped and seized the man's wrist with one hand. Stepping into him, he folded his arm over the man's wrist and levered it upward in one violent motion. He heard a wrist bone snap with an audible *crack*, and the assassin shrieked in pain. The knife clattered to the cobblestone path.

Just like training, Tyrwhitt thought. Except that in the CIA school at Quantico they hadn't been allowed to actually break bones.

The assassin backpedaled, trying to regain his balance. Tyrwhitt coiled, then drove the heel of his hand into the man's chin, putting all his weight into it. He felt bones and gristle crunch as the man's head snapped backward. He flopped backward onto the cobblestones and lay motionless. From deep in his throat came a low, gurgling death rattle.

Tyrwhitt whirled to confront the second assassin. He was crouching over the body of the informer. A dark pool was already spreading over the cobblestones from the body of his victim.

For a moment, Tyrwhitt and the assassin locked gazes in the darkened street. Tyrwhitt could see the man's face beneath the black kaffiyeh. He had a black mustache, a beak of a nose, dark, piercing wolf's eyes. He held the knife at the ready, seeming to consider whether to finish the job.

"Your move," said Tyrwhitt. He slid his hand beneath the *gellebiah*.

The assassin took a glance at his fallen colleague.

The man lay spread-eagled on his back, staring with sightless eyes at the night sky.

The assassin reached a decision. Keeping his eye on Tyrwhitt, he backed away, moving toward the yellow lights at the end of the passageway.

Tyrwhitt withdrew the Beretta from its holster beneath the *gellebiah*. He watched the man, not wanting to fire the noisy weapon, but prepared in case he produced a gun of his own.

The assassin whirled to run, but he was too late.

The shape appeared behind him, seeming to materialize from the gloomy darkness of the passageway. In the thin light Tyrwhitt saw something glint, a movement across the man's face—and he slumped to the ground.

The dark shape in coarse dark trousers and long, loose shirt stooped over the body. He wiped the blade of his *kukri* killing knife on the dead assassin's shirt. The man's sliced throat was gushing blood onto the cobblestones.

"It's about time you showed up," said Tyrwhitt.

"You didn't need me," said Mustafa Ashbar. "I was only worried that you might shoot him."

Which he had almost done, Tyrwhitt reflected, and it would have been a mistake. Street violence, at least with firearms, was not a common event in Bahrain. The Bahraini police would have come running.

Tyrwhitt checked the other two bodies. The first assassin lay silent, his head tilted back at an unnatural angle.

The informer lay in his own thickening pool of blood. He had been stabbed numerous times, it appeared. The front of his shirt was a sodden red mess.

Tyrwhitt shook his head in frustration. Damn it, he should have expected the attack. If he'd been alert, he could have saved the informer. He had almost gotten the story about the American prisoner when these ragheads popped up. A fucking amateur performance.

From around the corner he heard voices, shuffling footsteps. Curious locals would find the bodies and summon the police.

Time to disappear.

Mustafa was sheathing his *kukri*. Tyrwhitt stared at the weapon. It was nearly a foot long, with a wide, curved blade. He wondered how many throats it had sliced.

"Was it necessary to kill him with that thing?"

"Of course," said Mustafa. "He was a terrorist."

Well, thought Tyrwhitt, he couldn't argue with that. As usual, Mustafa made sense.

"I think it's time for a drink," he said.

USS Ronald Reagan

Dusk was settling over the Gulf. Through the tinted glass of the flag bridge, Maxwell could see the dark silhouettes of the *Reagan*'s escorting warships etched against the surface of the sea.

Hightree had sent the flag yeoman and his aide off the bridge. Maxwell and Boyce were alone with the admiral.

"It seems we have kicked over a hornet's nest," said Hightree. "I've been given orders—strictly verbal because none of this will be in writing—that everything we know or think we know about the POW matter is to be expunged. It doesn't exist. Nothing further will be discussed or sent through channels." He looked at Maxwell, then Boyce. "Is that understood, gentlemen?"

"May I ask from whom the orders come?" said Maxwell.

"No, you may not."

Maxwell felt the same old anger ignite inside him. What the hell was wrong with these people? He saw Boyce giving him a warning look. He knew he should just thank the admiral and leave the bridge. Follow orders and shut up.

"Admiral," he said, "that's a crock of shit."

Hightree looked like he had been walloped with a mallet. "Excuse me? I must have misheard you, Commander. Did you say something about a crock of shit?"

Boyce rolled his eyes and turned to stare out the tinted window.

"With all due respect, sir," said Maxwell, "I have spent my career believing that we didn't abandon our soldiers who were captured by the enemy. For some reason, our country is leaving one of our colleagues— yours and mine—behind. I find that deeply offensive, Admiral."

Hightree let several seconds pass while he composed his thoughts. His voice softened. "Just this once, I'm going to overlook your choice of words, Commander Maxwell. For what it's worth, I have the same feelings. But it's not our job as officers to interpret orders or to read things into them. As Battle Group Commander, I am expected to implement the orders that come down from my superior officers. If I'm not willing to do that, then I should stand down and ask to be relieved. The same is true of you, Commander Maxwell."

Maxwell's anger was spilling out of him. Hightree was right, he thought. He *should* ask to be relieved. Tell them to take this job and stuff it. These were orders his conscience wouldn't allow him to follow.

Something was holding him back. *What about Raz? How is quitting going to save him?*

He took a deep breath, trying to gain control of his feelings. He heard Boyce making a production of clearing his throat.

"Yes, sir," he heard himself say. "You are correct, and I apologize."

"Good," said Hightree. "We have to trust that our people in the intelligence services know what they're doing. Let's comply with our orders and get on with our jobs."

Hightree's tone made it clear the meeting was over. Boyce was already on his way to the door. "Thanks for carrying the ball on this one, Admiral," Boyce said. "Your point is well taken. Skipper Maxwell and I will put the matter behind us."

He gave Maxwell a meaningful look. Maxwell allowed himself to be towed out the door. He kept his mouth shut.

Manama, Bahrain

Just as Tyrwhitt expected, Bronson was pissed off. But this time he was more pissed off than usual. Something else was bugging him.

"It was you, wasn't it?" Bronson demanded.

There was no point in playing dumb, Tyrwhitt thought. "Sure it was me. What's the problem?"

They were in Bronson's private cubicle in the SCIF in Bahrain. Tyrwhitt hadn't yet written his report about the appointment with the Bu Hasa informer.

"Problem? An agent kills three Arabs in a semi-friendly Arab city in order to obtain one miniscule scrap of information that we already possessed. That's the problem."

More than one scrap, mate, thought Tyrwhitt to himself. The scrap about the American prisoner he was keeping to himself. One of those nice-to-know tidbits tucked away in his memory bank. Just in case.

"Actually, I only killed two of the buggers." It would just complicate matters if he mentioned Mustafa's share of the killing. "They jumped me in the back street behind the souk, and one of them took out the informer with a knife. I dispatched one with my hands, the other with the knife."

Bronson gave him a strange look. "Your hands?"

Tyrwhitt held his hands up. "Lethal weapons." He smiled.

A frown passed over Bronson's face. "The Bahrain chief of domestic security has already speculated that someone from this station did the killings."

"Clever chap, isn't he?"

"Our operations in Bahrain depend on cordial relations with the local government."

"Perhaps we should ask them to protect us against assassins."

Bronson's face darkened. "Don't be a wiseass with me, Tyrwhitt. I'm your immediate superior at this station. Your assignment was to meet an informer, ask specific questions, and report back to me. You were not authorized to commit executions at your own discretion."

Tyrwhitt was about to tell him that discretion had nothing to do with it, that the beady-eyed little fuckers were coming at him with knives.

He held his tongue. Bronson was a dickhead, and nothing he could say would ever change that. "Yes, sir, I understand. I promise not to kill anyone again without your permission."

He could tell by Bronson's blazing eyes that he wasn't buying it.

CHAPTER 20

THE SQUEEZE

USS Ronald Reagan
1905, Thursday, 18 March

Maxwell closed the door to his stateroom and took a seat at the fold-out steel desk. A stack of squadron paperwork lay on the desk. Beside it was a tray of unfinished correspondence.

The fatigue from the four-hour mission over Iran and the trip to the *Saipan* had caught up with him. A jumble of conflicting thoughts was crisscrossing his mind. He was still perplexed by the reaction from Hightree and the chain of command about the prisoner story.

He knew in his gut that the admiral was right. An officer's job was to implement orders, not interpret them. If he wasn't willing to do that, he should pack it in.

Well, damn it, maybe I will.

He opened the laptop computer on his desk and clicked it on. While he waited for it to boot up, he fumbled through a stack of CDs. He found a Berlioz—*Symphonie Fantastique,* his favorite. He slipped it into the player and let the music wash over him.

Claire was still on board the *Reagan*, and she would be wondering what happened to him. With her journalist status, she knew that the strike was finished and successful. She would know, too, that no jets were lost. He wanted to see her, tell her about the Iranian jet, tell her he loved her.

But not yet. He had some thinking to do.

As he usually did when he was fumbling for answers, he looked to the framed pictures on the bulkhead. Maxwell's heroes gazed at him from their framed portraits.

To the left was the bristling, energy-filled image of Theodore Roosevelt. A bit of Roosevelt, he thought, would be a good quality in every military commander. All the way up the chain, from Battle Group Commander to the Commander-in-Chief.

In the middle was a black-and-white photograph of a grinning young man in the cockpit of an A-4 Skyhawk. He was tall, lanky, wearing a dark, bushy mustache. At first glance, visitors thought the picture was Brick Maxwell. Then they read the handwritten caption on the bottom: LT. CMDR. HARLAN MAXWELL.

Maxwell's father, retired Vice Admiral Harlan Maxwell, had been a powerful but distant icon in his life. Only in the last few years had Maxwell and his father reconciled after years of estrangement.

To the right was a portrait of a man in eighteenth-century dress. He had a handsome, longish face, a wig, and a serious expression. In Maxwell's opinion Captain James Cook was the ultimate role model—explorer, scientist, navigator, man of action. Like the fictional Captain Kirk in *Star Trek*, Cook boldly went where no man had gone before.

What would Cook do? Maxwell wondered. Going boldly didn't seem to be a good idea now.

He closed his eyes and rubbed his temples with his fingers. He'd been in the Navy nearly twenty years, including his tour at NASA. He'd had several occasions to question his own suitability as a military officer. He would never be an unquestioning follower of orders like Admiral Hightree.

But Hightree might have been right about the CIA. The intelligence services—CIA, FBI, NSA—knew what they were doing.

The hell they did.

He thought of several calamities caused by flawed intelligence. The missed warnings about the coming attack on the World Trade Center in September 2001. The bombing of a wrong target—the Chinese embassy—in Yugoslavia. A strike against a pharmaceutical plant—misidentified as a weapons factory—in Sudan.

The worst, in his own experience, was in Yemen. A Navy intel officer conspired with a terrorist—Jamal Al-Fasr—to kill over two hundred sailors and marines, and nearly caused the loss of the *Reagan.*

He thought again of Al-Fasr, replaying in his mind the scene aboard the *Saipan.*

I have a proposition that may interest you.

What kind of proposition?

An exchange of prisoners.

Bronson had cut him off before Al-Fasr gave the name of the prisoner. It was possible, Maxwell supposed, that it might be someone other than Rasmussen. Someone they hadn't accounted for.

But there was the notebook. Raz's journal.

Maxwell kicked off his boots, then peeled off the sweat-caked flight suit. He slipped into a pair of nylon warm-ups and a T-shirt, then settled back into the padded desk chair. He picked up the folder and began reading where he had left off.

> *The Colonel—he doesn't allow anyone to use his real name—is a different breed of man than the guerrillas in his brigade. He has a western education and has been trained in the U.S. as a fighter pilot. I have not yet determined what drives*

*him—why he has taken up arms against the U.S.
and the developed countries. He doesn't seem to
be a religious fanatic like most of his troops.*

As he read, he found nothing in the notebook of a
sensitive nature—no details about his captors, or his
treatment, not even his geographic location. No surprise
there. Raz knew that anything he wrote would be read
and analyzed by his captors and used against him.

Symphonie Fantastique swelled as Maxwell wrestled
with his feelings. Raz and Al-Fasr. Each a prisoner.
Each wanting freedom.

A sense of purpose was settling over Maxwell. Raz
was alive. He was out there somewhere in Iran. No one
was going to do anything about it.

Except me.

An idea was germinating in his mind. It was still
vague, probably unworkable. It all depended on
whether—

A knock at the door interrupted his thoughts.

He swung the door open. In the passageway stood the
answer to his question.

"Why haven't you called?" said Claire Phillips.

As usual, she was flustered. She had another of those
cute little spiels ready to deliver. And as usual, it left
her.

"Oh, Sam, I was so worried about—"

He didn't wait for the rest. He pulled her inside the
room, closed the door, took her in his arms. He kissed
her, held it until she'd forgotten what she intended to
say. Then she clung to him for another minute.

"Thank God, you're back, Sam. It's been six hours
since you landed."

"CAG and I took a trip over to the *Saipan*."

She looked at him. "There was something different
about this strike, wasn't there?"

He nodded. "The good part was that everyone got home okay."

She sat in the empty chair next to his and listened while he told her the bare facts of the strike. By the careful way he talked, she knew there was more to the story. Critical details behind the bare facts.

She knew the rules. As a journalist she knew how to piece together stories from the snippets of information she gleaned from her contacts. With Sam Maxwell it was different. Between them was a tacit agreement that whatever he told her was off limits, unless he told her otherwise. She had never violated the agreement.

He finished telling her about the strike. After a moment, she said, "Something else happened, didn't it?"

He nodded. "Remember the rumor about an American POW in Iraq?"

"The one you asked Bronson about? What was his name . . . Rasmussen?"

"It's more than a rumor."

He told her about the capture of Jamal Al-Fasr. And about his proposition that he be exchanged for an American POW.

Claire kept her silence, knowing that what he was telling her was explosive information.

He handed her a manila file folder from his desk. "They found this in Iran this morning."

She opened the handwritten journal. As she scanned the pages, her heart began to pound. Then she came to a passage that made tears spring to her eyes.

I think today is my birthday.

I wonder if Maria and the children will remember. If so, what will they think? Will they regard me as only a distant memory, or a family figure they dearly loved and wish was back?

Do the children think of Maria's new husband

*as their father? Does Maria love him the same as
she did me?*

*Such thoughts are not healthy. I will no longer
observe such occasions. Dead men shouldn't have
birthdays.*

She closed the folder and looked up at Maxwell.
"This is your friend, Rasmussen? The one who was shot
down in Desert Storm? He's being held by the Bu Hasa
terrorists?"

Maxwell nodded.

"And the CIA won't agree to an exchange?"

He shook his head.

"What am I missing, Sam? Why?"

"I don't know. Maybe they think Al-Fasr is too valuable a prize, or he's too dangerous to turn loose."

"Or maybe they don't want to acknowledge that Rasmussen is alive."

She saw the answer in his eyes. "That thought has occurred to me," he said.

"But it doesn't make sense, Sam. Why isn't our country doing everything possible to get one of our own
back?"

"Maybe they just need a little prompting."

It still didn't make sense. "I don't see how—"

"Have I ever asked you for help before?"

"No," she said. "Are you asking now?"

"Yes. This is important."

"Important enough to blow your career? And mine?"

He nodded again. "It's not for us. It's for a guy named
Raz."

She chewed on her thumbnail for a while. The pieces
were beginning to fall into place. She could guess what
he had in mind.

"Okay," she said. "What do I have to do?"

*   *   *

She returned to her stateroom, her mind filled with turmoil.

As she packed her roll-on bag, she thought about Maria Rasmussen. She had met her once, back in the Washington days when she was a fledgling reporter and Sam was in test pilot school at Pax River. It was a Sunday afternoon, four years after Raz vanished over Iraq. Sam took her with him to visit Maria in Virginia Beach.

She was a pretty girl, black-haired with high cheekbones and large brown eyes. Behind the dark eyes, Claire remembered, was a look of sadness.

They talked about family things, how the kids were handling school, the garden that Maria had begun in the backyard, old friends who had gone on to new assignments. Maria was thrilled that Sam Maxwell was a test pilot.

"Raz admired you so much," she blurted. It was the first mention of her husband. "He said you were the smartest guy in the squadron, the one who was going on to great things."

Maxwell had been embarrassed by the compliment. "Raz was like my big brother," he said. "He took me under his wing when I came to the squadron, always watching out for—"

A man barged into the room, smiling, exuding friendly boisterousness. He went straight to Maxwell and stuck out his hand. "You've gotta be Brick. I'm Frank Gallagher. Maria told me you were coming by."

It was hard not to like Gallagher. He had the humor and easy confidence of a man who didn't take himself too seriously. He was older than Maxwell by about ten years, a successful land developer, a widower and father of a pair of teenagers.

Maria's eyes darted worriedly between the two men, watching for signs of disapproval from Maxwell. She was caught in a chasm between bereavement and guilt. She was in love with two men—one a ghost, the other a man who provided the kind of rock solid strength she desperately needed.

Claire was not surprised when she heard, a year later, that Maria and Frank were married. She hoped that the two would have a good life. Maybe some of the sadness would leave Maria Rasmussen's eyes.

Now Claire understood what Maria had gone through—and was going through all over again. What it was like to love two men. To choose between them.

Life isn't fair, she thought. No one should have to make a choice like that. Not Maria Rasmussen, not Claire Phillips. When a ghost appeared in your life, you shouldn't have to choose between him and a living person.

So who promised you that life would be fair? Welcome to real life, girl.

With that thought, she finished packing.

An hour later she was aboard a CH-53 helo back to Bahrain. Her excuse was that the major news story—the strike in Iran—had been reported, and she had to get back to the bureau office.

It was still early morning when she arrived in her cubicle on the mezzanine floor of the Gulf Hotel. Five minutes later, she had Phillip Granley, the vice president of World News Syndicate, on the satellite phone connection.

His voice was a hoarse croak. "Christ almighty. Do you know what time it is here?"

"You said to wake you up at any time if it was something hot. This is something hot, Phil."

She told him about Jamal Al-Fasr and Raz Rasmussen.

Granley took several seconds to digest the information. "And you say the CIA doesn't want to do a deal and exchange prisoners?"

"Correct."

"Why?"

"That's the question. And that's the story."

"How did you get this information?"

"Sources. Unnamed."

"And I presume that you can document the story?"

This was the slippery part. The only document she had seen was the copied pages from Raz's daybook that Maxwell showed her, and she couldn't reveal their existence.

"I have seen solid evidence that the American prisoner exists and is being held by the Bu Hasa. I know, also, that the terrorist leader, Al-Fasr, is in American custody. It hasn't been announced yet, but sooner or later they'll have to admit it. We can't prove that he wants to be exchanged, but we don't have to. It makes sense. What doesn't make sense is why we're leaving one of our own prisoners behind."

"Can you think of one compelling reason why World Wide News ought to get crossways with the CIA?"

"Phil, when you hired me, you said to report the truth, no matter how much better a lie would sound. Well, damn it, this is the truth. I know it, and the CIA knows it."

"Yeah, fine, but that doesn't include sticking our noses into national defense matters. Sometimes we have to use good sense and cut the government a little slack with the truth. This kind of thing could blow up in our face."

"I'm not suggesting we go public with it. Let one of your contacts at the Pentagon know that we know, and that the story *might* come out unless they go through with the prisoner exchange."

"Threaten them, you mean."

"In a nice way."

"No."

"This is a humanitarian thing, Phil."

"You're saying we don't get to run the story, but we

use it anyway to blackmail the government. What the hell kind of business do you think we're in?"

"There'll be a story when it's all finished and done. And we'll have the scoop."

"This is a thing that gets reporters like you black-balled and VPs like me canned. Let me go back to sleep, and I'll forget you ever called."

"Phil, I love my job, but my personal integrity is more important. This man has been held hostage for over a dozen years. What if it were you?" Silence. "If you don't do this, I'll find another contact."

"Another job, you mean."

"Whatever."

Another long pause. "You're serious about this?"

"Very."

"Shit." She heard him sigh over the phone.

"Phil, it's the right thing to do. Even if the details never emerge, you'll know you had a part in setting this poor man free. If the truth does come out, this could mean a Pulitzer."

Another silence while this sank in. She knew she had found the right button to push.

"All right," said Granley. "I'll see Duncan Medcalf tomorrow when I'm in Washington. He's the new Deputy Secretary of Defense. When I tell him this story, you're gonna hear a scream all the way from Washington to Bahrain."

"Thank you, Phil. You won't be sorry."

Medcalf's owlish eyes peered through the oversized glasses, revealing not a hint of reaction.

"Prisoner?" said Medcalf. "You're claiming that an American has been held there for over ten years?"

"Over a dozen years," said Granley.

"And you say we can get him back in exchange for some captured terrorist?"

"For Jamal Al-Fasr. Whom I happen to know you just grabbed in Iran."

At this, Granley thought he saw Medcalf blink. "May I ask the source of this information?"

"It wouldn't be useful," said Granley. "Anyway, the Iran operation got a lot of media coverage. You knew you couldn't keep the Al-Fasr story under wraps for very long."

They were sitting in Medcalf's new office in the Pentagon. Before his appointment to the number two job in the Defense Department, Dr. Duncan Medcalf had been dean of the School for International Studies at Columbia. His academic career had been punctuated with three tours of duty in the State Department and one stint as a National Security Advisor.

"Assuming this Al-Fasr story was credible—and I'm not saying that it is—why would we release a terrorist who is on our most-wanted list?"

"Because we want to get an American back."

Granley waited while Medcalf toyed with the Mont Blanc pen on the table. *Maybe he doesn't know about an American prisoner,* thought Granley. *Or maybe Claire Phillips has it all wrong.*

"If World Wide News has a story about some American prisoner," said Medcalf, "why haven't you gone public with it? After all, it would be quite an exposé. Cause a lot of heads to roll here in Washington."

Granley nodded. Now they were in the bargaining stage. "I've considered that. I've also considered that it might be more useful *not* to go public with it. At least not yet."

"Useful?" The owlish eyes fixed on him. "Let me see if I'm following you on this. You want us to make a prisoner exchange—Al-Fasr for this hypothetical American POW, right?"

"Right."

"And if we don't, you *might* go public with the story."

Granley shrugged. "Something like that."

"I believe that's called blackmail."

"I prefer to call it freedom of the press."

"I can have your network's access to the Defense Department severed with a single phone call. Is that what you want?"

"Look, Dunc, you and I go back a long ways. I came to you with this because you're a guy who believes in doing the right thing."

Medcalf's face hardened. He rose and walked back to his desk. For a while he stood with his back to Granley. "I'm still new in this job. There are a number of issues I'm not yet privy to."

"I understand."

"It will take me a little time to sort out the facts."

"How much time?"

"Give me three days."

Granley rose. The meeting was over. "You're still a good guy, Dunc."

Oceana Naval Air Station, Virginia

"You gotta be shitting me," said Captain Gracie Allen.

"No, sir," said the briefing officer, a commander from OPNAV—the office of the Chief of Naval Operations. "Your C-9 leaves Oceana at four-thirty, connecting with a C-17 at Dover Air Force Base. I suggest you pack for two weeks."

"Listen, I've got a strike fighter wing to run. I can't—"

"You were handpicked for this assignment, Captain, because of your knowledge of the situation and because you are personally acquainted with the POW. Your

Chief of Staff will manage your office here until you return. Your orders are to report to the *Reagan* Battle Group Commander ASAP and coordinate with him."

Allen shook his head in amazement. From the window of his second-deck office he had a panoramic view of the flight line at Oceana Naval Air Station. Row after row of F/A-18 Hornets filled the expanse of concrete on the base. They were all his.

Allen's title was Commander, Strike Fighter Wing Atlantic, which meant that all the Navy's F/A-18 squadrons on the East Coast came under his administrative command. Though he held the rank of captain, the office carried with it the honorific rank of commodore. It was the last and best flying job in the Navy for an aging fighter pilot like Gracie Allen.

Except that he was on his way back to the Gulf. And he wasn't in the cockpit of a fighter.

"Am I gonna get shot at?"

"There's that possibility," said the commander. "You will be accompanied by a unit of marines and whatever air cover is deemed necessary. And, of course, the CIA will assign personnel of its own."

"CIA?" Allen shook his head. "So who's in charge? Us or them?"

"As the officer-in-charge, you represent the Navy's piece of the prisoner exchange. The CIA will provide other assets, including intelligence and cryptographic support. One of their senior officers will accompany you during the actual exchange."

"That figures. Who is it?"

"The section chief in Bahrain." The commander glanced at his notes. "Somebody named Bronson."

Owwooooooooooo.

The long chorus of howling and baying commenced, as usual, when Dog Balls Harvey entered the officers' wardroom. It was nearly six o'clock, and most of the Roadrunners were already seated for dinner.

Owwwwwooooooo. The chorus swelled.

Harvey's long face reddened. His oversized Adam's apple bobbed like a counterweight. He flashed an embarrassed grin, then bent in a low bow, acknowledging the howling officers.

Maxwell watched from his seat at the head of the table. Harvey was handling the treatment pretty well, he reflected.

As much as Dog Balls had pleaded, he had been unable to shed the call sign that the Roadrunners hung on him. When they presented him with a flight deck vest with his call sign stenciled on it, he threw away the vest.

They replaced it. He threw it away. They gave him another. Finally he gave up.

Now they were howling.

"Sit down," Maxwell said to Harvey, nodding to the empty seat beside him.

Harvey sat. His face was still red.

The howling subsided, and the officers went about having dinner.

"These guys are merciless," said Maxwell.

Harvey shrugged. "They're having fun."

"I can tell them to lighten up on you."

"Thanks, Commander, but I'd appreciate it if you'd just . . ."

"Butt out?"

He nodded. "Yes, sir. You may find this a little hard to believe, but I've sort of . . . you know, gotten used to it."

"All that howling doesn't bother you?"

"Not really. You see, I've been an outsider most of my life. I didn't belong to a fraternity or any clubs where I went to college up in Minnesota. Didn't have many buddies going through flight training. And the crews in my old patrol plane squadron, well, they never seemed to kid around as much as these tailhook guys."

It was the longest speech Maxwell had ever heard Harvey deliver. "What you're saying is that you're actually enjoying it?"

"Yes, sir, something like that. All that kidding and howling, it doesn't bother me. It makes me feel like I'm one of the guys." Dog Balls's face reddened some more, and he turned his full attention to his dinner plate.

Maxwell smiled. "Congratulations, Mr. Harvey. I think you've broken the code."

USS Ronald Reagan

Petty Officer Carson was almost finished filling in the day's inspection sign-offs. He was alone in the QAR compartment, and flight deck ops were shut down for the night. This was the best time to do his work. He could massage the entries that DiLorenzo had earmarked, improving the results of the day shift's work so that two of the jets would be out of the inspection cycle early. They would be back on the line by tomorrow.

He had just hit the enter key, watching the sign-offs magically appear on the screen, when he froze.

Someone was in the compartment. He heard the door clunk closed.

As footsteps clumped across the steel deck behind him, Carson's fingers flew back to the keyboard, hitting ALT/TAB once, twice, once again until the corrosion inspection records were gone and a new display shimmered on the screen.

He turned to face the visitor, and his heart nearly stopped. *Oh, godawful flaming shit. What does he want?*

Of all the human beings on the planet, Carson was most of all frightened by the hulking, glistening-domed presence of his squadron executive officer. He knew it was an unreasonable fear, but he couldn't help it. There was something about Cmdr. Bullet Alexander—that dark brown face, eyes glowing like embers—that struck fear in his heart. The man looked like a cross between Godzilla and Mr. T.

He was in the compartment. *What in hell for? The executive officer never came down—*

"Can I have a word with you, Carson?"

Oh, shit. Carson stared at the XO. His head nodded up and down and his lips moved, but nothing came out.

Alexander's eyes flicked to the screen for a moment, studying the display, then riveted again on Carson. "That the corrosion inspection sign-off?"

"Y-y-yes, sir. I mean, it's in there somewhere."

"Can you show it to me?"

"Show it to you? Well, yes, I guess . . . which jet do you want to see? They're all—"

"The replacement birds from VFA-193. Aircraft 306, 307, and 309."

Carson fought back the panic that was buzzing through him like an electric current. "Ah, 306 was the mishap bird, wasn't it, Commander? That's been removed from the LAN display already. Maybe you could get a printout from the wing maintenance office."

"But the corrosion inspection *was* signed off on 306?"

Carson's head went into an involuntary nodding movement again. "Oh, yes, sir. No doubt about that."

"Did they find any corrosion when they did the inspection?"

"Umm, no, I don't think so."

"And how about 307 and 309? They came from the same squadron. Have those jets received the full corrosion inspection?"

"Well, yes, sir. I believe they have."

"Show me, please."

Carson nodded, and his heart pounded in his chest. He turned to the keyboard and paged through the displays until he came to the sign-off sheets for aircraft 307 and 309.

Alexander peered at the screen for nearly a minute. "Those your initials on the checkoffs?"

"Yes, sir. That's me, the quality assurance rep."

"Does that mean you actually looked at the jets?"

"Well, what it really means is, I make sure whoever *did* look at the jets did his job according to the maintenance tech order. I'm sort of the validator of the process."

"So your sign-off is our final validation that the job was done right?"

Carson didn't like this line of questioning. He felt like a man headed for the gallows. "Yes, sir, you could put it that way."

"And you're saying that everything was okay? No corrosion, no problems?"

"No problems, Commander. Uh, may I ask why you want to know about this?"

"I'm asking because I lost an airplane for reasons that were not determined. Not to my satisfaction, at least."

Alexander peered at the flickering screen for another full minute, seeming to look for some hidden answer. Then he switched his gaze back to Carson. "I'm sure you understand how important this job is, Carson. You know that we're counting on you."

"Counting on me?" Carson's voice was beginning to tremble.

"To give us good airplanes. The pilots in this squadron trust you with their lives."

"Oh, yes, sir. I am very aware of that."

Alexander gave him another of those looks that sent a tremor through Carson's gut. "Keep up the good work, Carson." He turned to leave the compartment. "You know you can always come to me if you have any problems."

Carson watched the XO stride across the deck. The door clunked shut behind him.

The pilots in this squadron trust you with their lives. Alexander's words replayed themselves like a mantra in Carson's mind. *Come to me if you have any problems.*

If he only knew, thought Carson. With a mounting sense of dread, he turned back to the flickering computer screen.

Rear Admiral Jack Hightree was a man who kept his emotions under control. Rarely did he burst into fits of anger. Today was an exception.

Maxwell was standing shoulder-to-shoulder with Boyce in the admiral's stateroom while Hightree blew his stack.

"Goddamn it!" said the admiral, pacing in front of his desk. "You gave me your word. I put my own credibility on the line by taking your problem up the chain of command. I thought I told you that the matter would go no further."

"Yes, sir, you did," said Boyce.

"Then what the hell happened?" He whirled on Maxwell. "You, Commander Maxwell. Did you go over my head and contact someone at the Pentagon?"

"No, sir, I did not."

"Captain Boyce, did you contact anyone?"

"No, sir. Absolutely not."

Hightree let out a snort of exasperation. For another long moment he peered through his rimless glasses at the two officers. "God knows what they're thinking back at OpNav."

Maxwell caught Boyce shooting him a sideways glance. They both knew what Hightree was really worried about. His career.

Hightree yanked a sheet of paper from his desk and

waved it at them. "Some O-6 named Allen is arriving from Oceana tomorrow. He's supposed to coordinate a prisoner exchange with Al-Fasr and some unidentified American prisoner. We have orders to facilitate the operation." He glowered again at Maxwell. "Could this by any chance be the same alleged POW you told me about, Commander?"

Maxwell forced back the grin that threatened to spread over his face. *It worked.* Claire's boss must have pushed the right button.

With a straight face he said, "I have no idea, Admiral. Captain Allen is the Strike Fighter Wing Commander. I know him well, but I haven't had any contact with him in over two weeks. You can check my e-mail logs."

Hightree squinted at him for another moment, then turned back to his desk. Some of his anger seemed to dissipate. "Maybe something good will come out of this. If this is for real, it's the right thing to do. If we bring an American POW home, it will make us all look good. The *Reagan* battle group may get a commendation out of it."

Maxwell and Boyce exchanged glances. Hightree was back to normal. Thinking about his next star.

Bandar-e Mah Sharh, Iran

The rubber hull of the Zodiac boat made a scrunching sound against the pebbly shore.

Mustafa held the boat against the retreating tide while Tyrwhitt hopped into the knee-deep water and waded ashore. A tiny sliver of moon hung in the western sky. Nightfall had settled over the marsh country, but Tyrwhitt wished it was blacker. Even in total darkness, traveling by foot through this territory was dangerous as hell.

Not only was he concerned that the Bu Hasa might

renege on the deal and start shooting, there were at least half a dozen other Arab and Persian rebel groups operating in this area, all armed and motivated to kill Westerners. Especially Westerners in the employ of the Great Satan.

Mustafa concealed the boat in a stand of reeds. Before they set out on the path into the marshes, Tyrwhitt pulled out his Cyfonika satellite phone. He keyed the pulse signal that would inform the Bahrain station— and Ted Bronson—that they were ashore and were proceeding inland.

Bronson was still a dickhead, Tyrwhitt reflected. Worse, he was a lying dickhead. That became obvious when he assigned Tyrwhitt to negotiate the prisoner exchange with the Bu Hasa Brigade.

"Exchange?" Tyrwhitt had asked. "Of whom?"

"Who do you think? Prisoners. One of ours for one of theirs."

Tyrwhitt had nodded, both of them acknowledging that Bronson's previous insistence that no such prisoner existed was a bald-faced lie.

"And you're assigning *me* to negotiate with the terrorists?" Tyrwhitt asked.

"You know the ground," Bronson had said, "and you speak the language. I want you to go in country, meet the Bu Hasa leader, a man called Abu Mahmed, and work out the details."

Tyrwhitt resisted the urge to ask what had compelled him to change his story. An unacknowledged American prisoner *was* being held. Had been held for years. Which Bronson had known—and denied—for years.

Long ago he had stopped being surprised at the duplicity of the CIA. Deception was a time-honored tradition in the business of espionage, but with Bronson it went a step further. Bronson had some kind of personal vested interest in keeping the prisoner's existence a secret. It was obvious that he was not pleased that the prisoner was coming home.

That was the part that puzzled Tyrwhitt. It meant that the decision to repatriate the American prisoner had originated several levels above Bronson's pay grade. And he was pissed.

Something slithered between Tyrwhitt's ankles. It made a squishing sound in the mud.

"Are there snakes in these marshes?" Tyrwhitt asked.

"Many," said Mustafa.

Just what he didn't want to hear. "Poisonous ones?"

"Cobras."

Fuck. Tyrwhitt had an abiding terror of snakes, rodents, spiders—things that crept and crawled.

He was plodding through knee-high weeds, ten yards behind Mustafa. Over his shoulder he carried an H&K submachine gun. In his hand he kept his Beretta nine-millimeter pistol ready for instant use. A hell of a lot of use they'd be against a snake.

All Tyrwhitt's senses were engaged. Every thirty or so yards they stopped while Mustafa listened to the night sounds and scanned the landscape around them. Tyrwhitt kept switching his attention from the bushes around them to the slimy, snake-infested muck under his feet.

He wouldn't have made the journey without Mustafa. The Iraqi had grown up in the Tigris-Euphrates delta, and could pick his way through the marshes like a swamp rat.

Three miles into the interior, they arrived at the rendezvous point—a brackish lake with an enclave of fishing huts on one side. Mustafa motioned for Tyrwhitt to remain crouched in the weeds while he reconnoitered.

Tyrwhitt waited, keeping the Beretta at the ready. His nerves were twanging like harp strings. Clandestine meetings in darkened back streets or souks or seamy wharves were one thing. He'd done plenty of that and could even feel a kind of exhilaration in the danger. This damned swamp was something else.

It occurred to him that it might be a trap. He trusted Mustafa—but only as far as he trusted anyone in this business. If you wanted to stay alive, you never stopped being suspicious. An agent could become a double agent and turn on you like—

Something rustled in the high reeds. He cradled the Beretta in both hands, ready to fire. From the reeds appeared the shadowy silhouette of Mustafa. In trail behind him came two men in black costumes, wearing kaffiyehs, each holding an AK-74.

For a tense moment Tyrwhitt and the men confronted each other, the blackened metal of their weapons barely visible in the darkness.

"Are you Tyrwhitt?" asked one of the shadowy figures.

CHAPTER 21

THE EXCHANGE

Southern Iran
2055, Monday, 22 March

"I am Abu Mahmed." He said it as if the name needed no further explanation. "This is my lieutenant, Omar Al-Iryani."

The second man gave Tyrwhitt a sharp nod.

Tyrwhitt was surprised that they would use their names. Abu Mahmed handled himself like a man accustomed to being in charge. In the darkness Tyrwhitt could see only his lean, beak-nosed features.

"For authentication, I must ask the name of the prisoner you are holding," said Tyrwhitt.

"You know his name. Rasmussen. He is an officer of the American Navy."

"An officer named Rasmussen was shot down in Iraq during the Gulf War. How did you gain custody of him?"

"You don't need such information."

"How do we know it is Rasmussen you intend to hand over?"

"You don't," said Abu. "Not until you have him in your custody." He nodded to Omar. The Arab reached into a rucksack and produced a file folder, which he handed to Tyrwhitt.

With a red-lensed penlight, Tyrwhitt examined the contents. The folder contained a blurry black-and-white photograph of a white-haired man holding a newspaper which, Tyrwhitt presumed, bore a recent date. A signature—*Allen Rasmussen*—was scrawled on the bottom of the photograph. In a bottom corner was an inky thumbprint.

"This will confirm the identity of the man we are holding," said Abu.

Tyrwhitt nodded. "Do you require proof that we are holding Al-Fasr?"

"We know you have him. If you are so stupid as to try to deceive us, you will not get your captured American back alive."

Abu unfolded a map and explained the details of the prisoner exchange. "Here," he said, pointing to a circled spot on the map. "This is an abandoned fishing village. In the center is a courtyard. Only two of your people and two of ours will enter the village with their prisoners. After we have verified each other's identity, the prisoners will each cross the courtyard and rejoin his own people."

"How can we be sure it won't be an ambush?" asked Tyrwhitt.

"We won't risk the life of our commander," said Abu. "We want Colonel Al-Fasr back alive, don't we?"

Tyrwhitt thought he saw Abu and Omar exchange quick glances. *Good question*, thought Tyrwhitt. He was getting an uneasy feeling. Something about Abu's manner—that haughty I'm-in-command tone. Not the demeanor of a faithful lieutenant.

Another thought flitted across Tyrwhitt's mind. *Why was I sent to do this?* The details of the prisoner swap were cut and dried. The deal could have been done by satellite phone, even by e-mail. Instead, he had been dispatched through this snake-infested swamp to make small talk with a swaggering terrorist.

The negotiations were concluded without disagreement. The time and place of the exchange were settled upon. Nothing further needed to be discussed.

No handshake was proffered, which suited Tyrwhitt. Something about Abu Mahmed repelled him. He watched as the two Arabs vanished back into the high reeds.

Tyrwhitt followed Mustafa back through the marshes toward the concealed Zodiac boat. As he slogged along in the darkness, trying not to think about snakes, avoiding the sucking mud and invisible sinkholes, his mind kept returning to the image of Abu Mahmed.

The Arab was slick. Too slick. Too sure of himself.

USS Ronald Reagan

"What the hell are you talking about?" said Lieutenant DiLorenzo.

All the salesman's warmth was gone from his voice. He whirled on Carson, his eyes blazing like coals. "Are you freaking out on me? You can't back out now."

It was after midnight, and they were alone in the closed QA space. Carson was shocked by DiLorenzo's outburst. "I just thought that . . . you know, we owe it to the squadron to do the inspections."

"You've already signed off on the inspection schedule. Are you saying we should tell the whole fucking world that the inspections never happened?"

"Well, I was just thinking . . ."

"Leave the thinking to me," DiLorenzo snapped. He let several seconds pass, then his voice changed to a more conciliatory tone. "Aw, hell, Carson, I'm sorry. You've got a short memory, that's all. This was all explained to you once. You just forgot for a moment how it's supposed to play out."

He flashed a grin, then turned away to let Carson know the matter was finished.

It wasn't finished for Carson. "I still think we ought to have those jets inspected."

DiLorenzo took a deep breath. He rose to his full height and turned to glower down at Carson's face. "You seem to have forgotten some facts of life. I'm gonna be blunt, Carson. Your last three evals were shitty. So shitty that you not only don't have a hope in hell of getting promoted to chief, you'll be lucky to get your twenty in before the Navy throws your ass on the street. This is your only chance to save your career."

"Maybe my career isn't that important."

DiLorenzo gave him a curious look. "What is this, some kind of crisis of conscience? Let me give you something else to think about. Do you know what the inside of a six-by-six cell looks like? That's where you'll spend the next several years after a court-martial finds you guilty of falsifying maintenance records."

"Your initials are on the records too."

"So what? Everyone knows how the system works. The QA officer doesn't do the inspections. He takes the word of the petty officer who reports to him that the job was completed. That happens to be you, Carson. If it comes to an inquest, I promise you that you will be hanging all alone in the breeze. You are in this by yourself, and anything you say to the contrary will be denied by me and Commander Manson. You will have no proof."

Carson let several seconds tick by as he contemplated his future. He had made a deal with the devil. He was screwed.

"Okay. I get the picture."

"Good. I always knew you were a team player, Carson. Remember that Commander Manson takes care of his team."

"Yes, sir."

Carson left the compartment and stepped out onto the red-lighted hangar deck. He knew in his gut that DiLorenzo was right. It was his word against that of two commissioned officers. No one would believe him, because he had no proof.

Or so they thought.

Manama, Bahrain

"Absolutely not," said Bronson.

"But I'm the logical choice to run the mission," said Tyrwhitt. "I made the deal, I know Abu, and I know the setup."

"You stay here," said Bronson. "That's already been decided."

"By whom, may I ask?" said Tyrwhitt.

"You may not ask. Washington has assigned this mission a level one priority, which means an operations chief will run it, not a contract agent."

Tyrwhitt just nodded. There it was again, the old class distinction between officers and agents. Bronson was in dickhead mode again, and it was pointless to argue with him.

They were back in the SCIF, the heavily bunkered underground facility beneath the old American embassy. The SCIF had a blast door and another squad of armed guards. The exterior shell of the facility was shielded against monitoring or electronic intrusions.

Tyrwhitt had just finished reporting to Bronson about his mission into Iran, giving him all the details of the meeting with Abu Mahmed.

Almost all the details.

For reasons he didn't yet understand, Tyrwhitt had not mentioned to Bronson the uneasy feeling he had about Abu. Something about the two terrorists—Abu and his thug lieutenant, Omar—was still bothering him.

Even Mustafa had gotten bad vibrations from the pair.
"Bad men," was all he would say. He made a slicing
motion with his finger across his throat. "Don't trust
them."

Well, thought Tyrwhitt, it didn't matter now. His part
in the deal was finished. He yawned and sank back into
the leather-padded chair. The fatigue of the all-night
foray into the marshes had caught up with him. To hell
with the Company. To hell with dickhead Bronson. If he
wanted to run the mission by himself, more power to
him. Who the hell cared anyway?

Good question. Though he couldn't explain it, he *did*
care. What he cared about, though, wasn't the deal with
the terrorists, or the CIA's political need to please its
bosses, or even the outcome of the mission.

He cared about the prisoner.

Tyrwhitt was unable to erase from his mind the image
of the gaunt, white-haired man holding the newspaper.
It had to be him, the one he'd met back in Abu Graib
prison. Even though he hadn't seen the American prisoner's face in the next cell, he knew.

Something about the prisoner—Rasmussen—still
troubled him. He wasn't out of trouble. Tyrwhitt didn't
know how he knew that—but he just knew. It was why
he wanted to accompany the mission back into Iran to
make the swap.

"This Iraqi that you hire . . ." Bronson was saying.
"The one who went into Iran with you—"

"Mustafa."

"That one. We ran a check on him, and it seems he's
worked for every employer in the Middle East. Saddam,
Arafat, the Mossad, the Kurds, you name it, he's
worked for them."

Tyrwhitt shrugged. "He's a professional. He's loyal
to whoever pays him."

Bronson gave him a pained look. "What makes you
think we can use people like that? That's not the way we

operate in the CIA. The man's a double, maybe a triple
agent. He'll sell us out."

"He saved my life twice. Got me through a secret police roadblock in Baghdad, and he killed a Hezbollah
assassin in Beirut who was about to put a knife in my
back."

"This is the CIA, not the Foreign Legion," said Bronson. "Get rid of him."

Tyrwhitt just nodded. Dickhead Bronson. The best
thing was to ignore him. "Sure," he said.

The debriefing was finished. Tyrwhitt was emotionally drained from the trip to Iran and the stress of dealing with Bronson. He left the SCIF, submitting to the
usual pat down by the security guards, then passing
through the metal scanner at the bombproof exit door.

Squinting, he walked into the harsh morning sun-
shine. Mustafa was waiting in the battered Toyota
around the corner.

"Let's get a drink, mate," said Tyrwhitt, sliding into
the passenger seat. It was time to exploit Mustafa's
weakness for Jack Daniel's. "I've got another job for
you."

Mustafa nodded agreeably. "Where are we going
now?"

"Not we, mate. You."

USS Ronald Reagan

The key players in the prisoner exchange—now designated Operation Raven Swoop—assembled in the
flag conference room.

Maxwell and Boyce arrived together. Behind them
came Admiral Hightree, followed by Gus Gritti and his
executive officer, Lt. Col. Aubrey Hewlitt, still wearing
float coats from their helicopter ride.

Over Hightree's objection, Maxwell had been

picked for the mission by Gracie Allen because Maxwell knew Rasmussen better than anyone else in theater. They were former squadron mates, and that made it personal.

As the Air Wing Commander, Boyce would lead a contingency air support package—just in case. After the lesson learned in Yemen, the *Reagan* battle group would not insert a team into terrorist country without on-call air support.

Gus Gritti was still fuming. When Hightree got wind of Gritti's plan to personally lead the marine TRAP team—Tactical Recovery of Aircraft and Personnel— to accompany the mission into Iran, he called the marine colonel on the *Saipan*. "What's this about you leading the TRAP team?"

"Admiral, this mission should be led by the toughest sonofabitch in the Marine Corps. That just happens to be me."

"Cool it, Gus. This is not a job for an MEU commander, especially a general-select."

Gritti argued until Hightree told him to knock it off. Reluctantly, Gritti backed down and assigned his XO, Lieutenant Colonel Hewlitt, to lead the team.

Ted Bronson entered the compartment, looking like a raging bull. Behind him came Chris Tyrwhitt in his customary wrinkled bush jacket. Bronson acknowledged the senior military officers.

He spotted Maxwell and went directly to him. In a low voice he said, "It was you, wasn't it, you sonofabitch?"

Maxwell smiled. "Hey, it's good to see you, too, Ted."

"You leaked the story, didn't you?"

"Ted, how could you think such a thing?"

"Listen, hot shot. You may think you pulled something off, but I've got news for you. You violated national security. Your career is toast. You're going to get twenty years in Leavenworth."

"Haven't lost your sense of humor, have you?"

Tyrwhitt stood behind Bronson, watching the exchange with a bemused expression. Bronson shot Maxwell one more baleful look, then stomped across the room and took a seat in the back row.

Capt. Gracie Allen took the podium and aimed a laser pointer at the illuminated chart on the bulkhead screen.

"The Karkeh River, gentlemen," he said, tracing the stream that flowed through the marsh country of lower Iran. "The same area where you grabbed Colonel Al-Fasr. Our CIA colleagues have made contact with the Bu Hasa Brigade and have worked out a method to exchange prisoners. They get their man Al-Fasr, we get an American POW back."

Allen's pointer stopped at a place on the map. "Here, where the river flows into the Hawr Umr Sawan lake, is a deserted village. That is where we meet the Bu Hasa contacts and where we make the prisoner exchange."

"Gracie, can you confirm the identity of the American POW?" said Boyce.

Allen nodded. "If our intelligence is correct, then it's . . ." his voice cracked for an instant ". . . a squadron mate whom we lost in action over Iraq in 1991." The map on the screen flicked off, and in its place appeared a black-and-white photograph of a grinning young man in a flight suit, standing beside an F/A-18. "Lt. Cmdr. Allen Rasmussen. Call sign 'Raz.'"

Maxwell stared at the photo and felt a lump rise in his throat. A silence fell over the room, and for a moment he and Gracie Allen made eye contact. They had the same thought. *After all these years, Raz. We're coming to get you.*

Allen went on. He would be the on-site commander, with a direct link to Hightree, the Battle Group Commander. The Raven Swoop team would consist of only six marines, plus Allen, Maxwell, and Bronson. The marine TRAP team—forty-two infantrymen with mortars, light and heavy automatic weapons, and a squad of the MEU's best snipers—would be aboard a CH-53, ready to move in.

By the terms negotiated with the Bu Hasa, only two members of each force were to accompany their prisoner to the exchange point. After authenticating each other's identity, each side would send its prisoner across the open courtyard of the village to join his respective countrymen.

Maxwell and Bronson would deliver Al-Fasr and retrieve Rasmussen.

Allen flicked off his laser pointer. "That's the plan, gentlemen," said Allen. "Questions or comments?"

"One comment," said Gritti. "Don't trust those assholes. Does anybody here remember Yemen?"

"That's why we'll have the TRAP team—plus air cover—just offshore," said Allen. "For anyone monitoring from a coastal radar, it'll look like standard cyclic night op, but in reality we can have them on target in less than fifteen minutes."

"What if our guys—Maxwell and Bronson here—walk into a trap?"

"We've got human intel in the area and national assets overhead. You don't need to know details. Just know that if the gomers try to sneak in a large force on us, we'll catch them at it."

Gritti nodded, but his expression showed that he wasn't satisfied.

Allen took a few more questions. The briefing was finished.

Maxwell headed for the door. He passed Bronson, who regarded him with a look of contempt.

"Hey, Ted, I'm really looking forward to working with a great guy like you."

"Fuck you," said Bronson.

Manama, Bahrain

"The Gulf lounge at six?" She wavered on the edge of indecision. *Just say no,* she told herself. *Hang up the damned phone and ignore it when it rings again.* Instead, she heard herself say, "Okay, see you at six."

She hung up and shook her head. *You never learn, do you, girl?*

Much as she had tried to rationalize her long relationship with Chris Tyrwhitt, Claire still didn't understand her true feelings.

Do you love the guy? No, at least not in the traditional sense.

Are you attracted to him? Indisputably. Perhaps fatally.

She'd gone the distance with Chris. He had entered her life a few weeks after she'd broken up with a test pilot and astronaut-to-be named Sam Maxwell. Tyrwhitt was working the Washington beat for an Australian news syndicate, and he was just what she needed. He was fun, good-looking, and had a good career going.

Not until later—after they were married—did she learn the rest. He was unfaithful, reckless, dishonest. He also drank too much. How could she love someone like that?

Not until he disappeared in Baghdad, supposedly shot and killed by the Iraqi secret service, and then reappeared in her life, did she learn the truth about Tyrwhitt. He was a spy.

But Chris Tyrwhitt would never change, she reminded herself. Not the philandering and drinking part, anyway.

Okay, so it wasn't love. But she had to admit there was some sort of magnetism there. Something kept drawing her back into his orbit, even when all her senses were yelling at her to run in the opposite direction as fast as she could.

She had an idea what it was, and she didn't like it.
You're attracted to outlaws. Chris Tyrwhitt was your
world class, unreformed, kickass outlaw, even if he was
in the employ of a Boy Scoutish outfit like the CIA. She
smiled, thinking that he probably lied to them too.

She gave herself a final inspection in the vanity mirror. Chestnut hair coiffed and sprayed into place. Light
red lipstick, the wet look, not the kind she wore for the
camera. Silk blouse, top three buttons open, tied at the
midriff. Her favorite Kate Spade shoes. Full-length
linen skirt, nearly diaphanous, the kind that flattered her
long legs and slender shape.

She liked what she saw. Not the prim Claire Phillips
seen on the evening news, wearing the phony little reading spectacles to make her look businesslike, reporting
a suicide bombing or an air strike or the assassination of
some PLO officer. This was the off-screen Claire
Phillips, the one who still turned heads when she
strolled into the Gulf bar.

Satisfied, she gathered up the oversize leather purse
containing the tools of her trade—tape recorder, digital
camera, notepad, Palm Pilot. You had to be prepared,
she told herself. Chris Tyrwhitt might be an outlaw, but
he was also a source.

CHAPTER 22

IN COUNTRY

Manama, Bahrain
1800, Tuesday, 23 March

She liked the Gulf Hotel lounge. The atmosphere was a funky mixture of *Casablanca* and Miami's South Beach, with a Filipino jazz pianist who sounded like a young Brubeck. The air had the ever-present scent of Drakkar cologne and sandalwood. A forest of palm trees lined the room, and a semicircular mahogany bar covered one whole wall.

She paused in the entrance and peered around.

Tyrwhitt was at the bar chatting up a pair of GAGs—Gulf Air Girls. The flight attendants for the local airline were mostly European women, non-Muslims, and unlike the local Bahraini women, they could go out alone. The Gulf lounge was one of their favorite watering holes.

Claire didn't know whether to laugh or turn around and leave. Tyrwhitt would never change. Even when he was trying to charm his wife—soon to be *ex*-wife, she reminded herself—he couldn't resist trolling for trophies.

He glanced up and saw her. He turned to the GAGs and gave them a low, sweeping bow, then kissed their hands. They both giggled.

Wearing a huge smile, Tyrwhitt strode across the lounge.

"Claire, my darling, you look absolutely smashing." He gave her a wet smack on the cheek.

She nodded toward the bar. "I'm sure you told those two exactly the same thing."

He glanced at the two women, who were still tittering. "Them? Oh, I was telling them about you, and they were quite impressed. They're great fans of yours, actually. Nice young ladies, both Kiwis."

She gave him an indulgent smile. The guy was full of bullshit, but she had learned that years ago. She'd gotten over the heartburn from her husband's endless flirtations. She was cured.

She could tell that he'd already had a few drinks. His ruddy face was ruddier than usual, and he seemed to be in exceptionally good humor. *Careful, girl,* she warned herself. That was one of Tyrwhitt's dangerous attributes. The drunker he got, the more charming he became.

He led her to a table in the corner, and she felt the curious stares from the girls at the bar. That was the downside to being a broadcast journalist. Wherever she went in public, someone was sure to recognize her. Even without the phony glasses.

The waiter showed up with their drinks—Scotch neat for him, vodka tonic with a twist for her. The piano player recognized her and gave her a wave. He slipped into a rendition of "Take Five."

"How does it feel being loved and admired?" asked Tyrwhitt.

"Being anonymous would feel better, thank you."

"Too late. Your gorgeous face is now in the public domain. Even with those silly specs."

They had a round of drinks, then another, Tyrwhitt outdrinking her two-to-one. She listened while he conducted a discourse on the convoluted politics of the region. In almost every country, he explained, the old ruling entities were in a contest with disgruntled religious factions. In Bahrain, the emir was hanging on by placating the rebellious Shiite majority.

She knew most of this, but she was impressed anyway. She'd forgotten that Tyrwhitt, despite his dissolute life style, had a solid grasp of Middle East affairs.

"Do they teach that stuff to the employees of the CIA?" she asked. A loaded question, but what the hell.

He didn't seem to mind. "Technically, I'm not an employee. Just an agent who performs services on call."

"Isn't that what you called—"

"A whore?" He smiled. "Of course. I'm a natural."

"What about your boss? What's his name . . .?"

"Ted Bronson. The station chief."

"Is he a whore too?"

"No," said Tyrwhitt, and he chuckled. "Bronson is what they call an operations officer, not an agent, which makes him a pimp, I suppose. We whores get to do the dirty work."

She had to laugh. She could still see Bronson's hard, dead-eyed expression. "He's a strange one," she said. "He gives me the creeps."

Tyrwhitt smiled, not replying.

"I remember the way he shut you up," she went on. "When you were talking about the American who you thought was in prison in Baghdad."

Tyrwhitt nodded, still keeping his silence.

"So," she said, keeping her tone light, "was he telling the truth?"

"About what?"

"About an American prisoner left behind in Iraq."

"To quote my esteemed employer, such matters are several levels above my pay grade."

She nodded and continued digging. "In other words, there is a prisoner, but the company line is that there isn't?"

"This sounds very much like an interrogation."

"Just friendly conversation."

"Ha. Don't forget, I'm a journalist too. I know when I'm being grilled."

She laughed and let him change the subject. For a while they chatted about old friends, about working the Middle East beat, about the good times in Washington when they were newlyweds and the dark clouds hadn't come to spoil everything. They delicately avoided talking about the bad times.

Claire felt herself slipping into a deliciously relaxed state. She realized that the stress of the past few days had dragged her spirit down like a leaden weight. The glamorous life of a broadcast journalist wasn't really that glamorous. It was tedious, tiring, deadening.

Chris Tyrwhitt was good company, even if he was full of shit. She'd forgotten how much she enjoyed his quick wit, that wacky, offbeat sense of humor. He made her feel like a woman, not a costumed mannequin to be positioned in front of a camera.

So does Sam Maxwell, she reminded herself.

But with Sam it was different. He didn't make her laugh, at least not like Tyrwhitt. He was a man of deeper, more guarded emotions. What went on inside him was a private matter that he didn't often share with the world. She could love Sam Maxwell, but she might never understand him.

With Tyrwhitt it didn't matter. It wasn't necessary to understand him. What you saw was what you got. Tyrwhitt was an eternal adolescent, driven by whim and hormones, damn the consequences.

They nibbled at an assortment of chicken wings and spring rolls, neither of them especially hungry. They kept chatting about inconsequential things, and Tyrwhitt ordered more drinks. Claire knew she was over her limit—she could hear her brain buzzing like a cicada—

but she didn't care. She was a working girl. She deserved to unwind once in a while.

The piano player finished with a jazzed-up version of "September Song." He lowered the cover on his keyboard and gave Claire a wave as he left the lounge.

They were the only ones still there. The GAGs had long since departed.

"Time for Cinderella to fade," she said. She gathered her oversized leather purse. It occurred to her that she hadn't used any of the tools of the trade that she brought along. Oh, well.

"I'll be gallant and walk you home," said Tyrwhitt.

"I *am* home. I live in the Gulf Hotel."

"Oh, yeah. Then I'll see you to your room."

"I know the way."

"This is Bahrain. A lady needs an escort."

She didn't argue. They rose from the table, and she made a determined effort not to sway or wobble, taking long, purposeful strides as they left the lounge, across the marble-floored lobby where a half dozen Bahraini men stared from deep leather chairs, to the row of brass-paneled elevators.

Riding to the sixth floor, conscious of Tyrwhitt at her side and, most oddly, not minding it, she had a thought: *I shouldn't be doing this.*

Another thought: *Why not? He's still my husband.*

The elevator hushed to a stop, and the door opened. They stepped out and walked down the long carpeted hallway.

USS Ronald Reagan

Carson fidgeted while the phone rang. It had taken three tries before he got his nerve up to finish dialing.

An hour before he had been standing on the flight deck, bracing himself against the twenty-knot wind that swept over the bow, watching the jets launch into the darkness. One after the other, Super Hornets lunged down the catapult tracks, off the bow, and into the horizonless sky.

As he watched the strike fighters leave the deck, the words of the executive officer kept replaying in his mind. *You understand how important this job is, Carson. You know that we're counting on you.*

This was the only life he knew. Now it was about to end. He wanted to put on the chief's hat—God knew he wanted it more than he had ever wanted anything—but the price had become too high to pay.

He had gone from the flight deck to the QA space on the second deck. For another twenty minutes he wrestled with his conscience. Standing there with the phone pressed to his ear, he felt like a man plunging over a cliff.

Finally he summoned the courage to make the call.

A deep voice came on the line. "Commander Alexander."

Carson fought back the terror that rose up in him. "Sir, this is Petty Officer Carson, the QA rep."

"What's on your mind, Carson?"

"I . . . ah, was just thinking about your visit to the QA space, sir."

"Yes? What about it?"

"You said to let you know if I had any problems."

"Have you?"

"In a manner of speaking, yes, sir. A real problem."

Alexander didn't reply for a moment. "Is it urgent? I'm supposed to have breakfast with the Air Boss in fifteen minutes."

More urgent than you can imagine, thought Carson. He had to do this now or he'd back out. "Yes, sir. Very."

"Can you find my stateroom on the O-3 level?"

"I'll be there in five minutes."

USS Saipan

The blades of the SH-60 bit into the damp air, lifting the helicopter from the flight deck. Maxwell could feel the rumble of the two turbine engines through his metal seat.

A pall of blackness lay over the Persian Gulf. Dawn was still an hour and a half away. The Bu Hasa commander had insisted the exchange be conducted in darkness, which, for the Americans, was fortuitous. With advanced-technology night vision goggles, they owned the night. The schedule also permitted an egress in the pinkness of dawn, which would provide enough light, if it became necessary, for Boyce's strike fighters to find *Sherji* targets.

"Hell of a thing for a couple of fighter pilots," said Gracie Allen, sitting next to Maxwell. "Trapped in a chopper full of snake eaters."

Maxwell gazed around the darkened cabin. Allen was right. The interior of the SH-60 was filled with face-blackened marines in battle dress, all clutching M16A2 combat rifles.

"Let's hope we don't need them." Maxwell also hoped they didn't need the rest of the entourage—the Cobra gunships and AV-8B Harriers escorting the SH-60, or Boyce's strike fighters flying high cover. Ditto the EA-6B Prowler, on station to jam and spoil any Iranian air defense radar activity.

The Cobras and Harriers would stay offshore while the SH-60 with the Raven Swoop team continued inland. The fighters would remain on station, rotating to an orbiting KC-10 tanker for refueling, for as long as the team was in country.

Maxwell and Allen were dressed alike, wearing camo BDUs. Each had a PRC-6725 field radio and a Trimble GPS navigation unit hooked to his belt. In a satchel they carried extra ammunition magazines and a set of PVS-7 night vision goggles.

Allen wore his standard-issue Beretta nine-millimeter in a web shoulder holster. He looked at Maxwell's sidearm, strapped in its faded leather holster. "What the hell is that?"

Maxwell slipped the pistol half out of the holster. "Colt .45. My dad passed it down to me."

Allen shook his head. "He should have passed it to a museum."

Maxwell shrugged and reholstered the weapon.

He saw Bronson watching them from across the cabin. His face was blackened like the others. He wore BDUs, with the same radio, GPS, and NVG kit hanging on his belt. Instead of a Beretta, he wore a Glock semi-automatic strapped to his hip.

It was odd, thought Maxwell. Since the mission began back on the *Saipan*, Bronson had changed. He seemed to shed some of his hostility, becoming businesslike, almost cordial. Maybe he had misjudged Bronson. He was still an asshole, but at least he was a professional asshole.

Close to Bronson sat Jamal Al-Fasr, his wrists bound with a tie-wrap, a black watch cap pulled down over his eyes. Bronson had taken personal custody of the prisoner, insisting that Allen and everyone else stay away from him. No communication, no contact.

Maxwell knew that the CIA hated giving up a valuable prisoner like Al-Fasr. He guessed that Bronson's people had already given him a thorough interrogation. More than thorough, probably. He would also bet that they had gotten nothing of value.

For forty-five minutes the big helicopter clattered through the night. The darkness outside was nearly total. It was as if the chopper and all inside it were swallowed in a black void. No lights, no hint of height or horizon or even stars outside the cabin window.

Lt. Col. Aubrey Hewlitt, the senior marine, stepped out of the cockpit and flashed two five-finger signals to his sergeant. He turned to Gracie Allen. "We just crossed the shoreline. Ten minutes to the LZ."

It meant the Raven Swoop team was on its own. No gunship escorts, no Harriers close at hand in case of an ambush.

Maxwell thought again of the operation in Yemen. They had blundered into a trap set by the same man they were now transporting to Iran—Jamal Al-Fasr.

He looked again at the dark shape of the terrorist commander, opposite him in the cabin. In a detached sense, he could understand Bronson's anger over the prisoner exchange. Al-Fasr had been one of the most wanted fugitives on the planet. Capturing him had been a coup for the CIA.

Now they were setting him free.

A thought came to Maxwell's mind. *Are we doing the right thing?* Al-Fasr hadn't changed stripes. Were they setting him free to wreak more atrocities on the world?

If so, Maxwell thought, he would have himself to blame. Through Claire's contacts, he had set the wheels in motion in Washington to force the exchange.

The whining, clattering noise of the helicopter's turbine engines changed pitch. Maxwell could feel the SH-60 slowing, maneuvering for a landing.

"Heads up, marines," called out Hewlitt. "Showtime."

Abu Mahmed was instantly alert. The familiar throbbing sound came from the south, from the direction of the sea. Even though his eyes had adapted to the darkness, he was unable to penetrate the inky gloom of the night.

His satellite phone buzzed. From the southernmost surveillance post came the excited voice of the sentry. "They're here, flying low up the river."

"How many?"

"Just one, I think."

"Are you sure? No escorts, no gunships?"

"I don't think so. Only one large helicopter."

"Where are they landing?"

A pause. "I'm not sure. I can't see them any longer. It sounds as if they are landing at the levee, near the mouth of the river."

Abu nodded. The CIA contact claimed he couldn't say the specific location of the landing zone. It depended on visibility and weather conditions, he said.

If they were alighting at the mouth of the river, it meant they were no more than two kilometers from the village. Fifteen minutes hiking time, twenty at the most.

How many troops? Abu wondered. Perhaps the sentry could count them. If they came in only one helicopter, they couldn't number more than fifteen.

Abu climbed down from the Land Rover and entered the darkened hut. The prisoner lay asleep, curled up on the floor in a corner.

Abu gave him a kick in the small of his back. The prisoner grunted and rose up on one elbow.

"On your feet," said Abu. "Move quickly."

The prisoner looked up at him. "Where are we going?"

"Shut up." Abu delivered another kick, this time to the prisoner's stomach. The prisoner groaned and doubled over.

"You will do exactly as I tell you or I will shoot you on the spot," said Abu. "It would give me great pleasure. Do you understand?"

The prisoner looked at him through dull, pain-filled eyes. He nodded his understanding.

With Al-Fasr gone, Abu had not felt constrained in his treatment of the prisoner, particularly after his attempted escape and the killing of the *Sherji* guards. No longer was it necessary to coddle the infidel, treating him as a fellow officer as that posturing fool Al-Fasr had done. The prisoner was a disciple of the Great Satan, an enemy of the Islamic revolution. He deserved neither pity nor respect.

Abu had already decided to put a bullet in his brain. But then came the strange message from the CIA officer, Bronson. A mission to exchange Al-Fasr for the American.

So now they were playing a deadly game. Though he and Bronson were mortal enemies, each was using the other for his own purposes. In the end there would be only one winner. Abu had already decided who that would be.

"Quickly," he said to the *Sherji* assembled outside the hut. "Take your positions. It is time to greet the infidels."

CHAPTER 23

REVELATIONS

Manama, Bahrain
0245, Wednesday, 24 March

She fumbled for her key.

The big leather bag was full of gadgets. The electronic room key was somewhere in the bottom. As she fumbled she was conscious of Tyrwhitt's familiar, rumpled presence. He was quiet, not his ebullient self.

She came up with the key. "Thanks for a very nice evening, Chris. It was good fun."

He didn't answer. Instead, he drew her to him. He kissed her, not the obligatory, sloppy social kiss he had bestowed in the restaurant, but a long, tender kiss that swept her back to the whirlwind courtship of five years ago.

She felt dizzy. The vodka tonics had kicked in, and so had Chris Tyrwhitt's potent outlaw charisma.

She let him take the key card from her and slip it into the slot in the door fixture. The green light flickered. He opened the door.

It had been a long time, she thought. They had not made love since their days in Istanbul, before she threw him out of the apartment. She couldn't even recall the particulars, only that it was another of his classic affairs, something involving the wife of a diplomat. A Scandinavian, as she recalled. Ash blonde hair, large blue eyes, the behavior of an alley cat. Tyrwhitt had a thing for alley cats.

Ancient history, she told herself.

The door was still open. *Say good night,* she ordered herself. *Get him out of here before it's too late.*

Then it was too late.

Before she could protest, he scooped her up and carried her into the room.

Haw Umm Qasr, Iran

The landing zone turned out to be an intersection of ancient cart paths near the southern edge of the lake. The blades of the SH-60 were kicking up a cloud of fine dirt and stones and dry weeds.

As the wheels of the helicopter neared the ground, the marines hit the dirt running. Within seconds, they had blended into the night.

Maxwell followed Gracie Allen out the door. Behind them came Bronson, yanking the prisoner along behind him. They stopped fifty yards from the helicopter, crouching beneath a low outcropping of rock.

In the darkness Maxwell heard radios crackling, low voices reporting perimeter positions secured, the metallic sound of automatic weapons being set up. The turbine engines of the helo settled down to an idle whine, the blades rotating in a slow whoosh.

Hewlitt appeared out of the darkness. He muttered something into his handheld transceiver, then turned to Allen. "Perimeter secure, sir. No sign of troop movement, no IR returns, no emissions. That's the best we can do. Your people are good to go."

Allen nodded. He looked at Bronson, then Maxwell. "I want position reports. Stay in contact all the way. Transmit 'Raven Swoop' when the deal is done. If I don't hear anything for five minutes, we're coming to get you. If things turn to shit, the call is 'Basher.' We hear that, and the grunts are coming in hot."

Allen clapped each man on the shoulder. "We do this right and we're gonna make a lot of people happy tonight. Instead of killing, we're going to bring someone back to life. Good luck, gentlemen."

Bronson turned to Maxwell. "I have to say something, Brick." His voice was low, almost respectful. "All that stuff between us back on the ship—well, that was anger and ego talking. I was wrong, and I apologize. I'm a professional, and from what I hear, you are too. Let's put it behind us and get this job done. Okay?"

He extended his hand.

Maxwell was caught off guard. He shook Bronson's hand, thinking that this was definitely not the Bronson he remembered. He'd been wrong about the man. "Okay. We're on the same team, Ted."

Bronson squeezed his hand for another second. "Good man. Now let's go make it happen."

He hauled the prisoner to his feet. Al-Fasr recoiled as Bronson pulled out his Glock semiautomatic and held it under his nose. "Stay in front of me. No communicating of any kind, not one word, no abrupt movements. I will not hesitate to put a bullet in your head. Got that?"

Al-Fasr nodded his understanding.

Bronson slung an MP-5N submachine gun over his shoulder, then prodded Al-Fasr to move on down the path.

Bronson and Maxwell each strapped on their NVG. They looked like alien creatures, the two eyecups and the long snout extending six inches from their faces, a faint green glow behind the eyepieces. Through the NVG, the impenetrable blackness became a greenish daylight. Maxwell could see the rutted path for a quarter mile ahead of them. Weeds, rocks, low-hanging shrubs stood out in minute detail.

The hood over Al-Fasr's eyes had been removed. Without NVG, he moved warily in the darkness, his boots scuffing the rocky path. Night birds flitted in the nearby low shrubs. In the reeds beside the path, the slow-moving river made a dull gurgle.

For six minutes they walked, stopping every hundred yards or so to scan the terrain. Rounding a bend in the path, they saw the squarish outlines of low buildings, huts, an ancient wall.

Bronson signaled a stop while he scanned the area.

"Somebody's home," he said in a low voice.

Maxwell peered through his own goggles. He saw no sign of life. The huts looked abandoned, the roofs partly gone, windows missing.

"What do you see?"

"On top of that building to the left," said Bronson. "Somebody watching us."

He gave Al-Fasr another prod. "Okay, let's go close the deal."

They followed the path through an opening in the crumbling wall, between single-story buildings. They stopped at an open space in the center of the village.

The courtyard. The designated meeting place.

Bronson scanned again, sweeping the area from side to side.

A voice came from the darkness. "Stay where you are. Identify yourselves."

At the sound of the heavily accented voice, Al-Fasr cocked his head, peering across the darkened courtyard.

"We have a gift from the sea," said Bronson, reciting the prearranged script. "There are three of us."

"Do you have Jamal?"

Bronson pressed the muzzle of the Glock into Al-Fasr's neck. "Tell him."

"I am here," called out Al-Fasr. "They speak the truth."

In the artificial green light, Maxwell saw figures appear on the far side of the courtyard. There were three men, two with weapons, one unarmed. The unarmed man was tall, moving with a shambling gait. He had nearly white hair. His face was gaunt.

Maxwell felt the excitement rise up in him. *Raz.* It had to be him. Thirty yards from freedom.

"The prisoners will advance," said the voice across the courtyard.

Manama, Bahrain

Like old times, thought Tyrwhitt.

She used to like being picked up like this. She always put up a token resistance, then relaxed and allowed herself to be carried inside the hotel room.

A flood of old memories came over him. He remembered the familiar feel of her legs on his arm, the chestnut hair brushing his face.

He let the door close behind them.

"Put me down, Chris. This is a very dangerous idea."

He continued holding her in his arms. "Begging your pardon, Madame, but it seems to me to be a perfectly good idea."

"Put me down, damn it."

He held her several more seconds, savoring the scent of her hair. As he lowered her feet to the floor, he noticed something on the sideboard behind her.

A vase filled with fresh roses. A card lay beside the vase.

"We are now at the point," he said, "when you're supposed to say 'mix yourself a drink while I get into something comfortable.'"

"You don't need a drink. And I'm in something comfortable."

He positioned himself in front of the roses so that she couldn't see them.

"Why don't you put on some music then? It'll help you relax."

"I'm already relaxed. Numb, in fact."

"Oh, humor me, darling. Just a little music, a quick drink, and I'll go. Promise."

She gave him a wary look, then went to the CD player across the room. "Still like jazz?" she said. "How's Sonny Rollins?"

"Good stuff. Play it."

While she loaded the CD, he turned to the sideboard and removed the card that lay beside the vase of roses. Even before he read the card, he knew who it would be from.

My dearest Claire,
Our anniversary, sort of. Remember this night a
year ago in Dubai? Wish I were there with you.
Duty calls, but not for much longer. See you soon.

All my love,
Sam

She was still fussing with the CD player. He wadded up the card, then pulled out one of his business cards. On the back he scrawled a hurried note.

To my darling Claire,
Like old times.
Chris

"What's that?" said Claire, turning away from the CD player.

He slipped the card onto the sideboard beside the roses. "Oh, just a little something," he said.

"Roses?" Her eyes widened. "Where did those come from? Did you . . ."

She went to the flowers, then picked up the card.

He watched her read the card. There was something about roses, he thought. When everything else failed—the booze and soft music and personal charm—you could count on roses. Roses were magic.

Of course, these weren't exactly *his* roses, but that was a technicality. It was the thought that counted.

She was smelling the roses, clutching the vase to her. "I'm very touched, Chris. Thank you."

"I remembered how much you love roses."

Her eyes were misting. "Still a romantic, aren't you?"

He smiled. "Some things never change."

"But a dangerous romantic."

"Not so dangerous. I'm the same chap you were in love with ten years ago."

"I don't know." She clutched the roses to her. "So much has changed in ten years."

"One thing hasn't changed. I love you as much as always."

At this, the hazel eyes became more misty. Her wariness seemed to be melting away.

He took the roses from her and returned them to the sideboard. Gently, he took her into his arms. Just like old times.

USS Ronald Reagan

"Holy shit," said Bullet Alexander.

He and Carson were in Alexander's stateroom. On the desk between them was Carson's digital recorder.

The device was not much larger than a cigarette lighter. Inserted in a shirt pocket, it could pick up every word spoken within ten feet.

"When did you record this?"

"Night before last," said Carson. "During the late shift. Lieutenant DiLorenzo and I were in the QA space."

"Anyone else with you?"

"No, sir."

Alexander stared in wonder at the recorder. "May I ask why you're giving me this?"

Carson looked at him. "I guess it was because of something you said. That you were counting on me. It got me to thinking about what was most important—my getting promoted, or having another of our jets go down, maybe taking one of the pilots with it. I don't want that on my conscience."

"Which aircraft were given the bogus corrosion inspections?"

"Numbers 306, 307, and 309."

"Number 306 was the bird I jumped out of."

"Lieutenant DiLorenzo backdated the inspection record. He did it after your jet had already crashed."

Alexander's eyes blazed. "Could that aircraft have been affected by corrosion?"

Carson winced. "Knowing what we know now, probably. From the wreckage there was no way to prove it."

For a moment Alexander let his mind drift back to the cockpit of his doomed jet. He could see the runway of Al Jaber rising up to meet him, the jet wobbling out of control, the sudden violence of the ejection. The taste of desert sand in his mouth as he hit the ground.

Those sons of bitches.

He picked up a clipboard on his desk. "Three-oh-seven is airborne now. Looks like CAG is flying it. Do you think that jet has airframe corrosion too?"

A glum look passed over Carson's face. "If we'd inspected it like we were supposed to, I could answer that."

Alexander glowered at the recorder. "And you're sure that both Lieutenant DiLorenzo and Commander Manson are in on this?"

"You heard the recording, sir."

"Yeah, I sure did." Alexander stood and rubbed his chin for a moment, still looking at the recorder. "Are you willing to testify against them?"

Carson nodded.

"Even if it means having charges brought against you?"

Carson swallowed hard. "Yes, sir."

Alexander picked up the recorder and slipped it into the pocket of his leather flight jacket. "You're relieved of your duties for now. Stay away from the maintenance offices and don't talk to anyone until I call for you."

"Yes, sir. What's going to happen to me?"

"That's up to the skipper. But I promise you one thing. I'm going to nail those other two sons of bitches."

Haw Umm Qasr, Iran

Al-Fasr's nerves were resonating like high-tension wires. In his career as a soldier he had been exposed to many threats, but he had always managed to control the circumstances. He had chosen his battles, calculated his chances, steered the outcome.

This was different. Never had he felt so vulnerable.

He took careful steps, moving deliberately toward the voice across the courtyard. His right leg was aching again, sending sharp pains up his thigh. On the far side he could see only vague forms. How many? Three? One would be the American prisoner.

He had recognized Abu's voice. His faithful lieu-tenant. His second-in-command. Abu was there to bring him back from captivity.

Or was he?

Al-Fasr's instincts were screaming at him. Some-thing—an inflection in Abu's voice, the peculiar venue of this exchange, an old, nagging suspicion—was send-ing him a warning signal.

Something wasn't right. But he was powerless, at least at the moment. His hands were still bound with the tie-wraps. He knew that Bronson's pistol was aimed squarely at the middle of his back. Across the courtyard waited Abu. With another pistol.

Abu is your comrade. Your fellow warrior. He is here to rescue you.

He had to believe. He had no choice.

In the gloom of the unlighted courtyard, he saw a shadow coming toward him. Shambling, moving with stiff-legged steps, like a man who'd lived for a long time in confinement.

Rasmussen.

His judgment had been vindicated. Accepting the prisoner as a gift from Saddam Hussein, using him as a bargaining chip—it had been a shrewd investment. Now it would purchase freedom for them both.

It was strange, he thought. He could feel a sense of camaraderie with the prisoner. He remembered the long talks with the American. Rasmussen had been an hon-orable and intelligent companion.

The dark form of the American materialized out of the gloom, shuffling toward him. Yes, it was definitely Rasmussen. Al-Fasr wondered whether he understood what was happening.

"Good luck, Navy," said Al-Fasr when they were three feet apart. "Perhaps we'll meet again."

The prisoner's face seemed to come alive. For a moment he stopped and looked at Al-Fasr. "I don't think so, Colonel."

Rasmussen shuffled past him, toward the waiting Americans. Ahead of Al-Fasr were the dark forms of Abu and someone else.

Who?

Then he recognized him. Omar Al-Iryani was an Afghan who had been at Abu's side since the Mujahedeen days. Al-Fasr suspected that it was Omar who had carried out the executions of the *Sherji* who were not loyal to Abu Mahmed.

A silence lay over the courtyard. Al-Fasr could hear Rasmussen's shuffling footsteps behind him. Over the rim of the low buildings, the sky was pinkening. Dawn was less than half an hour away.

Twenty yards to the edge of the courtyard. The ache in Al-Fasr's leg was sharper now. The hike from the helicopter had been pure agony for him.

In the thin light, he could see Abu and Omar watching.

Something was wrong. *What?*

Omar's eyes. The Afghan's eyes were darting from Al-Fasr to something else. Something off to the side, behind Al-Fasr.

Al-Fasr turned to look behind him. Rasmussen was still walking toward the far edge of the courtyard. Maxwell and Bronson hadn't moved.

He heard the soft *clack* of metal on metal. A rifle bolt sliding home. He turned toward the sound.

Then he saw it. Something dark, moving on the roof of the building across the courtyard. Out of the view of the Americans.

Al-Fasr had sensed treachery since he climbed out of the helicopter. That was why Abu had set this up. He wanted Al-Fasr as a martyr, not a commander.

"Sniper!" he yelled. He spun around, looking for

Rasmussen. He ran toward the American as fast as his crippled leg would move him. The sound of gunfire split the morning stillness.

He saw Rasmussen go down. In a low crouch Al-Fasr scuttled toward him. More shots rang out. He was almost there when a bullet thudded into his body.

CHAPTER 24

HUNCHES

Haw Umm Qasr, Iran
0520, Wednesday, 24 March

Maxwell was caught off guard. In the sudden chaos, he saw muzzle flashes, Rasmussen falling, heard Bronson's SMG rattle off a burst.

He dropped to one knee, snatching the .45 from its holster.

Across the clearing he saw a flash. In the next instant he felt the whir of the bullet sizzle past his right ear.

Holding the heavy pistol in both hands, he leveled the sights on the larger of the two forms and snapped off a round. The Colt sounded like a howitzer going off in his hands. In the greenish light of the NVG, he saw plaster fly off the wall of the building behind his target.

Shit.

Another flash from across the courtyard. Another bullet whizzing past, smacking plaster.

Steady. He aimed again, sucked in a breath. *Just like the practice range.* The problem was, he hadn't practiced with this damned, clunky NVG strapped on his head.

He held his breath, keeping the sights level on the silhouette across the courtyard. *Squeeze.*

Again the howitzer boomed in his hands.

This time he saw the taller man lurch backward, falling on his back. He lay writhing on the ground.

Maxwell swung his head, scanning with the goggles, looking for the second shooter.

Nothing. He was gone.

Holding the Colt out in front of him, he swung back to the building behind him. He saw Bronson scuttling across the dirt. He stopped, raised the SMG to his shoulder, fired a short burst at the rooftop.

A rifle slid off the roof and landed with a clunk in the courtyard. Two seconds later, the body of the sniper slid down, thudding into the dirt like a bag of laundry heaved from a balcony.

Bronson dropped back to the wall, scanning from left to right, sweeping the rooftops.

"Advantage America," he said. "We have the goggles, they don't."

"How many are there?"

"I killed two snipers on the roof," said Bronson. "How about the two across the courtyard?"

"One down. The other's gone."

"There'll be more on the way. We have to get the hell out of here."

Maxwell looked at the dark shape lying in the courtyard. "We've gotta get Raz—"

Bronson's portable transceiver crackled. "Raven, this is Gracie. What's going on there? Are you guys taking fire?"

"Affirmative, but we've got it stabilized," answered Bronson. "We're coming out. We need to leave as soon as we get there. Do you copy that?"

"We copy. Understand Basher. We're on the way."

"Negative, negative. Just be ready to pull out when we get there."

"Roger, Raven. We're standing by."

Bronson turned to Maxwell. "I want you to clear out

of the village. Go to the river and wait for me. I'll be a minute behind you to cover our exit."

"What about Raz?"

"I'll get him. Now you go!"

Maxwell glanced once again at the inert form in the courtyard, then rose and headed into the darkness outside the village.

It was all a deception.

That was the only conclusion Mustafa Ashbar could draw, watching the scene from his vantage point behind the low wall.

With the NVGs that Tyrwhitt had given him, he could see the shooters and the angle of the gunfire. *How many?* Two *Sherji* on the roof, plus Abu and Omar in the courtyard. Two Americans, both wearing NVGs.

He kept his own submachine gun firmly in his grasp, his finger crooked around the trigger guard. It was an Uzi, his favorite, donated by a grateful Mossad agent whose life he had saved one night in Damascus.

For a moment Mustafa considered interfering in the gun duel, but he quickly rejected the idea. It would just betray his presence to the other *Sherji* in the area. The truth was, he didn't have any vested interest in the outcome. The Americans were his current employers, but this mission was a private one. His only purpose here was to observe the event, then return to Bahrain and report the details to Tyrwhitt.

Tyrwhitt, the crazy one.

Mustafa felt no loyalty to the Americans, certainly no more than he felt to the Israelis or the Kurds or the Russians. He was a stateless person whose fealty was to himself and, in rare instances, to trusted comrades. Like Tyrwhitt.

He and Tyrwhitt were from the same mold, Mustafa reflected. They spied and informed and killed for money, nothing more. Certainly not for allegiance to a country. But they had risked their lives to save each other, which was the reason Mustafa had agreed to perform this mission.

He watched, remaining motionless, as the second American departed the courtyard. He saw the first one—Bronson, the American chief in Bahrain—move toward the two downed prisoners.

With a growing certainty, Mustafa knew what would happen next. And he could guess why.

Maybe he should use the Uzi.

No, he decided. Stay out of it. You are an observer, not a participant. Let it happen.

Nothing made sense anymore.

Rasmussen lay facedown on the cobbled courtyard. It was possible, he supposed, that he was dreaming. None of this was really happening. Or he was dead already and this was some version of hell.

Who was shooting at whom? *Why?*

Al-Fasr, whom he thought was dead, had appeared in the darkness, passing him in the courtyard. *Good luck, Navy.* What did he mean?

He hadn't understood why they brought him to the village at night until he heard the voices. *American* voices. Then he had done as Abu told him. He began walking toward the voices.

Toward freedom. For an incredible moment, he had let himself believe he was going home.

He should have known better. It was better to believe in nothing. Better no hope at all than to have his dreams dashed like cheap glass.

The gunfire had stopped. He sensed someone crawling toward him. He heard panting, the labored sound of deep breathing.

"Get out of here," said a raspy voice. "Run for it. It's a trap."

Rasmussen stared at the shadowy figure. It was Al-Fasr. He appeared to be wounded.

"You've been hit," said Rasmussen. "Who was it?"

"It doesn't matter," said Al-Fasr. "This is where I belong, but not you. You have to get out of this place."

Rasmussen rose to his knees to help Al-Fasr. He could see that he was bleeding. The bullet seemed to have penetrated his shoulder. Rasmussen bent over him, trying to locate the wound.

"For God's sake, run," Al-Fasr croaked. "It's your only chance."

Rasmussen couldn't make himself move. Run from whom? Where? His only chance for what?

He saw a dark silhouette coming toward him. The man looked like a predator, a black apparatus protruding from his face. He was dressed in camouflage BDUs. In one hand he carried a submachine gun.

"Who are you?" said Rasmussen.

The man didn't answer. He removed the device from his face, and in the greenish glow from the detached device, Rasmussen glimpsed the features of his face. He was not an Arab. He had cold, penetrating eyes and a hard set to his mouth.

"He's your worst enemy," said Al-Fasr.

The man peered down at Al-Fasr, studying him for a moment. He pulled a semiautomatic pistol from his belt and aimed it squarely at Al-Fasr's head.

"Noooooo!" yelled Rasmussen.

He flinched at the sharp crack of the shot.

Disbelieving, he stared at the body of Jamal Al-Fasr, who lay facedown, a pool of blood spreading beneath him.

The man turned his attention to Rasmussen. He swung the pistol and aimed it at his head.

Maxwell followed Bronson's instructions. Leaving the courtyard, he went as far as the crumbling old wall that bordered the far edge of the village. In the greenish light of the NVGs, he could see the path that ran along the river. The path to the helicopter and safety.

Then he turned around.

As a fighter pilot, Maxwell had learned to trust his intuition. More than once a hunch had kept him alive, hinted to him that something—the airplane, the weather, the enemy—was about to turn on him.

Something was wrong. He didn't know what it was, only that he was getting one of those subliminal warnings. It was wrong to leave their backup behind at the LZ. It was wrong to leave Raz in the courtyard.

He started running back toward the village.

An old dictum from test pilot school came to him: *Remember your first impression. It is almost always the right one.* It applied to people as well as airplanes. He remembered his first impression of Bronson—a cynical, ambitious man with a secret agenda. Except that in the last few hours Maxwell had been persuaded to change his first impression of Bronson.

Bronson is not what you think.

He ran faster. He was rounding the corner into the courtyard when he heard the pistol shot. The muzzle flash was amplified in the NVG, but from thirty feet away he could see everything.

"Hold it!" he called. He stopped in the shadow of the low building.

On the ground lay a body. He saw Bronson, pistol in his hand, aiming at a kneeling man's head. The man on his knees wore a dejected, resigned expression.

A man awaiting execution.

"Don't shoot him, Ted."

Bronson lowered the gun, but he didn't turn around. "I told you to get out of here. Now do it."

"Drop the gun, Ted."

Bronson didn't move.

Maxwell fired a round from the .45 over Bronson's

head. Bronson dropped the pistol. He still had the SMG slung over his left shoulder.

"This isn't your business," Bronson said. "Go to the helicopter."

"Not without Raz."

A deathly stillness fell over the courtyard. Bronson kept his back turned. Maxwell could see that he wasn't wearing the NVG. From the east, a pale light had begun to insert itself into the darkness.

Bronson whirled, catching Maxwell by surprise. The first burst from the SMG was wild, kicking up dirt ten yards away. Bronson was trying to find his target in the darkness beneath the building.

Maxwell forced himself to take his time. *Breathe in, hold it . . .*

He superimposed the sights over the greenish shape of the man with the SMG.

Another burst from the SMG. Plaster shattered from the wall behind him. Maxwell saw Bronson's eyes over the barrel of the submachine gun, looking for him.

Finding him. The muzzle of the SMG swung toward him.

Squeeze.

The Colt recoiled in Maxwell's grip. He forced himself to keep his eye open, ready to fire again.

It wasn't necessary. Through the goggles he could see Bronson. He was down, lying on his back, legs still kicking. The submachine gun lay beside him.

Maxwell walked to him, keeping the Colt trained on the spread-eagled body. He ejected the clip and rammed a fresh one home.

Maxwell removed the NVG and looked down at Bronson's body. He had a purplish cavity in the middle of his forehead. His sightless eyes stared up into the pinkening sky.

Rasmussen rose to his feet, wearing a stunned expression. "You called me 'Raz,'" he said. "Who are you?"

"I'm Brick Maxwell."

"Maxwell?" Rasmussen stared in disbelief. "You were my best friend."

Maxwell grinned at him. "I still am, buddy."

Rasmussen looked stunned.

Bursts of gunfire came from the river. Rasmussen still hadn't moved. He kept staring at Bronson's body.

"Who's that?"

"A bad guy," said Maxwell.

"An American."

"Yeah."

Rasmussen seemed to think about this for a moment. "Why did he want to kill me?"

Maxwell tried to think of a good answer. He couldn't, so he told the truth. "I don't know."

"And you shot him."

"Yeah."

It was more than Rasmussen could comprehend. For several more seconds he stood over the two bodies, staring first at Bronson, then Al-Fasr.

Another staccato rattle of gunfire, this time only a hundred yards away.

"We have to get out of here, Raz. We're in Indian country. Stay close and follow me."

He picked up Bronson's SMG, then handed the Glock to Rasmussen. Rasmussen looked at the weapon with disgust, seeming to remember that it had just been used to kill Al-Fasr. And almost used to kill him.

"C'mon, Raz," said Maxwell, taking him by the wrist. "We have to catch our ride home."

He led Rasmussen out of the courtyard. He retraced his steps back through the village, across the old wall, along the path toward the river. They stayed in the shadows, running from one patch of cover to the next. Sporadic bursts of gunfire along the river broke the morning stillness.

Around the first bend in the trail, they encountered three NVG-clad men, running at full tilt toward them. Two fanned to either side, kneeling and aiming their M16s at Maxwell and Rasmussen.

"We're Raven Swoop," Maxwell called. "We're coming out."

"Brick?" Gracie Allen walked up to Maxwell and removed his NVG. He stared at Rasmussen. "I'll be damned," he said. "You got him."

Rasmussen peered back at Allen, his face filled with disbelief. "Gracie? Is that you? Gracie Allen?"

"Yeah, Raz, it's me." Allen gave Rasmussen a hug. "It's been a while, pal."

Allen turned to Maxwell. "What the hell happened? I've been calling you on the transceiver. Where's Bronson?"

Maxwell nodded toward the village. "The deal went sour. Bronson's dead."

"Damn," said Allen, shaking his head. "There wasn't supposed to be any killing. Now we're in a world of trouble. The gomers showed up in strength at the LZ and the helo had to bug out. Now we've gotta find a new LZ so he can snatch us out of here."

As if on cue, another rattle of gunfire erupted nearby, somewhere around the bend in the trail.

Allen barked several terse commands into his transceiver, then listened to the reply in the earpiece.

"That was Hewlitt," said Allen. "His team is behind us a quarter of a mile. They're engaged with a couple hundred gomers, maybe more. We still have the NVGs and the advantage of darkness, but the sun is coming up. Real soon we're gonna be in shit city."

Maxwell peered into the pinkening sky. "This might be a good time to call for the cavalry, Gracie."

USS Ronald Reagan

"You wanted to see me, XO?"

Alexander looked up from his desk to see Splat DiLorenzo in the stateroom doorway. "Come in and close the door behind you."

DiLorenzo took a seat at the desk facing Alexander. "What's up?" He made a show of checking his watch.

The watch-checking he'd picked up from Manson, Alexander guessed. He'd never had a good feeling about DiLorenzo. Nothing specific, just a faint whiff of hostility that seemed to emanate from him.

DiLorenzo was older than the other squadron officers, having come up through the ranks as an enlisted man. He was polite enough, but around Alexander he always had an air of frostiness. That probably came from Manson too.

"I've just come across some disturbing information, Splat. I have reason to believe that someone in the squadron has been falsifying aircraft inspection records."

DiLorenzo let out a dry chuckle. "Now that's pretty hard to believe. Why would anyone do a thing like that?"

"I was hoping you could help me figure it out."

DiLorenzo shook his head. "I don't have a clue. Why do you think I could help?"

Alexander smiled, remembering how DiLorenzo liked to answer a question with a question. "Well, let's suppose someone wanted to get an aircraft through the corrosion inspection lickety-split, back on the line. They could just pencil in the inspection and be done with it."

"Does anyone use pencils anymore?" Another dry chuckle.

"The computer network then."

"It takes a password to get on the LAN. Whoever did it would have to be authorized."

"Unless it was someone who had stolen the password. Someone very clever."

For just an instant, he thought he saw a flicker of alarm pass over DiLorenzo's face. "What are you saying?" said DiLorenzo. "That one of my guys is hacking the computer?"

"Maybe. Who would be in a position to do that?"

"Only one or two people," said DiLorenzo, looking concerned. "If it was true, then I'm to blame. I've been told that I'm sometimes too trusting with my guys, but, you know, that's the way I am. I would just never have thought that . . ."

"How about Carson? Could he be logging the false entries?"

DiLorenzo nodded gravely. "I hate to say this about one of my own people, but, yes, I'm afraid it could be Carson. I've been worried about him lately. Poor Carson, he always tries to blame other people—me even— for his mistakes. He's had a bad attitude ever since he got those bad evals and didn't make chief."

Alexander had to force himself to keep his expression blank. This guy DiLorenzo was too much. All torn up inside over what one of his troops had done to tarnish the honor of the squadron. Blaming himself for not reading the danger signals. DiLorenzo deserved an academy award.

And then Alexander couldn't hold it any longer. He cracked up laughing.

"What's so funny?" asked DiLorenzo.

"This." Alexander reached across his desk and punched the play button on the digital recorder.

For five minutes DiLorenzo sat motionless, his face a frozen mask, as he listened to the recorded voices.

"Your initials are on the records too."

"So what? Everyone knows how the system works. The QA officer doesn't do the inspections. He takes the word of the petty officer who reports to him that the job was completed. That happens to be you, Carson. If it comes to an inquest, I promise you that you will be hanging all alone in the breeze. You are in this by yourself, and anything you say to the contrary will be denied by me and Commander Manson. You will have no proof."

"Okay. I get the picture."

"Good. I always knew you were a team player, Carson. Remember that Commander Manson takes care of his team."

The recording ended. DiLorenzo still hadn't moved. He stared straight ahead, not blinking, looking like a wax dummy.

Alexander tilted back in his chair, enjoying himself. "Okay, Splat, tell me again the part about poor Carson, the one who tries to blame everyone—you, even—for his mistakes. The one with the bad attitude."

DiLorenzo looked at Alexander as if seeing him for the first time. "I want a lawyer," he said.

CHAPTER 25

MAVERICK

Haw Umm Qasr, Iran
0620, Wednesday, 24 March

"About damn time," muttered Boyce into his oxygen mask.

His four Super Hornets were in a holding stack, ten miles northwest of the Raven Swoop site. Each jet carried twelve CBU-59 APAM—anti-personnel and material—dispensers, as well as a standard load of AIM-9 and AIM-120 air-to-air missiles and a full load of twenty-millimeter. For extra measure, Boyce and his wingman each carried one Maverick laser-guided missile.

In the pale light of dawn, Boyce could make out the undulating dark river, the deserted village, and the white smoke that the FAC—Forward Air Controller—had deployed to mark the bull's-eye reference point.

The voice of Snake Rafferty, the FAC assigned to Hewlitt's unit, crackled in Boyce's headset. "Your primary target is dug in, one-five-zero degrees, two hundred yards from bull's-eye. Troops, about two hundred of them, in a line southeast of bull's-eye."

"Galeforce Zero-one copies," Boyce acknowledged.

"Galeforce Two-one will push in fifteen seconds,"

called Rico Flores. His flight of four Super Hornets would leave the stack fifteen seconds behind Boyce's flight. The result would be a continuous rain of antipersonnel bombs on the dug-in *Sherji*.

"Galeforce Zero-one, Sea Lord," came the voice of the controller aboard the orbiting E-2C Hawkeye. "Picture clear. No threats."

"Galeforce copies." Well, Boyce thought, at least the gomers didn't bring air defense toys to the party. It meant that the strike three days ago had taken out Bu Hasa's serious assets.

He wondered what went wrong. It had been too much to hope for that the prisoner exchange would go without a glitch. There was always a glitch. In the war against terrorists, nothing went as you expected.

He wanted to ask whether they'd gotten Rasmussen, but he didn't. Better not put it on the radio, just in case. He'd wait until the team was in the helo, on the way home.

"Galeforce flight, check knockers up," he called. In sequence, two through eight, the Hornet pilots confirmed their master armament switches selected to the armed position.

Also inbound were the Cobra gunships, still ten miles away. They would stay low and out of the fight until Boyce's Hornets had laid down the cluster bombs. Then they would move in with their own rockets and Vulcan cannon.

The eastern horizon was glowing orange with the new dawn. Down below, Boyce could see the dark, marshy landscape punctuated by ribbons of morning fog. The smoke of Snake's marker was curling straight upward like a wispy white ribbon.

Through his HUD he saw the *Sherji* positions. Tiny sparks of light were already winking at him as he slanted down toward the target.

Good, he thought. Small arms fire. A few suicidal

Sherji were popping away with light assault rifles. That was fine with Boyce. It made their positions easier to spot.

He felt the low, purposeful heat of anger warming his insides. The *Sherji* were playing the same game as they had in Yemen. Use someone on the ground as bait, suck in a recovery team, spring the trap.

Sorry, gomers. Game's over.

The target swelled in his Head's-Up Display. He eased the CCIP—Continuously Computed Impact Point—cross in his HUD over the winking muzzle flashes and pressed the pickle button on the stick. Through the airframe of the Hornet he felt the *thunk* of the ejectors kicking off the CBU canisters.

Seconds later, "On target, on target. Good hits. Galeforce Zero-two, move your aim point thirty yards left."

Boyce pulled, grunting against the four Gs on his body. Over his shoulder he could see the next Hornet sweeping low over the target, laying a fresh swath of cluster bombs. He could visualize the destruction on the ground. Each dispenser deployed hundreds of BLU-77 bomblets that sliced through everything in their path—trees, vehicles, troops—like tiny machetes.

One by one, Boyce and his wingmen circled for their second and final pass.

"Galeforce Zero-four off target, Winchester." Winchester meant that all of his ordnance had been expended.

By the time Flores's Hornets arrived over the *Sherji* positions, it was over.

"Galeforce Two-one checking in as fragged."

"Hold fire, Two-one. The gomers are running," called Snake. "The survivors are heading for the marshes. Looks like CAG's flight got most of the job done."

"Galeforce is off target, Snake," called Boyce. "You can call in Cleaver." "Cleaver" was the call sign of the lead Cobra gunship pilot. With their high-velocity

Gatling guns, the Cobras would chase down the retreating *Sherji* like hawks chasing mice.

Thinking of the slaughter on the ground, Boyce felt one fleeting moment of regret for the loss of life. The moment passed. His thoughts were replaced with images of the ambush they had tried to set.

The trapped marines in Yemen.

The torpedoing of the *Reagan* in the Gulf of Aden.

The attack on the World Trade Center. On the Pentagon.

"Stick it to 'em, Cleaver," he called.

The new sun was spreading a pale glow over the landscape, casting shadows behind the ridges and levees of the marsh. Gazing down from five thousand feet, Boyce saw the three other fighters of his flight in a climbing rendezvous turn, rejoining the formation.

The target area looked like a wave of lava had flowed through it. All vegetation had been removed. A gray veil of smoke hovered over the ground. To the north, the Cobras were pursuing the escaping *Sherji*, flying in a line-abreast formation low over the terrain. Boyce could almost smell the stench of death.

And then he spotted something. To the west, concealed behind the low shrubs along the river.

A plume of dust.

As he arced his Hornet around to the west, peering down sun, he got a better glimpse. A truck of some kind, drab green, canvas top, driving on a levee concealed by weeds and foliage. It was kicking up a barely noticeable rooster tail of dust.

Interesting.

"Snake, Galeforce One-one. Do you have a vehicle exiting the target area to the north? Maybe three miles?"

"Negative, Galeforce. If he's leaving the party in that direction, he's one of the guests. You're cleared to engage. Cleared in hot."

"Galeforce copies."

He studied the vehicle as it sped westward. In another minute it would reach the high foliage of the marsh and be out of sight.

During the mission planning back on the *Reagan*, it had occurred to him that hauling a 670-pound antitank missile amounted to gross overkill. There wouldn't be any suitable target for a weapon like the IR-guided AGM-65F Maverick. But something—a nagging voice from his subconscious—told him to load it anyway.

What the hell, you never knew what you might find.

Sanctuary.

It was so close he could taste it. The stagnant redolence of the decaying swamp grass filled the cabin of the Land Rover, mixing with the dry dust smell coming up from the levee. Ahead lay the thick foliage and hiding places of the marshes. In this watery wilderness he would be safe.

Abu Mahmed felt almost giddy with his success. Again he had dodged the bombs and guns of the infidels. Behind him lay the ruins of the old Bu Hasa Brigade—the brigade commanded by the incompetent dreamer, Jamal Al-Fasr.

Al-Fasr was a martyr. In death he would be a greater figure than at any time in his life. Abu Mahmed was now the unquestioned leader of the *new* Bu Hasa Brigade. Under his direction, the Brigade would reform here in the ancient ruins of Babylonia. The holy war against the Great Satan would resume with greater fury than ever before.

It had been necessary to cooperate with the Americans—to let them *think* he was cooperating—in order to gain leadership of the holy war. The Bu Hasa Brigade had to be purified in order to save it. In one violent episode, Allah's vengeance had been dispensed on both Al-Fasr and the American CIA operative, Bronson. And, unfortunately, Omar.

In his overweening arrogance, Bronson had assumed that it was he who was manipulating events, using Abu Mahmed to his advantage. It was typical American insolence, thinking he was superior to his Arab counterparts.

He had been stupid.

Abu was driving the Land Rover. It was difficult keeping the vehicle on the narrow path atop the levee, trying to peer through the dawn mist and flat light. In the seat beside him was Ali, the *Sherji* who had witnessed the shooting of Al-Fasr by Bronson, and then the killing of Bronson by his fellow American.

That was the part that perplexed Abu. He knew that Bronson wanted Al-Fasr dead—that had been their bargain. The secret that Bronson had kept from Abu was that he also wanted the American prisoner, Rasmussen, dead.

Why? According to Ali, Bronson had been about to execute the prisoner when his fellow American shot him.

Very peculiar. But the Americans behaved in peculiar ways. They were a godless and barbaric society that would soon—

His thoughts were interrupted by Ali's frantic gesturing.

"What's the matter with you?"

Ali was a brave but ignorant Uzbek peasant. He was pointing behind the Rover. "Back there, something . . ."

Abu kept one hand on the steering wheel as he craned his neck around. He had only a narrow view through the enclosure in the back of the Rover.

The hairs on his neck stood up.

Framed in the rectangular opening was a smoke trail. It was zigzagging like a bat in flight.

Abu slowed the Land Rover, his attention fixed on the object behind them. *What is it?*

In the next instant he knew. The object swelled to fill the rectangular opening.

More from instinct than deliberate choice, he swerved the Land Rover, knowing as they careened off the levee that it was a futile move. He was vaguely aware of the scream that erupted from Ali's throat.

Abu Mahmed's last flash of awareness was of the cataclysmic ball of flame that transformed his body into molten protoplasm.

Mustafa heard the sounds of the jets fade in the south, replaced by the whopping noise of helicopter blades. The Americans had routed the *Sherji*, and soon they would be leaving.

The *Sherji* were stupid. Those who survived the air attack were running like rabbits to the northern marshes. Like most terrorists, they trusted too much in Allah and gave too little credence to the strength of their enemy. At least two hundred, perhaps more, had kept their appointments with Allah this morning.

He had remained concealed at the edge of the village courtyard while the tableau played itself out—each of the warring parties slaying the other until only two were left. When the two Americans departed, the courtyard was littered with the dead.

He was not surprised. After meeting Abu Mahmed and his lieutenant, Omar Al-Iryani, during the mission with Tyrwhitt, he knew what would happen. He had seen it in their faces. They were the same self-assured, dark-eyed fanatical faces he had seen in the other terrorist groups—Al Qaeda, Hamas, Hezbollah, Abu Nidal. They were men who worshiped death.

But something happened in the courtyard that *did* surprise him. An American, whom he recognized as the CIA chief in Bahrain, cold-bloodedly executed the Bu Hasa leader, Al-Fasr. When he was about to execute the

American prisoner, he was thwarted by the other American, the tall pilot called Maxwell.

Who killed Bronson.

Very perplexing. Mustafa had no idea why such a sequence of events occurred, but he could guess the impact it would have back in the paneled offices of the CIA. It was a story that would send tremors all the way to Washington.

Which, he understood now, was why Tyrwhitt had sent him on this unauthorized mission.

Mustafa continued to stare at the motionless bodies in the courtyard. The thin light of dawn was illuminating them. He could see the body of Bronson, face to the sky, the dark cavity of a heavy-caliber pistol round in his forehead.

In the distance he could hear the rattle of the Gatling guns on the Cobra helicopters. The *Sherji* were in full retreat. Mustafa knew what would happen next. The Americans wouldn't leave their fallen soldiers behind. They would collect the body of Bronson and, probably, Al-Fasr.

Mustafa reached a decision. It was illogical, dangerous even, but he was following his instinct. He scanned the courtyard for signs of life. There were none. He climbed over the low wall. As he scuttled across the courtyard to the motionless bodies, he slipped the nine-inch curved blade of his *kukri* fighting knife from its scabbard.

Rasmussen felt as if he were dreaming. Two burly marines, one on each arm, hoisted him into the helicopter.

He sat in the forward cabin, his back to the cockpit bulkhead. On the bench next to him were Gracie Allen and Brick Maxwell. One now a strike fighter wing commander, the other a squadron skipper.

Amazing.

These two had been with him on the mission into Iraq. The only one in the flight not here was his wingman, DeLancey. He wondered if DeLancey was still in the Navy.

It was funny how memory worked. He could recall with perfect clarity the details of his last flight—the blackness of the night, the winking lights of Baghdad on the horizon, the fiery tail of the missile he'd fired at the oncoming MiG. He could remember them as if they happened yesterday. Other large pieces of his life were gone like gaping holes in a floor. He was a Rip fucking Van Winkle.

The cabin filled with black-faced, grinning marines. They were high-fiving each other, shaking hands, full of themselves. Several wanted to shake his hand. A young corporal asked for his autograph. Their commander, a lieutenant colonel, told them to cool it and leave the guy alone.

They came to get me.

The reality still hadn't taken hold. *Why now? After all these years, why did they come now?* It was entirely possible, Rasmussen thought, that he was hallucinating.

His thoughts kept drifting back to the darkened courtyard. Something very unreal happened back there, and he was still puzzling together the pieces. Little by little, as in a complicated mosaic, he was getting a sense of what it meant.

Someone didn't want him to leave Iran. The American—the one who accompanied Maxwell and Al-Fasr—killed Al-Fasr. *Then he was about to kill me.*

Maxwell shot him.

At least that was what he thought he saw. It didn't make sense.

Rasmussen wanted to ask Maxwell what the hell really happened. Who was the other American? Why did he put the bullet in Al-Fasr? Why did he want Rasmussen dead?

And then he saw Maxwell watching him. His sober, intent expression was conveying a message. *Not now. Keep it just between us.*

Rasmussen nodded.

He heard the mechanical drone of the helicopter's turbine engines deepen. Through the hard bench seat he felt the vibration of the rotors changing pitch. The chopper lifted, tilted its nose forward, gathered speed.

He stared out the window at the cloud of dirt whipped up by the blades. The hard brown earth was dropping away like a vanishing world.

This was the moment he had deliberately shut out of his dreams. It had been the only way to keep his sanity. *Don't let yourself think about leaving. Dead men don't go home.*

Now he was going home.

The realization came over him like a thunderclap. He wasn't hallucinating. It was as real as the vibration of the big turbine engines, the whopping of the blades, the curious, self-conscious faces of the marines in the cabin. It was all goddamned real.

He hadn't wept for years. That was another thing he had learned to shut off. Dead men didn't cry.

He looked at Maxwell, then at Allen. There was much he didn't understand. But the knowledge that he was going home had taken hold of him. Over the din of the rotor blades, he said, "You . . . you came back . . . I thought I would never . . ."

He couldn't finish. His chest convulsed, and he began to weep uncontrollably. From deep inside the tears gushed from him, making muddy streaks down his dirty face. He sobbed—a deep, visceral moaning sound— coming from some dark place inside him.

Maxwell put his arm around Rasmussen. Gracie Allen unstrapped and walked across the metal deck. They sat on either side of him.

Rasmussen wiped his eyes on his sleeve. "I . . . was

supposed to be dead. You came back." Through his red-rimmed eyes he looked at Maxwell, then Allen. "Thank you."

Another wave of helpless sobbing shook him. The morning light was streaming through the port windows. The young marines were trying their best not to stare at him. Some were crying too.

Finally Rasmussen gained control of himself. "I'm sorry," he said. "I gave up. I shouldn't have, but I've been dead for a long time. I didn't think I'd ever go home again."

Maxwell nodded his understanding.

Allen leaned toward him. "We came as soon as we could. We didn't know you were alive, Raz. Not until a little while ago."

He forced himself to sit upright. Be a man, damn it. Show some dignity. He blew his nose. "Does anyone else know I'm alive?"

He saw Allen glance at Maxwell. "Yeah," said Allen. "And a lot of things have changed since you were shot down."

Rasmussen nodded. He knew what was coming.

"There are some things you need to know," said Maxwell. "Some personal stuff."

He braced himself. "Maria, you mean?"

Maxwell nodded. "Yeah. Maria."

"I know." He took a deep breath. "The Iraqis made sure I knew all the bad stuff."

"She thought you were dead, Raz."

"So did I."

"After what you've been through, it's—"

"After what I've been through," he said, his voice cracking, "I can handle it."

Maxwell squeezed his shoulder and left him to his thoughts.

Through the starboard cabin window the gray murk of the Persian Gulf was coming into view. Somewhere out there was a carrier—probably some super new carrier that hadn't even been constructed when he disappeared in Iraq.

Maxwell was right. A lot had changed in the world. It would take time to adjust to all the changes. He could already feel the pain of loss. He supposed it would be painful for Maria, too.

He used to worry that he might lack the courage to survive. Years of imprisonment changed all that. If he'd gained nothing else, he had learned an essential truth about himself. He possessed an inner strength that he didn't know he had.

It was true, he thought. *I can handle it. I can handle anything.*

CHAPTER 26

RECOVERY

Southern Iran
0640, Wednesday, 24 March

It was sweet.

Boyce had always wanted to fire a Maverick under real combat conditions. There was nothing more real than hosing a terrorist while the ragheaded sonofabitch was motoring across a swamp in a heat-emitting vehicle.

His wingmen—Flash Gordon, Hozer Miller, Leroi Jones—were in a loose trail formation behind him. They would rejoin during the egress from Iran, using Fiddle to identify each other and slide into formation.

Boyce called the FAC. "Snake, Galeforce Zero-one is checking out."

"Good work, Galeforce. I confirm a direct hit with the Maverick."

"Mighty fine. I've been wanting to—"

His transmission went dead. *Now what?*

Then he saw the red light on his UFC—Up Front Control. The number-one radio, the one with the Have Quick facility that synchronized with the control and surveillance inputs, was dead.

Okay, a pain in the butt, but no big deal.

He switched to the number-two radio. "Galeforce Zero-one flight, Galeforce Zero-one on the back radio. Be advised my front radio is tits-up. I won't be monitoring squadron common."

"Two."

"Three."

"Four," said Leroi Jones, then he added, "We promise not to talk about you behind your back, CAG."

Boyce grinned inside his oxygen mask. Wingmen always badmouthed their bosses on the radio when they thought they weren't being overheard. What the hell, let 'em run their mouths.

"Yeah, right. Galeforce flight, let's go strike frequency now."

Boyce checked in with strike control and passed the daily code word for the Return to Base signal.

"We've got you, Galeforce One-one," said the controller. "Call Marshal at fifty out."

Ahead, Boyce could see the coastline, the sunrise glinting off the network of streams that wound like veins through the delta. Crossing the shoreline, he would order his flight to "fence out"—check master armament switches safe, de-select weapons, shut down transponder squawks.

He disconnected the right side of his oxygen mask, letting it dangle from his helmet by the left fitting. The cold air of the cockpit air conditioner felt good on his sweaty face. He was still new to the Super Hornet, less than a hundred hours in type, and that was one of the things he liked about it. You could drop the mask and actually—

What was that smell?

Something electrical. Ozone? What the hell? He didn't see any smoke—

There was something else. His right MFD—multi-function display—was blinking on and off. With each blink he was getting a *deedle-deedle* in his headset. The master mode display was cycling from air-to-air to NAV.

Definitely not normal.

"Galeforce Zero-two, you've got the lead," he called. If he was going to lose navigational gear, he needed someone to find the ship for him.

Flash Gordon acknowledged, and seconds later Boyce saw Gordon's Hornet slide forward, past Boyce's right wing, taking the lead of the formation. Boyce slid down and beneath Flash, crossing to his right wing, re-balancing the formation with Miller and Jones on the left side.

He glanced again at the blinking MFD. It wasn't blinking anymore. It had gone blank, totally dead.

Shit almighty. This jet was going to hell in a handcart. Lucky for him it was daytime, visual conditions. Nothing bad could happen unless—

Uh-oh. What he was smelling wasn't just ozone, and it wasn't his imagination. Something oozing from beneath the consoles. The noxious smell of smoke.

"Galeforce Zero-one has a problem," he called.

USS Ronald Reagan

Bullet knew he should leave it alone, wait until Maxwell had returned and finished his debriefing, then fill him in on the bogus corrosion inspection mess. It would become the business of the Judge Advocate General and the ship's legal department.

But he couldn't, at least not yet. Something was smoldering like an ember in his gut. *The sons of bitches.* They had signed off flawed airplanes, then sent unsuspecting pilots to fly them.

The image kept coming back to him—smoke billowing from the floorboards of the cockpit, displays flashing on and off like cheap neon signs. The runway almost under him when the goddamn jet slewed out of control and—*wham*—an ejection at near-zero altitude.

He'd been lucky. He almost bought the farm. And they blamed it on combat damage when all along those two—Manson and DiLorenzo—knew the truth. Even worse, they were setting up somebody else for the same thing. The next guy might not be so lucky.

He caught Manson coming out of the maintenance office on the second deck.

"Craze, can I have a word with you?"

"Sorry, I've got business on the flight deck."

The guy never changed, thought Alexander. Disrespectful as ever. "It'll have to wait. I need to ask you something."

"What is it?" Manson made his usual show of looking at his watch.

Alexander glanced both directions, up and down the passageway. They were alone, at least for the moment. "The corrosion inspections on aircraft 306, 307, 309. Tell me why they weren't accomplished."

Manson gave him a wary look, then smiled disarmingly. "I don't know what you're talking about, XO."

"Sure you do. You're the maintenance officer. You're the guy who's supposed to be on top of those inspections. Remember, you said you'd work the shifts smarter so you'd get the jets through the inspection and back online?"

"And that's what I did. Is there a problem?"

"Yeah, if you think criminal falsification of records is a problem."

"What I think," said Manson, watching Alexander closely, "is that you don't know anything about squadron maintenance. If you'd done a tour of squadron officer duty like everyone else, you'd understand how the system works."

"Well, that may be true," said Alexander. "But I don't have to know very much to understand that your quality assurance officer and the QA petty officer are both guilty of faking the inspection records of those jets."

"That's a lie."

"And I understand enough about human nature to know they're not going to go down without taking their boss with them."

Manson's pudgy face changed color, reddening from the neck up. "What are you trying to pull? I don't know anything about any false records. You've been trying to make me look bad ever since you got to this squadron."

"You knew what they were doing. You told them to do it."

"How the hell would you know?" A look of cold fury covered Manson's face. The veins stood out like ropes on his thick neck. "You come here, not knowing shit about the real Navy, playing the minority card, a goddamn showboating carpetbagger—"

Alexander's fist caught him flush on the jawline, snapping Manson's head back, knocking the hat from his head.

As Manson sagged against the bulkhead, Alexander seized the collar of his flight jacket and hoisted him upright. He thrust his face within four inches of Manson's nose. "Maybe I didn't hear you clearly, Craze. I believe you said, yes, sir, you would cooperate with the investigation into the inspection matter?"

He gave him a shake, thumping him into the bulkhead. "Isn't that right?"

Manson looked at him with dazed eyes. "You can't assault an officer like this . . ."

Alexander heard footsteps clunking down the passageway. He released his grip on Manson's jacket and stooped to pick up his hat. "Oops, sorry to bump into you like that, Commander."

He was replacing the hat on Manson's head when he heard the footsteps stop behind him. He turned to see Holmes, a yeoman from the squadron admin office.

"Ah, Commander Alexander, I've been looking all over for you," said Holmes. The yeoman kept staring at Manson, who was wobbling on his feet, his eyes glazed. "The air boss wants you up in Pri-Fly right away."

"What's going on?" said Alexander.

"A problem with one of the jets, sir. Some kind of emergency."

"Who is it?"

"CAG Boyce. In aircraft 307."

USS Ronald Reagan

"Red, this is Bullet."

"I read you, Bullet. Go ahead."

Alexander was still catching his breath. He had climbed the ladder to Pri-Fly—the windowed space up in the carrier's island that had a panoramic view of the flight deck and the sea around them—three steps at a time. Aerobic workouts sucked, especially on a full breakfast.

"How bad is the smoke?" Alexander asked. He was standing next to the *Reagan*'s Air Boss, Cmdr. Jock Williams, seated in his high, padded chair.

"I've got the mask back on," answered Boyce. "Visibility in the cockpit is crappy. I've lost the right MFD and the HQ radio and—whoop, wait a minute. The radar just X-ed out."

Bullet swore under his breath. Boyce's jet was coming unglued, just as his had at Al Jaber. He took another second to catch his breath. He saw Craze Manson come into the compartment.

Manson took a place by the glass-paned window, watching the scenario with an expressionless face. Alexander noticed that the right side of his jaw was red and swollen.

"All right, listen up, Galeforce Flight," Bullet said

into the microphone. "Flash, you lead CAG back here fast, but do *not* go supersonic. You hear me?"

"Dash two hears you,"

"Set him up on a two mile straight in. The Boss—" He paused to glance at Williams, the Air Boss, who was following the dialogue. Williams gave him an affirmative nod. "—the Boss will have a ready deck for you. Galeforce flight, you all copy that?"

They all copied.

"CAG, you have to trust me on this," said Alexander. "You're in a no-shit emergency. After you roger this transmission, I want you to turn off your generators and battery, then secure all electric switches except for your good radio. Do not—repeat, do not—turn anything on until Flash signals you at three miles. Then just your battery, no generators. You can dirty up normally and fly a straight-in pass. Once you've stopped in the wires, turn everything off and shut down."

He paused for a breath. "If you understand, CAG, just say copy and turn the switches off."

Three seconds ticked by. "Copy."

The smoke was getting worse. It was billowing in a steady gush from beneath the console, making his eyes burn and flood with tears.

A thought flashed across Boyce's mind: *I'm too old for this shit.*

At fifty, he was the oldest active aviator aboard the *Reagan*. This was Boyce's swan song. Commanding an air wing was your last tactical flying job before they retired you or shipped you off to a padded chair behind a desk.

During nearly three decades as a naval aviator, he had seen his share of trouble—engine malfunctions, combat damage, fires, an ejection from an A-7 with a turbine section failure. He had handled them all with professional cool.

Yeah, but you were a young stud, not a balding old fart with weak eyes and a thick gut.

He shook the thought from his brain. *Stay focused. If you want to live through the next five minutes, fly this jet.*

His standby altimeter, which required no electrical input, showed that they were descending through 1,500 feet. The *Reagan* was ten miles ahead.

He took his eyes off Flash's jet for a moment and glanced up ahead. Through the veil of smoke in his cockpit and the haze over the Gulf, he couldn't see anything. Just a gray murk of sea and sky. He had gone to RAM/DUMP on his cabin pressure switch, allowing outside air to ventilate the cockpit. It was clearing some of the smoke, but not much.

Blinking against the tears, he locked his eyes on Flash's Hornet, twenty feet from his left wing. Flash was his only lifeline to the deck of the *Reagan*.

Another glance inside. The standby airspeed indicator—also nonelectrical—was dropping below 250 knots.

They were getting close.

Then he saw it, beneath the nose, the foaming white trail of a vessel. The wake of a carrier? It had to be.

Flash was giving him a hand signal. Time for the final act.

He reached for the ON/BATT switch, moving it to ON. He heard a *pop* in his headset, then the faint crackle of the radio.

He keyed the mike button. "Red's up. How do you read?"

"Loud and clear, CAG," came the voice of Pearly Gates, the LSO. "You're two miles on final. You need to go dirty. Do you have the ship?"

Boyce glanced through the front windscreen. Ahead lay the gray mass of the carrier, trailing a broad white wake. "I've got the ship." To Flash, he radioed, "You're cleared to detach."

Flash had taken him as close as he could. Now Boyce had to fly the final part of the approach by himself.

As Flash's jet peeled off to the left and accelerated away, Boyce reached up and lowered the landing gear handle. He heard the familiar *clunk* of the gear locking down. *Thank God*. At least the hydraulics still worked.

He lowered the flaps, then extended the tailhook.

The smoke was getting worse. He thought about blowing the canopy off, then decided against it. He didn't know if he could fly a carrier pass with the top popped and the wind howling past him at a hundred fifty knots.

Three green lights. The landing gear was down.

The ball—the visual glide path indicator mounted at the port edge of the landing deck—was coming into view from the bottom of the lens, rising toward the green "on glide path" datum lights.

"Runner 307, Rhino ball, fuel unknown."

"Roger ball, Runner," answered the LSO. "Wind is thirty down the angle."

The ball rose above the datum lights mounted in the middle of the lens, indicating that he was going high. Boyce nudged the two throttles back a tiny increment, easing the Hornet back down to the glide path. Without a full electrical system, he was flying without the Super Hornet's high-tech presentation—a HUD with its superimposed velocity vector symbol that gave him a precise picture of the Hornet's flight path.

Just like the old days. No fancy gadgets to make it easy for him. He'd do it the old-fashioned way—airspeed, ball, and line up. Hell, he could still—

"Pow-werrrrr," came the urging call from the LSO. He was settling low on the glide path. Pearly was using his best sugar talk, coaxing Boyce to be smooth.

He jammed the throttles ahead, feeling the thrust kick in—*shit, too much*—and yanked them back again.

"Eaa-sssy with it." More sugar talk.

Boyce forced himself to lighten up his grip on the two throttles. *Easy, goddamnit.* It was time for finesse, not jerkiness. He had to get this thing down on the first pass. If he blew it, missed a wire or got waved off, he was screwed. He'd pull up and punch out of the jet.

The smoke was thickening, obscuring his view through the windscreen. His eyes were brimming with tears, burning in the acrid cloud. He wished he had blown the canopy, gotten the smoke out. Now it was too late. He didn't dare remove his hand from the throttles.

Getting close. He squeezed his eyes shut for an instant, trying to clear the blur of tears. The blunt gray shape of the *Reagan* was swelling in the windscreen.

The ball was swimming in his vision. Moving up? Down? *Shit, he couldn't see.*

"Don't go high," warned the LSO. No more sugar talk. It was a command. "Right for line up."

He nudged the throttles back and dipped the right wing, following the LSO's call to stay aligned with the center line. He sensed the Hornet settling, the deck rising to meet him.

"Attitude!"

He pulled back on the stick, raising the nose, lowering the tailhook just enough . . .

Whump. For a sickening moment he felt the Hornet careening down the deck, toward the far edge of the landing area. Instinctively he pushed the throttles up to the stops.

Then the hard lurch. The Hornet shuddered to a stop, its tailhook engaged on the last wire.

He snatched the throttles back to idle and opened the canopy, letting the smoke billow out of the cockpit. He felt the sweet, life-giving rush of wind that flowed over the flight deck.

A flood of elation swept over him. *You're still alive, you old fart.*

He was reaching for the battery switch when he heard Bullet Alexander on the radio. "Welcome back, CAG. You had us worried."

"Aw, hell, son," he coughed. "That was a piece of cake."

CHAPTER 27

DEBRIEF

USS Ronald Reagan
1017, Wednesday, 24 March

Like most air intel officers, Cmdr. Harvey Wentz had a low regard for the cognitive skills of fighter pilots. They were single-purpose gladiators who were dangerous if they knew too much.

At least that was the impression Maxwell had always received from Wentz. He wasn't getting any different feeling now.

They were in the *Reagan*'s SCIF, buried deep in the interior of the ship, guarded by emission-proof bulkheads and two armed marines outside the door. On one side of the long conference table sat Maxwell, with Boyce at his left. Opposite them were Wentz and two unsmiling CIA specialists who had flown out from their regional office in Riyadh.

One of the CIA men, a man named Perkins, wore tiny, round-rimmed spectacles. He scribbled continuously on a yellow pad. The other, who introduced himself as Lambert, tended a digital recording device at the end of the table.

They let Wentz ask the questions.

"Okay, Commander Maxwell, let's do this again. Run

through the sequence of events from the time you arrived at the village until you rejoined the TRAP team."

"I just ran through it."

"Run through it again. You may have omitted useful details the first time."

Or you may trip yourself up, thought Maxwell. It was an old interrogation technique—get the subject to repeat his story, catch him altering the details, find out what he's hiding.

He went through the events of the mission again, describing how he and Bronson delivered Al-Fasr to the village, how the firefight erupted, how he and Rasmussen escaped.

Wentz watched him thoughtfully. "And Mr. Bronson? What happened to him?"

Maxwell felt the eyes of the CIA officers fixed like lasers on him. "I told you that too. When the shooting started, he was hit."

"By whom?"

"By someone with a gun."

Wentz shook his head. "Don't be flippant with us, Commander. Was it one of the snipers or someone else?"

"It was dark. There were several shooters."

He saw the two CIA men exchange glances. Perkins jotted something on his yellow pad.

"But you were wearing NVG, were you not?" said Wentz.

"Over my eyes, not the back of my head."

"What the hell is this?" snapped Boyce. He aimed his cigar at Wentz. "Are you guys running a debriefing or a goddamn inquisition? Get to the point."

"With all due respect, Captain Boyce, I have to remind you that this is more than a debriefing. A covert mission was compromised, and a senior intelligence officer has been fatally wounded." Wentz glanced at the two CIA men, who nodded back to him. "It's critical to national security that we gather every piece of intelligence from this operation."

"Then I suggest you act like an intelligence gatherer instead of a prosecutor. Brick isn't on trial here."

Wentz looked exasperated. They all knew that Boyce wasn't supposed to be a participant in the debriefing, but he had inserted himself over Wentz's objections. Wentz was also a pragmatist. Boyce was a Navy captain who happened to be the Air Wing Commander. He could turn Wentz's life into a living hell.

"Okay," said Wentz. "Let's try this again. Who fired the first shot?"

"They did," said Maxwell. "A sniper on one of the buildings."

"And what was your response?"

"I shot one of the *Sherji* who had brought Raz. Bronson took out the two snipers with his SMG."

"So what happened to Al-Fasr?" asked Wentz.

"Someone shot him."

"Someone? Who?"

Maxwell hesitated, feeling the penetrating stares of the two CIA men. He had a clear vision of Al-Fasr's shattered skull, Bronson standing over him with the Glock in his hand.

"I don't know," he said. "Someone who wanted him dead, I suppose. Who do you think that would be?"

Wentz shot him a baleful look. "What do you mean by that?"

"I mean, Bronson and company"—he nodded toward the CIA men—"were not thrilled about having to give Al-Fasr back, were they? Since Al-Fasr happened to get shot while we were giving him back, it might have some connection with Bronson getting shot in turn."

"What are you suggesting?" Wentz removed his glasses and peered at Maxwell. "That Bronson shot Al-Fasr?"

Both CIA officers were leaning forward over the table, watching him. Maxwell hesitated. *Careful,* he told himself. *Don't go too far.* "No, just postulating. Trying to make sense out of what happened."

"So are we. We're still trying to learn something from the bodies."

Maxwell felt his heart quicken. "Bodies?"

"The TRAP team commander sent a squad to recover Bronson and Al-Fasr's bodies."

Maxwell kept his face blank. He should have known. Of course, they'd try to recover the bodies. He wanted to know more, but he made himself remain quiet.

Wentz resumed the interrogation, but he said nothing more about the bodies. His questions seemed to lose their belligerence. The subject of Ted Bronson's death didn't come up again.

Finally, he announced that the debriefing had ended. The CIA men rose and shook Maxwell's hand, then Boyce's.

Boyce ignored Wentz's outstretched hand as he led Maxwell to the door. He glanced back inside the SCIF, then closed the door behind him. "Dipshits," he said.

Manama, Bahrain

Claire awoke feeling the pangs of remorse and a searing headache. The events of last night were replaying in her mind like a bad movie.

Oh, damn. Why did I do that?

Rays of sunlight were streaming through the blinds, filling the bedroom with a painful yellow luminescence. For a while she didn't move. Finally she forced herself to look to the other side of the bed.

It was empty.

Thank God. That was another thing about Chris Tyrwhitt. No matter how much he'd had to drink or how little sleep he'd gotten, he rose early. To his credit, he'd had the decency to get up and leave her alone this morning.

She went directly to the shower, trying to shut out the images of the previous evening. It didn't work. Chris Tyrwhitt's hypnotic voice kept inserting itself back into her mind.

Just like old times, darling.

Why not? After all, we're husband and wife.

Her mistake was in letting herself fall under Tyrwhitt's spell again. Her original assessment was correct. He *was* dangerous. Chris Tyrwhitt could charm the knickers off the queen.

Admit it. You didn't resist.

Not enough, anyway.

And that was the part that was causing her all this bad feeling. She didn't love Chris Tyrwhitt, at least not in the way a wife loved a husband. She was finished with all that. Tyrwhitt was trouble. He was an ex-husband in every way except by signed and stamped divorce papers, and those were in process.

So why did you sleep with him?

That was what bothered her. Maybe, just maybe, she thought, there was still a tiny grain of love for the man who used to be her husband.

Love? Or plain old-fashioned lust?

She wrapped herself in the big white terrycloth robe and then ordered coffee from room service. Her headache was fading. So was the remorse, replaced now by a sober recounting. She had to give the guy credit, he still knew how to disarm her. It was classic Tyrwhitt— the drinks, the funny stories, the easy charm. And then, the pièce de résistance.

The roses.

She looked around. They were still there. She picked

them up and smelled them again. The note from Chris lay on the sideboard.

She had to admit, it *was* a nice touch. Very romantic, very thoughtful.

And then she saw something else. On the floor, almost beneath the sideboard. Something crumpled.

She picked up the wadded-up card, smoothed it out, and read the note from Sam Maxwell.

In the next instant, all the charitable thoughts she had for Tyrwhitt vanished in a flash of rage.

"That son of a bitch! That devious, sleazy bastard! That no good, lying, deceitful asshole. That miserable, two-faced . . ."

She slumped into a chair, clutching the card in her hand. She didn't know whether to give way to uncontrollable weeping, or to laugh.

I can't believe I'm still such an idiot. After all these years, I fell for it again.

She let several minutes pass. Gradually she regained control of her emotions. She was thinking again.

She rose and walked to the window. The sun was glinting off the white plaster of the buildings outside. The light no longer hurt her eyes, and her headache was receding.

Out of every bad experience, she believed, something good had to come. If anything good came from her dalliance with Tyrwhitt, it was this new clarity of thought.

It all seemed perfectly obvious. Tyrwhitt hadn't changed. He would never change. He would always be the same charming lowlife weasel that he had been last night.

Nor would Sam Maxwell change. He was still the dashing, duty-bound, inarticulate guy she loved.

And had always loved.

Now she knew. Too bad she didn't figure it out before last night. She hoped it wasn't too late.

USS Ronald Reagan

Something was wrong with Manson's jaw.

Maxwell listened, trying to follow Craze Manson's rambling story, but he couldn't keep his eyes off his jaw. It was swollen, turning an ugly shade of purple.

"Seventeen years," Manson was saying. "No retirement, no benefits. I'm throwing away seventeen years of my life. I hope you're satisfied."

Actually, thought Maxwell, he was *very* satisfied, but he just nodded and said, "Go on, Craze. Explain why you're resigning."

Manson gave him a baleful look and went on. "I don't owe you any explanation. That letter on your desk says it all. I'm resigning from the Navy as of today. End of story."

They were in Maxwell's stateroom. He and Alexander were seated at the desk, while Manson stood facing them. He was wearing his service khakis, cap tucked in his belt.

Maxwell wanted to get this over with. Fatigue was oozing through him like a drug after the stress of the prisoner exchange mission. He was still in the camo BDUs he'd worn into Iran. In a corner stood his mud-caked flight boots.

Alexander had been waiting for him when he emerged from the intel debrief. The word had already spread around the squadron. Splat DiLorenzo and Petty Officer Carson were under arrest. Carson was in the brig and DiLorenzo was confined to quarters. Craze Manson was leaving the Navy.

Maxwell looked at Manson. "You may be called to testify at DiLorenzo's court-martial."

"I've got nothing to say."

"Well, I guess that's something."

"The deal is, I resign, I won't be charged."

"The deal is, you won't be charged with a violation of

the Uniform Code of Military Justice. That doesn't mean you won't be subpoenaed by DiLorenzo's counsel."

Manson shrugged. "If they expect me to tell them I knew about the corrosion inspection sign-offs, they can go piss up a rope. I had no knowledge, and they have no evidence."

Maxwell glanced over at Alexander, who was doodling on a yellow pad. They both knew Manson was probably right. The case against him was circumstantial, nothing more than DiLorenzo's word that he had been following Manson's orders. Court-martialing Manson would be a waste of manpower.

Alexander, for his part, was still furious about the deal. "That lying son of a bitch tried to kill me and the CAG," he roared when he heard about it. The only good thing was that Manson would be gone from the squadron, which was a blessing.

Carson was another matter. The petty officer had let himself get sucked into helping DiLorenzo—and at the eleventh hour had searched inside himself and found a sense of honor. Carson was worth saving.

By stretching his authority as commanding officer, Maxwell would conduct a captain's mast—a nonjudicial form of military justice. Carson would receive a demotion and a censure, but he would be spared a court-martial. With an endorsement from both Maxwell and Alexander, Carson would be allowed to remain in the Navy.

"When can I get out?" said Manson

The sooner the better, Maxwell felt like saying, but Alexander answered for him. "As soon as your papers clear admin, you'll get orders to report to the wing back at Oceana. They'll process you out. You'll be a civilian this time next week."

Manson nodded, then looked at Maxwell. "One more thing. I want a letter from you stating that my departure

from the squadron was under honorable circumstances."

"Sorry," said Maxwell. "I don't write bullshit documents. That's your department."

Manson's face reddened. "You're the CO. You have
to add an endorsement to my letter of resignation."

"I already have. I endorsed it 'approved.' "

Manson stood there for another half a minute, working the muscles in his discolored jaw. "You're pretty
smug, aren't you? Both of you carpetbaggers. You've
been trying to get me out of the squadron ever since you
came on board."

Maxwell listened in silence while the venom continued to spill out of Manson. He thought again about the
rule, dating back before the Roman Legions, he
guessed, that required every military unit to have someone like Manson. Some flaming asshole, just to keep
things stirred up. He hoped that Manson's replacement
wasn't on the way.

Manson finally stopped ranting. Maxwell said,
"Craze, tell me something."

"What?"

"What happened to your jaw?"

The color deepened in Manson's face, making the
purple bruise even uglier. "Ask him," he said, nodding
to Alexander. "Will that be all?"

"I certainly hope so. You're dismissed, Commander
Manson. Close the door behind you."

Manson spun around and left the stateroom, giving
the door a vicious slam. They could hear his heels hammering like drumbeats down the passageway.

Maxwell looked at Alexander. "Do you have any idea
what happened to Craze's jaw?"

"Jaw?" Alexander seemed to be studying a flake of
paint on the far bulkhead. "I didn't notice. Was something wrong with his jaw?"

*   *   *

Boyce got a good ember going, then wafted a cloud of gray smoke across the room. "Cohiba," he said. "Fresh from Havana, via Bahrain. Want one?"

"No, thanks."

"Good. You wouldn't appreciate it anyway." For a while he rolled the cigar between his fingers, absorbed with some new thought. "I presume you told Wentz and the spooks everything you knew."

Maxwell took his time. He could tell when Boyce was fishing. "Pretty much."

"They were curious about what happened to Bronson. You're the only guy who was in position to know."

"Not the only one. There was the guy who shot him."

Boyce nodded, still looking at him through the gray smoke. "Oh, yeah, him. Whoever that was."

"And Rasmussen. He was there too."

"Apparently he wasn't any help to them," said Boyce. "Said he had no idea who shot whom. He hit the dirt when the shooting started and missed the whole thing."

"Too bad." *Good for you, Raz,* he thought.

Boyce was giving him a look that he had come to recognize. Boyce said, "Now that Rasmussen has been freed, there are some things I've learned about our man Bronson that make me wish he was around to answer some questions."

"Like what?"

"Like he was the case officer back in ninety-three when they received intelligence that an American prisoner might still be in Iraq. It seems pretty clear now that Bronson knew the truth—that Saddam Hussein was holding Rasmussen after giving all the other Gulf War prisoners back."

"So why didn't he pull out all the stops to get him back?"

"By ignoring Raz's existence, the CIA could deny Saddam the use of the prisoner as a bargaining chip. For his part, Saddam couldn't go public with it because it would be clear evidence that he was violating the terms of the cease-fire accord. And after enough time had gone by, the CIA couldn't afford to admit that it had known about the prisoner all along or there would be hell to pay. It was a stalemate, and Raz was caught in the middle."

"Until Al-Fasr came along."

"Yeah. For Saddam, the prisoner became a liability, so he traded him to the Bu Hasa Brigade in exchange for a security deal on the eastern border. The Bu Hasa thought they could use the prisoner for their own bargaining purposes. Which, as you know, they did."

"Rasmussen for Al-Fasr."

Boyce nodded. "Except, as it turned out, the deal was rigged. Al-Fasr's unfaithful lieutenant, a guy named Abu Mahmed, didn't really want Al-Fasr back."

"And Bronson didn't want Rasmussen back."

Boyce studied the end of his cigar. "You said it, not me."

"So who besides Bronson knew that Rasmussen was alive?"

"Somebody a lot further up the food chain. Maybe quite a bit further. Probably better if we don't know."

More than ever, Maxwell was feeling the stress and fatigue of the all-night mission. He hadn't slept for— how long? Almost twenty-four hours. His eyes burned and his joints ached.

He rose from the steel chair and headed for the door.

"Haven't you wondered," said Boyce, "why they haven't determined who really killed Bronson and Al-Fasr? After all, they have the bodies, and they ought to be able to trace the bullets."

Maxwell was instantly alert. "Bullets? You mean—"

"Wentz and the spooks weren't telling you all the story. They said they recovered the bodies of Bronson and Al-Fasr, but that wasn't the whole truth."

Maxwell turned to look at Boyce. "May I ask what the whole truth is?"

"The truth is that there are no bullets. Presumably, both men were shot in the head. That's the problem."

"Why is that a problem?"

"Because there are no heads."

Maxwell felt a roiling sensation in the pit of his stomach. "No heads . . . ?"

"They were decapitated. It seems that someone sliced off their heads. The TRAP team never found the missing parts. The marine who told me the story had to stop and puke."

Maxwell thought he might do the same. "Why would anyone do that?"

"Terrorists have reasons that are beyond our understanding."

Maxwell was dazed. He was reaching for the door latch when Boyce said, "By the way, Brick, I was wondering something else."

Maxwell stopped with his hand on the latch. "Sir?"

"I was just wondering whether it might have been you who shot Bronson. Was it?"

For a long moment he looked Boyce in the eye. "No, sir."

"Good answer." Boyce returned his gaze through a cloud of smoke. "But even if you didn't, you should have."

A hush fell over the Roadrunners' ready room. The visitor entered and peered around. He wore starched khakis and the gold leaves of a lieutenant commander. He carried a newspaper beneath his arm.

"Who's in charge here?" he said.

Leroi Jones, the squadron duty officer, looked over to Maxwell, who had just come in to pick up his mail. Maxwell gave him a formation hand signal—touching his forehead and pointing to Jones. *You've got the lead.*

Jones shrugged and said, "Guess I am, sir."

The visitor said, "I'm Lieutenant Commander Scudder, the *Reagan*'s new Public Affairs Officer."

"What happened to the old PAO?"

"He's been relieved, shipped back to the states. I was sent out here to clean up some public relations problems."

"Public relations? What's it got to do with us?"

Scudder gazed around the ready room. His jowly face wore a look of disapproval. "It has to do with the call signs you people are so fond of using." He held up the front page of the newspaper. It was yesterday's *New York Post*, and on it was a photograph of flight operations aboard the USS *Reagan*. A figure in a flight deck vest and cranial protector headset was pointing down the deck as a jet was launching.

"Look at the man in the picture," said Scudder. "See the name on his vest?"

Jones took the paper and peered closely at the photograph. "Hey! That's Dog Balls!"

Scudder winced. "That photograph has been seen by something over a hundred thousand readers."

"Cool," said Jones. "Ol' Dog Balls is gonna be famous."

Scudder snatched the newspaper back. "There's nothing cool about it, Lieutenant. Things like this tarnish the Navy's public image. This is a public relations disaster."

"So why are you telling us about it? If you don't like it, just make him get rid of the call sign."

By now the pilots in the ready room had all maneuvered their way to the front, following the conversation.

"That *is* the problem," said Scudder. "He claims this squadron gave it to him, and he's not allowed to get rid of it."

Jones grinned. "Dog Balls really said that, huh?"

"It seems that Mr. Harvey actually *likes* the . . . disgusting name. He says he won't change it unless you give him one just as good."

Howling broke out in the ready room.

"Attaboy, Dog Balls!"

"Good for him!"

"What a guy!"

Scudder's face reddened. He glared at the pilots in the room. "Listen. You people don't seem to understand the facts of life. This is the new Navy. The Tailhook scandal is behind us. We have to do everything we can to portray a clean and wholesome image to the public."

"Clean and wholesome," repeated Jones, nodding his head. He was peering at the wings on Scudder's uniform. They were the gold wings of a naval aviation flight officer. "Hey, what kind of flying job do you have?"

"None anymore. I was a tacco on a P-3 during my first tour."

"So what was *your* call sign?"

"We didn't use call signs in our squadron."

"Well, now that you're here on the *Reagan*, Mr. Scudder, don't you think you oughta have a call sign like the rest of us?"

A wary look flashed over Scudder's face. "No, I don't think—"

"After all, you're working with fighter pilots now. If you want us to help you, then you really oughta get a call sign."

"Never mind that. I came down here to talk about—"

"In fact, we'd love to come up with one for you, wouldn't we, guys?"

Another chorus of cheering erupted from the back of the ready room.

"Hey," yelled Bud Spencer. "We'll even get you a vest with your new call sign stenciled on it."

Scudder sensed calamity rushing at him. He began backpedaling toward the door. "Well, this has been interesting, gentlemen. Thank you for your time. I have to go meet—"

"Scrotum!" yelled Flash Gordon from the back of the room.

Scudder stopped. His eyes filled with horror. "Scrotum?"

"That's it!" said Jones. "It's perfect. That'll look great on your vest. *Scrotum Scudder!*"

At this a fresh round of cheering and whistling reverberated from the steel bulkheads.

Scudder bolted for the door. He slammed the door behind him, but he was too late. Jones and half a dozen others were right behind him. The chorus followed Scudder all the way down the passageway and up the ladder to the next level.

"Scrotum! Scrotum Scudder! Hey, come back, Scrotum!"   •

Manama, Bahrain

I hate this business, Claire said to herself.

The red message light on the telephone was blinking like a fire alarm. It was the third urgent message from Phil Granley in the New York headquarters of the World News Syndicate. Each was the same. *Return this call immediately.*   •

She knew what Granley wanted.

She poured herself a coffee and stood staring out the window of her room in the Gulf Hotel. To the west she could see the sprawling harbor of Manama. Somewhere in the distance was the USS *Reagan.* The smaller ships of the battle group would be assembled like chicks around a mother hen. On one of the ships was an American named Allen Rasmussen.

Finally she picked up the phone and dialed Granley's number.

"Where's the prisoner?" he said. "Have you got an interview yet?"

"What prisoner?"

"You know damned well what prisoner," he roared. "The one you had me stick my neck out a mile for. He's been freed, right?"

"I don't know. The Navy's not saying."

"What do you mean, you don't know? The story's already been leaked to every news bureau in the Middle East. After what we did to make this happen, I expect you to get an exclusive on this one."

"They're keeping him secluded, Phil. The guy's life has been shattered. He's not on display."

"Lean on your military connections. You can do it, I know you can. Get in to talk to him."

"No."

A silence fell over the telephone line. Through the crackle of the satellite connection, Claire could hear Granley's deep breathing.

"What the hell's this all about?" he said.

"Ethics, Phil. It's called conducting ourselves like responsible journalists. We did something decent by helping get Raz Rasmussen out of captivity. Now let's do the decent thing by leaving him alone."

"Where are you getting this Mother Teresa shit? You're in the news business, not the goddamned sisterhood of bleeding hearts."

"Oh, and another thing, Phil. Tell our reporters to stay away from his wife. She's going through her own hell now, and she also deserves some privacy. If you want us to get credit for something, let's get it for doing the right thing."

Several more seconds passed. She could sense the heat of Granley's anger through the phone. She knew what was coming next.

It took five more seconds. "You're fired," he said.

"Okay."

"Whaddya mean, okay? You just blew what was once a very promising career."

"You're angry, Phil. You'll get over it."

"Not in your lifetime I won't." She heard the tinny sound of the satellite connection change. The line was dead.

She returned to the window. In the gathering dusk, the ships in the harbor looked like fish feeding in a stream. A serene image in a world at war.

Granley *would* get over it, she thought. He'd get over it first thing in the morning when she called him about the exclusive story she *did* get.

It came from out of the blue. An agent—an Iraqi named Mustafa Ashbar—had come to her, he said, on the advice of a trusted friend. In exchange for a reasonable payment, he was willing to share the details of a most incredible story, one that would eclipse the human interest story of the returning prisoner of war. Yes, it could be verified, he said. It concerned the Bu Hasa Brigade and a certain deceased CIA station chief.

CHAPTER 28

THE CAPTAIN

Manama, Bahrain
1730, Friday, 26 March

The four naval officers strode into the officers' club bar in the American Support Unit compound in Bahrain. With Rasmussen were Maxwell, Allen, and the *Reagan*'s Air Wing Commander, Red Boyce. All captains except for Maxwell, a commander.

"I feel like I'm impersonating an officer," said Rasmussen. The eagles on his collar glistened like newly minted silver.

"Get used to it," said Red Boyce as he bellied up to the bar. "Let's have a round." He signaled the bartender.

Boyce and Allen ordered Scotch and water, while Rasmussen and Maxwell had Heinekens.

"I still don't know how I got to be a captain," said Rasmussen.

"Do the math," said Allen. "Brick here was a snot-nosed lieutenant, and you and I and Red were lieutenant commanders when you got shot down in ninety-one. How many years is that? We all got promoted right on schedule."

"That has to be the only good thing that happened

while I was in jail," said Rasmussen. He could almost joke about it. Almost.

"Wait till you get your back pay," said Boyce.

"I'll drink to that," said Allen. He clinked his glass against Rasmussen's green beer bottle.

Rasmussen didn't feel like a captain in the U.S. Navy. After all these years, he didn't even feel like an officer. He definitely didn't look like one, despite the starched khaki uniform and the shiny eagles on the collar. The image in the mirror over the bar looked like someone's grandfather—sunken eyes, hair thin and gray, the once-muscular frame now gaunt and stooped. The short-sleeved khaki shirt hung from his bony shoulders like a shawl.

He was already feeling the beer, and not minding it. But he needed to sit down.

Boyce looked around for a table. He spotted one in the corner, occupied by a trio of uniformed junior Navy officers. While Maxwell, Allen, and Rasmussen watched from the bar, he walked over to the group, said something, and the three obligingly emptied the table.

"That was quick," said Rasmussen when he arrived at the table. "How'd you get them to leave?"

"I told them you were the sickest, most hungover fighter pilot in the U.S. Navy, and if they had any sense they'd get the hell out of here before you puked on their black shoes."

"They gave up that easy?"

"They're surface warfare types. I bribed them with a round of drinks."

Boyce fired up a Cohiba, then reached for the leather dice cup left on the table. "The game's five-of-a-kind, gents. Loser buys the next round." He slammed the cup down, starting the game with three deuces.

While the dice cup went around the table, Allen ordered a round of tequila shooters from the bartender.

The fifth deuce came up on Rasmussen's roll, which cost him the round.

"Welcome back to the real Navy, Raz," said Boyce. "Pay up and drink like a man."

Getting together for a farewell drink had been Allen's idea. Maxwell and Boyce had just arrived from the *Reagan.*

Rasmussen was having fun for the first time in—he made himself stop counting the years. His eyes were watering from laughing. He had to think for a moment to recall the Arabic expression, then it came to him. *Hayat jayeeda.* Yeah, that was it. *Life is good.*

And getting better, he hoped.

The dice went around the table and this time stopped at the lone commander. Maxwell groaned and waved to the bartender for one more round.

"They'll have to load me on the airplane with a forklift," said Raz. That was another thing he'd lost during his years in prison—a tolerance for alcohol. The booze was humming in his brain like a swarm of bees.

"We've got twenty minutes before they come to get us," said Gracie Allen, who was escorting Rasmussen back to the States. "There's no rule says we gotta be sober. Besides, you know the Air Force. There won't be any liquor on that jet."

It still didn't make sense to Rasmussen that they would send a C-20 Gulfstream just for him. On board was a staff doctor and two nurses, who would stay with him on the flight back to Ramstein in Germany. He was traveling under a fictitious name—Captain Richard Miller—to throw off the newshounds and curious GIs. After a few days in Germany, he and Gracie would board another special airlift mission, a C-17, to the United States. To his family. A new life.

The prospect filled him with a fresh wave of uncertainty.

Allen seemed to read his thoughts. "Have you talked to Maria yet?"

Raz nodded. "Sort of. It was tough, trying to say things on the phone, and I told her to take it easy, I'm not going to barge back into her life like Godzilla."

"The kids?"

"They're fine. Very excited. Seems strange to hear Joey's voice all hoarse and baritone, nearly grown up. Lisa sounds like a gushy, happy teenager. My kids are still my kids." An unwanted thought flashed in his mind: *But my wife is not my wife.*

An uncomfortable silence fell over the group while they all tended to their drinks.

He and Maxwell exchanged looks. Between them would always be the shared secret of what happened in a darkened courtyard in Iran. Rasmussen gave him a knowing nod.

Something else flitted into his mind. Something that had been bothering him all these years.

"What about my MiG?"

He felt the stares of the three men. Allen broke the silence. "Uh, *what* MiG?"

"The one I shot down before I got hit. Did I get credit for it?"

More stares. "No," said Allen, "you didn't get credit for a MiG."

Raz nodded. "It was DeLancey, wasn't it? I'll bet DeLancey claimed the MiG."

"Yes, he claimed the MiG."

Raz almost laughed out loud. Suspicions confirmed. After all these years of guessing. "When I heard DeLancey call a Fox One—after I'd fired my Sparrow at the MiG—I knew he'd claim it himself. You guys know DeLancey. That was something he'd do."

He could tell by the way they exchanged knowing looks that there was more that he didn't know. Shit, there was no end to what he didn't know.

"Okay, what else? DeLancey got credit for the MiG, and let me guess the rest. He got a medal for it, right?"

"A silver star," said Maxwell. "First kill of the war."

Raz shrugged and took a pull from the fresh beer. "I'm okay with that. I was supposed to be dead. Somebody should have gotten the credit. So where's my buddy, that asshole DeLancey? A CAG by now, no doubt."

"No," said Boyce. Raz saw him looking at Maxwell. "DeLancey's dead."

"Oh. What happened?"

Boyce glanced at Allen, then back at Maxwell. Maxwell shrugged.

"Killed in action over Iraq," said Boyce. "Two years ago."

"Too bad."

"Yeah," said Boyce. "Too bad."

He could tell by Boyce's tone that it wasn't too bad. And by the way he was looking at Maxwell, he guessed there was more to the DeLancey story.

Nothing surprised him anymore. He killed a MiG, but he was supposed to be dead. Now he was alive, and the man who took credit for the MiG was dead. The weirdness never stopped.

A petite female officer in dress whites came into the bar. She looked around, then spotted Raz. "Captain Allen and Captain Miller, I'm Lieutenant Berger from Admiral Dinelli's staff. I'm here to take you to the airport when you're ready, gentlemen."

"I'm ready," said Raz, and he tossed down the beer. The hum in his brain had swollen to a steady buzz. Damn, he'd have to learn to drink all over again.

With Lieutenant Berger leading the way, they walked outside. An unmarked white Mercedes was waiting at the door. Two marines in Service Charlie uniform, one the driver, the other an escort wearing a sidearm, saluted the officers as they emerged from the door.

The alcohol and the comradeship and his own emotions were catching up with him. One at a time, he gave his fellow officers a hug. For a long moment he held Maxwell in a tight embrace.

"I'll never forget," he said, his voice catching. "You're the man. You got me out."

"You'd do the same for me," said Maxwell. He squeezed his shoulder. "Take care of yourself, Raz."

Rasmussen climbed into the back of the Mercedes. He waved from the window as the car sped away toward his new life.

Claire busied herself writing notes while she waited. Through the window she could see the long rays of sunset bathing Bahrain in a soft glow.

It was still early. The tables at Cico's were only half filled, mostly with Manama locals. A small clutch of noisy westerners—American or European embassy staffers, she guessed—were gathered at the bar. One of them recognized her, and she could hear them talking about her.

Sam Maxwell had surprised her with his call. The *Reagan* was still at sea, not due to drop anchor in Bahrain for another day and a half. He had flown in on a COD for some kind of meeting. He glossed over the subject, but she could guess. The Rasmussen release was the number-one hot-button item on the wire services, and she guessed that Sam Maxwell had something to do with it.

It was frustrating. Even though she had played a backstage role in forcing the government to acknowledge Rasmussen's existence, she had to keep her silence about what she really knew. She attended the same press briefings with the other reporters, asked the same dumb questions, waited in line to—

She saw him come in the door.

This has to be love, she told herself. If not, then what other explanation was there for the way her heart fluttered when she saw Sam Maxwell enter a room?

How about guilt? The image of the roses and the crumpled card—and Chris Tyrwhitt—dwelled in her mind. She pushed the image away.

He didn't spot her right away. He stood in the foyer, gazing around, squinting in the subdued light.

She watched from the table. Maxwell's craggy features missed handsomeness by a couple of millimeters. Maybe more than a couple. He was wearing the same outfit he always wore when he came ashore—deck shoes, chinos, knit sport shirt. With that rangy, loose-limbed build of his, he could pass for a senior tennis pro. Or a ski bum. Maybe even a fighter pilot.

He saw her, and his face broke into a wide smile. Taking long strides, he came to the table.

"Don't you have anything better to do than hang out in bars?" His standard opening.

"Where else would I pick up sailors?" Her standard comeback.

He took her in his arms and kissed her, a serious one that lasted a full ten seconds. She didn't mind, and she didn't care what the embassy staffers gawking at them from the bar thought. Nothing mattered at the moment. Sam was safe, he was here, and she had him to herself.

"Thank you for the roses, Sam. They were beautiful." *There. I got it out.* She hoped he didn't notice the flush in her cheeks when she said it.

He didn't. "I'm glad you got them. I wasn't sure they would get delivered."

Another flush. *They almost didn't,* she couldn't help thinking. Again she pushed the thought away and steered him to the table.

He sat across from her, holding both her hands, while

she told him what had happened since she flew off the *Reagan*. She'd been summarily fired by her boss in New York, then rehired exactly eight hours later. The Rasmussen story had the press scurrying like mice after cheese.

"What are they saying about his release?" said Maxwell. "Any details about the deal?"

"No specifics. Only that a CIA officer named Bronson was killed in the operation. No one's made a connection yet between the Rasmussen story and the President's firing of the CIA director. One of the journalists had a rumor that an important terrorist had been captured, but the Central Command public affairs briefers just stonewalled it. They say they don't discuss details of antiterrorist ops."

"Good answer. But you know the story. What are you going to do with it?"

She smiled. "What story?"

"Thank you." He squeezed her hands. "I'll make it up to you somehow."

"You already have. You're here."

Maxwell caught the waiter's attention and ordered a bottle of wine. She remembered the last time they were here—and the wine they didn't finish. Maxwell had rushed back to the *Reagan*.

"How is your friend Raz?" she asked.

"Okay. Still a little befuddled. He's on his way to Germany. They'll keep him secluded for a while, nobody getting to him except his family."

"How's his wife handling it?"

Maxwell shrugged. "Not as well as Raz. He had years to deal with the fact that she's remarried. Maria has been an emotional mess since she first heard that he might be alive. She'll need some help."

Claire nodded. *Maria thought her husband was dead, and he wasn't. I know what she's going through.*

The wine arrived, a Gevrey Chambertin '96 Domaine Serafin, the same as they'd had last time. They watched the ritual as the waiter pulled the cork, proffered a taste for Maxwell's approval, then filled their glasses.

"To better times." Maxwell touched his glass to hers.

"Better than what times?"

"Better than the last time we were here."

"I'll drink to that. No interruptions tonight, Sam. We have the whole evening to—"

Wrong. Her eyes caught movement across the room, in the foyer where more guests were entering the restaurant.

She should have known. The script never changed. Whenever she and Maxwell wanted to be alone, someone spoiled it.

Someone she didn't want to see tonight, or any other night.

A shambling, bearded figure was coming across the dining room toward them. She heard a groan come from Maxwell.

"Well, fancy meeting you two here," said Chris Tyrwhitt.

Maxwell tried to hide his anger, but he couldn't. It was oozing from him like smoke through a crack.

Tyrwhitt didn't seem to notice. "Heard you were in town, old sport," he said, and pulled up a chair. "Something told me I'd find you here."

Maxwell could guess. The CIA had been present at the Central Command SCIF where he'd attended another debriefing, this time with the Fifth Fleet and Central Command spooks. Tyrwhitt knew he was in town.

Tyrwhitt helped himself to the new bottle of wine. After a trial sip, he said, "You should have gone for the '97. A superior year for the Burgundies."

And you should have stayed dead, thought Maxwell. Tyrwhitt was already signaling the waiter for another bottle.

"Is there any subject you don't know everything about?" Claire asked.

Maxwell was surprised by the sarcasm in her voice. She was glaring at Tyrwhitt as if he had sprouted horns.

Tyrwhitt didn't seem fazed. "No, not really. That's why I'm so indispensable to my employer."

"That's what they thought about your boss, Bronson," she said.

Tyrwhitt nodded gravely. "Ah, poor Ted." He held his glass up and looked at Maxwell. "Here's to Ted Bronson. A great American who perished in the service of his country."

Maxwell held his eye, trying to read his meaning. Did he really believe that crap? If so, Tyrwhitt was either drunk or delusional.

"Does anyone know what *really* happened to Bronson?" asked Claire.

Tyrwhitt's eyes fixed on Maxwell. "No," he said. "Supposedly there were no witnesses." He turned to Claire. "They're having the memorial service tomorrow afternoon at the embassy. Would you like to attend it with me?"

"Sorry. I have an appointment."

"Too bad. Business?"

"Personal business."

"The network?"

"My lawyer." She reached into her briefcase and withdrew a sheaf of papers. "I have to deliver these."

She shoved the papers in front of Tyrwhitt. "The place for your signature is marked with a yellow tag. Sign each copy, please."

Tyrwhitt looked perplexed. "What's this? What papers?"

"Our final divorce decree. It just needs your signature, then it will be processed and done."

"Claire, my dear, this is all premature. We haven't had a chance to discuss this. You and I have to decide what—"

"I've already decided. I love Sam Maxwell. I'm glad you weren't killed in Baghdad, Chris, because the world is a more colorful place with you in it. But not in my life. I want this marriage over and finished."

Tyrwhitt shook his head. He put on his most charming smile. "Claire, Claire, I know you're upset with me about—"

"Sign the goddamn papers!"

Both Maxwell and Tyrwhitt stared at her. People at other tables turned around. Maxwell had never heard that hard edge in her voice.

Tyrwhitt looked at Maxwell. "You know, old sport, I think she means it."

"You'd better believe I mean it." She thrust her pen at him.

All the bluster seemed to whoosh out of Tyrwhitt. For several seconds he sat staring at the document.

With a look of resignation, he took the pen and scribbled his signature on each of the papers.

After an awkward silence, Tyrwhitt seemed to regain his cheerfulness. He reached for the new wine bottle. "This calls for another toast." He filled their glasses. "To Claire, the love of my life, and to her future happiness."

Maxwell touched his glass to Tyrwhitt's, vaguely aware that Claire was smiling at him. He felt her hand reaching for his beneath the table. Her eyes were sparkling.

He tried to think of something bright to say, but nothing came. *Guess that's why they call me Brick.*

Tyrwhitt tossed down his wine and rose to leave. He

gave Claire a peck on the cheek, then smiled at them both. "Claire has made her choice," he said, "and I will respect it. The two of you have my blessing."

On his way to the door he stopped, seeming to have another thought.

He came back to Maxwell. "I nearly forgot," he said in a low voice. "My compliments, old sport. Nice shooting."

Robert Gandt

**A MILITARY WRITER WHO
"TRANSPORTS READERS INTO THE COCKPIT."**
—San Diego Union-Tribune

**Read all the
Brick Maxwell
aviation thrillers—**

With Hostile Intent
0–451–20486–7

Acts of Vengeance
0–451–20718–1

Black Star
0–451–21066–2

**Available wherever books are sold or at
www.penguin.com**